HUMANBORN

SHADOWS OF EIRELAND

BOOK ONE

JOANNA MACIEJEWSKA

Source France, 1 Av. Johannes Gutenberg, 78310 Maurepas, France.
compliance@lightningsource.fr

To friends left behind.

CHAPTER ONE

The air was thick with magic as I stepped into the street.

The overcast sky hung low like a drunkard hunched over after a rough night, and the steel-gray clouds scratched the rooftops. Even the Magiclysm couldn't change some things: winter in Dublin had to be dark and wet.

Several of the molekind stood on the far side of the street, leaning against the wall by the vibrant purple door. The protective wards stamped all over it emanated with power, though the color of the wood had nothing to do with magic, just the local habit of painting doors, which had amused me ever since I moved to Ireland. Red, blue, purple, gray... Each door different, even though the red-brick town-houses formed a line of uniform buildings along the street. Of course, now some of them bore the marks of curse-started fires or lay in ruins demolished by mindless giants' clubs, but I still remembered how they looked before the war. At the same time, I hardly remembered the people who used to live there as they came and went wrapped up in their own lives.

The molekind's crooked talons pointed at me as I passed by, and more than one evil eye inspected me. Gosh, I hated them. All the mythborn looked eerie, but those, short and hairy with their noses perking up like rodents', seemed more inhuman than most, though they adapted better than others of their kin. Dressed in tracksuits and jumpers like proper Irish knackers, they loitered in the rundown streets looking for trouble... or for victims.

Judging from the scraps of Irish language I had picked up over the years, they were discussing one at that very moment, and since there was no other living soul within sight, I had a pretty good idea of who that victim might be. Oh, the Liberties, the shittiest area of Southern City Center —but hey, it was home.

The molekind kept whispering, and at first I avoided eye contact, but then I caught a glimpse of a familiar brown-skinned humanoid amongst them. I made sure that one caught my warning glare before I passed them. Insults in Irish chased me down the street, but I also picked out words like "the Court" and "Kaja."

Right, you little shrimps, that would be me: Kaja, the humanborn female who sometimes spoke with the mythborn at the Court. It didn't matter that they would only meet me when they saw fit and that we rarely got past insult-infused pleasantries—I'd been to the Court at the other side of the river, and that was what counted. I only hoped I'd make it to the corner before they remembered that I was also a frequent guest to the human-only Trinity College.

The aroma of freshly baked bread enveloped me. Before the war I used to buy scones for breakfast in the local bakery. The owners died in the first months of the conflict, and a mythborn girl seamlessly took over. Her sleek face and bright eyes contrasted with the sharp teeth jutting from her lower jaw, and her hands were as big as Guinness pints, but she looked mesmerizing, not grotesque. We exchanged polite greetings, but I couldn't bring myself to shop there. Who knew what she'd been putting in the dough? The last thing I wanted was a nasty magic poisoning or allergic reaction to some mythborn spice.

As I turned the corner, I weaved my way through the makeshift stalls selling food, war memorabilia, and both magic and plastic junk, shouting out their sales to the mixed crowd of humanborn and mythborn customers. In the beauty salon further up the street, a female bridge dweller was getting her claws done and chatting cheerfully with a humanborn beautician who didn't seem bothered that her client had green skin and bulgy eyes and hardly fit into a chair. Kids ran through the crowd ignoring the divisions imposed by the adult world, and as I listened to mythborn and humanborn drunkards arguing over last night's match, the Liberties didn't seem as bad anymore: at least we'd learned to coexist, which wasn't necessarily the case up in the North Side or over in Dublin West. I took another turn onto Thomas Street, the nicest one in the area, though still shabby in comparison to the former city center.

The tall tower of John's Lane Church proudly reached for the gray sky, but a thorn bush crawled along its walls, and I doubted it'd be long before the majestic building would finally give in. In front of the church, a bunch of humanborn shook their charity buckets, so the meager coins inside rang in the rhythm of donation pleas. The priests did their best to protect the church, but their private war against the magical influence wasn't going too well. I knew they'd lose, and the magic thorn bush, a remnant of the war, would consume the building just like it consumed the nearby St. Catharine's. Unless, of course, the priests finally gave in and got some good amulets and offensive curses. With the dwindling flock of believers and magic still warping everything it touched, their holy water couldn't hold out forever.

I doubted their efforts would bear fruit, but I crossed the street and threw a coin into the ever-hungry donation bucket. I ignored the "God bless you!" that followed as I walked away. I was never one of strong faith, and the war had made me even less of a believer, but I did remember the countless times priests would let my squad in through the side door. They never asked questions, and they always had food and water waiting, as well as a prayer for those that didn't make it back. And for that, they'd have my coin until that bloody thorn bush finally claimed its victory, or until they'd ask me to find the best charm-crafter for them, so they could treat that thorny insult to architecture with the finest of magic.

I walked past the shops and meager cafes, some new, some old, no different than it used to be. Even before the war, only a few businesses lasted longer than a year. They remained the same at their core as charm-powered devices substituted for electricity, but with Dublin's population decimated, they were eerily empty. Even the influx of mythborn clientele couldn't make up for the numbers lost in the once-overcrowded city.

Thomas Street led me straight up to St. Audoen's Church, another one in the string of six or seven churches in the area. During the war, an angry mythborn mob had lured a giant toward it. Once the big'un was done with the building, the mythborn threw explosive curses all over the church. Even three years after the treaty, lonely figures still roamed the crumbled walls, holding their blood-bound charms and searching for loved ones' remains. Family, friends... Nobody could give the exact numbers, but folks said at least several hundred had sought refuge in the church back then, and almost anyone in Dublin with a relative missing during the war would walk through the ruins at least once in hope of finding their final resting place.

I looked away and picked up my pace. Moving on was so damn hard when every place screamed with memories and deep-buried trauma, but the closer to city center, the more Dublin had recovered from the atrocities, and it became a bit easier to pretend I didn't remember the past. I really should have moved somewhere else, but the rest of Ireland wasn't in any better shape after the Magiclysm and the war that followed.

As soon as I turned onto Dame Street, nostalgia gnawed at my thoughts. The street looked the same as it did during my early years in Dublin: crowded, messy, and chaotic, with a lot of cheap eateries, some convenience stores, and random businesses. That was, of course, if one ignored the otherworldly physique of the mythborn pedestrians.

I walked past a humanborn group. Fashion hadn't improved, with tacky and flashy outfits still the first choice of many people and sportswear or pajamas being the second. I refrained from staring at them, but then I caught a heated conversation.

"The explosion knocked out all the windows in the street," said a woman in a pink sweatshirt. The amount of makeup she put on her face would suffice to plaster a moderate-sized hole in a wall.

I slowed down, and since nobody paid any attention to me, I stopped nearby. From what I could see, they were mostly of Irish origin. I smirked at the thought that Ireland, even though multicultural before the Magiclysm, hadn't become a melting pot yet, so a few exceptions aside, it was still easy enough to guess one's nationality first by their looks, and then by their accent. Not that it really mattered after the war, but old habits persisted.

The man with a professional drunkard's face gave a throaty laugh. "Feckin' mythies! They can't even blow things up right."

I bit my tongue before reminding them that about half a century earlier, the Irish nationalists blew up Nelson's Pillar in the same fashion, with more damage to the windows in the street than to the English admiral's statue. Instead, I fished for more information, because news of an explosion in Dublin was disturbing. With the peace treaty signed, we didn't have many open acts of violence anymore. Even when the members of the Mythborn Protection Force got a bit out of hand, it usually ended with nothing more serious than some bruises and broken bones.

"Nay, this was serious. Folks say them bodies were found."

"Just gossip."

"But if it's true..." One man's hands curled into fists. "Blood for blood."

The others nodded with grim expressions.

It didn't seem I could learn anything more, so I walked away. I couldn't help a sarcastic mindset when some recent official announcements by Eireland Office, our governing body, claimed that Dublin had almost fully recovered from the atrocities, and everyone coexisted in peace now... Yeah, "recovered" my ass.

I picked up my pace and headed toward the familiar gray walls of the Trinity College. No wonder Albert had sent a message that he wanted to see me. The last thing we needed in this scarred city was another hate-driven riot.

CHAPTER TWO

I'd never visited Trinity College before the Magiclysm. Even though it was open to the public, the students' young faces made me think I'd feel out of place, and as my years in Dublin passed one after another, I felt less and less a tourist. My sense of curiosity and amusement faded as it was consumed by everyday life: job, grocery shopping, house chores, and drinks with coworkers in the local pub. I still went to see places on the weekends and traveled the countryside a bit, but I missed quite a few things in Dublin.

So I had no comparison to how Trinity College had looked before the war. Nevertheless, its massive size never failed to impress. The complex grounds spanned more than four blocks in the heart of Dublin, its buildings of gray stone including the modern additions to the historical parts. Inside the wall surrounding the former college, there were once parks and greeneries, but they'd since become training grounds or storage areas. People who populated Trinity had changed too. There weren't any innocent students anymore, replaced by seasoned veterans and inventors while Trinity's interiors were repurposed for the military and shelter needs.

The guards at the entrance gate wore amulet-enhanced gambesons, and their tireless eyes scanned the line of people. Two queues formed, one for the inhabitants, the other for guests, but I ignored both and walked straight to the broad-shouldered red-head who checked identity badges and inspected suspicious gear.

"The commander is waiting for me." I felt the hateful stares of all the humanborn I passed by. Sorry, folks, I wouldn't have skipped the queue if it wasn't important, and I knew it was important, because Albert wouldn't have called for me otherwise. "Kaja Modrzewska." I gave them my Eire-land ID.

Their mouths moved soundlessly when they tried to decipher my beautifully Slavic name. They should have been happy I wasn't born to the family of Szczyrek or Błaszczyk.

"I'm sorry, but you'll have to wait in the queue, ma'am," said the taller one.

"Are you going to explain to the commander why I'm late?" I asked in a blatantly passive-aggressive tone. The news of an explosion didn't put me in a patient mood, let alone an amiable one.

My question made them both flinch, and they exchanged worried looks. I really needed to remind Albert to make sure all the guards knew my name. I didn't mind standing in line with the rest of the honest folk when I was visiting, but making the man who ran Trinity College wait for me... That was plain rude, even for my respect-deficient attitude.

"Let her in." Orla Monaghan walked by, and both the

guards stretched in a formal stance at her sight. "The commander is waiting for her," she added in passing.

Before I could thank her, she strode away in her perfect outfit of spandex mesh, accompanied by a quiver and bow, of course. Her dark blond curls bobbed in a ponytail, and I didn't even have to see her face to picture that triangular chin, freckles, and pointy nose... and her lips, always pressed into a thin line of determination. If Orla lived a thousand years ago, bards would sing songs about her deeds. The kind you don't repeat to your children, but sing with the comrades sharing a fire on the night before the battle.

"You're welcome." Her voice came once more, again with no warmth to it.

Almost amused, I shook my head at her back then gently pushed my way through the guards to make it inside before their devices could pick up the arsenal of charms and amulets I wore and sent the two poor blokes into a state of panic.

The college's grounds were teeming with people. Some I recognized from wartime—their faces leaned over my wounds, and their hands passed me a piece of equipment or a warm meal. I waved to them and exchanged smiles when our eyes met, but I didn't stop to talk, and soon the shade of the entrance door swallowed me.

Albert's office was on the third floor, and as I passed several guards on my way there, I couldn't resist a smile. Old habits remained, and even with the peace treaty signed, the Trinitians still acted as if an assassin could walk in at any moment, but the veterans on a guard duty—their faces marked with scars and painful memories alike—let me through with as little as an anti-curse scan. They knew I'd be one of the last people to threaten Albert's life.

I knocked at the door, and when I entered, Albert rose from his seat. Tall and broad-shouldered, he kept his brown hair cropped in a military fashion, and even stuck in his office all day long, he still wore his street combat outfit. Should it come to that, he'd be ready to fight in shorter time that it took me to put all my charms and amulets on.

"Kaja, I'm glad you made it." His voice, low and deep, delivered words with a perfect British accent. The best way to seduce a linguist was to keep one's R's and T's soft and stretch the A's a bit, and because of his birthright, these came to Albert as natural as complaining came to me.

"Is it about the explosion?" I shook his hand, and he held mine a bit longer than needed.

"You already know about the explosion at the docks' market?" Albert arched his eyebrows. "We got word only half an hour ago."

"I stumbled upon the information. Nothing solid, but I thought you'd need me to find out more."

We sat at his desk, and he poured tea. Water steamed as the charm attached to the teapot kept it at perfect temperature.

"That's not why I called for you, but yes, I'd appreciate it if you could look into that too," he said. "The MPF are not claiming responsibility for this one."

I frowned. No one except the Mythborn Protection Forces, a self-proclaimed rebellious mythborn unit, would bomb a civilian humanborn place. If they didn't announce it as their victory in the war against Eireland Office and the vague "humanborn establishment" it supposedly embodied, someone else must have decided to influence the peace... or the MPF had some sort of a fallout. Either way, Albert needed to know before Liffey's waters flowed red.

"I'll see what I can find," I replied. "And the case you called me for?"

"A journalist went missing, supposedly in Dublin North." Albert pulled out a picture of a humanborn woman. Irish, from what I could tell, though she could have been of British origin too, like the commander himself. "She was supposed to write an article about the botanical gardens and never reported back."

"If she tried to sneak in there..." I shook my head.

"Let's hope she didn't." Albert let out a sigh.

No matter how many warnings were given, no matter how many dreadful stories circulated, there was always someone foolish enough to try to get to the gardens without the mythborn Court's permission. Sometimes mythborn delivered their leg or hand, or pieces of torn and bloodied clothes. Sometimes they didn't deliver anything.

"What's her name? Do you have any other info?" I studied the photograph. Slightly square jaw, full lips, determined eyes. She seemed like the type to wander where she wasn't invited, with a stupid conviction that she'd get what she wanted any way available.

"Emma Doherty. Here's her data, address, and contacts within *Eireland Times*." Albert handed me a large envelope. "From what I understand, she has friends on the North Side, so she might have been staying with them, but if she tried to get into the gardens..." His eyes fixed on me. "I'm more interested in ensuring the Court doesn't take offense than finding her remains."

I couldn't say Albert's lack of compassion moved me. With the delicate balance between the mythborn and humanborn, we didn't need some careless brat stirring things up just because she wanted to write a front-page story.

Before I replied, a knock on the door interrupted us, and a guard's head poked in.

"Commander, there's a mythborn lady waiting in the grounds," he said. "We let her into the courtyard, so the folks outside don't get any ideas, and Orla's watching her. She wants to speak with you, commander."

"Did she give you a name?" Albert asked, amused.

"She showed a ring with a strange symbol on it, but it reeked of magic, so we didn't want to risk bringing it up here." The guard hesitated. "She looks like one of the Court gals."

Albert sighed and rose from his desk, but I made a gesture to stop him. "I'll go and check her on my way out. No need to risk it."

"I could handle one assassin, even if she's a mythborn," he said as he waved the guard away. "You sound like some of my strategists bound on confining me to this office for my own safety."

I glanced at the windows overlooking Dame Street and the former National Bank of Ireland, a spot in the very heart of Dublin. "Not a very strategic point, to be honest. One sniper with a good magic bow, some cursed arrows, and you're dead." I mocked a pistol shot at his head. I didn't mention that I preferred Albert anywhere but his office. We didn't need to go the personal route.

"The windows held in the war." Albert stood by my side. "Why would it be different now?"

His scent reached my nostrils, and I refrained from inhaling deeper, from bringing back the uncomfortable, yet overly pleasant, memories.

"You're right, it probably wouldn't." After all, Trinity College had survived a direct hit from a tank. Well, from a mythborn equivalent of a tank... a sophisticated, portable cannon-like device spitting out curse-enhanced rocks. It took us a lot of planning and even more blood to stop that thing.

Albert's hand brushed my back, a gesture lost somewhere between a friendly reassurance and a seductive tease.

"Sometimes..."

The longing in his voice brought an unexpected pain, and I tore away from the window to escape the words to come. "Come, let's see what made the Court member desperate enough to visit Trinity."

He snorted and shook his head at my deflection, but he headed for the door with me nonetheless. On our way down, we didn't speak a word, but we didn't have to.

Because I too sometimes regretted that the war was over.

MOST OF THE Trinitians in the yard tried not to stare, but Orla openly glared at the tall, sleek figure who stood on the patch of grass too green to have been there an hour earlier. I almost expected flowers to bloom around and an entourage of butterflies to surround the mythborn female when she turned toward us, but Eithne ni'Crann knew better than to tease her guards with too much magic and give Orla an excuse to shoot.

"Albert, *mo chara*, I appreciate you coming down to meet me." Her voice jingled with the sound of silver bracelets while she fixed the two emerald pool-like eyes on the man by my side. "I'd hate to disrupt this place's energy with my presence."

Albert offered a courteous bow, and I offered my restraint from grimacing. As if she didn't already bring disruption. Every moment she stood on the Trinity's grounds meant the magic seeped through the protection the college inhabitants had built over the years.

"And Kaja, I'm glad to see you in good health." Eithne skimmed past my face.

Was there a stab hidden amongst her words? I exchanged a quick glance with Orla over the mythborn's shoulder, and for once, Orla and I shared the same feeling. We both wished for the Court bitch to try something, to try *anything* we could deem an assault. Between Orla's bow and my arsenal of charms and curses, Eithne's smug expression would be the last one she ever wore.

"As much as I appreciate your taking time to visit us, Lady Eithne, I'd rather get straight to business," Albert said while he shot Orla a warning glance. If I wasn't standing to the side, I'd have gotten the same treatment. "What brings the Court's messenger to Trinity?"

Oh, how the mythborn cringed at the title Albert used to belittle her. If there was anything I loved more than his accent, it was his ability to deliver diplomatic insults. Of course, I preferred the non-diplomatic ones myself, but it felt good to know peace didn't make Albert soft.

"I came to discuss the recent disturbing event. My brethren worry this provocation might affect the unstable peace between our people."

No doubt she was talking about the explosion. It seemed the news traveled fast on both sides of the river.

"Provocation, Lady Eithne?" Albert's voice was chilling. "I expected the MPF to claim responsibility for the attack."

Eithne moved with the grace of a leaf in the summer breeze, and her face expressed a well-staged hurt. "Mythborn Protection Forces had nothing to do with the explosion. I can assure you they wouldn't dare go against the Court's orders." She looked Albert in the eye. "We both know that many humanborn would be interested in putting the blame on the mythborn to limit our rights even more."

Albert tensed, and the muscles on his face twitched as he gritted his teeth. "Or you're here to deceive us, Lady Eithne. It wouldn't be the Court's first attempt."

Eithne's lips curled down into a perfect horseshoe of disapproval. "We're not at war anymore, *mo chara*. Even if some of your officers wish to believe otherwise." She glanced over her shoulder toward Orla as if reading Albert's officer's thoughts.

The Irish bow mistress reciprocated with a sneer and readjusted her quiver in an obvious tell.

I might have had my issues with Orla, and all in all I was for peaceful coexistence instead of mutual extermination, but I sure appreciated her unyielding approach to the sneaky backstabbers from the Court.

"My officers don't go around blowing up mythborn establishments," Albert replied. "I'll need something more than your word as proof MPF had nothing to do with the attack."

Her eyes flashed as if catching a forgotten ray of sun when Eithne turned to me. "Let Kaja gather information, then, and I'll pay half of her fee. How's that?"

The nerve of her! Did she really think she could use me like that? And that I'd do her a favor? If she wanted to prove the innocence of her brethren, she could do the work herself.

"I'm afraid I'm already overbooked when it comes to assignments." I didn't even bother pretending I regretted refusing her offer.

Eithne sent me a royal smile, the one a gracious queen bestows upon her subjects, and the perfect arch of her eyebrow lifted ever so slightly, but before she replied, one of Albert's men approached him.

"Excuse me for a moment." Albert bowed and stepped to the side, gesturing for Orla to join him.

While they listened to the lieutenant's hushed report, Eithne leaned closer. The scent of fir and something else sneaked up my nostrils.

"Have you tasted bark on your tongue yet?" Her whisper dripped poison. "When your saliva turns brown, it's going to be too late to do anything. I won't be able to help you."

And then she moved away with the grace of grass bending serenely in the wind. As if she was never close. As if she had never slipped the treacherous words into my ears.

"You smell good," she murmured, not looking at me anymore. "Like my childhood."

Eithne's words grated against my composure like claws across rock, and she stood unmoved, a mythborn statue.

Albert returned, and Orla resumed her spot behind Eithne's back. The Irishwoman's hand brushed her enhanced bow's grip with hope, and Eithne's lip quivered in amusement, as if she knew what went through the other woman's head.

"Apologies once more, Lady Eithne."

"I understand, *mo chara*. The Trinity's commander is never the master of his own time." Her head bent in a gentle nod. "I'd hate to keep you any longer, so if I can trust Kaja will take the matter into her capable hands, I shall depart."

Albert glanced at me, and I mustered a shrug. "Fine, I'll take it." If only I could wipe that smug smile off the other-worldly bitch's face. She'd better not expect a discount for my services. At the same time, I couldn't deny that her mention of help reignited a spark of hope. Even if it was a lie meant to make me agree, I couldn't afford to take the chance.

"Albert, Kaja, Orla." Eithne bowed her head threefold, and then she spun in place with the agility only mythborn could claim as natural.

Albert watched her departure with a frown. "I wonder what her play is. Why would she want us to investigate?"

"Maybe they want to get rid of troublemakers?" I suggested. "Wouldn't be the first time they tried to use us in their games." With Eithne gone, I ran my tongue against my palate, but my saliva didn't taste any different. Was she bluffing? Or was there still time? "I'll make sure she pays full price anyway."

"Weren't we supposed to split the cost?" Albert smirked at me, and I enjoyed his amused tone.

"And you'll split it. You get the discount part, she gets the full-price part." I chose to ignore what Eithne said about covering half of my expenses. After all, I got to decide what my fees were. Not to mention that if she knew a way to help me, she'd make me pay dearly for it, so doing the same to her was only sensible. And if her words were nothing but a deception, I'd have more money to search for something on my own.

Albert followed my gaze and studied both Eithne walking toward the main gate and Orla taking the initiative to follow her as a guard. "You've been wearing quite a few amulets recently," he said in a casual tone.

"The Liberties are not the safest part of town, and I often get back home after dark." I hoped my face held an emotionless expression, not to fool Albert, but to keep him from prying.

"It's getting worse, isn't it?" He turned to me as soon as Eithne disappeared out of the gate.

Right, I should have expected he wouldn't take the hint. I looked him in the eye. "It's fine for now. I'm just checking to see if I can get better results with new amulets." I forced certainty into my voice.

Albert took a step forward but then froze, all of a sudden conscious of where we were: not in his private office anymore, but on the Trinity College's open grounds, with half those present following his every gesture... and mine, for that matter, because I was sure gossip about me still circled, gossip about the outside woman with whom Albert was closer than to some of his fellow Trinitians. I had no doubt many veterans also shared other kinds of gossip about me and the commander.

"How much longer will they hold?" He kept his voice down. "And what if they fail?"

I hesitated, but another lie would get us nowhere, and I owed him the truth, not only for what was already in the past, but also in gratitude for keeping the details of my condition to himself.

"I don't know. And we'll see."

He stretched his lips thin, but I couldn't resist a smile when he gave a nod of approval. As much as he didn't like my answers, he appreciated I gave them.

"At least let our medics have a look at you. It can't hurt, and maybe they'll be able to help," he said.

The desperation in his voice stopped me from making a sarcastic remark about secrets not being secrets anymore when a bunch of medics would become privy to them. One thing that hadn't changed over the years, that hadn't changed since the war, was Albert's concern about his men. Even though I was hardly ever a Trinitian, he acted no different toward me than toward anyone under his command.

"Once I get the job done, I'll stop by Tadgh," I said, offering a compromise. Discussing my ailment with one trusted mythborn scientist seemed a better idea than revealing the secret to a bunch of humanborn eggheads.

Albert shook his head in disapproval, but his expression betrayed him. Like me, he cherished small victories we had over each other, and I just gave him one. "I'll have all the information on the explosion and necessary permissions sent over to you, and anything new on Emma too."

I arched my eyebrows. He already had something on the attack? "I can't believe you pretend you need my services. Even I can't gather information that quickly."

"But you start where we finish," Albert replied. "Drop by my office whenever you learn something." He glanced at me. "Or just drop by."

I didn't reply, enjoying the tone of his voice and his accent. Truth be told, I didn't want to ask whether he'd have Tadgh on standby to ensure I didn't disappear before the Trinity's only mythborn resident looked me over.

Another lieutenant approached, and his face reflected this kind of "I need to pee" urgency, so I took a step back, indicating my business with the commander had concluded. "I better go now, or your men will take me down just for the chance to talk to you."

Albert, already turning to the newcomer, glanced at me for the last time. "I meant it, Kaja. You better not wriggle out of this one."

I blew him a goodbye kiss as a reply. To all others, it might have seemed a nonchalant and discarding gesture, but Albert would know. It pained me to even agree to his terms, but I wouldn't try to cheat him out of the deal, not after he was letting me leave instead of dragging me to the medical wing.

Still, when I walked outside the gate, I sighed with frustration. Compromises... I hated compromises.

~

OUTSIDE TRINITY GROUNDS, College Green street led me straight back toward Dame Street, but I didn't follow it home. Instead I stopped at the small market in front of what used to be the Central Bank of Ireland. In the middle of the square, the Crann an Oir—Tree of Gold—stood as proudly as it had before the war. I'd always hoped that the sculpture, a metallic sphere of golden leaves, would actually start growing after the Magiclysm. The mere fact that it had survived the war unscathed indicated it had some sort of magic within... On second thought, maybe it also had some sort of hidden common sense, because I would bet the radical humans would have tore it down in no time if it displayed any magical features. Peace didn't mean we liked or trusted the mythborn any more than we did during the war, and some factions still tried to eradicate anything related to magic in any way they could. Acts of vandalism still caused tensions, and the careerists in Eireland Office pushed through countless magic regulations, unconcerned that those laws also hurt the humanborn, as if they could deny that most of us had changed after the Magiclysm. After all, there was a reason many of us, myself included, didn't call ourselves humans anymore: we had too much magic in our bodies, some dangerously unstable.

The market was full of makeshift stalls and blankets spread on the ground with wares piled on them, and the vendors promised a cornucopia of goods from fresh vegetables to weapons to half-active charms salvaged from the city's countless ruined buildings. I headed straight for the noisy corner of the market, where a humanborn kid stood by cages full of birds. His freckled face and red heap of unkempt hair revealed him as a local, and he grinned when I approached. If he was surprised I was in need of what he was selling, he didn't show it, though his main clientele had to be mythborn, because even with the temporary food shortages, the humanborn didn't fancy pigeons and seagulls.

"This one." I picked the fattest bird, trying not to think what it must have been eating to have grown that big. Before the war, seagulls fed on fish and crabs both in the river and at the seashore, but when the shamrock tides came, and the Liffey's waters turned black, their food sources disappeared. Unless—and I shivered at the very thought—those stupid birds still searched for their meals in the familiar waters. No wonder humanborn preferred more traditional poultry.

The youngster took the bird out of the cage. "Ya want yer bird dead?" When I shook my head, he tied its beak, wings, and legs with pieces of rope.

I handed him a few notes, but he brushed my hand away. Eireland's official currency, harps, wasn't trusted in the streets, and whoever accepted it usually asked a higher price than in barter. One had to be careful with money that could lose all its value overnight should the war start again or the Office fall for any other reason. The euro, the old currency back from when Ireland was still part of the European Union, had a better exchange value but was also scarcer, and only business who dealt with tourists had enough of it to trade.

"If you're paying with the bills, the price is double," he replied with a bold stare, even though I gave him the amount listed on the piece of cardboard. "But I could take one of these in exchange." His eyes locked on my amulets.

I snorted. "I'd have to buy all your birds to make it fair." I could part with the trinket and make a new one in less than an evening, but it was bad for business. Next time I came, he'd rip me off even more. "So, deal or no deal?" I held my hand out with the notes.

He took my money and handed me the seagull with an expression that was a mix of hurt innocence and a starving orphan. I got the message: I was the evil adult preying on his innocent youth and preventing him from making an honest living, and even though he couldn't have fooled me, I was certain, with a little bit more practice, he'd succeed in conning the less observant customers or tourists.

I took my bird and walked away.

"Old hag!" he called after me. "May you choke on it!"

It seemed the kid might have more to learn about business and interacting with customers than I thought. His shouts turned a few heads, and I caught glimpses of curiosity and disgust on passersby's faces, but I didn't care. I made my way through the Temple Bar down toward the river.

The city's party and tourist district had suffered in the war too, but as soon as the ink on the peace treaty dried, the rebuilding began. Mythborn charms seamlessly replaced electricity, providing light in the streets, though few venues could afford them for the neon, so the city drifted toward a more rustic look. Yet, utilities problem aside, it seemed that people couldn't live without their entertainment, and many pubs reopened their doors almost instantly. Around me, local humanborn mixed with human tourists who came to Dublin in search of magic and thrills, and for a pint of Guinness, of course, because some things never changed.

Any other day I'd stroll through Temple Bar and watch people wrapped up in their joy, be it real or illusory. I'd envy them their bursts of laughter and careless behavior, and at the same time I'd wonder how many of them were just desperate to forget the years of war. I could always fish out the veterans from the crowd, hunched over their pints with eyes blurred, watching the replays of past skirmishes in their heads. And then I'd rush home to search for my own oblivion.

But today, with the seagull in my hand, I made my way through Temple Bar without delays or trips down memory lane, even if every actual lane I walked brought memories. It was still early in the afternoon, but the gray sky darkened, and the sun would set soon. One of the things I hated about winter in Ireland... in Eireland: if you slept a few minutes too long, you could easily miss any sunlight that might shine that day.

I weaved my way through the narrow streets all the way down to "the Quays," the city's riverside area. I tried to ignore the Ha'penny Bridge as I walked past it. Once famous throughout Dublin, a metal and concrete link between the Temple Bar district and the clubs and restaurants on the other side of the Liffey, it now scared people away with foul smells and remnants of hearts pinned to its railing where the love locks used to be. Tourists watched from afar with morbid fascination on their faces, and later in the evening they'd come back for the "show." The bridge dwellers' practice of tearing a victim open and strapping his or her heart to the railing always attracted an eager audience, especially with the reassurances that the killed humans were all convicted criminals or volunteers. For me, any mention of this brought one of those rare moments I regretted the war was over. Without the peace treaty, I could gather several of my friends and be done with this place quicker than an Eireland bureaucrat pocketed a bribe. But with the treaty signed, all I could do was try to push Ha'penny Bridge's existence out of my head.

Or I could join the protesters under the Eireland Office chanting slogans about inhuman practices and throwing obscenities at the protesters standing at the opposite corner and loudly demanding respect for the mythborn cultural inheritance.

Truth be told, not all the mythborn rejoiced in their kin's murderous ways, and only the ones we called bridge dwellers seemed to treat humanborn as gourmet meals, though they weren't particularly vicious or predatory. They resembled more a pack of hyenas taking the opportunity to justify their tastes with a gruesome spectacle for tourists. If other mythborn liked human meat too, they were definitely more discreet about it.

I walked by several bridges on my way and approached the O'Donavan Bridge. The makeshift shacks clung to one another along both sides of the bridge, and since the middle became a place of gathering, cooking, and daily chores, passing to the other side meant weaving through countless mythborn and their belongings. And the bridge dwellers weren't always a friendly lot. They weren't necessarily vicious either, but close-knit and often distrustful, and, with their pack mentality, angering one dweller meant angering all of them.

Their faces were hardly humanlike, swollen and with bulging eyes making them look more like fanged frogs than sentient beings, and their green and brown skin covered with pustules only enhanced their repulsive physique. I held my face straight as I walked along the bridge, knowing better than to give them any excuse for hostilities. For some, even eye contact was an invitation to make claims of the observer's rude behavior.

"Kaja!" A friendly face, though no less green or fanged, popped from one of the shacks. "Come in!"

Three-Bones waved, but his eyes looked at me with wariness. Just like the night we'd met for the first time when a stun curse exploded nearby and sent me flying into a building. Out of breath and dazed, I fought to get up and run before a mythborn squad found me. When I regained some of my senses, I found myself being dragged across the street by a nearly six-foot creature. I could only hope it'd kill me before it ate me. On this matter, at least, bridge dwellers were better than giants: they usually killed and cooked their food, while the big'uns simply shoved living beings into their mouths.

Not only did Three-Bones not kill me that night, but he also nursed me back to health and kept the mythborn scouts off my back while I recuperated. So when months later an angry humanborn mob accused him of eating wee little Fiona, I was there to repay him for his kindness. It cost me a broken leg and quite a stash of curses, but I made sure the self-proclaimed judges listened to reason, and when some of them didn't, they listened to each other's screams as my curses hit their marks. Later, Three-Bones had been cleared of suspicion when the Trinitians caught the actual murderer... a humanborn one.

Ever since then, Three-Bones and I had been friends, and he kept an ear out for gossip and things that could interest me. He wasn't a mole, and he'd never turn on his own kin, but he understood that the aggressive and hateful elements needed to be rooted out if the peace was to last.

"You bring seagull," he said when I entered his shack. "No good."

I handed him the bird. "You know me too well, Tee-Bee."

"Need information, yes?"

Three-Bones' English had much room for improvement, but as long as we could communicate, I wasn't about to give him grammar lessons, especially since I wasn't really qualified to do so in the first place, seeing as English was a second language for me as well.

"Someone blew up a humanborn place," I said without further pleasantries. Our relationship was more that of business associates than socializing friends. "And the MPF is not claiming this one. Anything stirring?"

"No good." He clucked and shook his head. "But nothing here. Troublemakers sleep in winter."

"I wish it was true." I sighed. So much for easy clues and quick solutions. "Let me know if you hear anything, will you?"

Three-Bones gave me an eager nod, then pointed at a small pot in front of his shack. "You stay dinner?"

I inspected it with curiosity. Its dark contents bubbled somewhat cheerfully, and I'd feel tempted, especially that I knew Tee-Bee didn't fancy human flesh, but the fish and seaweed aroma of the rising steam made my decision for me. I'd be insane to eat whatever he caught in the river.

"Not today. Got more work," I replied. "Stay warm, Tee-Bee."

"You too, Kaja."

Judging by how often the bridge dwellers used that expression, "stay warm," they must have had more in common with frogs than just their faces. I weaved my way back through the bridge, and this time its other inhabitants paid me little to no attention. Yes, even if my fishing for information brought no results, being friends with Three-Bones definitely had its benefits.

CHAPTER THREE

If someone asked, I usually said that I don't know why I stayed.

When the battle dust and magic mist finally settled, and the magic-cocooned planes started arriving, the foreigners were offered the first seats to leave, and some hastily made their way to Dublin Airport seeking to flee this cursed land. Others, though... After four long years of bleeding out to prove our right to live here, most of us couldn't just get up and go. I'd witnessed my sister being crushed under a giant's foot and my friends dying by the hands of the mythborn. I heard their screams when enraged bridge dwellers ripped them apart, and I felt the battle lust when I helped to slay my first screech. No matter what country we were born in, what language we spoke, or what customs we cultivated, we were all Irish in a way. This was our home. We fought for it as hard as we could, so we bloody deserved to stay.

Yet this was not entirely true.

The memories of the day when the Magiclysm came never stopped haunting me. The clouds, thick and overcast, swirled like a shoal of frightened fish, twisting in the sky above and pulsating with colors. Then the rains came; some were cold, some hot, and some burnt our skin like acid. Wind lashed the droplets against the buildings and trees, and the officials on the radio and TV urged us to stay indoors. Soon their voices died out along with the whole infrastructure that didn't endure the moment when the magic had returned to the world. We sat in the dark, alone and unprepared.

And then they came: the mythborn, though back in the day we didn't know what they were. They spoke a weird language, according to the scholars, only slightly resembling old Gaelic, but they adapted quickly to our speech, taking Irish and English as their own. We didn't know better, so we tried to give them names straight from pop culture: elves, orcs, giants, trolls... Yet soon it became clear that as diverse as they appeared, they weren't multiple species, but one. Someone coined the name mythborn, and it stuck.

When the Magiclysm started, we all were in the "zero zone," in the epicenter of the magical breakout, and back then no one had any idea about protective gear, safety protocols, or other bullshit like that. The amount of magic-contaminated air I breathed in during the war would be enough to push me beyond the boundaries of what was considered "human," and the last thing I wanted was to become a quarantined guinea pig while some eggheads and bureaucrats decided whether it was safe enough to release me into the normal world. So I never claimed my seat on the evacuation plane.

Later, when it became clear that the return of magic affected most of the country's population, with some succumbing to quite drastic changes, our perception of ourselves shifted too. Some still grasped for pieces of humanity and purity, but others, like me, tried to embrace the new. A new term emerged, humanborn. Many people, especially those affiliated with the Trinity, still loathed it and refused to use it, even though in a way it was more accurate. We were all born of human, but some of us couldn't be considered human anymore.

Not that right after the Magiclysm we had time to ponder such things. The newcomers weren't a friendly bunch, and the initial lack of communication didn't help either. One incident here, another there, and before we'd realized, we had a full-blown conflict.

We waged it mostly with makeshift melee weapons and bows, since Ireland had a ban on firearms. Then we added magic items to our arsenal looted from our dead enemies: amulets for protection, charms for augmentation, and curses for killing. It took some trial and error before we figured it all out, and by then the mythborn were already gaining the upper hand in the war.

Back then we didn't understand why the rest of the world left us alone. With the countless international treaties, when NATO and the UN were supposed to step in, we felt abandoned. Only later did we learn that international forces made several attempts to aid us. First, the magic shrouding Ireland interfered with all the devices, forcing the world's military to rely on more primitive solutions. Then, when the first support squads reached Ireland, they were greeted by mythborn, not humanborn. And our enemies made it clear: if any international forces tried to interfere, they'd start slaughtering the civilians who up until then hadn't been threatened... At least not too often.

So we were on our own. Many of us fought in small guerrilla units, put together from people willing to defend their neighborhoods, but in the end we were all drawn to what used to be Trinity College and became the Trinity, a heavily defended fortress that under Albert's leadership changed the one-sided slaughter into a somewhat even death match. On brighter days, I mused that it was a British lad who led the resistance that fought for all the people in Ireland. On the darker ones, I gave him a short nod before his orders sent me out to places likely to claim my life.

But I'd survived, and the information I'd gathered helped to push the mythborn back across the river. They bled us out, one by one, but we stood our ground. We attacked their squads when they least expected, blew up their supplies, and for every dead humanborn, we sent three mythborn into nonexistence. They retaliated fast, and more blood, both ours and theirs, flowed through the gutters.

And then the unexpected came. Right when we were facing defeat, preparing for the last desperate defense, a mythborn messenger arrived to offer a cease-fire. A few weeks later the mythborn sat down at the negotiation table, and after eighty-four days of arguing, slinging suspicions, and bargaining, we had peace. After seven months more, we had a government voted in from among both of our kinds, the Eireland Office.

We had problems, too. Distrust between mythborn and humanborn, demands of reparations, and the Mythborn Protection Force still trying to wage war. But year after year peace lasted, and those who decided to stay, bound by their love for the country or shackled by the wartime nightmares, had adapted and learned to live with our new neighbors. And when I heard their odd accent in the local pubs and their laughter at humanborn jokes, I allowed myself a bit of hope that the wounds would close in the end, and the war scars on the city, those abandoned vehicles and destroyed buildings, would also vanish one day.

And now, with a single explosion, my hope shrank like ice on a child's feverish forehead. Whether it was the Court's play, or whether the most influential mythborn faction's concern was genuine, I had to uncover the truth, otherwise my dreams of a peaceful future would turn to nightmares.

CHAPTER FOUR

I spent five days traversing the streets of Dublin. Five days of prodding, pushing, playing games, bribing, and throwing around veiled threats, and the only thing I got for my efforts was confirmation that Eithne had told the truth. Mythborn Protection Forces weren't involved in the bombing, which in a way didn't make me happy at all. If the bombers had had any ties to the MPF, tracking them down would be much easier, while searching for a group, or even worse, an individual, with no associations would be both time-consuming and difficult.

I didn't feel like drinking, but I dragged my sorry bones to Temple Bar. Even though I had my net of contacts and ways of gathering information, I still appreciated the results yielded by simple eavesdropping or socializing with strangers. After all, without the Internet and the aid of social media, it was the best way to make connections.

Not that it made me happy. As I walked on the rain-glossed cobblestones, I cursed the bomber, the weather, and pretty much anything else that crossed my mind.

People around went about their lives, and even so early

in the evening, many seemed to have indulged in beer and whiskey a bit too much. I weaved my way through Temple Bar's streets, steering clear of any larger groups, both humanborn and mythborn. So far, things remained quite civil, but when alcohol chose the words spoken, problems were bound to arise, and I wasn't about to get caught in the middle.

The pub I frequented used to have a different name before the war, but after it survived the Magiclysm unscathed, the owners renamed it An Finscéal, the Legend. As the story went, on the day when Ireland changed forever, one of the employees spilled a keg of craft beer all over the floor, and what everybody thought to be a disaster and a waste turned out to be their salvation. For some unknown reason, alcohol partially negated the mythborn magic, and according to the locals, the accidentally spilled beer sank into the floorboards and had protected the pub ever since.

Some tourists frowned at the story, but I knew better than to question it. Before we learned how to protect ourselves in the battlefield, mythborn curses wreaked havoc among the human ranks, and not once or twice had a good swig of whiskey kept my comrades alive until a field medic arrived.

The interior of the pub never ceased to amaze me. Several small rooms were packed with tables and chairs, and were linked together by the inner courtyard also filled with furniture. People stood everywhere, and their chatter melted into background noise, bringing back memories of Friday nights in good ol' Dublin, and something from the past atmosphere still lived within the walls, as if the spilled beer preserved more than the building itself. If I ignored the groups of mythborn by the tables, I could almost believe I'd stepped back in time or into an alternate reality where the war didn't happen.

I liked to believe that feeling was what made An Finscéal so popular.

The bar was crowded, and it took a while before a young mythborn got to me.

"What can I do for ya?" she asked with a perfect Irish accent, which made me inspect her oversized ears and round nose once again. She beamed a smile that suggested she'd worked really hard to get those glances, to fit in.

She had my order ready in no time, and I left a tip with pleasure, not for the service itself but for her embracing the humanborn ways. I found a free part of a wall to lean against and scanned the surroundings once more. Big groups weren't promising, as they always ended up discussing generic topics like recent events or politics, and I wasn't in the mood for more effort. Besides, fishing out loners could be hit or miss. Three or four groups looked local enough, though some tourists were mingling with them.

I didn't get to pick my target. Heck, I didn't even get to finish my drink before a slight tremble unsettled the ground underneath my feet and the pub's inner magic flared up, setting off my warning amulet. Most guests didn't notice, though a few men and women looked around with sharp and searching eyes—veterans like me. When no threat came, they returned to their drinks and interrupted conversations. I couldn't just go back to drinking, and it had nothing to do with past traumas. I put my cocktail down and rushed to the door, collecting a handful of insults as I elbowed my way out of the pub.

Outside, above the buildings, dark smoke rose into the gray sky, and I broke into a run. The direction was obvious as I made my way against the stream of humanborn and mythborn scrambling to get away, and I soon stopped by a half-destroyed building. The magically lit sign over the entrance said "Greenleaf Inn,", and I preferred not to think how many guests might have been inside.

The war had definitely changed things in Dublin, as the only onlookers were groups of tourists brave or stupid enough to stick around, while most of the civilians had already cleared out. Only a handful of mythborn worked around the building, some of them fighting the blaze, some rescuing the wounded.

I pushed past the tourists and without a word helped one of the mythborn drag an injured comrade out onto the street. His grimace revealed sharp teeth, and he let out a quiet growl, but he didn't chase me away, so as he laid his burden down onto the wet cobblestones, I worked on stopping the bleeding from the biggest wound.

Another mythborn approached. "We don't need your kind here," she barked.

Focused on the wound, I hadn't realized there weren't any other humanborn around. The explosives were set in a mythborn-populated building.

"Look, he needs help, and you don't have enough people." I pointed at the mythborn lying in front of me. "You can chase me away when I'm done." I didn't add that I was counting on her gratitude in the future.

She narrowed her eyes, but I caught a spark in them. She must have recognized I knew what I was doing. At her mark, some other mythborn passed me bandages and some sort of salves, and without delay, they were off back into the building. I patched up the wounded the best I could and moved on to the next mythborn as the rescuers were pulling more and more victims out. What a career advancement, to move from an information broker to a paramedic elbow-deep in her former enemies' blood!

We worked without a break. With more and more wounded lined up for me to take care of, I didn't notice the dark day shift into a darker evening. I was never trained to be a field medic, but during the war one picked up various skills, and though I couldn't do much, at least I knew how to keep someone alive until help arrived.

When I finally lifted from my knees, mythborn medics were carrying the wounded into carriages, and the bombed building was dark, with no trace of fire. Along the perimeter stood a line of mythborn guards, and I hesitated, finally realizing how out of place I was.

I didn't have to wait long for someone to spot me, and I braced myself to confront the angered guard who was approaching fast like a summer storm.

"She came after the explosion," a familiar voice said. The mythborn female who let me stay approached. "And she helped."

The armor-clad mythborn hesitated, and I saw my chance.

"I have the Court's emblem in my bag if you let me take it out." Better safe than killed by an overcautious guard. "Lady Eithne wishes me to investigate."

"A likely story," the guard replied. "We have our own to investigate. The lady wouldn't have asked a humanborn to do it."

I slowly took out the emblem and let the mythborn inspect it. "There's been another bombing, but it was a humanborn place. This explosion might be connected." Or it might have been humanborn retaliation, but I knew better than to mention it.

The guard gave me a reluctant nod. "And what do you want?"

I didn't really know what I wanted. "Let me look around," I said. "I won't take anything, and if I find any clues, I'll share them with you."

The guard took another glance at the emblem, and I had no doubt he'd memorized my name etched onto the fine silver. "If you're lying, this is the last time you'll ever use this." He handed it back to me and walked away.

I looked at the mythborn woman by my side. "Were you here when the bomb went off?" I asked before she could walk away.

"Is that why you helped us?" The mockery in her voice was clear. "To get what you need?"

I didn't reply. Instead, I raised my hands still marked with mythborn blood and holding the emblem. Then I looked her in the eye, waiting until she understood. I didn't have to help to get what I needed. All I had to do was wait and show them my emblem, and she must have known that. I might be a humanborn, but the piece of intricate mythborn jewelry I carried forced many of the mythborn doors open whether they liked it or not.

Still, being nice often paid off. A humanborn helping save mythborn made a better impression than one doing nothing while mythborn died.

"I was at the counter," she said in a more amicable tone. "The bomb went off on the floor above, and my first instinct was to get out." She looked away, and her cheeks darkened. "I heard screams, and fire rose, so I went back in... You saw the rest."

Indeed, I saw it. The nails and sharp scraps of metal in the wounds were more dangerous than the burns. Like in the humanborn place, the bomb was meant to hurt living beings more than to destroy the building itself. Whoever did it wanted victims.

I considered my next question. She hadn't noticed anything suspicious, otherwise she'd have mentioned it already, but if the bomber wanted the mythborn to suffer... "Look around very slowly," I said. "And tell me if you see anyone who was here before the explosion."

She was a good actress. Her eyes skimmed past the meager crowd that watched from the perimeter, and as she looked back at the building, she said, "No one in the crowd, but there's someone in the shadow of the building to the right. Looks like a humanborn who left the inn before the explosion." Her eyes returned to me. "If I call the guards, he'll run."

I considered my options. I was supposed to gather information, not to go after the actual bomber, but if I did nothing, he'd get away, and I didn't count on the mythborn's memory to recall his face in detail. "I'll go toward the inn," I said. "Shout some insults at me, then complain to the guards loud enough to get everyone's attention."

"Can you catch him?" she asked with hope.

"I'll try." I gave her honesty instead of reassurance. "Ready?"

The nod was almost nonexistent, and I would have missed it if I wasn't looking for it. Then her face changed into a mask of anger, and she lifted her arm. I swatted at her hand in a discarding manner, spun on my heels, and walked toward the inn.

"You can't just do that, humanborn!" she cried out after me, and I envied her acting skills. "The Court will know about it!" She wrapped it up with a bunch of Irish insults strung together with such skill that I took a mental note to ask her one day for some lessons. Nothing gave me more linguistic pleasure than being able to express my frustration properly in multiple languages.

As I walked toward the inn, I took a chance and glanced at the shadows where the humanborn lurked. In the shade of the building stood a dark silhouette of a man, his head turned toward the mythborn complaining to the guard with her voice loud enough to reach the passersby on the other side of the Liffey.

Instead of going into the inn, I moved to the wall and stuck to it, preparing for the dash to come. Once I started moving, I wouldn't be able to hide anymore... I wished I had a stunning curse with me, but they always caused trouble at the checkpoints, and I rarely carried them after the war. The veteran in me cringed at that choice, as if giving up any wartime habits in times of peace was to become my doom. But if I gave in to those urges, I'd never get a full night's sleep, even in the safety of my warded apartment.

The grim thoughts of mistakes past weren't about to help me, so I pushed away from the wall and darted toward the hiding humanborn. At the same moment, a flare rose into the dark sky, bathing the area with magical illumination. In its light, the man I was after stared at me in surprise.

Damn those mythborn! If only they had waited a few minutes longer!

I took a good look at his face, a dark-haired Irishman with the red skin of someone who indulged in alcohol, and then he lunged around the corner.

I wasn't about to give up so easily, and in his footsteps I followed. My common sense whispered that turning the corner could cost me my life if he waited there with another nasty explosive, but the thought of losing my only clue urged me to take the risk. My amulets should keep me alive unless he used something really powerful.

But when I ran into the next street, there was no one in sight. Magically powered street lamps provided enough light, and even though shadows crawled in the buildings' broken windows, no one would be able to disappear in the open.

I slowed down. With the commotion behind me, I couldn't count on hearing his footsteps, and I didn't want to pass the black holes of prewar shop windows too quickly. My mark could be hiding in any of them, waiting for a chance to strike.

Then I caught an order given in Irish behind me. The mythborn guards spread across the street, throwing light charms into the gaping holes of blackness that used to be shops, restaurants, and bars.

"Kaja, isn't it?" Their leader approached. I nodded, but he didn't offer to introduce himself. "Bríd told us you carry the Court's emblem." He looked around, then his eyes focused back on me. "She also said you were chasing a suspicious humanborn."

"Your flare spooked him," I replied, "and he disappeared before I made it to the corner."

At the mythborn's command, other guards split in twos and searched through the ruined buildings, and I kept silent about how pointless it was. I only hoped they wouldn't try to pin the failure on me. It was their flare that warned the suspect, but blaming the only humanborn around would paint them in a much better light if anyone in the Court asked questions.

The mythborn guard kept watching me as if he tried to gauge his approach. In normal circumstances, I'd be at best chased away, at worst accused of conspiring with whomever had blown up their inn. But I had Eithne's blessing materialized in a shiny silver emblem, and Bríd might have mentioned I helped with the wounded, so if he went too far, he risked I'd complain to the Court.

As I was a firm believer that good deeds should receive a reward, I expected my earlier efforts to pay off. Not that I would let those mythborn die if I could help it, but since I did, I had right to capitalize on it. After all, catching that bomber would help us all.

"I take it you want to have a look inside?" he asked.

"I'd appreciate if you allowed me." I kept my voice humble. No need to antagonize him if he stretched his hand out first. "Of course, I'll share all my findings and won't take anything without permission."

The mythborn turned back toward the inn and gestured for me to follow. "Of course." He grinned over his shoulder. "But we'll search you when you're done nevertheless."

So much for mutual trust. I held off a sigh. *Baby steps, Kaja, baby steps.* At least they didn't play the mythborn pride card and throw me out.

WHAT THE BOMB didn't destroy, the fire ravaged, and in the light of the charms, the Greenleaf Inn looked worse than some of the buildings that didn't survive the war. The mythborn guard and I walked through the soot and pieces of shattered windows, scanning the destroyed furniture. The inn must have been a cozy place, but the wood used to decorate was also its doom. At least the rescuers had already removed the bodies.

We made our way up to the third floor, where, according to the witnesses, the bomb went off, and the destruction before my eyes made the previous corridors and rooms seem well preserved. I already knew the terrorist had used nails and pieces of metal to ensure the death count would be high, but I didn't realize that the pieces of the bomb must have been strengthened with some sort of a curse. The shrapnel not only peppered the nearby victims, but also went through the walls, ceiling, and floor to reach more targets. Was there an igniting curse attached to it as well, or did the blaze start by accident?

Even without the dead bodies and invisible bloodstains purged by flame, I had no trouble figuring out the dreary tale of destruction, and all of my instincts demanded I turn and walk away. But I needed to get to the point of detonation, so I kept going deeper through the inn's corridors, making every effort to ignore the images of carnage my imagination was painting.

The mythborn guard gave me a curious glance. "You fought in the war, didn't you?"

I snorted. "That obvious, eh?"

He gave a slow, almost respectful nod. "You're searching for details, and you're reading more than someone without experience would see. You also keep pressing on even though your face says you'd rather get out of here."

"I don't enjoy pictures of slaughter," I replied. "In the war, civilians were mostly kept out of the fighting."

I didn't mention that both humanborn and mythborn ignored that rule at the slightest suspicion of said civilians collaborating with the enemy.

"Mostly," he said as if his thoughts followed a similar line. "So, what do you hope to find here?"

"Anything, really." I saw no reason to conceal the truth.

He didn't comment on the chances of finding that "anything" in a fire-purged place. In the charm's light, his gold hair and amber skin looked even more otherworldly than outside, and I avoided staring. Most mythborn were quite pleasing to the eye, save maybe the bridge dwellers and the hairiest of the molekind, but their personalities and attitude would cool down any romantic notion, and I didn't have time for indulging myself with eye candies.

His eyebrow arched slightly as if he'd caught my extended attention, so I fixed my gaze at the corridor. The bomb must have gone off in what looked like a recreation area, and I stared at the remnants of the explosion and the marks that the fire failed to erase. The terrorist had definitely used a device enhanced with a lot of magic.

"There's nothing here," my mythborn guide said.

I was ready to agree with him when a dark, twisted shape on the ceiling caught my eye. I couldn't reach it with my hand, so I scanned the surroundings for anything solid enough to climb on. The mythborn by my side reached out, and with a gentle jump he made it to the ceiling and back holding his prize: a piece of a metal plate. He landed with agility that would spark envy in a squirrel and held the object out to me.

"I'm guessing it's a piece of the bomb," he said. "But it's too damaged to learn much from it."

I caught the disappointment in his voice and almost hoped he'd toss the piece away. But trying to sneak it out could prove troublesome, so instead I asked, "Do you mind if I hold on to it then?"

"What happened to not taking anything from the site?"

I put on my best smile. "I'm asking nicely, am I not? It's big enough to split, and we could both do some research."

He thought before replying. "I'll take it to the Court, but I'll let them know they should send you a piece or even all of it when they're done. If you work for Lady Eithne, that shouldn't be a problem."

"It could take them weeks," I complained. "And that's time we don't have."

He snorted. "We?"

I kept my face serious, ignoring his bait. "That man is out there. He already bombed a humanborn place, and now the mythborn. Do you think he'll alternate between us? Or was the first run an accident, and you're his real target?" If he wanted to play the enemies card, I had no remorse using his fellow mythborn's deaths as a bargaining chip.

The guard hesitated, then sighed. He wedged the plate under his boot and bent it until it split in two. "Better be worth it." He handed me one of the pieces.

"I'll do my best." I put the metal in my bag. "I'm done here if you want to escort me out."

We headed outside, and as soon as we left the inn, two more guards approached, but my guide waved them away.

"She can leave," he said.

I gave him an appreciative nod for not insisting on having me searched. Maybe after I'd proven I knew what I was doing, he was exercising some trust? Either way, I got what I needed. The face of the suspect remained fresh in my memory, and with the charred piece of bent metal, I might have a means to track him down.

CHAPTER FIVE

T he man I saw near the Greenleaf Inn was a humanborn, so he most likely didn't make the explosive. The metal, though bent and charred, bore marks of intricate mythborn writing, and even though it wasn't impossible for us to learn their arts, the craft's perfection suggested the terrorist had had someone else make the bomb for him.

As I leaned over my worktable and pulled the light charm closer, I couldn't shake the feeling of the situation being out of place. Why would any mythborn make such a device for a humanborn? We might not be at war anymore, but I couldn't conjure anyone foolish enough to give the former enemy means to sow destruction. And since I was at it... Why would a humanborn bomb a place of his own kind first? Were the two attacks even related?

The feeling that I was missing some important pieces of the puzzle nagged like a hungry dog, and I couldn't shoo it away. The war had taught me that ignoring instincts led to either a quick or painful death.

With a magically enhanced blade, I cut off a piece of

metal. The plate I got at the inn was big enough to make several charms, so I had spare bits in case I screwed something up, which was likely. After all, I was a self-taught explorer.

The humanborn might not have created the bomb, but he carried it, and he might have been emotional about his task. I hoped he was, since he stuck around to watch the aftermath. The sensitive device carried to its destination might have soaked up some of his own latent magic. He wasn't an Afflicted or even in stages close to it, but the Magiclysm affected us all, and I was betting that I could reinforce the link between the bomb's scrap and the one who planted it at the inn.

I wanted to get the fecker, but even if I didn't, merely working on a locating charm got me excited. The idea budded from the blood-bound charms used to find missing people with drops of blood from their relatives, and I could copy most of the markings from there. The real problem was ensuring that the weak trace of personal magic, that I could only hope still lingered within the bent plate, would bind to the charm and make it work. It all depended on how emotional the terrorist was when he carried out his plan, and how lucky I'd be in forcing the foreign mythborn markings to do what I wanted.

Armed with an engraving tool and the knowledge I'd collected meticulously in my notebooks from any available sources—mostly from scavenged wartime devices—I began the process. Magic, the chaotic magic within me that was destroying my body, flowed almost harmoniously as I channeled it into the engravings I added to the scrap of metal. The excitement of creating a new charm and the prospect of trying it out almost dimmed the anticipation of finally having the means to find the terrorist. You see, I might be self-taught, and my etchings looked like cat scratches compared to the mythborn finery, but over those few quiet years after the war, working with magic became a bit of a passion.

I worked for hours, ignoring my body's need for rest. My breaks were only as long as the water took to boil, and I'd return to my worktable with a mug of fresh tea in my hand. Tea might be an expensive commodity, but I couldn't live without it, so I paid the price for being well stocked and let the dark, aromatic liquid keep my body going long after it should have collapsed.

The night was already receding when I put the last marks on my new device. My eyes burnt as if rubbed with sandpaper, but I ignored it and held the charm over an old map of Dublin. To my surprise, it pulled my hand to the west side of the city. Not enough to pinpoint the terrorist's location, but enough to suggest the direction. That was, of course, if he wasn't traveling often. But if the charm worked, I'd get to him sooner or later.

A yawn that almost dislocated my jaw reminded me that after a sleepless night I wouldn't make it through the day on tea alone, so I gave up the idea of going out immediately. A couple of hours of sleep and some caffeine capsules I'd found in the newly opened pharmacy should suffice.

With the last conscious thought, I set my alarm, an old-style wind-up clock, and crashed. The dreamless slumber embraced me before my face even hit the pillow.

AFTER SEVERAL HOURS, I forced my eyes open, poured more tea down my throat, and left home. The tracking charm seemed to be working well, but I didn't want to risk its power fading over time.

The aroma from the nearby bakery teased my nostrils, reminding me that a sleep-deprived body needed a full breakfast, the very one I'd skipped in my eagerness to get to work. I hushed my stomach with a promise of a treat for dinner later, but it still grumbled with displeasure. I almost felt the mythborn female's eyes following me as I pretended to ignore her pastries' display. One day I'd have to muster some courage and try her products. Of course, I planned on buying something to go and having Tadgh check it before I'd bite into it.

The charm still pulled me westward, and I took the route along the river. I remembered the leisurely strolls I used to take there, but now the Quays were as dilapidated as the rest of Dublin, maybe even more so, since the Eireland Office didn't invest in anyplace far from the city center and its tourists. With Dublin's citizens decimated, it made no point to restore all the buildings, and the most populated areas got the first treatment. Not to mention that both humanborn and mythborn representatives kept arguing that their districts got less funding the last time and slowed everything down, so any restoration project was bound to get stuck in the bureaucracy's narrow pipeline, and with enough bad luck, it'd linger there forever.

I turned south by the ruins of the Heuston Station. I didn't want to ponder the ill fate of the almost two-centuries-old building that we destroyed when the mythborn figured out the workings of trains and made them run on magic. In the war it seemed simple: they were bringing more mythborn from the countryside to fight us, so we placed explosive curses at their gathering point and at some tracks outside of Dublin to break the supply line.

Now... Now it seemed like a waste and another poorly healed scar on the once-fine city.

I walked down the wide street, weaving my way through the wrecks of cars and double-deck buses nobody had bothered to clean off the streets. Their yellow and blue paint had faded, and they were pockmarked by magical rains and exploding curses.

The charm's pull became stronger, and I resisted the urge to pick up my pace. Even before the war I didn't know the area well, and barging in blind was the last thing any sensible veteran would do. After all, I wanted to find the knacker who had already blown up two places, not to go down in a not-so-heroic fight against an overwhelming number of opponents if the terrorist had companions.

The modern apartments towered on one side of the street, their glass exteriors shattered like dreams of a peaceful life, and their concrete skeletons dark against the ever-gray sky. The charm led me along the street, and I couldn't help eyeing those tombstones of old Ireland with wariness. Even though the area seemed uninhabited, it didn't mean a gang or some other bunch of ne'er-do-wells wouldn't pick it as their hiding spot. It might be safe enough in the light of day, so I walked in the open instead of sneaking by, but my scout's instincts demanded I at least made a quick scan of the buildings I passed in case anyone was lurking nearby. In the war, it often meant the difference between making it to the end of the street or not, and I had no reason to believe the peace treaty we'd signed meant Dublin was safe. Some parts of it weren't particularly safe even before the war. Besides, some people had no problem turning against other humans when external dangers faded.

I caught movement at the end of the street. A man came out of the last building, heading my way. He didn't notice me, since he was busy shoving something into his pocket, but even with his face tilted down, I recognized him.

Without hesitation I lunged into a sprint, and before he looked up, I'd already cut the distance between us in half. If he stood his ground, he had a chance of taking me down: I might have fought in the war, but without my curses I wasn't much of an opponent, and a strong man wouldn't have much trouble overpowering me. But just as I hoped, his instincts kicked in, and at the sight of someone darting toward him, he turned and ran.

"Stop!" I shouted. "By the commander's order!"

I didn't expect him to obey, and the words weren't meant for him. My voice carried through the ruins, echoing in the empty streets, and I hoped it would reach the nearby humanborn checkpoint. If they cut off the man's escape, I wouldn't have to risk losing him in some half-destroyed building like last time.

The guards at the checkpoint must have been either bored or very cautious, because four out of the six-person team came running from around the corner straight at the escapee. The man stopped, and to my surprise didn't try to find another escape route. Instead, he turned toward me and smiled.

"You can't win this one," was all he said in his heavy Irish accent.

He squeezed his fist, and before I had a chance to react, a curse activated. I was lucky it wasn't another explosive one. Instead, the magic item sent a jolt through his body, and he collapsed. The smell of burnt hair filled the air, and I held back the reflexive urge to retch.

As the guards approached from the other side, I fished out the Trinity's emblem. "I'm here by the commander's order," I said. "This man was a suspect in the recent bombings."

They exchanged glances, then nodded. "We can take care of the body. Do you need anything else?" asked the one with the captain's badge.

"I saw him leaving one of the buildings, and I'd like to check it." Trying to ignore the stench, I fished some keys and a wallet out of his pocket. "Can you spare two people to accompany me?"

Without a word, he gestured at two of his companions, a tall, dark-skinned man with a club and a robust female with a crossbow.

"Thank you." If there were any terrorists in the building, the three of us wouldn't likely be enough, but having some backup couldn't hurt.

As we backtracked to the destroyed building, I checked the man's wallet. Eireland ID in the name of Jonas Byrne, a few bank notes, and a picture of a red-haired woman. The photograph looked contemporary, so the creases on the paper must have been from Jonas handling it. My inner voice whispered that she probably didn't survive the war if he had to look at it so often.

The building's interior remained silent, and no movement disturbed the rather grim scene. The ground floor was a picture of destruction that suggested the place was a resistance point during the war, and after a quick check, we made it upstairs.

I spotted the right place in an instant. Only one apartment had its door still intact. The keys fit, and my amulets didn't warn me of any nasty surprises waiting inside.

"Wait here," I told my escort.

Whatever was in the apartment, it might not be for their eyes. The mythborn-made bomb in the Greenleaf Inn suggested that someone from the other side of the river might be involved, and if the rumor spread, it wouldn't help in preserving whatever trust remained between the humanborn and the mythborn. Better to keep only Albert and Eithne privy to the information, and let them sort out any diplomatic issues.

The apartment was a mess. It seemed to have survived the war in a fairly good state, but Jonas didn't come across as a man who liked cleanliness. Dirty clothes were scattered on the floor and dirty dishes on the table accompanied the stench of old food and stuffy air. Dust mixed with crumbs of concrete from destroyed walls gathered in the corners. The light seeping through the boarded windows provided some visibility, but I still activated a charm when I approached the small desk in the corner.

On one side lay two metal devices, and the familiar mythborn markings made their purposes dreadfully clear, but it was the pile of papers in an unfamiliar language that caught my eye. The text used some of the mythborn runes, but it didn't seem their version of Gaelic. On top of the pile lay a strange medallion: an Irish triskelion with its arms shaped into snake heads. The same symbol appeared on the documents.

Jonas's last words returned to me. *You can't win.* A dying man choosing such words could mean only one thing: there were more of them, and not all were humanborn. I stared at the document, painfully conscious I had a decision to make. If I gave the papers to Albert, Eithne would most likely deny everything, and we'd never learn much, but if I kept them secret... Would the Court representative spill some information in gratitude for not dragging the Trinitians into what could be inner mythborn matters? Even if some offshoot of MPF was using the humanborn as their mules, it didn't mean the conspiracy was reaching beyond mythborn politics.

It was not a decision I wanted to make, but it was one I had to make nevertheless.

With a quiet sigh, I hid the papers and the triskelion in my bag. I could at least try negotiating with Eithne and see where it would get me. If she refused, I'd tell Albert everything.

The rest of the apartment yielded nothing, so I stepped outside and locked the door. "There are explosive devices inside," I said. "Post guards downstairs and notify Trinity. They'll send someone to deactivate them."

We got to the ground floor and parted ways. I needed to send a message to the Court and then head for Trinity. Jonas was dead, and the threat of another bombing waned, but his last words and the weight of the documents in my bag reminded me I would be a fool to seek comfort in the terrorist's end.

We might have removed a pawn from the chessboard that Dublin had suddenly became, but the player who moved it remained hidden.

I WAS ALREADY WAITING at the Trinity when Eithne arrived. I sat at the table in one of the guest halls that Albert used to receive visitors he couldn't deal with outside and wasn't willing to let roam Trinity, let alone invite to his office. Come to think of it, the halls mostly hosted mythborn guests and Eireland Office representatives, which spoke volumes of whom Albert trusted.

I had a good view through the window. Escorted by one of the guards, Eithne strode through the yard so light and flowing she might as well have been levitating above the ground, and when she walked into the room, her presence filled it with magic instantly. It was much like in the old movies, where flowers bloomed and birds sang at the fair maiden's approach. The problem was Eithne didn't fit the maiden's role any more than I did. Her beauty might be deceiving, but her sharp green eyes left no doubt she was an experienced player, ready to sacrifice a lot to reach her goal. If she was to lead her people, I'd bet she'd be as good at it as Albert. It also made me wonder what kind of person pulled the strings in the Court, if such a cunning player was a mere messenger.

"Kaja." Eithne's voice had a pleasant ring to it, and she offered me a smile. "I've heard you've found the guilty humanborn."

Was there a hint of satisfaction in her last word? After all, I'd proven that the Mythborn Protection Forces had nothing to do with the attacks.

I gave a short nod in response, and she didn't ask any more questions. Instead, she sat at the table by my side, leaving the opposite side to Albert, as if she wanted to alienate him. Her eyes remained locked on me, and I could only guess whether she was performing some sort of an evaluation or simply aiming to make me feel uncomfortable. Knowing vibrant mythborn personalities, she was probably doing both.

"Lady Eithne, Kaja." Albert walked in and sat by the table. His arched eyebrow was the only comment on Eithne's choice of seating. "My apologies for not wasting time for pleasantries."

I leaned back in my chair and shrugged. My relationship with Albert had been anything but formal, and I liked it that way. We only played the show of formality for others.

"No need to apologize," Eithne replied. "Let's get to the matters at hand. As I understand, the threat has been dealt with?"

"Kaja located the terrorist, a humanborn named Jonas Byrne." Albert gave me an appreciative nod. "Unfortunately, he committed suicide before we got any information, but from what we've gathered, his motive might have been the death of his wife and unborn child."

Eithne's eyebrow arched in polite interest while I kept my face straight. Albert made this assumption based on the death notification letter his men found on Jonas's body and after checking the records in the Eireland Office. To him, it must have seemed the terrorist worked alone, struck with grief and hate, since I hadn't told him yet that I believed those emotions were merely used by someone else to push poor Jonas to violence.

"His wife wasn't of Irish descent, so she took the evacuation offer," Albert continued as I fought the need to share my suspicions with him. It had to wait until I talked to Eithne. "She was pregnant at the time and in the first group to leave the island. Things had gone wrong during the obligatory quarantine. It turned out she was one of the Afflicted, and something had triggered the change. She killed three people before the guards... neutralized her."

Silence fell after Albert finished. Even though I knew the story already, it still reminded me of all the things gone wrong, during the war and after it. As heartbreaking as Jonas's story might be, I doubted it was the most dramatic one.

"But why would he target both humanborn and mythborn?" Eithne asked.

"I believe he blamed you for the war, and us for his wife's death." Albert shrugged. "But it might as well have been a twisted mind's need to sow destruction and share the pain regardless of who the target was."

"I see." Eithne seemed satisfied with the explanation, as if some humanborn terrorist's motives were of secondary importance. "Is there anything else before we discuss Kaja's payment?"

Albert gave her a lukewarm stare. "Actually, there is. We've found two more explosive devices in his apartment. They were of mythborn make."

Her eyebrows arched ever so slightly, as if Albert didn't just throw a veiled accusation at her, but casually told her he saw a seagull in his office window.

"If the Court could have one of those devices, we'd do our best to track down its origin," she replied. "If someone among the mythborn is trading such things, we'll ensure they learn the wrongs of their choices." Her face hardened.

As much as I disliked Eithne, I had to admit she played it well. In one reply she ignored Albert's indirect accusation and made a claim the Court had nothing to do with it... even if they did.

"I'll see what I can do." The tone of Albert's voice made it clear he didn't like her response. "There's nothing else to discuss, then. We'll inform the press the culprit was apprehended, making it a joint effort of Trinity and the Court, if Kaja doesn't mind." He looked at me.

"I'm fine with that." I didn't need more advertisement, and if the news of the humanborn and mythborn working together could help to defuse the hostilities, I was all for it.

"Very well. Your usual rate?" he asked.

Eithne leaned forward. "If you don't mind, the Court will fully cover Kaja's expenses."

That comment earned her two surprised glares. Albert

must have been pondering the Court's sudden generosity, while I searched for Eithne's hidden motive.

"Fine with me," Albert replied first. "If you don't need my presence anymore, I'll return to my duties, but feel free to take however much time you need. A guard will be waiting outside to escort you to the gate, Lady Eithne."

As soon as he exchanged short bows with Eithne and left, the mythborn female locked her green gaze on me. Out of a sash by the belt of her embroidered silk dress, she took a small vial. A thick brown liquid washed against its glass walls.

"You'll receive the money as well, but I believe this is what you really want." She offered the vial to me. "Take one drop every day, diluted in any liquid."

I stared at the vial, unable to ask the most important question.

"It won't revert any changes," Eithne said. I wasn't surprised she knew what was on my mind. "But it can significantly slow them down."

My eyes widened. If I understood right, as long as I didn't get another curse thrown at me or imbalance my inner magic in any other way, I'd be as good as cured. My affinity for magic, the side effect of the change, never bothered me, while transforming into a drooling heap of destruction did. It seemed the vial was my salvation, but it also might have been Eithne's trap. Why would she part with such a drug? Why would she offer me a way out?

Eithne smiled, but I couldn't see past her mask. No hidden motives, no malicious intent... As if a friend had offered me a bottle of my favorite perfumes just because she was my friend. Her benevolence must have been driven by reasons I wasn't aware of, maybe even couldn't comprehend, but it also gave me an opening.

"That's very generous of the Court," I said.

"The news of your help at Greenleaf Inn reached us, Kaja," she replied.

So it was a game after all, and she had something else in mind. Saving several insignificant mythborn couldn't have made a significant difference. I didn't reply, just waited for her move.

"You did more than you were asked to." She inspected my face with sudden interest. "You seem tense, though. Do you not trust the medicine?"

Of course I didn't entirely trust the "medicine," but I had ways to check it later, and if I wanted to get answers from her, I had to be open up about what really bugged me. Without a word, I slid the triskelion out of my pocket and placed it on the table between us.

Eithne's face became still, and I caught that subtle shift in her impenetrable mask. She stared at the medallion for a long, silent moment. "Albert doesn't know." She didn't ask— she had figured it out.

"Not yet." I let her read a clear warning in my voice. If she brushed the matter away or lied about the triskelion, I'd go straight to Albert.

To my surprise, I didn't get a sarcastic comment or a jab about my distrust toward everything and everyone, but the friendly smile she gave me instead worried me. It meant venturing into the uncharted waters of my relationship with her, where one mistake could sink my hopes of learning more. And I needed to know more, since her reaction had already confirmed the Court knew the symbol. I could bet they also had information about the ones who wore the triskelions, because there had to be more of them.

She reached for it, and I let her take it. I had copied the symbol, and the papers too, just in case I needed them.

"Come visit me at the Court, Kaja," she said in a casual, friendly tone. "You'll receive the payment we owe you, and we'll talk more if you wish to. Show my emblem to the guards, and they'll let you in."

I raised a brow at that. An invitation to the Court sounded like a promise of information, because I had no doubt the payment was only an excuse. Whatever the snake triskelion meant, Eithne didn't intend to discuss it at Trinity, and I could relate. I wouldn't spill my secrets either in a place that could have unwanted ears about.

"It'll be a pleasure, Lady Eithne," I replied in a formal tone. "Would tomorrow at noon suit you?"

"Perfect." She got up from the table. "Until tomorrow, then, Kaja."

Her departure was as smooth and flowing as her arrival... as if the triskelion I gave her never shook her composure.

My excitement at learning something fought with the guilt of keeping secrets from Albert. In the past, I'd never even considered it—but in the past, we fought against the mythborn together. If I told him now, Albert would insist he'd handle it, either because of the ill-conceived need to protect me or because he believed such things should be handled by the Trinitians, and I wasn't one of them. Since Eithne wouldn't have admitted anything openly, I made the hard call. With my officially neutral position, even as dubious as it was because of my strong ties to Trinity, she might give me at least a few scraps of information. The memory of the snake symbol, unsettling and with a sinister feel to it, convinced me that we needed to know what was going on. Even if that meant removing Albert from the loop for the time being.

I smiled at the thought of how pissed he'd be if he knew.

Not even because I'd left him out, but because of the risk I was about to take. For all I knew, Eithne's luring me to the Court could be an attempt to remove me from the picture. I'd go to the North Side but never return, becoming one more disappearance in the unstable Dublin, and no one would ever find a proof it was Eithne's doing.

I brushed those thoughts aside. It wouldn't be the first time I'd gambled my own life to get the information Trinity needed, and taking initiative without going through the proper channels was always my trademark.

Before I left the college grounds, I paused at the inner yard. Maybe I should at least mention to Albert I hoped to get some information from Eithne? This way he'd have a trace to follow in case something happened. I pondered how much I could share with him, but the image of his reaction dealt with my doubts faster than a seagull gulped a crab. Albert would deem it too risky or insist I told him all I knew. Both cases could blow my chances with Eithne. I doubted she had spies so close to Albert, but she seemed to know a lot about the life in the former college, so I wasn't willing to take that risk.

I walked out into College Green and merged into the crowd that headed toward Dame Street. I'd tell Albert once I had some solid information.

CHAPTER SIX

Before the Court became the Court and was a Museum of Decorative Arts and History, I visited it often. The square building with a large yard in the middle made me feel like I'd stepped back in time, and its extensive exhibitions always caught my attention. But after the war broke out and then ended, I didn't come around too often. The museum stood on the north side of the river, and venturing into the mythborn-controlled territory was risky. Besides, the Court guards wouldn't let anyone in who hadn't been invited by Lady Eithne or some other influential mythborn. Even when I did assignments for them, carried messages from Trinity or requested information, I'd only be allowed as far as the inner courtyard. Eithne would come down to me, and I'd never get to see the Court's interior or the mythborn who ran it. I heard of some humanborn stupid enough to try sneaking in, but I wasn't one of them.

It was almost noon when I approached the gate, and the armor-clad guards barred my entry. Their usual reaction put me at ease, because I still didn't know whether I'd be walking out of the Court alive.

"My name is Kaja Modrzewska. I'm here at Lady Eithne's invitation." I showed them the silver emblem.

Their leader gave it a quick glance but didn't inspect it closely, and I took it as a good sign. They might have been informed I'd be coming. "You'll have to leave all your amulets, charms, and curses in there. We'll return them when you leave." He pointed at the door in the archway.

I tensed. Before, they were never that strict with their security, at least not when one could walk only about fifty steps into the courtyard. It might have meant that Eithne wanted to have a private talk. But no matter the reason, I couldn't agree to their terms. I had a few charms and curses I could part with for a while, even if I didn't like the thought of mythborn getting a close look at them, but the rest had to stay on. I wouldn't risk my affliction getting worse at Eithne's vague suggestion she'd sate my curiosity. Not to mention that if I was walking into a trap, giving up all my protection seemed foolish.

"I'm afraid I can't remove all of them," I said in an apologetic tone. "Is there any other way?" Trinitians had their scanners to check for malicious curses, so maybe the mythborn had something similar they could use?

It seemed that my tone wasn't apologetic enough, or the mere fact I didn't want to remove all my magical items at once made them suspicious. The mythborn guards enclosed me in the four walls of their massive shoulders. Their stern faces and teeth jutting from their lower lips told me there was no way I'd talk myself out of this one, even if I wanted to leave the Court's grounds, forgetting all about the deal with Eithne.

"Is there any trouble?" Another mythborn approached.

If I was to describe him with a single word, I'd pick "gray." Not only because he wore the uniform that matched the color of most ruins in Eireland, but he also had short, ash-like hair and skin resembling Irish skies on the gloomiest of winter days, though its texture seemed more like dried-up, cracked mud.

And the emblem on his chest, the only patch of black, had the symbol I knew so well from the times of war: ribbons of smoke weaving into a blade, the symbol of the Scáthanna—the shadows. If mythborn had anything that could be considered "special forces," its member stood before me, but at least he didn't seem hostile, his face expressing a mixture of caution and amusement.

"Lady Eithne's guest," one of the guards replied. "She refuses to surrender all the magical items she carries."

I gave the newcomer what I hoped was my best defiant stare. No way he could convince me to take off even one of my trinkets.

"I see." He glared back at me with those quicksilver-hued eyes, too intense to even resemble human ones. Then he turned to the guard. "If you're concerned about safety, I could spare a moment and escort our guest to Lady Eithne's office." His English, clear and precise, had that unfamiliar ring that I called "the mythborn accent," and I had to appreciate he didn't insist on using Irish.

"But the charms..." the guard muttered.

The gray mythborn gave no reply except for a stern look, and to my surprise, the guards took a step back.

"As you wish, Master Riagán," said their leader.

I wished I could say I kept my face straight, but I only hoped I didn't gape like a clueless child. He was *Riagán*?! The mythborn sharpshooter whose testimony of skills were the countless bodies of Trinitians and other humanborn, shot from unbelievable distances and at impossible angles. Only his arrows, all marked with a gray band, sticking out of our fallen comrades proved that Riagán was more than a tale spun by campfires.

His smirk told me he'd figured out what I was thinking, and the arch of his eyebrow confirmed he wasn't just some random mythborn who happened to have the same name.

"Shall we?" he asked with the courtesy I didn't expect from someone like him, and then he offered his arm.

I stared at it probably longer than would be considered polite. I reminded myself we were not at war and fought against the temptation to march off toward the Court's door, forcing him to catch up. Then I took his arm, because, Scáthanna member or not, he seemed like the lesser evil compared to the overzealous guards. Of course, he might just be confident that he'd put a quick end to any scheme I might have been trying to pull off.

"I don't believe we've met before." He led me through the courtyard toward the Court's entrance.

Two more guards stood there, but they paid us no attention, as if Riagán's presence was all the credentials they needed.

I bit my tongue before replying that obviously we hadn't, since I was still alive. The war was over, and if he could act civil, so could I. "Kaja," I replied. "Kaja Modrzewska."

He repeated my name as if tasting it, and his pronunciation was close to perfect. "Is this your first visit to the Court?" he asked.

We walked through the vast corridors of what used to be the Museum of Decorative Arts and History, and even though I'd walked its halls many times, I didn't recognize it.

Everything inside had changed—the corridors' layout, the rooms' size, and their furnishing. Intricate paintings hung on the walls, depicting events of glory and greatness in otherworldly sceneries. Ambient lights, small lanterns encrusted with gems, and carved benches decorated the interiors, all matched perfectly. Whoever was responsible for the Court's furnishings had superb taste.

And, of course, there was magic too, subtle but ubiquitous, teasing my senses to the point I considered how it would affect my body. Yet my own magic remained quiet, as if the Court had soothing effects on it.

"To the Court... yes," I replied. No point mentioning I saw the place before the mythborn claimed it for their own.

"Then I won't distract you with attempts at conversation, and let you take it in," Riagán said.

I sent him a weak smile that I hoped would suffice to show my appreciation. His offer was probably nothing more than a mythborn boasting of the grandeur of his own people, but it allowed me to take in all the beauty and marvel before my eyes. It also provided an escape from the small talk during which I'd have to steer clear from any sensitive subject: the war, the mythborn, the Court... so, pretty much anything, unless we wanted to discuss the weather at lengths it most certainly didn't deserve.

Once we stopped by the door guarded by a single mythborn, he took a step back. A smile still lingered on his lips while he held my hand, and I silently swore that if he kissed it, I'd slap him silly, no matter the consequences.

He let go. "It's been a pleasure, Kaja." He bowed to me and then nodded to the guard, who opened the door without a word. "I hope we meet again."

I swallowed a hostile response and reciprocated the bow. "I'd hate to take more of your time," I said in a tone that, with a huge dose of tolerance, could have been considered polite.

He burst out laughing, and I found no malice in his tone,

only amusement like the one a parent has for a stubborn child.

"Riagán?" Eithne stepped out through the door, and then her gaze turned to me. "Kaja."

"The guards had concerns about her amulets and charms, so I took it upon myself to escort your guest to you, my lady." Riagán bowed. "Unless you need me for anything else, I shall take my leave now."

The look Eithne gave Riagán I could only describe as a warning glare, as if he was overstepping some boundary known only to the two of them. Then her face softened, and with a gesture she invited me into her office. Whatever the whole thing was about, it seemed I wasn't supposed to know, and I couldn't care less for their squabbles when I wasn't the one in trouble.

The room smelled of old oaks with its walls and floor covered in wood. Some, decorated intricately in nature motifs, had delicate marks of green paint, making the carvings resemble fresh leaves, but other than that, Eithne's office proved to be quite monochromatic—a large desk made of wood matching the walls, and so empty it could satisfy even my OCD-driven coworker from the prewar times, and two carved chairs that resembled uncomfortable thrones.

The only splash of color was a set of two cups and matching jug made of white porcelain, which I believed I'd seen on the museum's display back in the happier, more stable times. It seemed that with all their pride and looking down on the humanborn, the mythborn weren't beyond recycling our art pieces.

Eithne poured clear liquid and passed a cup to me.

I dipped my lips into it, more as a courtesy than of a need to drink, and the smell of alcohol and plum hit my nostrils. If not for the color, I'd believe the mythborn lady had served me Asian plum wine, which I hadn't drunk for years. I took a cautious sip and savored the sweet alcoholic taste.

Eithne's eyes shone, and she took a drink from her own cup. "The secret of brewing veenya belongs to the mythborn alone," she said. My linguistic knowledge in the matter was limited, but I was certain "veenya" wasn't a Gaelic word. "And it always tastes different, depending on who drinks it."

Magic... I should have known. Hiding my regret, I put the cup down.

"Don't worry, you can drink it safely," Eithne added.

Maybe I could, but plum wine was strong, and I preferred to be sober in her presence. "You invited me here for a reason, didn't you?" I asked, even though we both knew the answer already.

Eithne opened one of the drawers and put two vials on the desk. Their familiar dark brown color made me hold my breath, but my voice of reason whispered these would come at a high price.

"I wanted to thank you for not mentioning the symbol to Albert." She pushed the vials toward me. "These are for you to use as you see fit." The way she said it reassured me that she guessed I wouldn't be drinking it all myself.

"I hope you'll clean your own... house, Lady Eithne," I replied in a rather dry tone, and didn't reach for the vials. I didn't keep her secret out of courtesy or for personal gain, but to avoid igniting animosities between former enemies and out of hope she'd shed some light on what was going on.

Eithne sighed, and I couldn't figure out whether the sadness on her face was genuine. "I intend to do so, though the issue, as you saw for yourself, is not limited to the mythborn," she said. "I'd like to ask for your help in our investigation."

So the vials were either a bribe or an advance payment for my future services. Maybe even a way to keep me under her thumb and ensure I didn't pass any information to other factions in Dublin, especially the Trinitians.

"Will you have me running blind, or can I expect some... briefing?"

Eithne's laughter filled the room like the sound of wind chimes on a hot summer evening. "I'll tell you what you need to know," she said sincerely. "I trust you won't go about revealing anything to anyone outside the Court without my permission."

"Fair enough," I replied. As much as I'd prefer not to agree, if I wanted the knowledge, I had to play by her rules. "But you'll tell me everything. No scraps, no leaving out uncomfortable details."

Her lips stretched in another smile, though her expression was that of a seasoned player, and then she said, "Of course." She pointed at my cup sitting alone on the desk. "Make yourself comfortable—it's quite a story."

The carved wood pressing against my back made it clear I should abandon all hope for any comfort while I sat in the chair, so I reached for the cup. Since Eithne had gone through the trouble of giving me two vials of a substance I desperately needed and served me an expensive drink, she must really want me to listen... and to help.

"Centuries ago, when we left this world, when we sought shelter in another realm, we took most of the magic with us," Eithne said. "It seemed fair to do so. Humans were pushing us out of our home, but we wouldn't leave behind that what they craved the most. Only a few of the skilled ones stayed behind, adapting their magic to the new, limited ways and to the new religion."

I gave a slow nod. I could appreciate that Eithne gave me a shortened version instead of debunking the tangle of Irish myths. Especially that most of them were probably born after the mythborn had already left. I could always ask for the details later, and I had to trust she wasn't about to leave out the pieces of the story I needed.

"Have you heard the story of Saint Patrick?" she asked.

"The one where he got rid of the snakes?" I replied. "That's obviously a myth."

Eithne gave me an amused glare.

Right, magic and mythborn-like beings were nothing more than a story too, but the latter sat in front of me, more real than any myth should be.

"Indeed, there were no snakes in Eire, ever," she said. "But Saint Patrick did rid Eire of something... Sadly, unlike the legend says, he didn't drive it into the sea."

My jaw dropped, just a little, when I connected the dots. "He sent it to your world." The snake-head triskelion made sense all of a sudden. "Fomoire?" I used the old Irish word, instead of the modern one or its English equivalent, Fomorians, but Eithne shook her head.

"Something more primal that gave birth to Fomoire before even my people's times," she replied. "When we still lived here, we conquered them in wars and reduced them to a handful, but when we left, there wasn't anyone to stand guard, and we didn't leave you enough magic to keep them at bay. I can only guess they bred, and their numbers grew again."

"And Saint Patrick?" I asked, though I suspected the answer.

"He used whatever magic he had left to drive them out of this place once and for all." Her voice turned bitter.

"Into the same world you sought your refuge in," I finished for her.

"They thrived there as much as we did. We fought wars for centuries, and there were many glorious battles to sing about..." Her eyes lost focus, but then she looked sharply and gave me a somewhat apologetic smile. "But there are also tales of loss and fall, and those of betrayal too, and as time passed, they started to outnumber those of victory."

I remained silent. Eithne didn't lie when she promised me the whole story. I wouldn't be surprised if I was the first human... humanborn to hear what had really happened: why the Magiclysm broke out and why the mythborn returned.

"We were falling," she whispered. "Coming back here... coming back home was our last desperate attempt to save our kind and to lock the three-headed snake away in the wasted world. We hoped that we would find a way to coexist, to share the gift of magic with humans in return for a safe haven."

Instead, the Magiclysm raged, and now I understood why. Upon their return, they must have siphoned all their magic back, and it was just too much for the world that had become industrialized and rational.

Eithne gave a nod as if she followed my line of thought. "We forgot that time doesn't stand still in either of the worlds, and we were unprepared for what awaited us here..." She shook her head. "Before anything could be done, we were at war again, and the rivers of spilled blood divided us and the humanborn."

I knew this part of the story all too well, and with the memories of my friends dying still fresh, I couldn't offer any sincere comfort, especially not with the bitter certainty that both the mythborn and humanborn only entered peace negotiations because they were bleeding out. Maybe the mythborn would have gotten us in the long run, with most of Eireland under their control, but then the rest of the world would likely retaliate, wiping them from the face of the planet. It was only a matter of time for the world scientists to learn how to counter the magic distortions over Eireland, and the world's armed forces would be upon them. They were strangers, they were powerful, and they were a threat. No chance humans would leave them alone.

Eithne's expression became serious. "It's our home too, Kaja, and we won't let anyone force us to leave again," she said. "We will fight for it, and we won't let the humanborn subdue us. But for the same reason, we wish to protect it."

"The three-headed snake," I said.

"Somehow, it has found its way back here. We don't know how, but we're certain Jonas Byrne couldn't have been the only one." She leaned forward in her chair, her eyes fixed on me. "Your net of information is wider than mine. I need your help in finding the Snake's agents... in finding the one who passes this blight on to the others. Who gives them dark thoughts and means to destroy what we're trying to build here."

"So the devices don't come from mythborn?" I asked.

"Not that I know of," Eithne replied with a sincerity I didn't expect. The Court's representative admitting to her lack of information... That was both surprising and serious. "Their design is of the Otherworld, of the Fomori's hands, but I can't be certain that some mythborn hadn't... converted."

She didn't have to add that it happened before. Her own mention of betrayal made it clear that the Snake and its

Fomori children could sway the mythborn to join their side, and Jonas Byrne's example proved that humanborn weren't above suspicion either.

Eithne sat silent, as if waiting for my reply. My eyes slid down toward the desk and the vials filled with the dark fluid. Why did she even bother asking? Why did she bother with all the show of making an impression on me or trying to convince me? She had me already. She must know that I'd do almost anything for every single drop of my salvation; that I'd agree, especially after the tale that reassured me that I wasn't only helping the Court. I was helping save everyone in Eireland and preventing the war.

"How long do you think you have?" Eithne asked all of a sudden.

I cringed, not happy she'd voiced my own fears. As if she needed to drive the point home. "A year," I sourly replied. "Maybe more, if your remedy is as good as you claim."

"A cautious but quite accurate estimation." The fact that Eithne didn't discard my number wasn't comforting. "And then what, Kaja?"

I didn't want to tell her that I thought about it every night when sleep wouldn't take me. I didn't want to admit to the fear eating through my composure. She already had a hold on me, so I had no reason to give her more ammunition, and I definitely wasn't about to tell her that I'd already prepared. Among the many charms I wore, one wasn't to protect me from attacks. It was to protect others from me, should it come to that. A quick and hopefully painless death locked in the shape of a metal pin.

"That brings me to the second matter I hoped to discuss with you here," Eithne said when I didn't reply.

Another topic she wanted to talk about away from Albert or anyone else eavesdropping. A topic that somehow involved me and my problems. A cold shiver went down my spine when it occurred to me that all the show she'd put on so far, including entrusting me with the mythborn stories and secrets, might have been only a prelude to what we were about to discuss now.

Eithne leaned back in her chair, and I couldn't tell whether she was confident she'd get what she wanted or was trying to throw me off balance. Countless scenarios and multiple possibilities ran through my head as I searched for a latching point, for anything that would even the playing field.

But despite my increased intellectual effort, when Eithne started to speak, I listened to her offer speechless and dumbfounded.

CHAPTER SEVEN

When the conversation was over and Eithne walked me to her office's door, she showed quite the understanding toward my sudden lack of eloquence and spared me a smile out of her usual arsenal of humiliating expressions.

"Take your time making the decision," she said with unfamiliar softness in her voice, as if her offer was something more than a business proposal, more than a way to gain what she wanted. "I'll have someone escort you to..." Her words faded and her face returned to its familiar stern expression.

She wasn't looking at me anymore, so I followed her gaze. Riagán was leaning against the large window frame. He didn't even pretend to be watching the courtyard, and as soon as Eithne noticed him, he offered a bow.

"Weren't you supposed to be gone?" she asked without warmth.

"Our guest will need an escort to the exit," he replied in a casual way, as if Eithne's somewhat hostile expression didn't bother him.

The tension between them was clear, though I didn't have high hopes for learning what was going on between the two. The Court's politics were as unexplored as the mythical Atlantis. The mythborn could be slaughtering one another within the former museum's walls and no living soul outside would hear a thing about it.

"And you were concerned I wouldn't find a free guard around?" Eithne's eyes narrowed, and I caught a warning between the lines.

"I'm also here because one of our own asked to see our guest," he replied. "Connor, if you recall him."

I almost breathed out with relief when Eithne's expression lost its threatening edge. The last thing I wanted was to witness two mythborn fighting, especially in the middle of the Court, where I couldn't strategically withdraw to a safer place.

"Connor? I remember him." Eithne gave a nod. "Very well—take Kaja to him if she wishes to go." Then she turned to me. "It's been a pleasure, and I hope you'll visit us soon, regardless of whether you have any information or not."

I bowed. "Thank you for your hospitality, Lady Eithne." Funny how I turned to playing by the rules, but after the conversation we'd had, and after I'd agreed to work for her, I had to keep my attitude in check.

When I lifted my head, her office door was already closing. The lone mythborn guard stood unmoving, so, with no other choice, I turned to Riagán, who approached with the smile of a confident cat. I swear he was only missing whiskers, and I half expected him to lick his lips like a feline that had just caught a mouse.

"The mythborn I mentioned, Connor, wishes to discuss a private matter with you," he said. "Do you mind sparing a moment of your time for him?"

He couldn't have been more vague... Or maybe Connor didn't tell him much? It sounded like an assignment offer, and even though the Court members rarely sought my services, this one might be desperate enough to do so. I nodded and indicated for him to lead the way, but as soon as we started walking, he matched my pace.

"Did the meeting with Lady Eithne go well?" he asked like someone making small talk.

"I preferred when we walked in silence." I might not have been polite in my reply, but I had things to digest and consider, the very things said meeting was about, and I didn't feel like focusing on a conversation with a mythborn whom I knew only by his kill count.

Riagán's lips twitched into something that might have been a mocking smile, but he respected my blunt request.

He took me one floor up and stopped by a door as inconspicuous as all the others along the corridor. He opened it without knocking, and with a gesture invited me to step in.

The room must have been a workshop of sorts, with multiple tables and shelves filled with what I believed were protective amulets and offensive curses. A thought of snatching one up crossed my mind, but I wasn't about to give in to the temptation with Riagán behind my back and another mythborn in front of me, hunched over a table. This must be Connor.

Before I spoke any words of greeting, he stretched and turned toward us. I took note of an intricate, harness-like device that webbed his left thigh with countless amulets. As he took a step forward, his leg remained stiff, throwing his body slightly off balance, but I wasn't paying attention to it anymore. I looked at Connor's face with its peach complexion marked by darker, marble-like veins, and memories from the war swarmed me in an instant.

The heavy steps of an approaching giant that set the ground into a gentle quake, my squad hastily retreating, and myself dashing away from them back into the middle of the street. Their voices, heavy with urgency, calling my name. The red trail of blood as I pulled the wounded mythborn warrior into a nearby gate. And the longest five minutes of my life as I sat beside a bleeding mythborn nurturing a fool's hope that the giant wouldn't follow the scent of blood.

Once again I felt the helplessness of those moments. I knew I wouldn't be able to drag the mythborn deeper into the apartment complex, that we wouldn't be able to escape fast enough. And the desperation in the mythborn's eyes when he tried to reach for his knife. The mythborn might have used giants as a part of their warfare, but they didn't control them, and if they weren't careful, they fell victim to the big'uns' hunger too. In any other case, I wouldn't have pitied the enemy, but no one, not even a mythborn, deserved to die by a giant's hand—or its mouth, to be more precise.

Connor stared back at me, and I couldn't shake the feeling he was reliving the same moment.

I still remembered the overwhelming relief when a distant scream pulled the giant's attention in another direction before he got to the blood trail and sealed our fate.

"I wanted to thank you in person." Connor's eyes were darker and dimmer than I remembered, and his voice carried the sort of tiredness only seasoned warriors had.

I bit my lip. I'd left him back there in that apartment complex as soon as I made sure he wasn't about to bleed to death. A thing I felt uneasy about, patching up a mythborn, but after we'd survived the giant, it seemed like a waste to let him die there. Not that I'd have sticked around to nurse him back to health, but he must have understood that. He was, after all, an enemy.

"Nobody deserves to die by a giant's hand." It sounded stupid, but what was I supposed to say?

Connor's eyebrow arched, and for a moment he resembled the other mythborn from the Court, sardonic and confident, not the war veteran with a numb leg. "You had a choice."

I gave a short nod. I didn't want to explain why instead of finishing him off I tried to save him, contradicting the effort my squad made mere moments earlier to ground him and his comrades. A quick skirmish like many others, and I'd have left him to bleed until his last drop if the giant hadn't come. I didn't want to tell him I did it because of how my sister died. No mythborn needed to know that about me.

"As odd as it may sound, I'm glad you made it," I said.

He glanced at his harnessed leg, the one I remembered to be badly injured back then. "I was lucky."

"We both were," I replied. If the giant hadn't changed his route...

His facial expression shifted, and he opened his mouth, but the words didn't come, as if he'd changed his mind. He offered me a smile instead, and silence fell in the room. Connor broke it first. "I didn't know whether you made it out alive until recently," he said. "As you can see, I don't go out much anymore, but when Riagán mentioned you were at the Court, I asked him if he could arrange a meeting."

I glanced over my shoulder at the mythborn archer who stood by the door, watching the scene without what I already considered his usual smile.

"I appreciate the effort." Sure, it was nice to learn he survived the war, but what on Earth was I supposed to talk about with a mythborn who lived only because I'd had a moment of weakness? Because the sight of Ela's body crushed under a giant's foot, and the screams of Paul being eaten alive, never ceased to haunt me, always returning whenever I pushed them away for too long.

He hissed and shifted his weight back to his healthy leg. "I apologize, but I need to adjust the harness. I've been testing new amulets, and they seem to enhance the pain rather than numb it." He limped deeper into the room and sat at a chair. "It's been good to meet you."

I had to appreciate the way out he offered. "Likewise," I replied with honesty.

RIAGÁN WALKED me down the stairs and into the courtyard, but I was so deep in my thoughts I didn't pay attention to him. Meeting Connor had made my memories resurface, and my mind was back in the war, swarming me with all the images I worked so hard to forget. Still, I wasn't unhappy that I got to meet the mythborn I had saved. It gave me hope the peace could be maintained, and that the gruesome and disturbing experiences wouldn't come back in another outburst of mutual slaughter.

"I apologize if meeting Connor distressed you." Riagán's voice pulled me back to reality. "I should have explained what the meeting was about, but I feared you'd refuse."

"I'm fine," I muttered, hoping the mythborn would take the cue and shut up. My war scars weren't a suitable discussion topic.

The look he gave me indicated he doubted my honesty, and I didn't bother proving him wrong. We had made it through most of the courtyard already, so I would be free of his company soon enough.

The guards at the gate looked up, but their attention wasn't on us, and out of the corner of my eye I caught Eithne approaching. Had she remembered something I needed to know before I left? I slowed down but didn't get to do anything else as one of my charms activated. I wasted precious seconds staring at it, because since the war had ended, it wasn't useful anymore. I still had it only because I couldn't be bothered to remove it from my coat. So many other amulets and charms adorned it that one more didn't make a difference. It seemed that my laziness was about to save my life.

I searched for a possible source, and the guard post at the entrance seemed the logical choice. The warning charm activated within certain distance, and the gate was the only place I was getting closer to as we walked.

"Explosives!" I yelled.

As if my voice was what had set it off, a ball of fire rose within the gate and engulfed the mythborn guards before they could even comprehend the meaning of my words. The war had trained my instincts well enough, and I had never stood frozen in the face of danger, but the size and speed of the expanding flames reassured me that we neither had a chance of outrunning it nor would my amulets hold against it, so all I could do was stare at my own death approaching to devour me.

Riagán moved. He was a mythborn, so he might have a chance if he tried to run, but he grabbed my arm instead. Then, in an eye blink, he stood in front of me with his back to the flames, and as the blast hit us, he pressed his body to mine, wrapping his arm around me. His smile was gone, replaced by focus.

Magic surged around us, his and my amulets activating, and we fell to the ground when the blast hit us. His arm cracked under our combined weight, and I lost my breath when he landed on me. The flames rolled over us, licking at the magic cocooning us, and then the fiery storm dissipated.

Eithne stood nearby with her arm raised and fingers closed around a single item, a blue-hued mirror. Even from the distance, I sensed the magic crackling around her.

Then guards surrounded me and Riagán with spears pointed down. I could swear if they moved any closer, the metal tips would poke my eyes out.

"One move, humanborn, and you die," barked the mythborn female who lead them. The intricate helmet covered most of her face, but her green eyes shone with hate.

I should have expected to be the one blamed, and I knew better than to argue. To prove my innocence, I had to stay alive.

Riagán rolled off me with a grimace of pain, but he lay beside me and didn't try to pull his arm from under my back.

"Are you hurt, Master Riagán?" the guard leader asked. "Did this humanborn wound you?"

I almost snorted at the idea I could have injured one of the Scáthanna, and Riagán seemed to share my amusement.

"She didn't, but I broke my arm, and your order is making it difficult to pull it out from under her." His voice was a mixture of pain and sarcasm.

"Step away, Aisling." Eithne approached. She still emanated with magic, but the amulet she held before was gone. Too bad, since I wouldn't have minded getting a closer look at it. "If she didn't yell a warning, I'd be dead."

And if Riagán hadn't stepped in front of me, *I'd be dead.* I glanced at the gray mythborn at my side and, the guard's order be damned, lifted my back enough for him to pull his arm out. He sighed with relief as he got back onto his legs, cradling his broken limb. The guards tensed, but they didn't react. Yet, regardless of Eithne's words, as soon as Riagán stepped back, the spear tips moved closer to my face.

"You shouldn't approach, my lady! She might try to kill you again," Aisling said. If words could kill, I'd already be burning on the pyre of hate.

I opened my mouth, pondered my options, and closed it again. Eithne seemed to believe me, and she was the one calling the shots. I wasn't about to blow my chances by saying anything.

Eithne grimaced. That was all she did. At her single grimace, the spears withdrew to their normal positions beside the guards' bodies. The mythborn still gave me hateful glares, but as Eithne's protégée, at least for the time being, I wasn't in immediate danger anymore. But I was still lying on the ground surrounded by their distrustful faces.

"How did you know about the explosives?" Eithne's voice, though devoid of threat, was firm and decisive. I had no doubt that if my answer didn't satisfy her, the guards would be back at me.

"I have a charm." I hoped the interrogation wouldn't take long. The courtyard's stones were cold. "It warns me about proximity triggers. But something isn't right."

"What do you mean?" she asked.

"If it was a proximity trigger, the guards at the post would have set it off," I replied. "If it was set for a particular distance, Riagán and I would have set it off."

"What makes you think you didn't, humanborn?" Aisling barked.

"We were already deep in the blast zone when it activated," I explained, doing my best to not sound snappy. Then I locked my eyes on Eithne. "I think it might have been you who triggered it, my lady." She was the only other person walking toward the post. "Unless it was someone outside walking toward the Court, but I doubt it. If it wasn't activated by the guards or by us, then it had to be set to trigger when a particular person approached." I didn't add that such devices were difficult to manufacture and expensive. It wasn't a makeshift bomb put together from wartime scraps. If someone went through all the effort to make it or have it made, they wouldn't have used it on anyone insignificant.

Aisling must have come to similar conclusions, because her face twisted into a mixture of shock and horror. "Grainne, Donal, take the lady to safety now," she said.

Her words confirmed my suspicions that Eithne had more pull in the Court than only being a spokesperson would imply. Two guards moved to her side in an instant, but she ignored them.

"This is the danger I spoke of, Kaja," she said.

I gave a slow nod. "I need to warn Albert about the explosives. Trinity could be next."

Her green eyes narrowed, as if she was about to refuse, but then she nodded. "I trust you'll know which information to share with him."

And which to not share... Yeah, I got the unspoken message. I lifted myself from the ground and unpinned my warning charm. "You'll need it to check the Court's grounds." I offered the trinket, three beads on a safety pin, to her.

"Why would you give it to me and not to Albert?" she asked with genuine curiosity.

"The Trinitians have plenty of them, while I'm not sure if you have anything to warn you." Seeing as she'd almost walked into a deathtrap, I was quite certain she didn't.

Back during the war, I told Albert I found a mythborn civilian who owed me a favor and would provide useful charms to Trinity. Over time I supplied all the Trinitian squads, but the charms didn't really come from a craftsman. Even Albert didn't suspect they were my own invention, and I never shared the design with any mythborn. I tried not to think that I was about to give one of my secrets away. My craftsmanship was crude and unrefined: a clear indication that a mythborn didn't make the charm.

Eithne took it. "You have my gratitude, Kaja." She walked away, shadowed by her two guards, and giving orders to Aisling and the rest of her men.

I stood in the middle of the charred courtyard, once again alone with Riagán. He watched me with an inscrutable expression.

"I owe you for saving my life," I said. "If you have something in mind I could repay you with, let me know."

I half expected him to refuse my offer, not only because I suggested a proud mythborn could need anything from me, but also to keep my debt over me like a ticking bomb.

Riagán's eyes flashed with interest. "How about we settle it the old way?" he offered. "A kiss and a token from the lady who was saved?"

I could only guess that my face didn't look like it belonged to someone smart, but I struggled to keep my jaw from dropping. It wasn't about how well versed he seemed in human culture. To kiss a mythborn was at best risky, with magic emanating through their bodies and mixed into their breaths. I'd heard accounts of those brave enough, and even though they'd recalled the experience as pleasant, they also admitted it was quite intensive and addictive, as if magic enhanced pheromones. Ever since I learned that, I'd kept my own curiosity at bay and my distance from the mythborn —not that they were a friendly and inviting bunch anyway.

Riagán leaned forward, but his face only brushed past

mine, and I almost released the breath I held... until I felt his lips on my ear, with magic tingling like static in the dry air. First I froze, fighting the urge to slap him as several mythborn were already handling the explosion area. Then I readied a rant about manners the self-proclaimed knight was supposed to have.

"I think I'll take one of these," he whispered playfully, and pulled on my earring with his teeth.

I snapped my hand upward and pushed it between his skin and mine. He smelled of pine and campfire smoke mixed with magic, so I tried not to inhale it too deeply. "Wasn't it the lady who chose the token?" I asked.

Call me petty, but life debt or not, Riagán wasn't taking my favorite earrings, and the only keepsake I had of my sister. I'd rather part with all the amulets and charms I wore than give him one earring.

Riagán murmured his disapproval into my ear, a low, wordless groan that almost made me draw a deeper breath at the promise hidden within it. But he moved away, slow and with his cheekbone brushing mine, letting his magic tease me even more. I stood motionless, determined not to give in and jerk backward, but damn, I hated the mythborn games. I was sure if I reacted, I'd receive a full array of his mockery at my retreat.

While he took his time to move away from my face, I unpinned my brooch. Pure silver, with intricate Celtic weavings, it served me well both as a decoration and an amulet, and I'd have lied if I said I didn't regret parting with it. But most of my other trinkets were made of scraps, and it didn't feel right to offer the mythborn a tangle of wire and wooden beads.

I made a show of pinning it to his clothes, a glimmer of silver on his gray uniform, and then it was my turn to lean forward. With my eyes locked to his, I lifted to my toes, but at the last moment I moved my head enough to kiss his cheek.

As soon as my lips connected with his skin, a jolt of magic traveled through me, setting off at least two of my protection amulets.

Once, over a glass or ten of whiskey, I'd asked Tadgh what really happened when a humanborn kissed a mythborn. I found seduction magic as believable as love at first sight, and Tadgh gave a long lecture of humanborn inert magic responding and synchronizing with the more intense mythborn magic. The rest, he claimed, was just the simple biological reaction accompanying any kiss. Biology my ass... Now that I'd felt it, I loved the idea of calling Tadgh out on his lie, but unfortunately, that would require admitting I had firsthand experience.

My deeply buried instincts demanded I stayed close to Riagán, and I fought my own body to peel away. As I moved back, Riagán's lips were trembling in a restrained smile, but I didn't care if he was having fun at my expense. As soon as his magic waned, I got to experience the less pleasant part of the kiss. Yes, the addiction-related one. Every nerve seemed to be screaming at me, demanding I got closer to the mythborn again.

"I should save your life more often," Riagán said.

"You should see about that arm." I pointed at his broken limb.

I wanted to kiss him again, to smell his magic and let it envelop me. I could only be grateful he didn't move his head when I made my evasion, because the prospect of having kissed him on the lips became suddenly more dreadful. At the same time, my brain could hardly focus on the conversation, as the thought of tasting the magic on his skin was pushing all else away.

"You're right, I do need to pay a visit to the infirmary," Riagán said, as if agreeing with me only out of courtesy. His fingers brushed the brooch I gave him. "Your debt is settled now."

"Thank you," I replied. "Now, if you'll excuse my rushed departure, I need to warn Albert of the threat."

"Of course."

His voice made it clear he didn't believe me, but I didn't care. I matched his courteous bow, happy that mythborn rarely shook hands, since the idea of touching his skin made my blood freeze in fright and boil with anticipation at the same time. I rushed toward the Court's side gate untouched by the explosion, and I felt Riagán's eyes on my back all the way until I turned the corner. I was sure he laughed at my hasty retreat, and his friends would have a good time listening to his story of how I couldn't resist his charm, but as long as I didn't have to be there for it, who cared? I didn't have that many clients in the Court anyway, and I was quite certain Eithne was only interested in whether I could find the Snake's agents, not how epically I failed in maintaining my composure.

I was alive, I was free of a life debt for a reasonable price, and I had two vials of the drug secure in my bag. I checked for cracks as soon as I got out of sight, but apparently the magically enforced glass endured crushing better than Riagán's arm.

Yet, when I drew a deeper breath, as if hoping for the wind to bring the scent of pine and campfire my way, and when my thoughts detoured toward pondering whether kissing Riagán on the lips would have been that bad, I knew Albert would have to wait. First I needed to find a way to fix myself, and if there was anyone who could help me, it was the humanborn I'd planned to visit anyway.

I really hoped he was home.

I MADE my way along the Quays on the north side of the river. So late in the winter afternoon, the darkness had already taken rule over the world, and the south bank would have been safer, but I didn't feel like wasting time going back and forth, especially not with some of the bridge dwellers preferring nighttime activity and daytime repose. I guessed in winter time it really didn't matter when one was awake, since the chances of seeing the sun seemed almost equal before and after dusk.

The water in the Liffey was calm, a black mirror reflecting the street lights as if the sea puked its tide into the riverbed and froze. Only around the bridges, where green wisps danced above the liquid darkness, did the water ripple like a grandmother's frowning forehead, and it reminded me that a rough touch of western winds would change this smooth obsidian into boiling tar. Shamrock tides? Nothing but a lure for tourists: herd them to the shore after the sunrise and let them gape. But everyone in Dublin knew that since the Magiclysm the Liffey had a dark soul and only two states: slumber and hell. I liked both.

Getting from the Court to the O'Connell bridge was a forty-minute stroll, but I made it in under half an hour. Then I took several turns, pulling away from the river and into the narrow streets on the North Side. Most of the buildings looked like they were about to fall apart, and truth be told, they didn't change much compared to the times before the Magiclysm. Sure, many walls bore marks of fires or curses, but without them, the area wouldn't look much better. I expected the Eireland Office to do something about renovations, since the Docklands, the newly rebuilt tourist haven of expensive hotels and venues, was around the corner, but all the work ceased where the money ended.

When I finally stopped in front of the three-story building with a crude sign saying "Max's," the lights at the shop were out, but a single window on the top floor glowed yellow. I gave a firm tug on the bell chain, and the chimes above me rang with urgency. It took another ten minutes of persistence before Max stopped ignoring the noise and looked out the window.

His mouth opened, but he didn't say a word, and the enraged expression faded from his face. Within seconds he was away from the window, and the light went out. I waited outside until the shop's interior brightened, and at the backdrop of a magic lamp's glow, Max's silhouette opened the door for me.

"I guess you vouldn't bother vith the social call. Something vrong?" he said with his heavy German accent.

Before the war, Max was a chemistry student, and he made money on the side by mixing experimental and not-so-legal substances—and, come to think of it, the Magiclysm didn't change much in his life, save preventing him from getting a degree. This thin, dark-haired German embraced the returning magic and its effects with the excitement and curiosity of a mad scientist. Every new substance or liquid, every weird plant that sprouted in places warped by curses, made their way to Max's shop, and he brewed them into potent salves and elixirs. And drugs, because his ethics didn't bother with the substance's purpose so long as it was useful in some way.

If Max wanted, he could be a drug lord, or even *the* drug

lord of Dublin, but instead of running his own crime organization, he devoted all his time and energy to chemistry and let others play the power games. His position had remained unshaken since the first years of the war, and both humanborn and mythborn sought his services.

That wasn't to say he was an angel, either. I had no doubt that the tale of how he'd poisoned five members of a humanborn gang when they tried to force him to work for them was every bit true. Max offered courtesy only to paying clients. The rest could either leave him alone or die by one of his alchemical experiments, whichever they preferred.

"Please tell me you have something for that mythborn poison," I pleaded as soon as I walked in. The other business I had with him had to wait.

"Mythborn poison?" He arched his eyebrow. In the lamp's light his eyes looked even more sunken than usual. "You need to be more specific."

I didn't want to be more specific, but he had a point. "I kissed a mythborn," I muttered. I really, really hoped I didn't blush, and I chased Riagán's memory away from my thoughts.

"*You did vhat?!*"

"Don't give me that 'you're pregnant and drinking' look." I waved him off. I came for an antidote, not a lecture.

"It's vorse than drinking vhile pregnant."

I was sure he wanted to add some more scolding, but I gave him a very stern look. I'd told him I suffered from the affliction shortly after the war, not because we were friends, but because he was as bound on finding a remedy as I was.

"Very vell, give me a moment." He rummaged through the countless shelves and drawers, and placed several vials on the counter. Then he dumped them all into a huge mug, topped it with way too much whiskey, and, after a short stir, handed the mixture over to me. "Drink it all. You're going to have a huge headache tomorrov, the mother of all hangovers, but it'll help."

I guzzled it instantly, not even arguing that the hangover could have been avoided if he had been moderate with the whiskey. The alcohol burnt my throat and made it impossible to recognize what else Max had put in the mix, but as long as it helped, I'd drink a bottle of pure vodka mixed with bog water.

Max watched me, amused. "You knov, you could have just... vent all the vay." His telling smile made it clear what he meant. "Or did you decide he vasn't vorth it?"

"Who said it was a he?" I teased while the contents of his mixture settled in my stomach. The relief was close to instantaneous. Riagán's face still danced before my eyes, but my body stopped acting like a crazed junkie out of juice.

Max laughed. "You're not the type to attract those ethereal mythborn ladies," he replied. "Anything else?" The tone of his voice suggested I should pay and go, or even just go.

"Actually, yes." I pulled one vial out of my bag. "This slows the effects of the magic affliction. If you can figure out the composition and how to make more..."

I didn't need to finish. When the Magiclysm broke loose, nobody knew what effects the magic would have on human bodies. We fought and we hid in the invisible clouds of pure magic; we breathed it in unaware it would poison us. Some turned out resistant, but they were the minority. Most had their bodies changed and warped, while others adapted, absorbing the magic, but even the resilient ones needed some kind of protection or drug, and neither Max nor I were an exception. The only difference was how much we were affected, how far along in suffering from the affliction. He was the lucky one... On the other side, I had a brush with instant death in the form of a lobbed ball of sparking magic.

Max's face livened up, as if the information was an energy boost. "Hov did you get that? I've been trying to get a hold of anything like it for ages." He waved me off. "Never mind, I don't care. Hov much can I take?" His voice rang with anticipation. He didn't question the validity of my claim, didn't ask if it really worked. I wouldn't be wasting his time on gossip and quackery.

"All yours," I replied. "If any humanborn can figure out its ingredients, that would be you. Just don't get too greedy on the pricing."

Max grinned. "I vill make sure it's reasonable enough, and you still get your cut. Or a lifelong supply, if you vant." He studied the vial. "Vouldn't you prefer to keep at least some of it? As much of a genius as I am, I still might come up empty-handed."

"I'm good for a while," I replied. "But don't expect me to pay tonight."

Max rolled his eyes, and I found his sigh rather theatrical. "I vill go bankrupt one day because of you."

I couldn't help laughing. Always the entrepreneur, he was. "I don't suppose you could spare me more of that anti-dote?" I pointed at the empty mug. I didn't intend to be anywhere near Riagán for a while—or even better, forever—but it didn't mean I wouldn't get attracted to any other myth-born's magic, and I preferred not to make a fool of myself again.

He became serious. "It's not good for you," he replied. "If you can't resist kissing more mythborn, you're better off seeing the affair through. Less side effects."

"But more other consequences." I didn't even want to dwell on the idea of "seeing it through" with someone like the mythborn killer. I also doubted Riagán was or would be interested in anything more than a bit of fun at my expense.

"Look, the addiction vears off as soon as you satiate it," Max said. "Vell, at least it falls to manageable levels, anyvay, like alvays vith love," he added. "The antidote messes up your body's magic. It cuts it off for long enough for the addiction to be cut off too." He looked me in the eye. "I don't think I need to tell you vhat happens vhen all that blocked magic rushes back in."

He let his words sink in. I already had trouble keeping myself balanced, and with every month I wore more and more amulets to keep the magic from warping me into a crazed heap of deformed meat.

"Right, I better stay away from any amorous mythborn, then." I forced a cheerful tone. Max didn't need to know what had really transpired. "Thanks for tonight."

He lifted the vial up. "Anytime."

I was about to tease him that I'd take his offer literally, but I doubted I'd shake Max's composure. I suspected he rarely slept anyway, too engrossed in his research and with a multitude of substances available to substitute for the unproductive hours of slumber. I left his shop convinced that leaving the vial with him would inevitably contribute to his sleeplessness.

CHAPTER EIGHT

The downpour outside almost made me step back into the half-ruined corridor of the apartment building I called home. I'd heard it all morning, the steady staccato of raindrops against my windows, but in my naivety I'd hoped the rain would let up before I got ready. I wasted a lot of time in the shower, taking advantage of the fact that nature refilled the water tanks I had installed on the building's roof, and that my charms heated it up as it came. A much more efficient hot-water supply than the prewar heat-it-overnight solution that made me calculate all the time, trying to remember how much I'd already used. There was nothing worse in this chilly and damp country than showering in lukewarm water and trying to get all the soap off before it got too cold.

The rain hadn't stopped while I showered, and it was still pouring as I munched on my breakfast, fighting off nausea and headache. Max's "mother of all hangovers" didn't even begin to cover how I felt, and my meager stash of painkillers waged a long-ago-lost battle against it. Considering the variety and amount of pills I shoved into my mouth upon waking up, though, I wouldn't be surprised if the painkillers made an alliance with the hangover instead of fighting it.

Needless to say, the weather wasn't helping, and I could hear my bed calling me, lonely and forlorn, but some visits couldn't be postponed.

I braved the first few steps, and one of my amulets activated, preventing my clothes from becoming drenched, though it did little to prevent me from feeling every bloody drop of cold rain hitting my face, and once more I considered spending time inventing a magically enhanced wind-resistant umbrella. I'd likely make a sizable fortune in a country where winds could render an umbrella useless in less than a minute.

As I walked through somewhat less populated streets, the water splashing from deep puddles reminded me the roads weren't in a good state to begin with, and war only added holes and cracks in the already uneven asphalt.

I made my way to the Trinity as quickly as I could, and when I approached the gate, the guards just waved me in while they argued with some tipsy fella who kept insisting the Trinitians were barring him from entering his home. I gave him a closer look, but the odor of alcohol and urine coming from him hushed my suspicions. Whoever had orchestrated the bombings would be too wise to use a drunkard as a pawn. Not only did the man's rowdy behavior draw attention to himself, but in his state he had more chances of failing his task than succeeding at it.

Nevertheless, I picked up my pace. Without Riagán around, I didn't want to test my luck should another magical bomb go off. As I rushed through the inner courtyard, the thought of the mythborn reminded me he was also the cause of the massive headache that ravaged my skull like a stampede of rhinos.

With my mood no better than when I left home, I climbed the stairs and knocked on Albert's office door.

He looked me over as he invited me inside. "You look horrible. Rough night?"

"Side effect of information gathering." I let him draw his own conclusions. It was better letting him believe I spent yesterday drinking with my contacts than revealing that my poor state was a result of one kiss on a cheek. "But what I got was worth it."

He pointed at the chair, and while I hung my coat on the hanger in the corner, he made some tea. Of course, I had to snatch the mug before he added milk to it. Regardless of how much time we'd spent together, he still didn't remember this little bit about me. Polish people in general, and me in particular, didn't put milk in their tea, and no years on the Emerald Isle or sleeping with a Brit would change that.

"Does it have something to do with the explosion at the Court?" He sat down.

I nodded. News traveled fast.

"You've already heard about it?" Albert sipped his tea. "Will I ever know something sooner than you do?"

I smiled at the compliment and the familiar tone in his voice. In the past, that light, almost playful note was reserved for the more intimate moments we shared, but now I couldn't even take it as a promise. As much as we both sometimes regretted how things had turned out, I was the one who chose to avoid the Trinity, and Albert was the one to move on. I might not live on the college grounds, but it sure didn't mean I had no information and gossip about what was going on, including those about a young and promising researcher that supposedly visited Albert's office more often than her work required. Though even I wasn't rude enough to pry as to whether any real feelings were involved.

"I was there," I said. "The bomb was rigged to trigger at a particular person approaching."

"You were there?" He arched his eyebrow.

He had to, he just *had to* cling to the least important part of the information I brought! As usual, he latched on to any indication I might have put myself in danger. I almost wondered how he had managed to send me out on all those dangerous missions, but in the war, things were different. Sex back then had the taste of a desperate need to forget, and nobody had time for too many feelings or too much caring.

"Eithne had another job for me." I chased away the thoughts that after the truce was signed, those feelings we'd been pushing away erupted like a well-shaken bottle of Coke. And as such a bottle, they made a mess but didn't taste good. "But that's unrelated." It felt bad to say the truth only to add a lie to it, and on top of that, to hide the information from the man I trusted with my life and who had always trusted me with his, but I had to play by Eithne's rules. "Trinity might be next. You need to sweep the place for explosives... especially in the places easily accessible by outsiders."

I didn't dare to mention that a traitor might be one of his own people. If mythborn weren't resistant to the Snake's lure, how could I expect the humanborn, even as dedicated as Trinitians, to resist? Jonas Byrne might have served the Snake because of his need for revenge, but a good incentive could convince anyone to do things they would have never considered before. I knew it myself, didn't I? After all, I'd agreed to work for Eithne and keep her secrets from Albert in exchange for the medicine she offered.

"There's a new threat, then," he said.

"Eithne believes it might be a part of some bigger plot." Was I crossing the line already or still had some wriggle space? "That Jonas wasn't working alone, and someone wants to push both sides into war again."

Albert narrowed his eyes and looked at me in silence for longer than I found comfortable. "Or it could be the Court's games. Or the MPF got out of hand again."

I shook my head with certainty, but Albert's questioning gaze made it clear he'd need more than my personal conviction. Yet I couldn't give him anything without revealing what Eithne told me to keep secret. "They had victims," I said when a sudden thought struck me. "They wouldn't be killing off their own. I saw it close enough to tell you it wasn't a trick." The memory of the flames and Riagán's focused face as he shielded me returned, but I pushed it away.

"How close?" he demanded.

"I almost got caught in the blast," I replied honestly. Caught in his insistence, I couldn't fabricate a lie quickly enough. "If my trigger charm hadn't gone off, I'd be well done. The guards that were at the post when the bomb went off didn't stand a chance."

Albert stood up and paced around the desk, as always when he was in thought. I found comfort in knowing that his habits hadn't changed. "I'll have the guards double the security and make sure everyone wears the amulets."

"You and Orla might need to walk the grounds yourselves," I said. "From what I understand, the bomb in the Court was rigged to go off when someone of significant position approached."

My own words made me wonder yet again how much influence Eithne had in the Court. We always considered her nothing more than a spokesperson for the mythborn, with no real power, as hardly any of them would stoop to contact with humanborn or risk a journey through the still-unstable city to talk to Albert. But what if she was the one to make decisions all the time? The things she revealed to me and the offer she made indicated she had more say in the Court than I or Albert—or likely any other humanborn—thought.

"If we trigger it, people might not be able to get away in time," he said.

"If you don't, they'll die anyway when you walk past it. At least this way you can minimize the loss." It would require some logistics and emptying the areas of Trinity that Albert and Orla were about to check, but in my opinion, it was better than an accidental explosion that would annihilate everyone nearby. I was sure Albert would eventually come to the same conclusion.

"I'll have it sorted out," he said. "And I'll get someone to find you a room. You're staying with us until it's safe."

I opened my mouth, closed it, then opened it again when I was ready for some words other than a string of invectives. "I'm not staying. I have things to do."

"That's not negotiable, Kaja." He gave me a stern glare. "I won't let you put yourself in danger."

"I'm not a target." I locked my eyes on his and refused to look away first. "And while you and Eithne try to keep people safe, someone needs to be out there looking for clues."

Albert stood motionless, and his posture made it clear he wouldn't budge. "You almost died at the Court, you said it yourself. And if word gets around you're investigating it, you *will* be a target."

"Look, I understand." I really did. Albert was trying to protect me. "But it's not going to work. I'm useless stuck in here, while out in the streets I can do a lot. Do you think I'd have the information about the explosion if I stayed safely tucked in the Trinity's bed? You need me out there, commander." I probably shouldn't have said the last word, reminding him that he used to send me on dangerous missions all the time.

A grimace spoiled his handsome face. "Don't use that card against me. We're not at war anymore."

"Will you really wait till we *are*?" I demanded.

"What makes you think I'd send you out then?" His lips trembled in a constrained smile. "You've become a civilian, Kaja, and I only give orders to my troops."

"Oh, curse you!" I muttered. Of course the war wouldn't change anything. "I was hardly a Trinitian, even during the war." My squad might have worked with Albert, but we were always as independent as we could be. We started out as guerrilla, and we didn't feel we'd fit into the more structured military that formed in the Trinity College. "Let's not run in circles. You know you can't convince me to stay, so you'd have to lock me up."

"That can be arranged," he teased, though his face made it clear he was seriously considering it.

I almost breathed out with relief. We were in more familiar waters now, the ones with the port called "compromise," and we steered away from the whirlpool of an argument or worse.

"I promise I'll be careful," I said. "But if we don't find whoever is planning those attacks, no one will ever be safe, and at some point either mythborn or humanborn will snap."

"I know." He let out a heavy sigh. "At least let me get you an escort back home."

I resisted rolling my eyes, because this was the moment when we arrived to the safe, though quite uncomfortable, haven of compromise. I wasn't happy with a Trinitian accompanying me home, for all the residents of the Liberties to be reminded of my affiliations, and neither was Albert, though for different reasons. An escort back home was laughable when one considered that the danger came from triggered bombs, not from assassins.

"Sure," I said with somewhat forced ease. "I'll let you know as soon as I find anything." At least, I hoped I would, because if Eithne decided to keep all the information exclusive, I wouldn't have much room to breathe.

"But before you go, you'll visit Tadgh, won't you?" he fired back, and he grinned at my reaction. "You hoped I'd forget, didn't you?"

I gave him a sincere smile. He knew I had, because our compromises only ran as long as the more interested side enforced them. Yes, I had agreed to meet with Tadgh, but I never claimed it would be on my priority list or that I'd make an effort to make time for it.

"I'll go. I have business with Tadgh anyway, or with anyone you consider the best of your researchers." I could only hope that Albert would be reasonable enough not to point me toward Jemma, because no matter how brilliant she might have been, I didn't feel like dealing with Albert's gossiped-about lover. Before he could ask the question, I pulled out a vial of the drug. "It slows the effects of the affliction. If anyone here can figure out the ingredients, you could start helping people."

"How did you get it?" He inspected the vial.

"By being out in the streets and doing my job." I couldn't resist the stab.

He didn't flinch and instead gave me an unpleasantly inquisitive glance. "And your visit to the Court has something to do with it?"

"I got it through honest means." I didn't waver. "But I can't give you any details."

I could read Albert's displeasure from his posture. "There were times when you didn't keep secrets from me."

It stung, and I cringed. "It was part of a deal I made. And to be honest, to get my hands on it I'd do a lot more than promise I wouldn't betray my source." I hated myself for misleading him again, as Albert would most likely conclude I had an informant in the Court. "Our solutions keep failing, and this"—I pointed at the vial—"at least gives us hope."

"You didn't say it's the cure."

"Because it's not. But it works better than anything else I've tried, and maybe, just maybe, it can stop the progress." I didn't think we really needed the cure. Before it destroyed us in the end, the affliction enhanced us. I wasn't sure I'd give up my magic and the skills I'd worked hard to learn only to be considered "cured." As long as I knew the affliction wouldn't claim me in the end, I was fine with who I was... with what I was.

Mentioning it to Albert would only spark another argument, and it was one more reason to keep my independence. As much as both he and Orla were politically correct when it came to contacts with our former enemies, they didn't trust the mythborn and would rather keep the gap between us and them. Excluding Tadgh, the Trinity consisted only of humanborn staff, and no one so far had even mentioned the possibility of changing that.

Albert narrowed his eyes. "You said you tried it?"

Why, oh why did he always pick on my slips? "Yes. It's working, and it seems safe." I gave a short reply in hope to avoid a lecture.

"Seems?"

I rolled my eyes. The headache was returning, and I wished I could just go home. "Look, I wouldn't have come to you with something I wasn't sure about," I said in a quite insistent tone. If only Albert could trust me on that. "I'm alive, I didn't mutate, and we have something that will help many people in this city as long as you can make more of it." My stare was as firm as a stone, and I made it clear I wasn't about to discuss my choices. Albert was neither my commander nor my father, and couldn't make decisions for me.

His jaw moved, and I could almost hear his teeth gritting. "What if we discover it has side effects?"

"Then I'll worry about them." I took a deeper breath. I could cut the discussion short in one way—the one that would undoubtedly spark another argument. "I need it, Albert. I need it... badly."

His face changed, and the ire disappeared, replaced by concern. "You should have told me," he whispered.

"And what would you do? Keep me locked up here?" I was unable to keep the bitter tone away. "Look, I got it sorted, at least for now. You don't have to worry anymore."

"I won't stop worrying until we find a cure," he said. Before I could reply, he took a step forward and leaned over me. "Don't keep those things away from me."

The softness and concern in his voice caught me unprepared. It was anything but the tone of a man who had moved on, and I couldn't help wondering whether he hoped I'd finally make a decision to settle in Trinity. But then there was Jemma, and my sources were quite adamant the gossip contained more than a grain of truth. It still didn't mean she was anything more than a distraction or a means to keep his bed warm.

"I'm sorry." I looked away as I gave my apology.

"Can you at least promise me you'll come here when it gets too dangerous?" he asked. "I prefer to deal with the terrorists than with the news of your death."

"You can count on it." I offered a meager smile. "It's what I've always done, isn't it?" Over to the safety of the Trinity College's walls whenever I couldn't run anywhere else, and out again when the danger had subsided. Not that I'd remind him of the latter.

Albert let out a sigh, and I didn't have to read his mind to know his thoughts must have followed a similar path. "I'll get someone to escort you back home while you're with Tadgh before I decide that locking you up is a better option."

I knew him well enough to stay silent while we were still anchored in the safety of our compromise. But as he walked out through the door, I watched his broad shoulders, those of a warrior, not an office rat, and couldn't help wondering whether he still hated those compromises as much as I did.

TADGH DIDN'T INSIST on having his own laboratory, but with the distrustful approach of the Trinitians toward the myth-born, he ended up in solitude anyway. As I knocked at the door, his pleasant, voice devoid of any accent, invited me in.

"Kaja." He seemed genuinely pleased to see me. "The commander mentioned you might be stopping by."

The commander. Tadgh never called Albert any other

way, even though the Trinitians' leader didn't insist on keeping such a distance. Many veterans called him simply by his name, but not Tadgh. In general, the only Trinitian mythborn seemed to be withdrawn when it came to relationships with humanborn, yet at the same time, he offered help to anyone who asked.

I couldn't help remembering how he ended up in Trinity. I wasn't around for the show he involuntarily put on, but the tales of him leading a group of over fifty humanborn to the former college's gates circulated long enough for everyone to hear them at least a dozen times. It was a miracle that nobody shot him, since he'd approached at the head of a ragged and malnourished group.

He inspected me with his intensive hazel eyes, and his expression left no doubt that Albert had also mentioned the nature of my visit. I'd been grateful for Tadgh keeping a friendly demeanor instead of launching at me with his tools of his trade.

"I wish I could give you some good news," he continued as he looked me over. "But I don't have any."

I closed the door behind me, though I had no doubt the mythborn had the place warded against any eavesdropping. All the mythborn, even when they weren't crafters, seemed to possess some basic skills at ward-making.

"I might have some for you." I took out the vial.

His eyes widened. "The Court's alchemists finally figured it out, did they?" My suspicion must have shown on my face, because he laughed all of a sudden. "Oh, Kaja. It's not a secret everyone is trying to find a cure, and this vial bears the Court's mark." He inspected the liquid inside. "So, did they really make it? Is it the cure to the affliction?" He could hardly contain his excitement.

I shook my head. "It slows it down. It might stop it altogether, but it won't revert the changes. Or so I've been told."

"I should have expected the Court wouldn't be handing out the cure freely, when—" He paused abruptly.

"When they have other means," I finished for him. "I'm surprised you know about it, stuck in here." Even though I trusted Tadgh's wards, I wasn't about to mention the details.

The hazel hue in his eyes dimmed, and he looked away as if I'd struck a sensitive chord. "How much of this can I take?" he changed the topic. "Because you want me to try to copy it, don't you?"

"It's all yours, unless Albert wants you to share it with someone else." I took a step forward. Not enough to disturb his personal space, since Tadgh might be the only mythborn who comprehended that idea, but enough to make it clear I wouldn't let this one slide. He knew of things no one spending all his time at Trinity would know. At the same time, he would likely dodge any direct question, so I chose another approach. "I've been wondering, why are you still here? The war is over, and you could go back to your people."

His laughter sounded more than bitter. "I'm sure they'd greet me with open arms... and shackles ready."

Of course, with all my paranoia and suspicions, I'd forgotten why Tadgh stuck around in the first place. The humanborn he'd led to Trinity were prisoners of war: civilians suspected to be supporting guerrilla squads. The mythborn warriors had corralled them into a building and intended to execute everyone, women and children included. Tadgh, who was a field medic for that squad, opposed such genocide, and according to the rescued people, none of the warriors had woken up, and their faces remained unnaturally still when the rebellious mythborn led the prisoners away. He killed his own brethren to save humanborn.

"Mythborn don't have anything like amnesty?" I inquired, though I should have known better than to employ sarcasm. "Have they heard about forgiveness?"

I could admit I was grateful he let those veiled insults slide. I shouldn't have let my mood after the confrontation with Albert affect my relation with the one mythborn who actually seemed likable.

"I'll search for forgiveness when I find it necessary," he replied. "Until then, I'm happy where I am. And you... You should seek for what slithers in the shadows instead of worrying about me."

A gasp escaped my mouth, but I didn't say anything when his throat clearing sounded like a warning. It wasn't that he knew of the Snake that shocked me; after all, mythborn had fought its servants back in the other world. What gave me pause was that he knew *I knew*, which meant he must have been in contact with the Court somehow.

"You've been trusted with secrets, Kaja." Tadgh put the vial on the table. "It's the only reason we're having this conversation."

"I'd almost rather we didn't." The mere thought that I wouldn't be able to tell Albert he had a Court spy in the very heart of his organization made me question where my loyalties lay. I agreed to keep things away from him in hopes Eithne would share her knowledge, but it seemed I'd gone too far.

Tadgh inspected me as if he knew what was going through my head. "I don't give secrets away, I just... receive some every now and then. I thought I'd hear the news of the remedy and its formula, but it seems it made its way over here by other means."

I gritted my teeth when the pieces fell together. Eithne had used me. She must have known I'd share the vials with the Trinity, so instead of risking Tadgh's cover if he was the one to discover it, she'd simply handed the remedy to me. I wouldn't put it past her to have anticipated I'd also bring a sample to Max, so she gave me two vials, ensuring I wouldn't ponder for too long how to split the drug.

"My duty and loyalty lie here," Tadgh added. "I made it clear that if I was to make Trinity my home, I wouldn't be serving two masters."

"And she agreed?" I tried to picture the calm mythborn standing up to Eithne. She couldn't have been pleased.

A smile crossed his lips like a lizard running through grass. "Did I mention the shackles that would wait for me were I to go back?"

"But you could seek forgiveness," I pressed.

"Maybe one day. When we have real peace, and it doesn't matter anymore whether you're a mythborn or humanborn, and which place you call home."

His voice rang with so much pain and bitterness that I had to suspect he didn't believe in the peace lasting. To ask him for the reasons of his pessimism seemed too cruel, especially when my own instincts urged me to prepare for another war. It felt like the peace we had was nothing more than a nationwide game of pretending we didn't hate one another.

"If we want that to happen, I better get to work," I offered. "Maybe we can find the threats before they grow into another conflict."

I headed for the door, but Tadgh called my name.

"If she made you a certain offer, you should take it," he whispered. "The remedy is unlikely to change much at the stage you're at."

I didn't ask how he'd managed to diagnose me without even touching me or using any of his tools, and I understood his message, not that I was ready to follow his advice. I also had another, more pressing concern. "What will you tell Albert?"

"The truth. That you're stable, and the remedy you received is helping." He smirked. "And that to learn anything more, I'd need you to undergo a days-long checkup to which you very adamantly objected."

I almost chuckled. Yes, Albert would have no doubt I objected to anything that was longer than an hour. "What if he asks you to estimate how much I have left?"

His face changed, widened with a broad smile, and he almost looked human. "I am, as you humanborn put it, a scientist. I won't play guessing games without any reliable data to extrapolate from." He looked me in the eye. "A secret for a secret."

He said it playfully, as if it was some sort of a trade. But at the same time, my mentioning to Albert that Tadgh still had ties with the Court was as dangerous as his telling Albert about the real state of my affliction... and about *my* ties to the Court. If we were enemies, things could turn ugly, but it seemed we had a common goal: peace. We did what we needed to maintain it.

"So be it," I replied, not that amused. "A secret for a secret."

CHAPTER NINE

Sean was polite and formal, but most importantly, he was a boy who joined the Trinitians after the war, so he'd never experienced a real battle. As we walked along Dame Street, he tried hard to look confident and intimidating while I screamed inside. I couldn't blame Albert for that. He passed the escort request to his officers, and one of them decided that the commander's whim wasn't worth more than the necessary minimum. That meant one guard to accompany me home. A decision that I would have welcomed with gratitude if they'd assigned a veteran to me. We'd stroll home exchanging stories and draw much less attention than the freckled blond teenager who made escorting me into some sort of display of masculinity.

And, of course, all my attempts to send him back early failed as my guard insisted he needed to see his order through. I walked with a grim expression, and as the painkillers I'd taken in the morning finally declared their defeat against the hangover, the headache returned with all its might, souring my mood further. I didn't even want to think whether the kid would make it back to Trinity unscathed. I wouldn't be surprised if some local mythborn wanted to add a few bruises to his innocent face, and I wouldn't blame them. His uniform, posture, and proud face were like a blunt invitation for violence.

I couldn't have been more relieved when we finally reached my apartment building. I forced a smile and stretched out my hand, but before the insincere words of gratitude left my mouth, Sean spoke first.

"I should accompany you all the way to the door," he said with the dutifulness of someone who followed his orders to the letter. "There could be an ambush inside."

After one glance at his determined baby face, I gave up on explaining how explosive curses would be much more efficient in a confined space of a corridor, and even if someone decided to kill me while I unlocked my apartment door, a greenie like him would be of no help. I just marched inside the building, letting him rush after me.

Upon turning the corner, I stopped at the sight of the familiar mythborn leaning against the wall right outside my apartment. To my slight disappointment, his arm was neither in a cast nor a sling, already healed. Of course Sean bumped into me, and as soon as he spotted another person in the corridor, he reached for his sword. Riagán's smile, predatory and anticipatory, made my blood congeal. His bow was secure at his back, and he didn't make a move, but I would bet he was only waiting for the Trinitian to give him an excuse.

My hand snapped toward Sean and closed on his wrist. "It's fine," I said. "I have business with him."

Sean gave me a doubtful glance, as if no one in their right mind would do any business with a mythborn, but he didn't pull out his sword, and that was all I cared about.

Explaining to Albert how my escort died would only fuel his arguments to make me stay at Trinity.

While I rushed to unlock my door in hopes that it would relieve Sean of his duties, he and Riagán had a staring match, and the boy held longer than I expected... Though it was probably because he didn't recognize who the mythborn was. If, instead of Sean, I was accompanied by a veteran, there was no way this encounter wouldn't have ended in blood—a small blessing in this whole mess.

"I told you to come in the evening," I said to Riagán, and he shrugged, smart enough to go along with the lie instead of acting surprised. "Come in." I pointed at the door.

The mythborn's arched eyebrow sufficed for a comment, but he peeled away from the wall and entered, ignoring Sean. I turned to the Trinitian. "Thank you for your time," I said with a forced smile. "I'll be fine now."

Before he could say anything, I walked inside and closed the door, so he couldn't insist on checking my apartment for me. I firmly believed that if anyone ever managed to get past my wards, they deserved a shot at me.

The light coming from the living room indicated Riagán didn't wait for me to make himself at home. He stood in the middle of the room, taking it in.

"What are you doing here?" I asked.

He reached to his chest pocket and pulled out a pouch. "I brought you painkillers," he replied in a casual tone. "I thought you'd need them."

"Thank you for your concern, but I have my own pills," I muttered. I didn't even bother denying I had a headache. I wasn't that good of a liar.

"I brought you painkillers that will actually help," he said, amused. "Unless, of course, you like the idea of suffering in the name of…" He cocked his head. "Of what, exactly?"

"And what interest do you have in helping me get rid of my headache?" I fired back.

"A business one and a personal one." Riagán grinned. "Lady Eithne burdened you with a task, and I don't think your headache will help in fulfilling it. I also hope that, relieved of pain, you'll be grateful enough to not ask me to leave immediately."

I stared at him. I caught the sincerity in his voice but couldn't resist wondering why he'd like to stay in my apartment in the first place. He stood motionless with the pouch in his hand, and I finally accepted it.

"Take it with hot water," he said as I headed to the kitchenette and flipped the kettle on.

Since the war had ended, Eireland Office worked hard to rebuild the much-needed infrastructure, but the Liberties in general, and the building with a total of three residents in particular, weren't at the top of their list, so my appliances ran on customized charms rather than on actual electricity.

I dumped the contents of the pouch into a mug and inspected the bluish powder, but all I could tell was that it did look like some of the drugs mythborn used. Without Max's expertise I wouldn't be able to figure out any deception, so after a moment of hesitation, I poured steaming water over it. If Riagán wanted me dead, he could have watched me die in the explosion, and with the headache throbbing through my head like a hand drill through a brick wall, whatever the powder would do to me couldn't be much worse anyway.

Sipping the blue tea, I walked back into the room.

"Why do you keep these?" Riagán pointed at my TV set

tucked in the corner. "Did humanborn find a way to broadcast again?"

I shook my head. "Nope, your magic did it good. Still no television, radio, phones, or the Internet," I replied. "But I never used it to watch the news. It's for games."

"Games?"

His confusion offered me a bit of satisfaction. He might have studied humanborn history and tried to understand our culture, but he still didn't know it all.

"Let me show you." I reached toward the devices and activated the charms. As their magic substituted for electricity, my TV and game console came to life. "Have a seat." I pointed at the couch while I grabbed the controller. The game was already in, and I grinned while Riagán watched the loading screen with fascination. "You're going to like it."

It had taken me some time to find a copy that survived the war, and then I paid more than a ridiculous price for it, but it was my favorite of all time, so I considered it well worth the five amulets I traded for it. The epic fantasy with a vast world to explore never failed to entertain me back when I was nothing more than a Polish immigrant living in a mundane Dublin working a boring office job, and even now, when I could do a bit of magic on my own, and I lived in the twisted fantasy world that Dublin had become, I still launched it every once in a while. It was much easier to be the good guy, or the good lass in my case, in a video game than it was in the not-so-black-and-white reality.

Riagán watched the screen with all the fascination of someone seeing magic for the first time, and it must have been true in a way. Once the Magiclysm wiped out our mass media, the mythborn could only learn about television and other things through humanborn accounts. Some people might still own laptops and powered them with charms if they could afford it, but it was unlikely any mythborn had a chance to see such devices working. And hardly anybody would waste resources on having a working TV, unless they really loved their movies or games.

I loaded my saved character, and as I explained the concept of the gameplay, I made my way through the beautifully rendered scenes. I killed several enemies, showed off my character's magic spells, and explained the key points of a complicated storyline I'd been following. Riagán seemed to listen with interest, and when I exited back to the main screen, he looked disappointed.

My headache subsided, and a sudden idea struck me. "Now, let's make you a character." I grinned. That was a great opportunity to get back at him for all the teasing. "Don't worry, you can play an elf with a bow." I picked the new game from the menu and handed him a controller while briefly explaining the action buttons.

"Maybe I should play a handsome humanborn instead?" he suggested with more confidence than I expected.

I shrugged. "Your game, your choice." I didn't even bother to correct his mistake. Back in the times when we still had video games, the concept of a humanborn didn't exist.

I helped him with character creation, tried to explain how he wasn't supposed to name his gray-haired elf with a bow with his own name, and then I cut him loose. He died eight times before he made it through the tutorial, and then three times more on the way to the first village, but he didn't give up. Like a child presented with a puzzle, he tried over and over again with the focus I had seen only on true gamers' faces, and even though I had intended to ridicule his every failure, I ended up sharing tips and giving suggestions.

"So, why have you come?" I asked when one of the dungeons was loading.

He looked at me. "I was wondering if you were planning to move to Trinity." The game loaded, and I expected his attention to revert to the screen, but instead, he paused it and sat silent, as if in thought. "I hoped I could advise against it."

I arched my eyebrow. "Let's hear it." A mythborn trying to convince me I shouldn't stick with my fellow human-born... that had to be good.

If my sarcasm threw him off, he didn't let it show. "You're safer here," he said. "You're not a target, and you've been on your own long enough to know how to survive."

I couldn't help wondering whether he'd had a way to overhear my conversation with Albert, since he was throwing my own arguments at me.

"Also, if you move over there, you'll be seen as aligning yourself with Trinitians, which might... not sit well with some of your informants," he added. "And lastly, you agreed to aid Lady Eithne in her search. If you stay neutral, the Court can and will provide help and resources, but if you became one of Albert's people, our support would become greatly limited."

He didn't say anything I hadn't considered myself, and his last argument confirmed what I hoped to be true—that Eithne was ready to cooperate rather than treat me as a backup source of information.

Riagán stretched on the couch and returned to the game.

"That's it?" I couldn't resist.

He flashed one of his smiles. "You weren't planning to move there anyway," he said. "Otherwise you wouldn't have sent that Trinitian child away."

I chuckled. "I sent him away so that he wouldn't give you a reason to kill him," I replied. "But you're right, I'm not moving there."

"Even if Albert asked you to?" he asked with what seemed a genuine curiosity.

I cringed, both at the unvoiced suggestion in his words, and at the fishing for information. The gossip of Albert's relationship with me still circled, but hardly anyone outside of Trinity knew how much of it was truth—and whether it was still truth.

"I'm not moving to Trinity," I stated with certainty. I wasn't about to explain my personal life to him. "That should be enough for Lady Eithne."

The corners of Riagán's lips curled in a smile. "Who said I was asking for her?"

The tone of his voice, playful, but also resonating with the addiction that Max's mixture supposedly countered, reassured me the mythborn was back to playing his games. Before I could consider anything pleasantly discourteous, like throwing him out of my apartment that very instant, the video game provided unexpected succor.

I pointed at the screen. "That spider is about to eat you."

It worked like a charm. Riagán's attention instantly reverted to the screen, which allowed me to dodge the question in a way that didn't give him an opening for the next one. I did, however, think of ways to cut his visit short. The headache vanished, but the prospect of curling up in my bed and relaxing was very appealing. The wintertime sun had already disappeared behind the jagged line of Dublin's destroyed buildings, and I could use an early night.

While Riagán fought to stay alive on the screen, I closed my eyes, relaxing. The game had captured his attention, so I decided I'd let him play a little longer and then kick him out.

~

I WAS warm and somewhat comfortable, but when the scent of pine and campfire smoke filled my nostrils, I lifted myself from the pillow. My head hit an obstacle, and when my bed moved beneath me, I snapped my eyes open.

"Don't get up." Riagán moved his elbow away from my head. Was I still asleep, or did I catch a hint of regret in his voice?

Of course, his request could have only resulted in me doing the opposite. The blanket I didn't remember pulling over myself slipped down on the floor, and Riagán gave me an amused look.

"You seemed tired, and the game was interesting, so I thought I'd let you sleep." He pointed at the TV, where his character boasted what I instantly recognized as magical armor and quite a powerful bow. He had definitely found his footing in the game.

The morning light pushed its way through the curtains, which meant I'd slept for the whole night. I eyed Riagán with curiosity, ready to ask how he'd managed to sit so many hours motionless, but then I remembered who he was. A picture of the gray mythborn squatted down, motionless, watching for his prey, waiting forever to take his shot, appeared in my mind, and I didn't need to ask any more. Though I still gave him a suspicious glare. I should have at least woken up when he reached for the blanket and covered me. Unless, of course, the painkillers he'd offered me had side effects he'd forgotten to mention.

"I guess you're staying for breakfast?" I offered reluctantly.

"Depends on what you have. There's a bakery on the corner."

I shook my head, resisting a grimace. "I'll pass on mythborn-made bread," I replied. "But I have some fruit preserve and oatmeal." Before Riagán replied, a knock on the door got both our heads turning, and I rushed to the corridor.

Not fully awake and embarrassed by having slept on the mythborn war hero's lap, I thoughtlessly opened the door, expecting one of the many messengers who knocked on it daily bringing news or job offers. Instead, I stared at Orla's stern face. She wore her full gear, so it wasn't a social call. Not that she'd ever made one anyway.

"Glad to see you're alive," she said in a half-mocking voice. "And somewhat conscious, too," she added after looking me over. "Sean brought news of a mythborn waiting for you here. I take it he was no trouble?"

"No, everything's grand," I replied in hopes she was just passing by, and I wouldn't have to invite her in, but Orla's eyes were fixed on something behind me, so I glanced over my shoulder.

On the coat hangers, right beside my all-year jacket, hung an enhanced bow. One glance at the charms attached to it would make it clear that it wasn't the weapon of an ordinary mythborn. But, of course, the quiver beside it was even more of a tell, full of arrows with very distinctive fletching and gray bands on the wooden shafts.

"Come in, Orla," Riagán called out from my living room, burying all my hopes of defusing the situation before it got out of hand. "I'm looking forward to finally meeting you face to face."

Orla tensed, and her hand, so far leisurely placed at her

bow, closed around its curve. As I moved to let her in, she sent me a glance I couldn't quite decipher. I watched her back disappear in the room and allowed myself a silent sigh of relief before I followed her. They both must have known that as long as they stayed in my place, doing anything foolish wouldn't end well for either of them. Of course, later I'd have to deal with the questions of what a mythborn killer was doing in my place, and I wasn't looking forward to it.

"Lady Eithne was concerned about Kaja's safety, so she sent me to check on her." Riagán rubbed his eyes sleepily. "And Kaja insisted I shouldn't be wandering the neighborhood in the middle of the night."

I kept my face straight, grateful for Riagán's subtle lie: the game was turned off, and the blanket partially wrapped around his waist and legs suggested he had just woken up. Thankfully, my couch was definitely too narrow for two to sleep on it, so at least I wouldn't have to deal with any questions on that front.

Orla glanced at me. "I'd have kicked him out. Hopefully some knacker would have dealt with the problem." The tone of her voice made it clear whom she meant by the last word.

"Why don't you take care of it yourself?" Riagán arched his eyebrow and spread his arms, indicating he wasn't armed.

I held my breath. I suspected that even without his bow, he was a powerful opponent.

"We're not at war anymore," she replied with a slight curve of her lip that I desperately wanted to be a sarcastic smile. "And even though I might question the choice of company Kaja keeps, you're her guest."

Riagán nodded, and when he stood up, I couldn't help

wondering how much self-control Orla had to muster not to twitch at his movement.

"As are you." He took time to look her over. Finally, he stretched his hand forward in a typical human gesture. "As odd as it may seem, I'm glad to have this opportunity to meet you."

Orla didn't hesitate, and shook his hand. "Likewise."

I watched them with curiosity, two sides of the same coin: one humanborn and one mythborn. Cherished by their own kin and feared by their enemies, they both excelled in archery, but never got to meet on the battlefield, never got to claim superiority over the other. And now, by fortune's whim, they got to meet on neutral ground. I could only regret that the neutral ground happened to be my home.

"Will you be staying for breakfast, Orla?" I offered.

"Oatmeal and fruit preserve?" She knew my habits well. "I'll have some."

I retreated to the kitchenette, letting the two archers handle their own uncomfortable silence, but to my surprise, instead of lingering in a gloomy stillness, they quickly engaged in a discussion about bows. When I came back with three bowls of the best oatmeal one could get in a country with supply issues, Riagán was leaning toward Orla and explaining some technicality while pointing at a detail of his own bow—a charm, if I wasn't mistaken. I arched an eyebrow at that. Were they really sharing their trade secrets?

Riagán raised his head and moved away, letting me put the bowls on the table. I still couldn't read Orla, but at least she didn't come across as hostile.

"Did you know that, during the war, Orla once saved a whole regiment of mythborn?" he asked in a playful tone.

"I find it hard to believe," I replied. What did he want to achieve with such bait?

"So do I," Orla said in her dry tone, and I read a warning in it. She wasn't interested in his games.

Riagán stretched on the chair, grabbing the spoon I offered, and before he dug into the oatmeal, he gave Orla a teasing smile. "It was during the standoff at Donnybrook," he said after swallowing a spoonful of food. "We were barricaded at one end of the street, and the humanborn camped at the other. The mythborn ceannasaí considered an offensive. He wanted to reach the half-destroyed fortification midway between the two. Once claimed, it would be an advantage in taking down the humanborn defenses down the street." Riagán paused and watched me put several spoons of fruit preserve into my bowl, then he did the same. "I suggested that a head-on attack might not be the best idea, since we were well within bow range."

Orla's lips curled as she listened, eating her oatmeal. She must have known where the story was going.

"I got to suffer through a very long rant, one that listed my cowardice and overestimation of the enemy in so many words. He shouted that there was no way even the best humanborn archer could be a threat at such a distance," Riagán continued. "And the very moment he said that, an arrow whistled and went straight through his ear." He enhanced the story with gestures. "Twice the distance he claimed to be safe." Riagán looked at Orla. "His second-in-command proved more reasonable... I guess it had something to do with your well-placed arrow, so we withdrew with no more losses on our side. Trust me, I was never so happy about a mythborn dying as I was back then." Amusement flickered in his eyes, and for a moment he made me forget about all the death and destruction the war had brought.

"Your gratitude didn't last long, did it?" Orla gave him a mocking glare, and I feared she hadn't forgotten about the spilled blood at all. "Three months later, on Nicholas Street?"

Riagán's smile didn't waver. "Would you prefer I had killed you instead?"

She shook her head in disbelief, and then looked at me. "My squad was taking in some thugs who were trying to make a profit off the civilians," she said. "We were past St. Patrick's when I heard a familiar sound, and someone shouted 'archer!' We ducked, and someone screamed. Familiar fletching was sticking out from one of our prisoners' arse." She pointed back at Riagán's quiver in the corridor. "But the thug was still alive, and he screamed like a girl, so for a moment I stared, unsure whether I just saw the famous mythborn archer miss his mark for the first time."

Riagán ate another spoon of oatmeal, the smile never leaving his lips. He glanced at me, as if telling me to wait for the end of the story.

"Moments later we heard loud rumbling, and a giant rolled out from around a corner. Of course, he headed straight for the screaming thug." Orla stared at Riagán. "Because one supposedly grateful mythborn decided to lure a giant to us, we barely made it out of there alive."

"But you did make it out of there alive," Riagán pointed out in an amused tone. "And you did shoot that mythborn ceannasaí, no matter how thickheaded he was."

To my surprise, Orla laughed casually. "I guess we *are* even."

I sat in my chair motionless as the memories resurfaced: a giant closing in on me and the wounded mythborn, the overwhelming smell of blood that gave the monster a clear trail straight to us, and a scream in the distance that lured the danger away. With Orla's part of the story, my and Connor's incredible stroke of luck, including his survival after I'd left, finally made sense. I gritted my teeth when I realized Riagán had never mentioned he knew of it when he led me to Connor, even though he must have recognized me the very moment we met at the Court.

"Kaja doesn't seem to approve of my sense of humor," Riagán said, but I caught a warning in his voice. He didn't want me to bring that up in front of Orla, and I could relate. I wasn't keen myself on announcing what had transpired back then.

Orla looked at me with curiosity, and I cursed myself for not being able to keep a straight face, but it wasn't every day one learned secrets that redefined an event from the past. And the fact that, in the new perspective, Riagán had saved my life not once, but twice, wasn't helping either.

"I'm sure there's more to it," she said. "And I'd love to hear the rest of the story, but I better get going. If I don't report back soon, Albert might send half of Trinity to check on both of us." She took her bow and headed for the door.

"I'll let you out." I rushed after her, though leaving my apartment was much easier and safer than trying to enter it.

We stood in the narrow corridor while I undid the locks.

"Thank you," I whispered. "For not making it difficult." Sometimes the Trinitian bow mistress surprised me with her tact. Other times, she comforted me with her bitchy attitude—that one thing unchanging among the uncertainties of the world.

"The war is over," she replied, her dry tone offering some understanding. "And some secrets can remain secrets now."

WHEN ORLA LEFT, I sat back at the table, silent and sorting through my mixed emotions. Riagán's presence became unnerving, but to make him leave I'd have to speak, and I was less than ready to do so without letting words escape my mouth uncontrollably and in a rather offensive manner.

"You weren't supposed to know." He was the first one to break the silence, with his voice quiet and devoid of the usual teasing.

That was more than enough for me to snap, "So that you could call on that in a more opportune moment? No wonder you let me get away with the other debt so easy. You knew I'd still owe you anyway."

He tensed. "You weren't supposed to know," he repeated in a firmer tone.

Yeah, I figured that much, thank you. I bit my tongue before the anger got the better of me. At least I could do that much in terms of gratitude.

"If you're not happy with having a debt, we can settle it now," he offered in a friendly manner.

I couldn't help smiling at the memory of the last agreement. "I can spare another amulet, but I don't think I want to take my chances with another kiss," I replied with grim sincerity.

Riagán chuckled, and the mood shifted. My anger evaporated, as if the mythborn saving my life in the war was nothing more than another lighthearted bargain, as if what he had done for me and Connor didn't really matter any more than keeping a door open or picking up a dropped umbrella.

I shook my head. "I should repay you properly," I said, though it was the last thing I wanted to say. I really wanted to be done with him, but life debts shouldn't be treated so lightly.

He gave me a hiss of disapproval. "You're no fun, but let's have it your way, then." He leaned forward with a cunning smile. "I call on your debt now."

In the silence that fell, I could hear my own teeth gritting. I should have known better than to expect a mythborn to be accommodating. "Fine. What do you want?" My voice expressed every bit of the discontent I felt. I'd prefer not to guess what he'd make me do.

Riagán's smile widened. No doubt he was enjoying it, and I could only curse myself for getting myself into that mess. I should have kicked him out instead of trying to be fair.

"You'll show me upstairs," he said, and my eyes widened, as nobody knew my apartment had any "upstairs." How did he learn about it? "And I take one thing from here. One thing I choose, and you don't get to bargain like the last time."

I tried not to grit my teeth again; dentists were a rare commodity nowadays. Instead, I clenched my fists and ran an inventory of all the most expensive charms and amulets I had. A costly price to repay a debt, but I could part with one, and at least I could hope he'd pick one of them over one of my personal trinkets or memorabilia.

"But not the earrings. And how do you know about upstairs?" I demanded.

"When you fell asleep, I thought I'd put you in bed, but that thing you have in another room looks more like an intruder trap than a bed," he replied. "And since we're on the ground floor, it only makes sense that you have something above. Then I found the ladder in the closet."

I drew the air sharply. Had he tried to climb it, I'd have

had a dead mythborn and a lot of explaining at the Court to do.

"I figured I'd better wait for your invitation," he replied as if he'd read my thoughts. "So, shall we?" He stood up.

Reluctantly, I did the same. As much as I didn't like his demand, I wasn't in a position to bargain, and all in all I preferred to be done with the debt as soon as possible... Before Riagán came up with some even more unnerving way to make me pay it off.

"Wait here," I warned before climbing up the ladder.

I flipped on the lights upstairs, and the whole area lit up with the warm amber glow of magic-powered lamps. When I'd set it up, I knocked down most of the inner walls, creating a vast open space. The main design of what I called "the den" was my very own signature mess: workshop-like tables covered with junk, unfinished charms, and other projects. The rest of the furnishings were two wardrobes with clothes, and a bed made of two smaller ones nailed together, covered with countless blankets and pillows.

I stretched my arm down below the floor level and toward Riagán. "You'll need to hold my hand all the time you climb."

"Can't you just deactivate your protection?" he asked with curiosity, but followed my instruction. His hand was warm in touch and rough, with the cracks in his skin rougher on the edges.

"It's not meant to be off. Nothing enters or leaves this place without me." I let go of his hand as soon as he stepped outside the ward. "So if someone betrays me, they can expect a long and lonely death," I added as a warning.

Riagán looked around, and I let him take in the surroundings. Not only my mess and private belongings, but also barred windows and symbol-covered walls. Since he was already upstairs, I could give myself the pleasure of boasting of the den's protections. The whole building could collapse and this place would survive unscathed.

"You've been busy." I caught a new tone in his voice. Awe?

"I only paid for the work."

His expression made it clear he didn't believe me even for a second, but instead calling out my lie, he took several steps forward to inspect my worktables.

"And you pay for unfinished pieces too?" he remarked.

I didn't grace him with a reply, and he didn't prod me any further, as my wall display caught his eye. He walked over to the corkboard and stood there in silence. I was sure he recognized several pieces in my collection, a few strong amulets by the finest mythborn craftsmen, and a curse or two that I'd acquired during the war, mostly from the enemies who had died before they could use them. And as Riagán gaped at my treasures, I chased away the thought that I'd be parting with one of them soon.

"I'm surprised Albert let you keep these." Riagán finally tore himself away from the display. "I'm sure Trinitians would kill for all the knowledge they could gather from them."

"Albert doesn't know I have them. In fact, up until now, nobody knew." I locked my eyes on him, hoping the meaning of my words would sink in. If somebody tried to rob me or offer me a deal, I'd know who tipped them off.

He arched his eyebrow, unmoved. "I thought you'd have invited *him* here."

It was hardly a veiled suggestion about my relationship with Albert, but I didn't intend to give him details on why the Trinitian commander never stopped by.

"I made this place after the war." I gave the reply that helped me hold my own bitterness at bay. After the war, Albert rarely left the Trinity, wrapped up in running it and focused on the Trinitians and their problems. Since I chose not to be one, our intimacy had faded, and even though we remained friends, the distance between us grew. "Ready to go downstairs?" I asked, hoping Riagán wouldn't dig deeper. I wasn't about to pour my heart out in front of an arrogant mythborn.

He walked over to the ladder, and I extended my hand, but he didn't take it. Instead, he studied the markings around the opening on the floor.

"You warded it against inanimate objects too. A smart move," he said. "You should talk to Connor sometime. He might give you a few tips."

"I'll keep it in mind." I gave up on keeping the façade of having paid for the wards. He must have figured out my condition and that I channeled the unstable magic in my body into something more stable. I preferred not to think about how the amount of wards and trinkets in my den also told him how far along I was. Eithne said that I had about a year left, but would her estimation be the same if she'd seen what Riagán saw?

I held his hand as he went downstairs, and as I climbed down myself, I asked, "So, do you know already what you'll be taking with you?" He didn't insist on anything while we were in the den, but I had no doubt he would be able to name every single item displayed.

"These."

As soon as I faced him, he lifted his hand to show me my keys. The very ones I always mindlessly dropped on the table. Out of all the items in my place, priceless amulets included, he would have to pick this. *Kurwa mać!* Yes, sometimes I still cursed in Polish, especially in the privacy of my mind, where no one could judge me.

Before I opened my mouth, Riagán lifted a finger. "You're not allowed a bargain, remember?" he said.

His remark buried my hope that he'd grabbed the keys to offer one himself. I stood silent while the implications of his choice sank in. He'd be able to enter my place on his own, to get past my wards downstairs, and poke around at will. Not to mention leaving things that went boom or other nasty surprises if the flame of war ever reignited. Still, it wasn't the worst possible outcome. I could picture him demanding that I spy on Albert or sabotaging the Trinitians... I should consider myself lucky that Riagán was more eager to torment me personally than to come up with more elaborate plans to cause harm to other humanborn.

"I'll get you the spare set." I cherished the surprise on his face. He clearly didn't expect me to give up that quick. "If you eat any of my food, you replace it. If you make a mess, you clean it." Such rules coming from someone who kept her den in a state of permanent disarray... Yet I didn't consider myself a hypocrite—after all, this was my place and *my* mess. "And having keys doesn't mean you're moving in." I gave him what I hoped was a stern look.

"Deal," Riagán replied. "But you won't try to change the locks or ward me out of here."

I gave him a nasty glare. "I wouldn't," I replied. "As much as I hate it, it pays off my debt."

Riagán took a sudden step forward, and even though he didn't touch me, in the limited space of the former closet I felt pinned to the ladder behind me.

"Do you really hate this deal that much?" he asked in a low, deep voice. "You seemed quite comfortable sleeping on my lap."

He stood so close to me that I could smell his breath, sweet and full of magic. I drew a breath deeper than I intended, and when my lungs filled with the promise his closeness carried, I almost wanted him to kiss me. At least we'd be done with his games, I'd suffer through the consequences, and then move on.

His gray eyes stared intensely into mine, but he didn't move, and when I readied a snappy reply about invading one's personal space, Riagán stepped away, laughing.

"You're toying with me." I let my frustration talk.

Riagán smirked. "It's in my nature to play." He turned and walked back to my living room. "But I've taken too much of your time," he called out from there, "and you have an important decision about your future to make, haven't you?" he added as he stepped back to the corridor with his bow and quiver slung across his back.

I should have expected he knew the details of my conversation with Eithne, but the fact he spoke about it in such a casual way, as if he was in on the secret, left me speechless. I rushed over to the small desk and opened the drawer. I held the spare key set out to him and my other hand empty.

Riagán gave me my keys back without hesitation, but when he reached for the other set, his fingers brushed my wrist instead, in a gentle, almost caressing way. Then, before I made any comment, he swiped the keys from my palm and offered a bow.

"It's been a real pleasure." He didn't give me a chance to reply and left the apartment.

CHAPTER TEN

After I closed the door behind Riagán, I headed back upstairs. His scent lingered in the room, and to my surprise, I regretted he hadn't stayed longer. Sure, his games drove me mental, but otherwise his company proved interesting and entertaining: two things that were missing from my life for quite a while, save the job-related interactions. I was certain Riagán had ulterior motives for visiting me, and taking the keys to my apartment had to be a part of yet another game, but a fraction of me wanted to see where it was all going. Did he do it for some personal gain, or was Eithne pulling the strings he danced on? Seeing as Riagán knew of my conversation with her, I leaned toward the latter, especially with the mythborn lady trying so hard to be friendly and forthcoming with me.

This brought me to his parting words. No matter what his real motives were, Riagán was right: I had a decision to make.

I went over my conversation with Eithne and the way out she'd offered. It wasn't a cure for the magic affliction, a solution she claimed to be impossible. Magic, once awoken, couldn't be taken away, but there were means to stabilize its flow before it destroyed the owner's mind and body. According to her, I could remain as I was; to wit, I could retain the magic skill I had learned to control, but without the fears that consumed my sleep.

The hot water in the shower didn't ease the tension that churned my stomach after Riagán had left.

Eithne hadn't hidden the risks. The ritual could stabilize my affliction, or it could morph me into the very being I feared I'd soon become: a crazed, distorted, and violent Léanmhar—the Afflicted. So my choice was between slow certain death and a quicker but not so certain salvation. She'd also mentioned possible physical changes, nothing so severe as what awaited when the affliction finally claimed me, but she could tell me neither their extent nor their nature. She claimed it depended on the individual, on their adaptability, and on the stage of the affliction. I could change as little as getting a new hair color or become uglier than a bridge dweller.

And as if it wasn't bad enough on its own, the longer I waited, the greater the risk became.

With a sigh, I rinsed shampoo out of my hair. Next things to consider were the consequences of my choice. If I refused Eithne's offer, nothing would change, and I'd approach my own demise at the same pace every day until the curse I wore triggered and granted me a quick death— the prospect I thought I had embraced, but Eithne's words reminded me of how much I wanted to live, truly live, thinking about the future and planning for it, not just existing with the thought of death greeting me within a year.

The mythborn ritual she spoke of could end in my death as well, but at least she'd given me hope, a solution instead of an everyday struggle to keep going with no way out. At the same time, it meant I'd become tied to the Court in ways I couldn't even begin to imagine, because I didn't believe such a generous offer didn't come with strings attached.

I wasn't ready to make that decision. My amulets still protected me from myself, and the drug I got from Eithne seemed to be working even better. I had time to think it through and to talk to Albert.

I froze at that realization, and the stream of water hit my skin like hot needles. I would have to tell Albert about it, and the prospect of his reaction sank heavy into my heart. He'd never agree to such madness, to trusting the Court and allowing the mythborn to make me into... something else. But it would be worse if I made a choice and went ahead behind his back. We weren't lovers anymore, but he still cared about me, and I owed him the truth.

I left the bathroom, fished out fresh clothes, and made a mental note about mundane chores, namely laundry, catching up with me. I needed a distraction, but playing a housewife wasn't going to cut it.

I should have known better than to hope for something that would take my mind off uncomfortable thoughts. I should have heard the cruel giggle of fate when I wished for it, but I didn't, and when two hours later a pounding on the door brought me a distraction, I wasn't prepared for what it was.

The boy, not older than twelve, wore a Trinitian uniform, and his face showed fear. "The commander sends for you," he said. "Eireland Office was attacked." He pointed beyond the corridor. "I have a horse waiting. How quickly can you come?"

I was out the door in less than five minutes.

I didn't like horses and always believed the feeling was

mutual, though it also might have been the animals reacting to the magic I hardly contained. In any other situation I'd insist on going on foot, but with the grim news and the urgency of Albert's call, I wasn't about to make a fuss... unless the stupid animal decided to freak out at my approach.

"He's trained to handle magic," the boy said with pride. "Even a mythborn could ride him."

I mounted it with a bit of struggle. The boy climbed on in front of me and took the reins. I didn't protest and clutched the saddle instead.

"So, what happened?" I asked as we rode through the streets. They looked normal enough, but the uncertainty seemed to be hanging in the air, heavy like smoke from burning tires. People must have heard the news as well and worried about the war breaking out again. I shared their fears.

"Four 'splosions in the Office, and the building went down," he said. "The commander sent help, four squads, but no news from them when I was leaving."

I didn't need a vivid imagination to figure out how bad it could have been: some killed by the bomb, some buried under the rubble. I should have thought that the Snake would target the Eireland Office. Both the humanborn and the mythborn considered it, no matter how reluctantly, a government, and with it gone, Eireland could plunge back into war. With either side blaming the other one for the attack, things could turn gory quick.

As we approached Trinity, I sensed the change: no civilians queuing to enter, tripled guards, and familiar routines I remembered from the war. Albert hadn't wasted time and put everyone on a high alert.

I jumped off the horse the very moment it stopped, but

came to a halt as I approached the gate. The Trinitians' firm glares made it clear I wouldn't be able to skip a security check this time. It didn't make me feel better that my guide went through the same process.

Their captain lifted a charm-covered rod, and I spread my arms with a sigh. The device flared with alarms, reacting to every single amulet and charm I wore, and I felt grateful for resisting my instinct to grab several curses before I left the house.

"You wear an awful lot of magic, Miss..." He eyed me with suspicion.

"Modrzewska," I coldly replied. He wasn't one of the old-timers, or at least I hadn't fought alongside him, so I had no intention of making things easy for him. "If you insist on my removing even a single one, you can tell the commander he can meet me here."

His grimace made it clear he wasn't used to others challenging him. Without a word, he pointed at the waiting area, and I shrugged. His choice. I needed to see Albert, but I wasn't about to get myself in trouble by arguing with an overzealous officer.

"Do something sketchy and you die," he said, and at his signal, two guards accompanied me. Another one hurried off through the courtyard.

I shook my head in disbelief but took a seat on the bench with the two armor-clad watchdogs by my side. And Albert still couldn't understand why I hadn't stuck around... With nothing else to do, I allowed myself the pleasure of staring at the guards. It didn't take long for the other guard to return. He whispered to his companions and tried not to look in my direction too much.

The captain walked over, and I could swear he intentionally set a slow pace to irk me. "You may enter." The tone of his voice suggested a physical pain accompanied expelling the words from his mouth. "Sergio will escort you."

"I know the way." I walked past him.

"No civilians on the grounds without an escort," he barked.

I didn't slow down. "Then he better keep up." Was it Albert's order, or was the captain trying to get back at me? Even in the worst years of the war, civilians were allowed to roam freely through many parts of Trinity, except for the several off-limits areas, of course.

I passed through the courtyard followed by the clinging of armor that suggested Sergio preferred his position behind me. Orla stood at the entrance to the building and waved at me.

"Come, Albert is waiting." She threw one glance at the guard behind me, and the sound of rushed footsteps told me the man had walked away without any questions.

"How bad is it?" I asked while she led me through Trinity's corridors. We didn't climb to Albert's office, which meant he had to be in the tactics room, just like during the war.

"At least thirty humanborn dead, but twice as many are still unaccounted for," she replied.

I bit my tongue before I asked about the mythborn death count. The Trinitians were readying for war, which meant they didn't care about losses among the ones they perceived as the potential enemy.

Orla glanced at me. "We don't know the other numbers," she said after a brief silence. "With the way things are, I'm surprised we can even work together on the site."

She opened the door, and I walked into the room I'd hoped to never see again. Multiple maps covered the walls around three large tables in the middle. Most of them were photocopied and hand-taped to parts of the city plan, but some displayed the whole of Eireland or other towns on the island.

Albert stood among his men giving assignments, and they left one by one. Orla nodded at Albert and left as well.

"You sent for me," I said once we were alone.

Albert's face was a mask of pain, yet his eyes remained focused. Like in the old times, when his orders sent people to seek their deaths in skirmishes, assaults, and civilian-protecting missions. "I need someone to reach the Court," he said. "And you're the only person I can think of that might have a chance."

I took a deeper breath. "What's the message?"

"The Eireland Office is gone," he said. "So it's up to Trinity and the Court to maintain peace... If the mythborn even want that peace. We need to establish communications and keep rogue squads at bay before it gets out of hand." He rubbed his temples. "You can take whatever you need from our supplies, and I'll give you a team..."

I shook my head before he could finish. "Trinitians on the North Side would be like a war declaration."

He furrowed his brow. "Going alone is suicide."

I couldn't resist a laugh. "If it was, you wouldn't have sent for me."

"I'm still considering sending someone else." He looked me in the eye. "I have no right to ask you to risk your life."

"No, you don't." I returned his stare. "But you can offer me a job and pay for it. You know I have the best chance of surviving a trip to the Court and returning."

"That's assuming the Court didn't have a hand in that bombing." His hands curled into fists. "If it's their play, I'd be sending you to your death."

I bit my lip. If only I could tell Albert about the Snake

and the outside threat, but I felt Eithne wouldn't accept the extraordinary circumstances as an excuse for revealing her secret. "Eithne needs me," I said instead. "I don't think she'd kill me."

Albert snorted. "I'm surprised you trust a mythborn."

"It's not trust—it's business." I shrugged. "She wants something from me, and she offers a fair price. And even if she didn't, I'm more valuable to her alive." I sighed. I could only hope I wouldn't end up as her hostage if everything she'd told me turned out to be a lie. "Look, I better get ready. The sooner I set out, the better chance I have." I didn't have to add that things could get out of hand at any moment, and if Albert dragged us into an argument, it might destroy our chances for any contact with the Court.

Orla walked back in, and I caught a single arrow in her hand. "The Court is trying to make contact too."

Albert looked at her in surprise. "Did they send someone?"

"A message." She lifted the arrow and showed a roll of paper tied to its shaft. "I had Tom scan it for magic, but I assume it's safe."

"How so?" Albert arched his eyebrow.

A sarcastic smile stretched her thin lips. "Because Riagán only misses when he wants to." She pushed the paper down the shaft and revealed the gray band beside the fletching.

I held off a snort when I caught the telling tone in her voice. The arrogant mythborn must have aimed the arrow close enough to send a clear message: she'd be dead if he wanted her to be, and he wouldn't have missed his mark only to resort to poison or other indirect means. After all, it would be bad for his legend.

Orla unrolled the paper, skimmed it quickly, and passed

it to Albert. While he read, I threw a questioning glance at the arrow, and she shook her head ever so slightly. She hadn't told Albert about the chance meeting in my apartment, and I wasn't about to reveal it either. Some secrets were better left secrets, especially as we were at the brink of war again. If someone knew Orla had met with an enemy just before things went south, their trust in the bow mistress could waver. And if they knew the same about me, I wouldn't be a reliable source of information anymore, even if I was a neutral civilian.

"That's interesting." Albert looked up from the paper. "Eithne says the Court had nothing to do with the attack on the Office, which I would expect them to claim even if they did orchestrate it... But she also says she believes we didn't stage it."

I bit my tongue. The Snake. Its agents were behind it, and stopping Jonas Byrne did nothing except removing a pawn from the board. The real player had just moved other pieces around.

"What does she want?" I asked.

"She offers to keep the mythborn on a short leash if we do the same with the humanborn," he replied with his eyes back at the letter. The he looked at me again with an unfamiliar spark in his eye. Suspicion? Concern? I couldn't tell. "She wants you as the messenger."

I caught the unvoiced question in his words. "I'm not surprised. I'm as neutral as she can get without trusting an outsider." Albert's stare still pierced me, and I sighed. "That explosion in the Court... She would have died too if I didn't warn them." I had to give Albert something, but guilt clenched my throat. If I hadn't overstepped the line of keeping the secret yet, I was bloody close to it.

His face hardened. "And you only mention it now? Which side are you on, Kaja?"

I gritted my teeth. He knew where to stab. "If you don't trust me, tell Eithne you want someone else to handle the communication." This wouldn't help, but I couldn't resist. We locked eyes and stood in silence, two stubborn idiots unwilling to give in.

"Did you join the Court?" he eventually asked.

Such a question couldn't remain unanswered, and I sighed again. "Eithne gave me an assignment and offered good payment for it." I felt like I was repeating myself. "I can't tell you any more except that it's nothing aimed at the Trinitians or humanborn in general. If she said she wants peace, I think she means it." I took a step closer. "I haven't forgotten what they did during the war or all their schemes after it ended, but if we want to keep the peace, we have little choice. We have to cooperate with the Court, and you know it, because you sent for me."

Albert opened his mouth, but then glanced at Orla and closed it. She offered a dry smile.

"I appreciate your trying not to drag me into your personal issues," she said, "but we're stuck until you make a decision. So either tell Kaja you care for her too much to risk her life, or that you don't trust her enough with the mission, or tell her to get bloody going before the mythborn lose their patience."

"The voice of reason," I muttered against my better judgment.

Albert only shot her an angry glare. He paced around the table, and his lack of concern for the fact I could see all their tactical maps made it clear that trust wasn't the issue. He stopped and nodded at Orla, and she left without a word.

"She's right," he said when the door closed behind the bow mistress. "I'm looking for excuses that would let me keep you here." He walked around the table and stood in front of me. "And I admit, I feel a bit... betrayed. There were times when we kept secrets from others, but not from each other."

I looked down at his unspoken accusation. "I'm supposed to at least pretend I'm neutral," I replied. "And that means protecting the secrets of all my clients."

He hissed with ire. "Why, Kaja? Why do you need to stay neutral? There's a place for you here. There always was."

Right, a clichéd guilt trip to add to the argument, an ungrateful Kaja abandoning Albert and refusing his offer of a life together. Except there hadn't been any life together since the war ended, and my moving to Trinity wouldn't change much. Albert was so engrossed in running the place that I'd become nothing more than a familiar face waiting for him at the end of the day. If we talked, it was about the ongoing problems of the Trinitians, and even though I tried, I couldn't find my place in Trinity. I didn't fit in with the military; even during the war, my subordination only went as far as necessary. I also hated the administrative tasks and bureaucracy in general, and I was close to useless at scientific research. I was a scout, and I gathered information, so after months of trying to become a Trinitian, I understood it wasn't the place for me. Albert didn't.

"You're going to send me to the Court, aren't you?" I ignored his questions.

His face hardened, and once again it was the commander looking at me, not my former lover. "I have no choice. You're the only person both Eithne and I trust."

"Now that's the Albert I know and admire," I offered with honesty. The commander who could make difficult decisions and at the same time inspire people to trust him to make the best choice.

A sad smile lingered on his lips. "I miss you," he whispered. "Once you're done with Eithne, come back here... for good."

I wanted to believe the promise in his voice, that everything would be different this time, and we'd be able to rebuild what we had. I was ready to promise him to think about it, to really think about it, and maybe try to see if it could really work. But before I could say anything, the door swung open, and a woman walked in.

Her light brown hair framed a face a bit too round, but nonetheless pleasant. She wore a white lab coat over her full curves and looked every bit groomed like someone who led a sheltered, comfortable life.

"Albert, you need to see this!" she exclaimed. "That drug is close to miraculous!"

"Jemma..." One word from Albert's mouth, and his irritated tone seemed to freeze her in place.

I hid my smirk. It seemed that Tadgh had had to share the drug with the humanborn researchers, but at least it appeared that she had some progress to report—well, I hoped she did. I took a step away from Albert, aware how intimate we might have looked so close to each other.

"I better get going," I said with an ease I didn't feel. "I'll get Eithne to cooperate and try to convince her she should speak directly with the Trinitians."

I didn't wait for a reply, and he was smart enough to let me leave. As I walked toward the door, I ignored Jemma's curious glance and kept my face as relaxed as possible, even though my anger was on the rise. Not at her, not even at Albert. I was mad at myself, because I'd allowed myself to forget that the only reason I'd consider going back to the

Trinity had already moved on with his life. I couldn't even blame him. After all, I was the one who'd left, right?

~

IT WAS dusk already when I dragged my feet home, but on the other hand, wintertime in Eireland felt like it was always dusk. Sometimes I wondered whether the Magiclysm had affected the weather too, because even though winters before the war were similarly dark and wet, we'd have at least several days of somewhat clear sky and a few hours of sunshine—not that anyone had ever noticed them, they were so busy complaining about the rain.

The Liberties looked different, quieter and dismal, and I didn't need to guess that the news of what had happened in the Eireland Office had already reached the neighborhood. On the bright side, I didn't spot any signs of riots, which meant local mythborn and humanborn preferred to wait the struggle out instead of taking it out on each other.

My mind wandered back to meeting with Eithne. I was right that she wanted me, because she trusted me enough to tell her the truth about Albert's intentions: whether he'd be working to keep peace or preparing for war. Since I knew about the Snake, I believed the mythborn weren't willing to go to war over the Eireland Office's fall, but hearing it from Eithne herself put most of my concerns to rest.

I was grateful she didn't inquire why I'd insisted the Court and the Trinitians should have appointed their own people to communicate instead of using me as the intermediary. She accepted my vague explanation of making it look good in the eyes of civilians while I'd have more time to focus on the more important task. As much as we needed to do everything to preserve the peace, we would eventually fail if we didn't deal with the Snake's agents.

After that, all I had to do was to escort her representative to Trinity, and at the gates I asked for Orla. Ignoring the inquisitive glare of her narrowed eyes, I handed the myth-born over to her and rushed away with the excuse of having another task to do. I didn't really care whether she fell for it; all that mattered was that I avoided meeting Albert. I wasn't sure if I could get through another argument.

At least I got all that sorted and could go back home to get some well-deserved rest after a hellish day, except that it seemed my day wasn't over yet.

A small figure stood by my building, and I slowed down. There wasn't anyone else in sight, but I couldn't resist the feeling of multiple eyes watching me just like in the good horror movies.

When the stranger lit his cigarette, in the flicker of light I recognized one of the local molekind, and a shiver went down my spine. This couldn't be good. But to walk away meant showing weakness, and I'd only encourage those waiting in the shadows to chase after me, while if I walked closer, I could run into the safety of my apartment.

"*Tráthnóna maith agat,*" he said when I approached. His tone sounded polite, and his face, covered in short brown hair, expressed neither malice nor hate.

"Good evening," I replied in English. I wasn't about to ridicule myself with my meager Irish. "Can I help you?"

He pointed at the entrance to the building. "There's blood on yer door," he said, switching to English as well. "We tried to explain them fellas breaking in wasn't a bright idea, but them fools didn't listen. We cleared them bodies, but we didn't want to touch yer door."

I gave a slow nod. "I appreciate it."

"So... No hard feelings, eh?" He displayed a row of his half-rotten teeth in a smile. "No one wants more fightin' around here. Them Courts and Trinitians can do slaughter all they want, but here are the Liberties. None of their business."

I smiled at the unexpected development. The local molekind might give a hard time to the humanborn living in the area, but at the same time it felt like they had no interest in encouraging riots. I tried to imagine a day when the peace shattered, and the Liberties declared themselves a neutral zone. The mythborn's determined face told me they'd do a lot to make it work, and I could only hope the local humanborn would do the same.

"Will you keep an eye out on any other troublemakers?" I asked. "Both humanborn and mythborn."

His grin became wider. "Sure, pet."

I had to smile at being called a pet, so Irish of him, but I was certain he knew. The mythborn, with all their pride and disregard for our ways, were at the same time adept at absorbing them when it suited them. "I'm Kaja." I stretched out my hand.

"Padraig... But call me Paddy."

We shook hands.

"I had a hard day, Paddy, and all I want is dinner and bed, but if you ever need anything, just knock on my door," I said. "They don't kill unless you try to break in."

"See ya around."

Before I walked into the building, I could swear the whole street breathed with relief. It felt nice to be respected enough to be left alone.

~

WAR LEAVES SCARS, but I'd always convinced myself I was over them. Those on my skin might remain, but the inner wounds healed over time. Sure, I got nightmares every now and then, tossing under the blankets, or I stared into the night too scared of what waited under my eyelids if I were to close them, but these nighttime struggles resembled a distant echo of what was never to come back. I smiled, I joked, and I cherished the peace. I claimed to have moved on.

I lied to myself.

I didn't even have to see what was left of the Eireland Office. The news alone sufficed in bringing all the memories back, and the images I'd worked so hard on forgetting resurfaced like swollen dead bodies, both humanborn and mythborn ones, that flowed down the Liffey making their last journey to the sea.

When I finally collapsed onto my bed after a long and trying day, I hoped the dreamless slumber would claim me without delay, offering both the needed rest and an escape from what I knew already lurked at the edge of my mind.

Instead, I lay submerged in a shallow sleep, like an offering to the gods of nightmares, and they came with their claws grating against my composure.

Once more I knelt down beside Sonja with my hand on her chest, feeling her heartbeat becoming slower and slower with her every passing breath. She wasn't conscious anymore, so I didn't have to look into her icy blue eyes, and she couldn't read on my face that I had no way of helping her. Instead, my gaze was shackled to the side of her head, where a pool of thick, dark blood formed. One wrong turn in the war-torn city, one curse whizzing by, and she lay on the ground. While her body still clung to the last scraps of life, her mind seemed already gone.

Then my own physical pain dimmed the emotional suffering of seeing a friend die, and my mind recalled the desperation that overwhelmed me when I realized I also had been grazed by a curse. My hands were shaking as I generously poured whiskey over the wound on my arm, and the alcohol burnt like a promise of survival. Then multiple hands and arms on me as my comrades pulled me away, and the field medic applied simple healing charms we'd been stealing from the dead mythborn.

I still felt the thick line above my elbow, a reminder of a that wound.

But what came next made all the other nightmares fluffier and cuter than an Angora rabbit. I must have woken up as soon as the heavy thumps started in my dream, because I remembered gasping and staring at the dark of my den, but then slumber pulled me back into the treacherous quicksand of dreams. With my mind half-awake, I hoped to break free, to force the nightmares to shift and show anything but that.

Thump, thump, thump.

The heavy steps of a giant just around the corner had Ela's eyes widening. She was ducking in the middle of a street behind a pile of rocks that used to be the second floor of a nearby building. With curses whizzing by, she couldn't tear herself away, and I shouted her name. The image that had been haunting me, both in my dreams and while awake, once again played before me.

Ela peeled away from her shelter in a mad dash among the magic projectiles. She made it three steps, reaching her hand out to me. I stepped from around the corner of the building, ignoring the curses, and had outstretched my own arm. *One more step, one more step, sis!*

The giant's foot smashed her into the uneven cobblestones.

Time slowed, as if my mind wanted to ensure I could recall every single detail of my nightmare. I must have screamed back then, because ever since then my screams had woken me up countless times, but I couldn't remember it. My companions dragged me away from the giant and from the curses the mythborn kept throwing at us while I watched helplessly how the monstrous creature lifted Ela's limp body to its mouth. The thick fingers pushing on my dead sister was not an image I was ever to forget, and then a crunching sound followed, even though I could swear no bone in her body could have been left intact after the stomp. It always returned in my nightmares like a haunting echo.

I tossed in bed, and darkness whispered my own guilt and helplessness to me. One event, one explosion, and all the wounds I'd been pretending were healed burst open, spraying emotional pain all over my life. The thought that with the Eireland Office gone, the war would return, not only in my dreams but also in reality, was cutting deeper than any memory could.

I kept opening and closing my eyes, undecided whether I wanted to face more nightmares or my own haunting thoughts. The den, with its boarded windows and secure wards, resembled a tomb, even though I usually welcomed the peace and quiet it offered. During the war, we all jumped up at every sound, so silence guaranteed uninterrupted rest on those nights when the slumber-time horrors didn't claw at me.

I gave up and switched the charm-powered lamp on. The table by the wall lured me with the sweet promise of oblivion waiting in the manual work, but instead I went down to the kitchen. I wasn't one for using drugs, but Max had reassured me his mix didn't have any side effects, and some nights needed a treatment provided by that superb German invention. The vial stood half-empty in the cupboard, a silent witness to how often I needed sleep medicine, and as soon as the water boiled, I measured a teaspoon into a mug. So far, I hadn't gotten addicted or grown any extra limbs... Not that I was particularly concerned about the latter, since the affliction was bound to grow me an extra something sooner or later.

I chased away the grim considerations and inhaled the rich aroma within the steam. It promised me a night of deep sleep without any subconscious guilt trips. Max reassured me that I'd sleep even through another Magiclysm, and I had no reason to doubt his bold claims. I returned upstairs much calmer and already drowsy from the mixture. When I hit the bed again, even the most tenacious of nightmares had no chance.

CHAPTER ELEVEN

Mallory owned a small pub on the south side of the river, in the area where even before the Magiclysm tourists didn't venture too often, so most of his clientele were local humanborn and those few mythborn who lived in the area. Most of the pub's furniture bore the marks of war, charred by an incendiary curse that fell through the window or broken when some angry mythborn wanted to punish Mallory for "aiding the enemy of Eireland," as anyone who sided with Trinitians had been called during the conflict.

People hiding inside back then, most of them regulars, snuffed the fires before they could ruin Mallory's Ales, and as for the mythborn mob... I couldn't resist a smile, because even as I entered the pub, some humanborn was telling the story of "Mallory's courageous defense."

"... And then the biggest fella gave Mallory an ugly glare. Ya know, one of them shut-up-and-do-as-I-say glares." The humanborn waved his hands and twisted his face into a grimace that I guessed was supposed to imitate a mythborn.

"And then... *pow!*" His palm smacked against the other one. "Mallory swung his maul and sent the bastard flying!" More gestures followed. "I tell yous, teeth popped from the mythie's face like popcorn."

Several other men and women cheered at the story, but I didn't stick around to listen. On my way to the bar, I passed two mythborn sipping their stout at the table, and their amused faces promised that no trouble would stir from them, so it didn't even matter whether they enjoyed the story too, or secretly laughed at the silly humanborn recounting some unimportant event as if it was the battle for the O'Connell Bridge itself. But significant or not, the brawl in the pub had grown into a legend, and Mallory's maul, since then adorned with extra charms for better balance and pounding power, hung by the meager display of alcohol bottles. I had no doubt that, if needed, Mallory would swing it again at anyone who threatened him or his patrons, be they humanborn or mythborn.

Without asking, Mallory poured me a pint of cider as soon as I sat at the bar. "Want some chips with that? Drinking with an empty stomach isn't a good idea."

"Sure, I'll have some."

Before the war, it used to be "fish and chips," but with way too much magic contaminating the Liffey and the shamrock tides washing against the seashores, only potatoes remained of the local staple meal. The thick-cut, stick-shaped chunks had nothing to do with the elegant, thin fries served in American fast food chains, and even though those "chips" weren't my favorite, I'd learned to appreciate them, especially at Mallory's, where they weren't covered in salt and drowned in vinegar.

He disappeared into the rear and returned with a bowl full of golden goodness. He served it with small sachets of vinegar, salt, and ketchup on the side. If I closed my eyes and ignored the humanborn divulging the details of every single swing that took place during the brawl, I could almost believe I was transported back to the less magical times.

Mallory leaned forward while I ate, as if he was watching his patrons and listening to the story as well.

"There's been a man comin' 'round here lately." He spoke casually but kept his voice low enough. From a distance, he must have looked like he was making light comments about weather or life. "A bitter one and very wordy. He'd been goin' on 'bout how we should get our home back... how we should act. You know, the usual hate speech."

I swallowed a piece of a fried potato. If Mallory was sharing the story, it was anything but "the usual" stuff.

"He went on for a while, and I admit, I prodded him with a word or two." His smile made the wrinkles on his face swirl like cream in coffee. "When I got him drunk enough, he told me, in great secrecy, of course, that some folks are gettin' together, and if I'd be interested, I can find him at this address."

With a straight face he passed me several paper tissues, and I made a show of wiping my mouth while I slipped the note he hid between them into my sleeve.

"Harps or something else?" I reached for my purse. I usually paid for both food and information with the official currency, as Mallory used it to compensate his suppliers, but with the uncertainty following the collapse of the Eireland Office, it was only fair I offered him a choice.

"I'll take the bills. Hopefully they'll still be good tomorrow," he replied grimly.

I handed him the money. Much more than I'd pay

bartering items or services, which spoke volumes on the country's financial stability.

"You haven't finished your cider," he said as I stood from my chair.

"It's too early for so much alcohol." Information gathering meant I drank more than I liked and more often than I wanted to, especially since, contrary to common belief, the amount of beverages consumed had no effect whatsoever on stopping the affliction. "I only come here for the chips, really."

He laughed heartily, catching the attention of other patrons. "Take care!" He waved.

I got the subtle warning hidden in his voice. He must consider the man dangerous. "I'll see you soon!" I replied with a forced cheerfulness. My thoughts already circled the information I had.

The man Mallory mentioned might be just another disgruntled humanborn, maybe someone gathering friends to talk and complain together. On the other hand, he might be the Snake's agent. I wasn't about to check the address myself, especially after Mallory's warning, but Eithne seemed to be ready to handle the confrontational side of the search. I was fine with it. Not only did I not have to risk my own life to confirm my intel, but it also wouldn't draw Trinity's attention if things went south.

I crossed the nearest bridge, paying a handsome toll when I insisted on using the harps, but I still considered it a fair deal. Unlike Mallory, I didn't hold much hope in Eireland Office's rebirth, and with them gone, the official currency would lose a lot of its market power. A quiet voice in my head insisted that we'd lose much more. As useless as those bureaucrats were, at least they'd given us a sense of being a state, a country, not a war-torn island without any centralized government that everyone would somewhat respect—or at least pretend that they did.

I kept close to the river for as long as I could. It was enough that a walk through the North Side brought back unwanted memories. I didn't need equally unwanted encounters with some feisty local mythborn who wouldn't necessarily respect the Court's emblem. Eithne seemed to hold as much authority over the mythborn outside the Court as Albert did over the non-Trinitian humanborn: most obeyed the set rules when pressed but ignored them whenever there was some gain in doing so and they could get away with it.

The gray edifice of the former museum rose in front of me soon enough, and I couldn't help checking my proximity trigger charm. It remained silent as I approached the gate, and I tried to ignore the voice in my head reminding me it wouldn't trigger at *my* approach. I could be caught in a blast just because some important mythborn walked by.

"I've got some information for Lady Eithne." I flashed the Court's emblem to the two guards.

Interesting—even with the threat of another attack and the Eireland Office's fall, the mythborn didn't seem to have tightened their security. I might have been missing some subtler measures, or they could have used some additional magic as protection, but I wouldn't be surprised if Eithne actually hadn't done anything. To double the guards would mean to show weakness and fear, and I had no trouble imagining the proud mythborn lady refusing to yield.

"Kaja, yes?" the bulkier of the guards asked. "The lady should be in her office now. Do you know the way?"

I gaped, oh I did. I couldn't help it. Last time they'd hardly allowed me to step inside the courtyard and fussed about my charms, and now they were allowing me a free entry? I bit my tongue before replying "yes." Even if I thought I could find Eithne's office, I didn't want to risk getting lost. With the way things were between the human-born and the mythborn, and with my all-too-obvious ties to the Trinitians, I wouldn't be surprised if they branded me a spy for taking a wrong turn.

"I'd appreciate a guide," I said.

I half expected Riagán to show up, but as the guard whistled, another mythborn approached. She must have been molekind, because the tip of her head didn't go higher than my shoulder, but she gave me a smile much friendlier than the local Liberties' shrimps could ever muster.

"Take our guest to Lady Eithne's office," the guard ordered her, and the mythborn girl nodded hastily. It seemed not all the Court mythborn were spoiled, self-absorbed nobles.

She led me through the corridors, and this time I paid attention to the route. It seemed that my guide was as uninterested in making polite conversation as I was, so we made it to Eithne's office in silence. She knocked on the door and waited for permission to enter.

"My lady, you have a guest." She stepped aside, letting Eithne see me.

"Kaja, come in." Eithne wore a lush gold dress that made her look like a living statue. "And you"—she turned to the mythborn—"please find Ceannasaí Cathal and ask him to join us."

The mythborn girl rushed away, and I sat down.

"I have information that might be useful." I pulled out the slip of paper as I relayed to her what I'd learned from Mallory. "Might be worth checking."

Eithne seemed satisfied. "I appreciate you brought this to me instead of going there on your own."

I refrained from shrugging and bit my tongue before mentioning I had agreed to deliver information to her, not to die trying to single-handedly take down the Snake's agents.

Knocking on the door saved me from having to reply, and Eithne's face brightened as a tall mythborn walked in. I recognized the gray uniform in an instant, but it wasn't Riagán.

"Ah, Cathal," Eithne said. "I'm glad you found time."

He bowed, but without extreme servitude, and I got a moment to inspect his short-cut, dark hair and wiry muscles. There was a military-like air around him, and in a way, he reminded me of Albert. Minus, of course, the sexual attraction and emotional attachment I had with the commander... Still, I couldn't resist wondering whether he, too, spoke with a British accent.

"Is she the humanborn you've mentioned before, my lady?" His accent, of course, was that of a mythborn.

"Yes, this is Kaja. She'll be bringing you information about the Snake's agents," Eithne replied. "Kaja, Cathal will show you the Scáthanna's quarters, and from now on you'll work directly with him."

I stood up and offered him a bow. His face, rectangular, but quite pleasant for an inhuman visage, remained stony while he inspected me. I expected a derogatory comment or at least a telling grimace, but he only gave me a short nod. Not one of approval, of that I was certain.

"If there's nothing else, my lady, I'll take her now." The way he spoke made it clear I shouldn't expect any more personal interaction. "She can tell me what she's got while I show her around."

It seemed that I shouldn't have counted on any introduction, and the mythborn I was supposed to be working with wanted to keep it as formal and impersonal as possible.

"Lady Eithne." I stood up, bowed, and headed for the door, following my new guide.

Cathal led the way and didn't grant me a single glance over his shoulder, though I was almost certain I wouldn't be able to sneak away if I wanted to. He was, after all, one of the Scáthanna.

"So, what do you have for us?" he asked as we exited the building and stepped into the courtyard. The tone of his voice, ever so slightly derogatory, grated on my composure.

"An address," I replied as we headed to the door in the southern wall of the Court. "The man who was passing it out seemed to match the profile of the people we're looking for."

"That's it? Nothing more solid?"

"No," I almost barked. My response was quite civil considering the witty alternatives that almost slipped from my lips in reaction to his subtly aggravating aura.

Cathal seemed to release my worst instincts and strengthen all my war-bred hate toward mythborn. With that attitude of his, I could bet he and Eithne were best friends.

"This is where we live," he said as we entered a narrow corridor. "This is our day room." He indicated the door to the left. "If I'm not in there, ask any mythborn to find me and wait."

"Got it." I didn't feel like being more amiable. "Anything else?" I held out the piece of paper to him. The sooner we parted ways, the better.

It seemed my cold display amused him, and he didn't take the address from me. "Come back tomorrow in the afternoon. You'll be going with us."

"The hell I will." The words escaped my mouth before I could jail them. "I was only supposed to gather information."

"And gather information you will," he replied, "including places you're sending us to."

I found no argument. His perspective made sense, and the only alternative I could offer would be going alone. Needless to say, I wasn't looking forward to walking on my own into a place that could be a terrorist cell, and I was too old to give him attitude and storm out of the Court. But it didn't mean I liked the idea of spending more time with him.

"Fine. Tomorrow afternoon, then. Any particular time?" I wasn't about to give him an excuse to complain that I arrived late.

"Around dusk will be fine," he replied. "Others should be back by then."

I knew better than to ask where they would be coming back from. "I'll see you then."

I offered no bow, but I didn't think he expected one, and got no reply to my dry farewell. In a way, my interaction with Cathal summed up the situation between his people and mine: a shaky peace full of half-veiled animosities with a threat of hostility thick in the air.

Working with him would be so much fun, I had no doubt about it.

~

I SAT with Riagán on the top floor of a ruined apartment building. He peeked through the window with his bow and arrow ready, and his serious expression suggested I wouldn't have to suffer through his teasing or annoying remarks. The clouds slid across the sky, and I watched their shapes, illuminated by the moon, through the destroyed roof. Down in the street, the rest of the Scáthanna approached an abandoned apartment block that faced the building we were hiding in.

"You're not happy to be here," Riagán remarked casually as if making an interesting observation.

"There's no real reason for me to be around."

No matter how one would want to put it, I was useless after I'd gathered the information; even during the war I fought only when I had no other choice. Cathal's insistence on my joining them must have been a way to remind me of my place, nothing more.

"We're killers," he said. "We're effective, but we don't see things the way you do: as clues. You proved yourself at the Greenleaf Inn, and Cathal's hoping you'll find more than we can."

I wasn't surprised he knew that I was checking the bombed inn. Mythborn seemed much better at communication than humans ever were. "I'm sorry you have to babysit me," I changed the topic. "Instead of..." I indicated the street below us.

He shook his head. "I always stay behind," he replied. "Going hand to hand would be a waste of the bow."

I held off a chuckle at the thought that Riagán just admitted he had weak points. "I thought the Scáthanna were supposed to be the best." I couldn't resist.

"We are." The confidence in his voice made it clear I should have been wiser than to ever question it. "But each of us has different skills. Mine are with stealth and bow." His eyes tore away from the streets to glance at me, and his face lost the serious edge. "Besides, you aren't a burden. I saw you fight... and run."

I smiled at the tease in the last word. "And you never got a clear shot?" I knew the answer. I might have done my best to stay out of sight during the war, but I was out in the open many times, vulnerable and an easy target for sure, so if Riagán had seen me, he must have had more than enough chances to take me down.

"Several times." He resumed scanning the street. "It was never worth taking it. I'd kill a mere scout and reveal my position or jeopardize my mission."

I didn't think he was even trying to sound believable, but the place and time weren't ideal for digging. We had an assignment, and my curiosity wasn't going to kill me, especially since his decisions likely had something to do with my saving Connor. They didn't look like brothers, so maybe they were friends? I stayed silent. Asking more questions could wait.

"I might tell you why, one day," he said as if replying to my thoughts.

Then his body tensed, and his focused face made it clear the conversation was over. The Scáthanna were going in.

We sat in silence, and I couldn't chase grim thoughts away. Mallory could have been wrong, and I might have sent a team of mythborn killers against an innocent humanborn. Cathal had reassured me they wouldn't kill anyone unless necessary, but trusting a mythborn's words was setting myself up for disappointment.

"It's clear. Let's go." Riagán rose from his spot.

I stared at him in surprise. Only a few minutes had passed since his comrades went in. He gave me a grin, and there was nothing modest about it. Yes, his smile said, they were that good.

We made our way down, descending the half-collapsed stairs. Riagán went first, and even though I admired his agility and speed, I must have done well enough myself, because when we reached the ground, he threw me a look that seemed to be saying "not bad for a humanborn." At least, I hoped it did.

One of the Scáthanna waited for us at the entrance to the apartment block. Her ethereal beauty mesmerized me, but her expression made it clear I shouldn't stare, even if in awe.

"Second floor, to the left," she threw out as we passed her by. She never ceased scanning the darkness.

When we made it to the apartment, its door shattered on the floor, another mythborn stepped to the side, allowing me to enter, and I held off a cringe at a very intense odor of blood inside. Of course they'd had to kill their target. I could only hope there weren't any bystanders inside.

"There were two of them." Cathal stood in the corridor, cleaning his sword. Red stains marked his uniform and equally gray leather armor, but it wasn't his blood. "A Léanmhar and a mythborn."

The apartment was in disarray, and it told me about the uneven fight the Scáthanna had gotten into. The Léanmhar, or the Afflicted as we humanborn called them, were never easy to kill, but even though the opponent must have taken them by surprise, the Scáthanna had still managed to defeat him quickly and quietly.

"Laoise took a hit, but she'll be fine," Cathal added, looking at Riagán as if making clear I wasn't a part of the team.

"And the mythborn?" Riagán asked.

"She tried to run, and when we cut her off, she killed herself."

While they talked, I activated one of my charms and scoured the apartment in its light. Multiple symbols of the

Snake branded the walls, and on a kitchen table sat a stash of explosive curses and plans.

"Rotunda Hospital." I held it up for the mythborn to see. So much for my supposedly superb investigative skills and a reason to be here in the first place: even the blind wouldn't have missed that.

Cathal cursed in Irish, and I couldn't have agreed more. From the very beginning of the war, the hospitals were the few neutral zones. Humanborn doctors and mythborn medics who joined them made it clear they'd only help the wounded if nobody asked which side were they on. If the Snake's agents planned to blow up the Rotunda, they must have grown desperate to reignite the conflict.

The Afflicted man lay in a pool of blood, and I forced myself to kneel by him. His face, deformed by the rapidly released magic, wasn't pleasant to look at, especially since it reminded me of what I was to become myself. Touching him couldn't affect my own condition, but I still hesitated before searching through his blood-drenched clothing. The multiple cuts and burn marks told a story of the fight, making me grateful I never got to meet the Scáthanna on a battlefield.

With no additional clues, I moved to the mythborn woman. Alive, she must have been beautiful, with her silky blue hair and shimmering skin, but now her face was twisted in a grimace, and her fingers still clutched the killing curse. Beside her, a bag filled with explosive curses and documents, all of them with the same information on the hospital.

"She seems to be a courier," I said. "We didn't get the mastermind, but at least we damaged their supply and information line."

"Can you learn anything from here?" Cathal asked.

"It looks similar to what I found in Jonas Byrne's place. I don't think we'll find any leads." I rubbed my chin. "But if you clean this place up, it might be a good spot for an ambush."

Cathal nodded. "Whoever sent the courier won't know what happened and where." He turned to Riagán. "Get the humanborn home. We'll handle things here."

No goodbye, no appreciation, no words of gratitude, only a dismissal.

I held off a sigh. I might have provided them the information about this place, and I might have had a good idea about setting a trap, but I felt that even if I found all the Snake's agents in Eireland, I still wouldn't deserve being called by my name, nor any other sign of courtesy. To them, I was a humanborn and nothing more. At least I didn't get to hear I was useless.

Since he seemed to have lost all interest in me, I didn't bother with goodbyes as I made my way out of the apartment. Riagán threw some hasty words in Irish, which I believed were the equivalent of "see you later," and then he followed me.

"I can get home on my own if you want to stay," I offered when we got outside. We weren't that far from the river, and I could go through the bridge where Tee-Bee lived. The bridge dwellers there knew me enough to ask for a reasonable toll, or even let me through without one when they were in a good mood.

"Was that some way of telling me you don't want my company?" Riagán arched his eyebrow. In the moonlight, his gray hair, skin, and uniform looked as if they were made of silver. "Because I was given an order, and I'll follow you nevertheless."

I shook my head and forced a smile. "I thought you

might prefer the company of your comrades instead of being stuck with me. It feels like your ceannasaí meant sending you with me as punishment."

Riagán's laughter echoed through the empty street. "It's nothing like that. You did well today. You proved your worth with the information you provided us, and you didn't flip when Cathal baited you. I'm here because he wants to make sure you're safe. Otherwise he wouldn't bother sending anyone, hoping you'd get killed on the way home, and he doesn't have to work with you anymore."

"Your ceannasaí has a strange way of showing appreciation." I couldn't resist the comment.

"You'll get used to it." Riagán seemed unconcerned. "You've earned enough tonight for Cathal to keep you around. And that's not something the Scáthanna grant freely, not even to the mythborn."

"You're forgetting the part where I'm useful." I didn't fall for his praise.

"Because it's irrelevant." A shrug accompanied his words. "If he decided your insights weren't worth the hassle, we could have come up with multiple reasons to keep you away."

I couldn't argue with his logic. Riagán was right—if Cathal considered me a nuisance, he wouldn't have bothered taking me on their mission.

"What if he decided to send me home alone?" I asked.

My question brought a wide smile to his face. "I'm sure I could find a reason to go out scouting in the area."

THE MORNING after the outing with the Scáthanna was supposed to be my job catch-up. Even though finding the

Snake was a priority, I didn't work exclusively for Eithne, and I had to maintain my net of contacts. Every day messengers arrived, bringing news, requests, and information for trade, and I had to at least sort through it, otherwise I risked overlooking something important.

Sipping tea, I faced the piles of papers, some of them crumpled and worn, brought over from all the corners of Dublin. Many were requests of information about relatives and friends, and I put them into a box I'd later take to Trinity. Albert was trying to maintain the list of Trinitians, war veterans, and even associate civilians, so I shamelessly used his resources. Addresses were sometimes outdated, but at least I would know if the people in question were even still alive.

Then I had reports and information offers from my contacts, which I had to sort depending on how interested I was, or how much money they were asking. The task was rather mundane and tedious, but in a way, I enjoyed it. Back when I was still an office employee in the non-magical Dublin, I worked with a lot of data, both entering it and providing analysis, so sorting through piles of documents reminded me of the past life. Of course, back then I'd have a computer and the Internet to aid me, and if I missed anything, technology provided easy access to information and quick means of communication. Now everything seemed to take ages...

I picked up another piece of paper and scanned through it, so that I could decide which pile or box it had to go to. I wasn't paying attention to the text, searching only for the keywords, so the meaning of the message escaped me until I got to the signature: Václav.

Why would my old squad friend would be writing to me? I knew the obvious answer, but hoped he had another reason. I returned to the beginning of the letter and rushed through the greeting and few courteous questions. Then I read the part that confirmed my fears.

I guess I won't fool you with that empty blabber, because you already know why I'm writing. The time is coming, Kaja, so I'll be saying goodbye to the few of my friends who are still alive. Drop by if you feel sentimental.

Below, there was an address... Václav lived closer than I thought. After the war we tried to keep in touch, but I was still trying to find myself a place in Trinity while he fought his nightmares by moving a lot. Back then he planned to go south and settle in some remote part of Wicklow Mountains. Involved with Albert and Trinity, then wrapped up in my work, I didn't know if it failed to work out or he simply changed his mind.

The letter was from five days earlier, assuming he sent it the same day he wrote the date, and I froze at the realization I might have gotten to it too late. Like me, Václav's affliction was in an advanced stage, and he must have felt the magic within him getting out of hand. The only question was how much time he gave himself for the goodbyes, and his message didn't specify any time frame.

Within fifteen minutes I dashed out of my apartment, heading southwest. Even if the Snake's agent stepped in front of me, introducing themselves, I wouldn't have stopped, and I kept running through the streets as if it could change anything. Either Václav was well enough to be still alive, or my mad sprint was pointless.

The area where he was supposed to be living looked abandoned, and I had no doubt he'd chosen it on purpose. We couldn't control exactly when the affliction would claim us, and if something unexpected was to happen that would speed up the changes, he'd at least ensured there wouldn't be too many victims. Before he would get to the more popu-lated areas, guards at one of the checkpoints would spot him, and, with little luck, he'd die before killing anyone.

I cringed at the thought, but becoming an Afflicted meant becoming a senseless monster bound on destruction. That was why everyone I knew chose poison to leave the world on their terms.

I knocked at the door, wondering whether Václav was still alive, and the sound of heavy footsteps inside brought a wave of relief. Then his face with a square forehead adorned by a heap of light brown hair appeared in the door.

"Look who finally shows up!" Václav grinned at me.

With a gesture, he invited me in. He stood tall and straight, towering over me at almost seven feet. If I hadn't read his letter, I wouldn't have guessed how far along he was, but when I passed him in the narrow corridor, his distorted inner magic told me more than I wanted to know.

"I've been wrapped up in things." It wasn't much of an apology.

"As usual. Business going well, I take it?" He poured whiskey into glasses while I took a seat by the table.

The living room we were in looked shabby and unkempt. Not enough to leave an impression that Václav was a slob, but clearly house chores weren't his top priority. I couldn't blame him. If I knew I was to die, I wouldn't bother with cleaning up either. The pile of blankets on the couch suggested he slept in the living room, and the half-destroyed shelf presented a collection of books—all thrillers and horrors, judging from the names on the spines.

"I can't complain."

We raised our arms, and when the glasses clinked, the whiskey swooshed inside, washing against them. "To the fallen ones," we said in unison.

"Do you know how many are still alive?" Václav asked after we downed the first round. The bottle that he caressed with his fingers suggested that we'd be drinking for a while.

"Not sure. Hardly anyone stuck around." I didn't have to mention that even if we'd tried at first, we hadn't really kept in touch with each other. Everyone in our squad had their own way of forgetting the past, but we all agreed that seeing each other would not help the memories to fade. "But Patricia finally decided to leave. She got all clear after the quarantine and was out of here before her 'goodbye' stopped ringing in our ears."

Václav snorted. "I'm surprised she lasted that long. I knew her before the Magiclysm, and she was homesick all the time. When the war ended, I was making bets with Mark how soon she'd leave. After all, there are two types of immigrants." He grinned. "Those who adapt…"

"… and those who go back home," I finished for him.

I saw it even before the war: my constantly homesick compatriots, missing their families, friends, culture, and whatnot. They complained about weather, talked Polish whenever they could, and mostly kept away from non-Polish immigrants. Sometimes it was years before they decided to pack and go home, sometimes only a few months.

Then there were people like me or Václav, who missed Czech even less than I missed Poland. We spoke English most of the time, made friends across nationalities, and ate our homelands' food because we felt like it, not because we wanted to get a glimpse of being back home. After all, we were already home.

Václav poured another round, and I didn't refuse. It wasn't the first time I'd said goodbyes in that manner, and getting smashed seemed to be the part of the ritual.

"To long life!" He raised his glass.

I hesitated. That toast was meant for me, even if we both knew I was bound to follow in his footsteps sooner rather than later. But at the same time, I had just learned that there could be a way out of it, and I couldn't keep it to myself.

I put the glass down and put a half-full vial of the drug between us. "This could help you," I said. "One drop a day slows down the affliction. It won't give you much more time, but there might be another way..." All I needed was for Václav to live long enough for me to visit the Court and beg Eithne to grant him the way out she'd offered me. He needed that chance more than I did.

"Another way?" He looked at me, confused.

"It's not guaranteed, but the mythborn—"

"I've heard enough." He pointed at the vial. "That drug's theirs too?"

With a heavy heart, I nodded. I already felt I wouldn't be able to convince him, but I couldn't give up. "But it isn't a trick. It's working."

"Then you should keep it for yourself." Václav slid the vial toward me. "You should also check if that way out of theirs is worth anything. So that the toast won't go to waste." He raised his glass again, insistence clear in his posture.

I raised mine. "To long life." The whiskey tasted more bitter this time. "Why?" I whispered as soon as the glass clanged against the table. "It's not because you hate them, is it?"

At first, he didn't reply. He poured another round and stared at the liquid in his glass, swirling it in thought. Then he lifted his head and looked me in the eye. "Because I see no point. The last years have been... a struggle. I can't find a place for myself in this new world. With that much magic in me, I can't leave, and nobody needs a software developer here. I don't feel like just surviving. I'm tired." He sighed. "Even if the affliction hadn't gotten that far, I'd probably be thinking of that poison anyway."

I remained silent. In a way, I felt the same about staying in Trinity after the war, and my "poison" was leaving its walls.

"Maybe I'm not as adaptable as I used to brag," Václav continued. "Or maybe it's just that one step too much. If you bend too much, you break." He shrugged and raised his glass. "To peace."

I toasted with him. Back in the war we used to say "to victory," but as soon as the treaties were signed, we changed it. Peace was more precious than proving our superiority.

"I've spent the last few days drinking and remembering all the dead people and stupid things we did in the war, so I've had quite enough." He leaned forward with a hunter's smile. "Got any interesting gossip instead? Like where you got that drug or how you know what the mythborn are plotting."

"I have a better one for you." I couldn't resist a grin. "I kissed a mythborn."

Václav burst out laughing, and this sound made it worth sharing the memory of my humiliation. He was right to cut the war memories short. One shouldn't depart this world with grim thoughts. "The one you rescued from a giant?" he asked after he caught a breath. "I didn't know you were looking for him."

"Not him, and I wasn't." I held out my glass to him. "I hope you have more than just the rest of this bottle, because my story is worth a lot of whiskey."

"Oh, don't you worry, I have something better." In a few heartbeats he made it into the kitchen and back, and held out his prize to me. "Real Czech Becherovka. Probably the last bottle on this whole bloody island."

I mimicked a bow of respect. "That's definitely worth a tale. Sit down, oh brave warrior, and listen to the tales of one scout's misfortunes."

I stayed with him all day, telling stories and drinking, because after the staple Czech alcohol, Václav produced even more bottles of various beverages, all of them strong enough to burn any memory out of one's brain. It must have been around the evening when my comrade finally looked at me.

"I appreciate what you're doing, but you'll have to eventually go home," he said in a soberer tone than I expected.

"I'm hoping to get you drunk enough to agree to the drug," I replied honestly. That battle had already been lost, but it didn't hurt to try. After all, alcohol could have weakened Václav's resolution.

Besides, leaving meant I would never talk to him again. Once all the goodbyes were said, it was bad manners to come again.

Václav shook his head. "Let it go, Kaja. Save yourself." He made another trip to the kitchen and returned with a small bottle.

I arched my eyebrows. "Where did you get all that stuff?" I was staring at a well-preserved bottle of Żubrówka, bison grass vodka made only in Poland. Local stores used to import it before the war, but I hadn't seen one in years.

"For you." He set it before me. "Thank you for coming."

As much as I didn't want leave Václav alone, I knew it was time to go. If for no other reason than to give him time to die in peace. If I stayed and he turned, his last conscious thought would be realization that he was about to kill me. I didn't want that for him. With a heavy heart, I packed away the vial and the bottle.

"It was good to see you." He offered me a genuine smile.

We hugged, long and strong, and then I was out in the street. Lightheaded from the alcohol, I slowly made my way through the dark streets, fighting the need to return to Václav's place and force the drug down his throat. He'd made his mind, and I had to respect that. After all, this wasn't the first goodbye I'd said.

CHAPTER TWELVE

For three days I tried to forget about the meeting with Václav. I focused on finding clues about the Snake agents' whereabouts, checking old sources and making new friends, but it seemed that taking out the courier had damaged the communication lines between the agents. It meant they weren't about to attack another place, but it also made them harder to track. And as time passed, I feared the next clue would lie in the ruins of another blown-up building.

That was why even though I didn't feel like visiting the Trinity again, I had to let Albert know that "the unknown terrorist cell" might have chosen a new target. Walking toward the former college building, I ran various scenarios through my head, as if I could foresee which words and phrases would help us avoid another argument. Yes, I was that pitifully desperate.

The security at the gate remained tight, and as I approached, I recognized the captain I'd run into last time I visited. His face twisted into a vicious smile. He hadn't forgotten me, and I could count on him making my entrance as difficult as possible. I wasn't in a rush, so I lined up in the queue, catching the disgruntled glance of a veteran, by the name of Marcus, if I recalled correctly, who happened to be on guard duty. His posture made it clear that if it was up to him, he'd let me in without any fuss.

The day was quite warm, especially for winter, and the sun peeked out from behind the clouds as if unsure whether it wanted to look at postwar Dublin or not. I turned my face to it, basking in its illusory warmth and trying to remember the last time I got to enjoy it. With a book and coffee from a local store, on a bench in the park... I allowed nostalgia to flow through my thoughts, but I didn't let it take over.

The captain called the humanborn one by one, letting them in with as little as checking their Eireland ID and doing a quick scan. But once my turn came, he took his time inspecting my documents, and one of the poor guards had to scan me thoroughly, with the detector going off every five seconds.

"This is ridiculous," I commented.

He lifted his gaze from my ID and looked at me. "That's exactly what a mythborn spy would say. Do you have something to hide?"

I endured his scrutiny and shrugged. "Nothing. Take your time. I'll make sure Albert knows how you treat veterans."

He cringed. "Veterans, you say? All I see is a spoiled civilian who thinks she gets special treatment because she got us some information during the war."

Behind his back, my fellow veteran's eyes widened. Trinitians had always shown respect to those who risked their lives in the war, both fighting with the mythborn and protecting civilians, and many guerrilla squads worked together with the organized military units Albert had formed.

"I've heard enough about you. Insubordinate, untrustworthy, and loyal only to yourself," the guard spat. "You only came here for protection and disappeared as soon as it was safe, never lending a hand. Not a true veteran, but a coward. That is what you are."

I arched my eyebrow and mocked polite interest. There were at least a few officers in the Trinity whose opinions of me were as low as the temperatures around the North Pole, but I didn't think any of them would go so far as to brand me a coward, so it must have been the captain's personal addition.

"Your name, captain?" I asked in a dry tone.

He laughed at me. "Like I'd give it to you." He handed me my ID back. "I regret it, but we cannot admit you to Trinity. Have a nice day."

I snorted. Did he really think he could get away with that? I took the document and walked several steps away, then leaned against the metal fence and turned my face to the sun. "I have time. I can wait." I didn't even offer him a glance. "Your shift ends soon." If he thought I didn't know the guards' current schedule, he was wrong. Albert changed the roster around enough to confuse outsiders, but we'd come up with that system together back when I was still more involved.

"Remove her," he barked. "If she resists, throw her in a cell."

I opened my eyes enough to see the gate, but the captain's men hesitated.

"Captain, with all respect... She *is* a war veteran," Marcus said.

"Being a veteran is something more than joining some

rogue squads and feeding off Trinity's aid," the captain barked. "There are enough cowards around claiming the title. We don't need another one. Now get her out of my sight."

Marcus sighed as he walked over to me. "I'm sorry," he whispered. "He'll be gone at half one—come back then."

I let him take me by the arm and lead me around the corner. "Half one," as the locals said it, meant one thirty, and I could wait an hour. "Does he treat other veterans the same way?" I asked.

Marcus gave me an apologetic smile. "Captain Foley can be a bit rough sometimes. He's real military, and those who are... less conventional soldiers tend to irritate him more."

"That would be pretty much everyone in Trinity." I didn't hide my dissatisfaction. "I'm surprised he can even stand the commander." I'd always believed that Albert had some military background because of the efficiency he organized the Trinitians and strategized during the war, but he also had an understanding of the people under his command. He adapted quickly to the more chaotic structure and lack of discipline of the temporary units, making the best of what he had, and he didn't shy away from seeking the assistance of the multiple guerrilla squads that formed across Dublin. He gave us supplies and shelter, and we carried out his orders, fighting in the areas we knew like the back of our hands. And more importantly, as much as Trinitians saw themselves as a kind of humanborn elite, Albert had always treated the outside units as equals.

"I don't think he does," Marcus replied quietly.

I sighed. "I'll make sure Albert knows he's been disrespectful. I don't care if he has a problem with me, but he should at least treat Trinitian veterans well." I might be petty, because I *did* care about how he treated me. But if I wanted to do something about it, I needed to pretend I was selfless.

I let Marcus escort me further away, and once we were out of view, I shook his hand. "Thank you for standing up for me."

He smiled. "I still remember you got us out of Drumcondra when things went south."

I held off a snort. He'd brought up the very deed of mine that on the courage scale couldn't have been any further from the cowardice Captain Foley accused me of. It was also close to "stupidity," but I wouldn't admit it aloud, not after my getting Marcus's unit out of the mythborn siege was deemed "daring but successful." Of course, in the privacy of my own common sense, I'd later sworn never to do something like that again.

I was polite enough to wait for Marcus to go back to his post. He didn't need the scolding for what I was about to do.

I moved away from the building, making sure I had a good view of one particular window. I'd never perfected the art of whistling, but I'd kept my token from the war. Even though it had become one of my amulets, I could still blow air through it.

The sound shrilled through the air in the rhythm of an urgent message. I didn't want to put the whole of Trinity in a state of alarm with a different coded tune. People in the street turned their heads, their expressions worried, as the sound of the whistle must have brought back memories.

Within seconds, Albert stood at the window, and his confused stare was exactly what I'd hoped for. I played a little pantomime for him: pointed at the gate and shrugged. I didn't do anything more, because Captain Foley himself came running out of the Trinity, and his angry red face indicated the trouble I'd gotten myself into.

"You insolent... coward!" he spat. It seemed that his array of insults was severely limited. "How dare you use our signals for your personal gain?!"

I stared at him with as straight a face as I could manage. At this point he was on the verge of hyperventilation, and deep down I hoped he'd choke on his own hate and die. It surely would solve many problems, mine and Marcus's included.

But apparently I hadn't been a good enough girl, because no higher power granted my wish, and the captain kept shouting, "I'll have you jailed! I'll have you stripped of your privileges. I'll..."

I looked up at Albert watching the scene, his office window already open. It was his call.

"You'll have Kaja report to my office immediately, captain." His calm but firm voice came like a last-minute rescue. "And you'll escort her in person."

Albert could have spared me the further company of the thickheaded ingrate, but the look on Foley's face was worth it. He swallowed hard with his head at an angle, trying to make sure the voice was indeed Albert's.

"Yes, commander!" he replied loud enough for everyone to hear. Then he gave me a hostile glance. "This way."

As if I didn't know. Within the last month, I had probably been in Albert's office more times than Foley had ever visited it. I still fell in behind, letting him lead the way. Getting my payback now would destroy the image of the mistreated veteran I'd tried to paint myself as, hoping Albert would ensure Captain Foley never overstepped the boundaries of his post again. I wasn't a Trinitian, so I only had to put up with him every once in a while, but the plight of many of my former companions was a whole other matter, and for them I didn't hesitate to play on Albert's sentiments.

We walked in silence, disturbed only by the sweet music of Foley's gritting teeth. When we reached Albert's office, the door waited open, and he was sitting at his desk.

"Captain Foley, Kaja, come in please." I didn't fall for his pleasant voice, as his tightened face told me enough about his mood. "Has Kaja been causing trouble?" he asked as soon the captain closed the door behind us.

"She..." Foley glanced at me. I didn't think he recognized Albert's question as a trap. "I believe it might have been a misunderstanding."

With clear disrespect for all the military-like regulations, I snorted. Being a civilian definitely had its advantages. "Captain Foley refused me entry to Trinity. Along with accusing me of cowardice and abusing my veteran status."

Albert's eyes flared up, and if I could, I'd cheer him on. Always in control of his anger, he funneled it into his words enough for anyone to recognize it. "Captain Foley, explain, please." That cold, piercing voice of his. I loved it... when I wasn't the one he spoke to.

The officer's face became even redder. "This woman is an insult to any military organization." He was cornered, but he surely didn't hold back. "She has no respect for Trinity and its members, and she disregards all the rules. She's a coward who only seeks to leech off the benefits we offer to our veterans, and therefore offends all the brave soldiers who laid down their lives defending this country."

Albert arched an eyebrow as if in polite interest.

"I'd agree with being an insult and disregarding rules," I offered in a mediative tone, careful not to burst out laughing.

"I'd be surprised if you didn't." Apparently, Albert also couldn't resist a bit of sarcasm. Then he looked at Captain Foley. "I suggest you broaden your knowledge, captain. Ask our historians about the Drumcondra retreat, the defense of the O'Connell Bridge, the ambush at Portobello. I'm sure Kaja's name will come up in every single case." He stared his officer down. "And that's only the most widely known ones." Albert stood from his desk and paced around us. "You might question Kaja's methods, you might loathe her attitude, but ever since her unit agreed to work with the Trinity, she's always provided us information worth much more than the supplies we offered in exchange. Moreover, even though she is a civilian and her line of work requires neutrality, she openly favors us when it comes to the flow of information."

Through the whole rant, Foley stood silent, his face remaining a solid block of red. "I apologize, commander," he uttered when silence fell. "It was poor judgment on my part."

Albert didn't let him get away with that mockery of an apology. "I believe you should address Kaja, not me."

With a huge dose of goodwill, I could say the captain looked at me. But his face barely turned toward me, and his eyes were fixed at a point somewhere above my shoulder. "My apologies," was all he mustered.

I gave a nod, and Albert waved at him. "Dismissed."

Captain Foley made it through the door so quickly he could have simply vanished into thin air, and Albert's attention was focused on me. No, he wasn't impressed.

"You had to make a show, didn't you?" His voice wasn't even a degree warmer than when he spoke to Foley. "Did you enjoy humiliating my officer?"

I gave him a nasty grimace and a matching stare. "It's the second time he made it difficult for me to enter Trinity. I don't want to risk his slowing me down one day when seconds count." My tone was far from friendly, but I didn't care. I didn't get that bitchy often, but Foley seemed to have struck all the right chords. "It's not even about me. I can just walk away, and you'll find someone else to get you the information you need, but the ones who decided to stay in the Trinity can't. They need to suffer his jackassery on a daily basis."

His eyes narrowed. "Now that's too far. Just because he dislikes you, doesn't give you the right to accuse him of mistreating all the veterans."

"Maybe if you left your office more often, you'd notice —" I bit my tongue a bit too late. I raised my hand. "I'm sorry. That wasn't fair." Albert was spending a lot of time behind his desk managing Trinity, but my emotions must have gotten the better of me if I'd insinuated he didn't care about his people. "Talk to Marcus or other veterans who are assigned to Foley. See for yourself." I could only hope it would suffice for an apology.

Albert stared at me for a painfully long moment, then nodded. He returned to his desk. "So, what brings you here?" he asked in a semiformal tone. "You haven't been visiting us lately, so I'm guessing you're bringing some important news?"

I ignored the stab. We'd just wrapped up one argument, and I wasn't about to start another one. Especially not the one that ventured into more personal territory.

"My sources suggest that the terrorists might target the hospitals next," I said.

Albert drew air with a sharp wheeze, and his eyes widened. "How good is that source?"

I knew he didn't question the news, but hoped that it was more circling gossip than confirmed information, and I regretted that I couldn't give him the luxury of such doubt. "As good as if they had told me themselves," I replied with a heavy heart. "Rotunda's name was mentioned, but I have no idea if it's their only target."

Albert rubbed his chin. "I'll send the word to all the hospitals. If Rotunda's name surfaced, it might be a smoke screen to draw our attention away from another place." He looked up at me. "Anything else?"

I shook my head. "Not that I've heard. How are things at the Eireland Office?" I asked.

His forehead furrowed as if dark clouds covered his thoughts. "Nothing has changed. We're still digging up dead from under the rubble. The total death count for both us and the mythborn has reached eighty-two. Dozens more in hospitals... which you say might be next on the hit list." He smiled, though the curl of his lips seemed forced. "At least we still have peace."

Things weren't looking good, and his mention of peace sounded like a desperate attempt at finding something positive. I wanted to stay, maybe offer my help, but I needed to be out in the streets. I needed to find that one Snake agent who'd orchestrated everything and coordinated the attacks. Catching minor players did us no good.

I was about to say my goodbyes when somebody knocked on the door, and after Albert's reply, Orla walked into the office.

"We have a problem," she announced. "Shrieks."

Albert pulled the map from under countless other papers. "Where?"

"Donnybrook, Rathgar, and Dolphin's Barn," Orla replied.

It took me only a second to match the names to locations. "They shouldn't have been so spread out," I whispered. Shrieks always came in threes. Over time they might separate, sometimes due to humanborn and other times mythborn efforts to hunt them down, but to be found so far from one another was suspicious.

Albert marked the points on the map. "We don't have enough units trained for that. We could cover the first two, but Dolphin's Barn will have to wait." He looked up at me. "I'm sorry. I know it's the closest one to your home."

"It's also the least populated area." I didn't like my own words, but sending inexperienced soldiers would only make things worse.

The chill ran down my spine, and I couldn't chase the memories away, not anymore. In the second year of the war, when those creatures were still plentiful, they plagued both humanborn- and mythborn-controlled territories. My unit stumbled upon one when we were retreating from a night raid. I still remembered taking the corner with my companions and staring straight into the creature's eyes. Half of the people hadn't made it out of the street when the shriek released its frost breath, trapping them in ice, and the rest of us ran in twos or threes, hoping the shriek would follow someone else. We were lucky it didn't scream, else no one would have made it.

Even without its scream, we wouldn't have survived the night if we hadn't run into the Trinitians setting up a trap. They had drawn the shriek away from its closest victims, and yelled at the rest of us to keep moving toward the nearby square. Even though the Trinitians did their best, my unit lost more than two-thirds of its numbers before the shriek fell.

Since then, we'd learned a lot about shrieks, and we'd lost fewer and fewer people taking them down, but a shriek hunt was always a risk.

I snapped out of the unpleasant recollection, only to catch Albert's intense stare. He must have known what I was thinking about... He was the man who'd offered me water and words of comfort when I made it to the Trinitian-held square gasping for breath.

"Maybe you should stay here until we confirm it's safe," he offered. "Once we're done with the first two, the teams will join and take the third one. Unless we suffer too many losses, it should be done by morning."

I shook my head. "I'll be fine. If they're spread out so much, they likely won't move any more."

Why would they separate? Was it the Snake's doing? I mulled over the questions in my head, but no answer presented itself. These things should have been near extinct and long gone from Dublin area, infesting only the less populated countryside, though from what I knew, the mythborn hunted them with equal if not greater ferocity. And suddenly we had to deal with them in the very heart of Dublin.

I leaned over the map again. "I might know some people who'd be interested in a shriek hunt. They could take the Dolphin Barn's one."

Albert gave me a long, considerate stare, then shook his head. "I don't want to risk civilians' lives. And if things go wrong, the shriek might follow them into a more populated area."

I couldn't resist a smug smile. The people I had in mind definitely weren't civilians. "They're experienced, all veterans. You know, the sort that get bored without a thrill every now and then. They won't charge in without a plan just hoping for the best."

Albert hesitated. His face told me he didn't want to agree, but pushing his own people to do two shriek hunts in a row was something he wanted to avoid. I weighed my next argument: if I told him too much, I risked revealing whom I had in mind, but without more arguments, he could turn the offer down. Before I decided on anything, I received unexpected aid.

"I think I've met one of the people Kaja's speaking about." Orla arched her eyebrow as if seeking confirmation, and I gave her a nod. She did, but we both knew better than to share the details with Albert. "They shouldn't cause any trouble and might actually help."

Albert sighed. "How much is it going to cost us?"

I stared at him, dumbfounded. The very thought that Trinity would pay the Scáthanna would cause serious brain damage if one pondered it long enough.

"Kaja, I might be spending a lot of time in this office, but I'm not oblivious to what's going on outside these walls," Albert said in a tired voice. "I know some veterans started organizing mercenary groups."

"Oh." I didn't do anything to correct his assumption. If he believed he knew whom I'd be contacting, he wouldn't ask uncomfortable questions. "Don't worry about the money. It's between them and me."

He gave the nod I was waiting for. "So, anything else you need?"

"The Trinity's badge and papers confirming they're on a mission for you would be nice," I replied. "You know how guards at the checkpoints are sometimes."

I planned on leading the mythborn to the area myself, but that wasn't something Albert needed to know. If he did, I'd be grounded in Trinity for sure until they dealt with the threat.

Albert took out a document and a badge, and I ran through the text. Standard permission and authorization from the Trinity's commander, but it would do the trick.

I placed them in my bag. "I better get going."

Orla threw me a curious gaze, as if she wondered whether I really intended to ask the mythborn for help. I sent her a smile. For all I knew, the Scáthanna would discard the idea as ridiculous, but it wouldn't hurt to try.

"Send me a message on how it goes," Albert said. "If your team bails out, I'll have my people ready."

I nodded. "I should know by evening. Safe hunting." I had no doubt Albert and Orla would lead the teams themselves, and since I wasn't about to risk his figuring out that I intended to partake in a hunt too, even if only as a guide, I left in quite a hurry.

Out of Trinity and back home, where I needed to pick up few amulets and charms. Even if I wouldn't be hunting the shriek myself, going in unprepared would be more than foolish. Then, as soon as I had my gear, I would head straight for the Court.

When I walked into the room, all the mythborn inside looked at me in hope. Even Cathal had some interest flash across his face. I could imagine that for the Scáthanna, idleness was worse than death, and it'd been days since I'd had any information to share. Eithne's contacts had probably come up empty as well, so they must have been stuck waiting at the Court. From what I understood, they normally dealt with a multitude of issues across the still-unstable Eireland, but since catching the Snake agents took priority, they'd likely ended up on standby.

They sat at a long table, and the unfinished meal suggested the food was only a pastime.

"Have you found something?" Cathal's plain voice revealed no emotion.

I shook my head and caught several grimaces of disappointment on their faces. "But I have something else that might be of interest." I allowed myself a smug smile. "There was a shriek sighting."

In an instant, all their attention was on me. Their eyes stared with hunger and anticipation, and I recognized them for the primal hunters they were. The Scáthanna might act civilized, and at first glance differed little from other mythborn, as proud and arrogant as all of them, but at the very mention of a worthy prey, they reverted to instinct-driven predators.

"We would have heard about it." Riagán's voice sounded calm, though his eyes shone. They all wanted my news to be true.

I gave them what they desired. "It's deep in the South Side, in a primarily humanborn area. I doubt the news has reached the Court yet."

Cathal gave me a long glare. "Then aren't the Trinitians handling it?"

"They will eventually," I replied. "But they're tied up with the other two, so that one is... unassigned for the time being." I pulled out Trinity's badge and Albert's document from my bag. "If you want, I can get you in and out."

"Doing the job for the humanborn?" The broad-shouldered one, Faolan, snorted.

"Do you have anything else to do?" a black-haired mythborn female retorted.

Then they both glanced at Cathal, making it clear whose decision it would be, so I looked at him too.

"All three of them appeared quite a distance from one another," I said. "As if someone manipulated them into splitting." If they needed an excuse, this one was perfect: we had to know whether the Snake's agents were involved.

Cathal snorted, and I guessed he must have come to a similar conclusion. "Albert knows who you're asking for help?"

"I told him I know a team that might be willing to risk a shriek hunt," I replied. "He was happy enough that someone would deal with it, so he didn't ask too many questions." I didn't mention that Orla had her suspicions, since I wasn't sure whether Riagán had talked about his meeting with the others. If people started having any more secrets, I'd have to keep notes to make sure I didn't reveal something by accident.

Cathal nodded and then looked at his companions with a calculating glare. They kept their faces straight, but I could sense the tension.

"Get ready," he said. "I'll talk to the lady."

The efficiency with which they disappeared from the room was impressive, and I found myself alone with Cathal.

"I trust you brought your equipment?" he asked.

"I have what I need, but I'm your guide, not a warrior." I didn't look away. There was a difference between being a coward and knowing one's limits. "I'm going with you to get you past the humanborn checkpoints without too many questions asked."

"But you've taken on a shriek before."

That was hardly a question, and I couldn't help wondering whether he guessed or knew I'd had a run-in with one. "I know what to expect," I replied drily. "I won't be a hindrance, and in case something goes wrong, I can help, or get out of the way, whichever you prefer." I wasn't part of their team, and in such a case, staying out of the fray was often better.

Cathal smirked and nodded as he stood up. "I don't expect more. Wait here. Others will be back soon." He glanced over his shoulder on his way out. "The food is not going to poison you, so help yourself if you're hungry."

I stood dumbfounded by both the trace of humor in his voice and the offer itself, as opposed to the "… and don't touch anything" I'd expected from him, so I sat at the table. I wasn't hungry and didn't plan on stuffing myself right before setting out on a hunt, but the fruit platter caught my attention. They had grapes! It had been years since I'd eaten them. Their price, like most imported goods, was too much for me, and I wasn't about to go bankrupt for a mere handful. It seemed that the Court could either afford such extravagance or had a cheaper supplier. And I wouldn't put it past them to use magic to grow them in Eireland.

I didn't hesitate. If Cathal offered the food, it was only courteous that I accepted, wasn't it? The grapes tasted better than I remembered, sweet and juicy, and I chewed them in slow appreciation.

"Aren't you afraid these are magical?" Riagán reentered the chamber in full gear and with a bow at his back. I had to give a nod to his speed. In the time it took me to eat a handful of grapes, he'd gotten battle-ready.

With some regret, I swallowed the last grape. Speaking with one's mouth full was hardly polite. "Cathal told me they're safe to eat." That covered both the question about my fears and the unspoken one: whether I had permission to touch their food.

Riagán set his bow aside, and sat, or rather leisurely stretched, on the bench with his back against the table. As he leaned to reach for a plum, his face moved close to mine. Uncomfortably close, if somebody asked for my opinion, but no one did. Of course, it would be too much to expect he'd move away as he ate the fruit, and I couldn't help wondering whether it was another of his games.

"You better not scare her away, Riagán." The black-haired mythborn female entered. I was almost certain her name was Laoise, though no one had ever cared to introduce us. "She's our guide, and if she runs away before we get to that shriek, you'll be my practice target." Her hand skimmed across the knives at her belt.

"I don't think she scares away that easily." Riagán glanced at me, and the tone of his voice made it clear he meant our previous meetings. He wiped the juice off the corner of his mouth, his eyes still on me. "At least for a humanborn."

Laoise laughed and slapped his arm casually, and Riagán moved away to a more acceptable distance. Meanwhile, she leaned over my shoulder, and her face almost brushed against mine when she half whispered, "Don't mind him. He's just bored."

The mythborn didn't seem to comprehend the idea of "personal space." At least not when it was convenient for them to ignore it.

"We all are." Faolan entered, and right behind him was Sadb, an almost ethereal mythborn female. Her hair, tied in a high ponytail, resembled thick ribbons of sun-gilded mist.

The two more, a male and a female who followed, were Lorcan and Caitríona, but my knowledge about them ended at their names, and their gear didn't give any clue as to their roles in the group. Not that I had much idea about others either, since Cathal's orders always kept me stuck with Riagán, away from the fighting. Even though I had no reason to complain, it did mean I had yet to really see the mythborn special forces in action.

"Ceannasaí's not back yet?" Lorcan asked.

They reseated themselves around the table, and I found

myself surrounded by them. In hindsight, sitting down might not have been the best idea.

"So, tell us about that shriek." Faolan played with a cup made of cut glass, but his attention was on me.

"Shouldn't we wait for the ceannasaí?" I didn't feel like repeating myself or taking the scolding for sharing the information before he came back. Because if someone was to be blamed for anything, it would certainly be the only humanborn in the company.

Faolan gave me a displeased glare, and Sadb snorted.

"She's learning quick," she said.

"Good." Cathal entered, and all heads turned to him. He was, like all the others, in full gear already, and he held a rolled parchment. "Make some space on the table."

The plates and bowls disappeared as if a magic wand whisked them away, and I resisted a smirk. During those recent quiet days, the Scáthanna must have become really desperate for some action.

As Cathal approached, Riagán moved to the side, and the mythborn commander leaned over the table right beside me. Did I mention the personal space issue? I could swear they were all doing it on purpose.

"Show us," he said as soon as he unfolded the parchment.

I stared at the map with all its unfamiliar names, partially in mythborn runes, partially in Irish and English, but once I found a point of reference, the lines of streets and the shapes of various areas became the city I knew well.

"Southwest from here, Dolphin's Barn, near Grand Canal." I pointed at the area. "The report wasn't very detailed."

"We'll find it." Cathal's voice rang with confidence.

"There are humanborn checkpoints here and here. It'd be better if they fell back."

I bit my lip. Convincing a bunch of militia lads and lasses that they had to abandon their post wouldn't be easy, especially with a bunch of mythborn by my side. But Albert's document gave me some wiggle room, and if I played it right, I could make them believe I brought orders from the Trinity. They didn't need to know the clearing team didn't consist of humanborn.

"I'll see what I can do," I promised.

Cathal nodded and focused back on the map. "We'll go this way." His finger traced a route.

It wasn't the fastest way to the area, but I had no doubts he picked the abandoned neighborhoods and back alleys for a reason. A squad of mythborn marching through the Liberties and other populated places would cause quite a commotion that neither they nor I wanted. I liked the idea of going in and out as quietly as possible. Taking a shriek down wouldn't be quiet for sure, but at the same time, hardly anyone would dare to get close. Before we'd even get there, Albert's messengers would carry the warning to the people in the surrounding areas to keep clear. The best way for the civilians to stay alive was to close their doors, activate the protective wards, and let the military handle the shriek.

Cathal rolled the parchment back up and looked at me. "Kaja, talk to Cait about your gear. She'll see if you're missing anything essential."

I almost gaped when he said my name instead of addressing me as "the humanborn," but I was smarter than to argue I was already well equipped. When it came to shrieks, one could never have enough gear, and the mythborn probably had better charms and curses than I could get on my own. If they were willing to share, even if only for the night, I wouldn't refuse.

At Cathal's gesture, everybody stood up and left through the door.

Caitríona matched my pace as we walked through the courtyard, and her vibrant blue eyes inspected my outfit while I tried not to stare at her azure hair sneaking out from a tight beret. I didn't need to read her mind to guess how the evaluation had gone, because compared to their tailored uniforms and matching gear, I must have looked like a tramp. She probably didn't expect me to have any equipment she'd consider useful.

"Standard Trinitian set, isn't it?" The tone of her voice confirmed her evaluation.

I wasn't even surprised she knew what the Trinitians usually carried. After all, the mythborn and the humanborn had warred long enough for the Scáthanna to have a good idea about the gear Albert's people used.

Oh, the grin I gave her. Maybe it was childish, but I couldn't resist. "I've got several delayed-ignition heat charms, three short-range stun curses, and at least five shield amulets, including two ranged ones, plus two warmth sphere charms and enhanced earplugs." With every item I listed, Caitríona's face became longer, and I caught curious glances over other mythborn's shoulders.

"Good distraction kit." She gave a reluctant nod, but the tone of her voice betrayed her surprise. "Nothing for offense, though."

She must have known I had never been a warrior, so the comment had to be bait. Bait I decided to take, though not as she expected. "I see seven capable mythborn. Do you think it not enough?"

Faolan, who walked only a few steps ahead of us,

snorted. "The humanborn is getting cheeky." He gave a quick glance over his shoulder. "Let's see how fast she runs when we face the shriek."

"I'll get out of your way as quickly as possible," I offered.

A short burst of laughter came from the front, and one of the females chuckled. As Riagán's words came to my mind, I had no doubt the Scáthanna had once again tested me, and I hid a smile. I might have won some favor with them by not getting worked up by their teasing.

A grin flashed on Caitríona's lips, but I couldn't figure out what brought it on, my response or some mythborn joke I wasn't privy to. Either way, I had to appreciate that she didn't belittle my gear by comparing it with what the mythborn had available. I might have better amulets and charms than the "standard Trinitian set," but it was likely nowhere near what they brought.

Laoise fell behind to walk with us. "So, Kaja. Will you only watch and run, or do you want to help?"

I arched my eyebrow. Had I just been invited to participate? "I'll help if needed, but you've all been working together for a long time. I believe there's a reason I'm usually staying in the back with Riagán."

She seemed satisfied with my answer. "If you want the thrill, you can run with me." Her serious face made it clear the offer wasn't a joke. "If not, I'm sure Riagán won't complain about having company."

The reasonable thing to do would be to politely refuse. I wasn't a warrior, and my part of the job didn't include risking my life, but the prospect of seeing the Scáthanna in battle up close had a lot of appeal. I could also become the first humanborn to live and tell about it. If, of course, I didn't die some stupid death via shriek.

I smiled. "Count me in."

~

I STOOD by the rubble of what used to be a humanborn checkpoint, and the human-shaped pieces of ice around suggested I shouldn't expect any survivors, but I searched the area anyway before waving for the Scáthanna to approach. They waited by one of the ruined buildings while I planned to send these people away from danger... except that the shriek had gotten to them first.

The mythborn approached with serious expressions. What was supposed to be a somewhat challenging but in the end straightforward task had shifted into a game of the unknown. Before, we had a good idea of where the shriek roamed and a solid plan to lure it into a trap. Now, we could be walking straight into death's embrace if the creature lurked nearby. Without any words, everyone pushed magically warded earplugs into their ears. They filtered in speech and casual sounds, muffling them only a little, but at the same time shielded eardrums from the shriek's cries.

I stood silent and waiting. It wasn't my call, and if Cathal decided to withdraw, I wouldn't blame him. The mythborn ceannasaí stared at the ice shards that used to be living beings before the shriek's breath had frozen them.

"Laoise, Riagán, try to find it. We'll set up here," Cathal said.

Two mythborn set out in two directions, while Caitríona handed several small curses to Lorcan. They split, with Faolan and Sadb following with their weapons drawn. The two pairs made their way around, and I guessed they were working on setting the trap.

I stood alone with Cathal, feeling quite useless.

"The second humanborn checkpoint," he said. "Do you

think you can get there? If they're still alive, I need them out of the way."

I didn't ask why. The plan had already changed, but the Scáthanna still had a chance of luring the shriek into a place of their choice. A group of unaware humanborn barging into their hunting grounds could send everything astray.

It wasn't an order, and I appreciated he offered me a way out. There was a difference between luring a shriek alongside an experienced mythborn, and taking an assignment through the creature's territory without any information about its location. I could run into it around any corner, and I didn't have time for stealth.

"I'll do it," I said. Not for the thrill for which I'd initially joined their hunt, but because it was a job only I could do. And if I refused, I risked everyone's lives. Mine, the mythborn's, and the people at the checkpoint's as well.

He pulled out the city plan and held it up while I memorized the quickest route and took note of possible obstacles.

"When you ensure the humanborn are out of harm's way, try to make your way back here," he said. "Until we find that shriek, it's the safest point in the area." He reached to his belt and passed me a small metal tube. "And if you run into it, aim the flare at the sky and press it at the bottom. Riagán and Laoise will get to you as soon as they can."

I accepted the gift with gratitude. "Anything else?"

"If you can, lure it toward us. But if something goes wrong, just get away from it." His face was serious. "We'll handle it."

"Understood." I wasn't part of their team, and the quick rundown of their methods Laoise had given me on our way here didn't cover all the possible "things go to feckin' hell" scenarios, the very one we were experiencing now included.

I clutched the tube in one hand, and a shield amulet in

the other. Then I took off, deliberately ignoring the voice of reason that said being alone in a place where a shriek hunted meant my chances of survival had dropped faster than a seagull diving after a fish.

In wartime, I was most often on scout or messenger duty. I'd sneak through the streets, staying by the walls of half-destroyed buildings and quietly making my way through piles of rubble. I only resolved to speed when there were no places to hide or the enemy had already spotted me. This time I was about to make a run through a dangerous area, ditching all the precautions the war had imprinted in me.

The surroundings were eerily quiet, and as my fast footsteps beat a steady rhythm, my imagination worked hard to give me the scare of my life. As if I needed anything more than the desolate neighborhood and the thought the shriek was somewhere out there.

I kept a fast pace, but I didn't run. I'd need my breath and all my strength in case the shriek found me.

Regardless of my pessimism, nothing unexpected happened, and even though I kept my guard up, fear lessened its grip. The checkpoint was only two streets away, and once I ensured the humanborn had withdrawn, I'd be able to go back to the Scáthanna much faster.

I turned into the last street and breathed out with relief at the familiar shape of makeshift fortifications and several humanborn around. I'd made it!

A smile froze on my lips when a ball of red light rose in front of it—a heat charm, and a big one... What the heck were they doing?!

The surroundings trembled when the echo carried a powerful screech through the streets, and the humanborn at the checkpoint covered their ears. From this distance, I couldn't see their faces, but I didn't have to. I'd seen people who suffered that pain before. They weren't wearing the earplugs that saved me from sharing their fate.

Halfway between me and the checkpoint, the shriek ran out from the adjacent street. It was barely a humanoid, with a huge head magnified by the heap of tangled white hair. Its limbs, thin and wiry, resembled a tangle of birch twigs, but the fragility of the creature's body was illusory. It could take a hit and dish out one as well.

The shriek darted toward the checkpoint like a homing missile. Their eyesight wasn't good, but any strong source of heat could lure them from quite a distance.

I was reduced to the role of a helpless spectator. Nothing I had on me would pull it away and give the others a chance. They still stumbled around, dazed with pain, when the shriek released its breath. With the warmth sphere already fading, they froze within seconds.

The creature didn't crush the icy statues and didn't gnaw on the cold meat. I gritted my teeth. The shriek wasn't hungry, and it had only attacked because of the heat explosion. The humanborn might have lived if that charm didn't go off. Why did they use it? Or was it ...?

Another thought came, but I didn't dwell on it. I had a shriek less than the length of a block away from me, and if I didn't hurry, it could roam away.

I aimed Cathal's tube at the sky, activating magic within it, and in seconds a magical flare rose above me. It turned out I didn't even have to use a heat charm, because the sudden light was enough for the shriek to spin in place. As it inspected me with its glowing blue eyes, a low growl rose in its lungs. I didn't waste time staring at its ugly face and the icepick-like teeth guarding its mouth.

I turned and ran.

Shrieks rarely hunted in silence, so its low screech

followed me as I made my way back toward Cathal's group. Preserving my energy earlier paid off. I sprinted almost without effort, keeping the distance between me and the creature.

With Laoise's earlier advice in mind, I threw my first delayed-ignition heat charm at the end of the street. It rolled along the curb while I took off in the opposite direction. I counted seconds as I ran, and at the tenth the charm activated. The shriek cried out and headed toward the new lure. Of course, when the magic died out, and it didn't find the desired target, I'd become its prey once again, but until then I had a dozen seconds or so to gain a bit more distance. According to Laoise, shrieks were capable of long sprints if they gained enough momentum, and anything that gave them pause worked in favor of their target's survival.

Another screech, resembling a scream of fury, tore the air. It must have realized the heat charm wasn't a living being, and its real prey was getting away.

An arrow whizzed by, and the howl of pain told me it reached its target. Riagán stood at the nearby intersection, waving at me to take a turn. "I'll take over." He took off, holding a heat charm in his hand. Once it went off, he'd be a much more promising target, and lure the shriek straight into the trap.

I ducked into the side alley, but didn't stop even at the sound of Riagán's charm activating.

This might have been what saved my life.

The shriek didn't follow him. It ignored the stronger heat signature and rounded the corner, heading straight at me with speed I couldn't match. Had I stopped earlier, I wouldn't have had the precious seconds it took me to release the warmth sphere charm. When the shriek's freezing breath reached me, it was nothing more than a chilling breeze—unpleasant but not lethal.

I fired up the shield amulet soon after that, and the creature's claws bashed against the magic protection, but I was pinned down, unable to either put distance between us or take it down. Caitríona was right—my kit was good for distraction, not for hunting a shriek, and if I'd been alone, I'd be as good as dead.

The shriek clawed at the shield, but it would hold for a few minutes more. Suddenly, it paused mid-move and a howl of pain stretched its wide lips. As it twisted, it revealed arrows jutting from its back, but even though Riagán seemed to have been firing one after another, the shriek didn't turn away from me.

Over its growls, Riagán's heavy cursing reached my ears. Things weren't going as planned, not at all.

The air cooled around me, and I'd fished out another warmth sphere when I heard footsteps behind me. Sadb approached with her sword drawn. She must have circled the block or made her way through the ruins.

"When you're ready, take down the shield, and when I attack, run to Riagán," she said.

I didn't waste time asking questions and arguing. There must be a reason she hadn't told me to run to where she came from. Too much rubble? A trap set by the others? I took a deep breath and held my arm up with the amulet in it.

"Three. Two. One." I snuffed the magic, and the shield dissipated.

Sadb darted forward before I even started to move, her sword shining from a curse I didn't recognize, and engaged the shriek, drawing all its attention. I took the opportunity she gave me, trying to forget that usually the idea was to get *away* from the shriek, not *closer* to it. As I ran past the creature, the air cooled even more, but Sadb must have known it was about to breathe again. My warmth sphere might hold a little longer, and I hoped the mythborn warrioress was prepared for when it vanished.

Riagán waited for me at the end of the street, and as I reached him, he pulled me into a ruined store, throwing a charm behind us. "Quiet," was all he whispered.

The semi-translucent wall rose in front of the shop, with ice shards almost crystallizing in the air, and through it I watched Sadb run down the street with the shriek on her back. She took a sharp turn and led the creature toward the opening where the rest of the Scáthanna must be waiting. Riagán stood by my side with the bow ready, but neither he nor I moved, and the creature didn't pay any attention to us. The wall of cold air and magic worked as camouflage.

Riagán got to the shop's entrance as soon as the shriek passed us. "If you want to watch, it's safe now."

The sound of several curses activating reached my ears, and I joined him by the shattered door. In the opening where the checkpoint used to be, the shriek trashed within curse-made fiery walls, and Faolan and Sadb danced around it. Their swords shone with flaming magic, and each strike left a dark mark on the creature's body.

"They're toying with it." Riagán's voice expressed dissatisfaction.

Their strategy was so different from what the Trinitians did. Even though the humanborn trapped the shrieks in a similar way, they preferred to keep away and let fiery projectiles or flame curses to do the job. No one would even consider going hand to hand with one of them, and definitely wouldn't be *toying* with the creature.

As if they could hear Riagán's comment, the two mythborn rushed to a coordinated strike, and when Faolan's blade took the shriek's head off, Sadb had sliced its body in half. The headless corpse fell to the ground, and both mythborn leaped back, taking a defensive stance. I almost smiled at that. Even with the opponent dead, they didn't assume the fight was over.

I followed Riagán back to the opening while Caitríona placed flaming curses on the shriek's remains. They ignited within seconds, and the air filled with the stench of burnt flesh.

"Well done, everyone." Cathal skimmed past all the team members, and each of them earned a short nod. When his gaze stopped at me, he gave me the same meager praise as others. Then his face tensed. "Where's Laoise?"

"She never made it to the flare," Riagán replied.

The mood around changed in an instant, with all the faces becoming stern and concerned.

"She didn't fire hers," Lorcan said.

Then I remembered how the whole mess had started. "There's something more. When I got to the humanborn checkpoint, a heat charm went off. It lured the shriek straight to them. I thought it might have been an accident while preparing a trap, and they set it off too early, but they weren't wearing earplugs."

Cathal nodded. "Cait, take Faolan and see what you can learn there. Try to find that charm, or what's left of it."

I stood silent as realization sank in. Someone had left a delayed-trigger heat charm at the checkpoint to lure the shriek, which meant they might have been around, waiting for another opportunity to strike, and the creature's death might have been nothing but a hitch in their plans. What if we had walked straight into the trap? I watched the two mythborn walk away with my doubts rising.

"You think it's a bad idea, don't you?" Cathal pierced me with his eyes.

I knew better than to question a leader in front of his own people. "It's your call, ceannasaí." In a way, he was my leader too, even if only for the day.

Riagán snorted, and the glare that he threw Cathal was hardly respectful.

Cathal ignored the other mythborn's reaction. "Since when have you become a diplomat, Kaja?"

The situation seemed relaxed enough, and he addressed me by my name, so I allowed myself a smile and a bold reply. "Since I hang out with the mythborn who can kill me faster than I can take my words back."

His short laugh echoed within the buildings' walls. Then he became serious again. "I'm not in the habit of explaining my decisions, but I can't expect you to have the same trust in me that my team has," he said. "Cait and Faolan should be fine, and I was willing to take the risk to get us information we need. But that came with a price."

I understood. "You're not sending out anyone to find Laoise."

He nodded. "Not until they come back. Unless her flare goes up. Speaking of flares..." He produced another tube from his pocket. "You'll need another one. Keep it if you don't use it today."

Surprised, I accepted it. I could see reasons to give me one while we were in somewhat hostile territory, but the offer to keep it suggested he was fine with my using it when the Scáthanna weren't around. Or maybe I'd missed something? I'd have to ask him later. The last thing I wanted was to get on Cathal's bad side, especially when he started treating me as something more than a human-shaped information delivery service.

The sound of footsteps got us all to turn, and Riagán held his bow at the ready, but everyone relaxed when Laoise came into view. She glanced at the ashes not far from us, then looked straight at Cathal.

"We had some trouble. Everyone's fine," he replied to the unvoiced question. "What kept you?"

"I've found something you need to see." She glanced at me. "Kaja too. I stayed behind to ensure the area there was clear. We might have been walking into a trap."

Cathal nodded, then looked at Riagán. "Join Cait and Faolan, let them know what's going on." He waved at the other mythborn. "Lorcan, you're with us."

Riagán took off, and I fell in with Lorcan. The mythborn looked at me, but didn't say anything, making it clear he wasn't the conversational type. Laoise walked by Cathal and Sadb, and from the scraps of Irish I gathered they were filling her in on the shriek's hunt. At some point she glanced at me over her shoulder, surprise in her eyes. She turned away before I had a chance to inquire.

I didn't expect any explanation, but Lorcan said, "We haven't seen many humanborn pinned down by a shriek and keeping their cool." His voice was dry and coarse, and a sardonic smile curled the corners of his thin lips. "In fact, you'd be the first."

I couldn't help wondering whether the mythborn liked to gamble—and if they made bets, what my odds had been —but I probably wouldn't like his answer, so I resolved to stay silent. Even if they seemed to treat me better than when we'd started working together, walking alongside four myth-born and relying on their help to survive still had that eerie feel of a nighttime dream turning too real.

~

THE PLACE LAOISE led us to wasn't far away in a straight line, but when she was canvassing for the shriek, she must have weaved her way through countless streets before she got there. A flash of light caught my attention when we approached. An unusual thing in an abandoned area, and an even less likely sight on a shriek's hunting grounds.

Laoise led us inside, and Cathal gestured for Lorcan and Sadb to stand guard by the entrance.

Our boots crushed the red bricks of a collapsed wall, and the building resembled many others in the area. Some trash, destroyed furniture, and darker marks where the offensive curses hit. An aftermath of the initial years of war, when both mythborn and humanborn didn't care about the destruction if it meant we could get the enemy down quicker.

"I found it like this," Laoise said when we entered the sad remains of what could have been quite a cozy living room. "The light charm on, the egg cracked, and the body half-eaten."

Cathal squatted down by the pieces of shell, much bigger than any egg I'd seen before, but then, a shriek had hatched out of it, and it was the size of at least a humanborn teenager—or a mythborn molekind. "Fascinating. I didn't think it was possible."

I glanced over, curious if anything else would follow.

"Shrieks lay their eggs conjoined, in threes," Laoise explained while Cathal inspected the eggshells. "And three shrieks hatch. Separating them was considered impossible."

"That explains why the creatures were spotted at such a distance." My anger rose. My suspicions had turned out right. We were walking into a trap, even if it wasn't one meant specifically for us.

"The shriek hatched before he got away," Laoise said.

I walked over to the half-eaten body. The organs of the mythborn male were missing, and the claw and teeth marks on the ripped abdomen left no doubt the shriek got him. It had also chewed on his limbs, but the bones remained intact.

I knelt down, fighting the need to throw up at the stench of blood and bodily liquids. The mythborn's clothes, red and sticky, provided no clues.

"He's not from around here," Laoise said. "Local mythborn wear different clothes."

"He must have brought the eggs from the countryside." Cathal stood up from the shells. "Set them up one by one, leaving the delayed ignition charms at the checkpoints and probably also other populated places."

I cringed. "As if blowing up places wasn't enough."

"Shrieks cause more terror," Laoise said. "We'll have to find the place where they breed them."

"I'll speak with the lady about it." Cathal's brief reply made me wonder whether he was keeping something to himself.

I slid my hand inside the mythborn's pocket, and my fingers closed on a metal object partially wrapped in a scrap of paper—a bronze snake-head triskelion and a note. I scanned the text.

"Looks like we have a lead." I passed it to Cathal. "I don't get the Irish part, but there's an address here."

He read it in silence. "The note is nothing more than instructions to go to that address for help."

I stood back up, brushing the dust off my pants. "I'll check it tomorrow."

Cathal shook his head. "It's a mythborn-only place. You'd only be let in if you were in a company of one... and the nature of that company would make it difficult to gather information."

I didn't argue. Last thing I wanted was to be seen by a mythborn's side in a situation implying I was his lover.

"There's one more thing." His face became serious. "We'll destroy all the evidence here, and if anyone asks, the group you contacted never took the job."

My fists clenched in an instinctive response. How could I lie to Albert again? But on the other hand, how could I refuse Cathal? They had taken care of the shriek that would have otherwise killed many more humanborn.

"The more I lie to Albert, the more likely he's going to figure out something. He's already pressing me for answers." Maybe if I could convince Cathal that Albert should know more, he'd help me to change Eithne's mind on the matter.

He seemed unmoved, and gave me a firm stare. "It's your problem. If you don't think you can work this way, I'll let Lady Eithne know she no longer can rely on your services."

So much for my hopes. "I'm still in," I replied in a neutral tone. In the end, Albert *was* my problem, and if I stayed as neutral as I claimed to be, it would never be an issue. Instead, I constantly balanced between not being affiliated with anyone and keeping close ties with the Trinitians. The mythborn might tolerate my dubious neutrality, but they wouldn't make it easier, and I shouldn't have expected them to.

"I'm glad to hear that." His voice warmed up a notch. "Tomorrow evening we'll check Faoin Crainn. You're welcome to join. I'll make sure your presence is permitted."

Even as he spoke, Laoise placed curses on both the egg and the body. The magic flames consumed the evidence within heartbeats.

"I appreciate it," I offered with sincerity. A good working

relationship with them was of benefit to all, especially when Cathal started to treat me more like a team member. And the sooner we caught the Snake's net of agents, the sooner I'd be able to stop lying to Albert.

"Laoise, done?" He glanced over his shoulder. "I want to be out of here before someone spots us."

She walked over. "It seems clear, but I haven't searched through all the nooks."

Cathal nodded. "That should be enough. With the obvious clues gone, no one will bother with searching the place."

I gave the area one last look. The darker layer of dust and ash where the egg and the body had been looked like two more scars from wartime magic, and with enough wind and rain, they'd soon melt into one with the rest of the rubble.

"Let's go." Cathal's voice snapped me out of my thoughts, and I followed the two mythborn outside.

On one thing, I agreed with him: the sooner we got out of the area, the better. Even with the shriek gone, the air still felt colder than anywhere else.

CHAPTER THIRTEEN

I peeked through the window over Riagán's shoulder. Down in the square the crowd thickened, but I still spotted Cathal and Sadb. The ceannasaí looked like himself, though he'd swapped the gray uniform for what I recognized as a mythborn nobleman's clothes, but Sadb... If I didn't know whom Cathal came with, I wouldn't recognize the ruthless warrioress in the ethereal lady who clutched Cathal's arm. Her clothes, jewelry, and makeup suggested she belonged to the spoiled nobility who'd spent the whole war tucked safely in the Court and other mythborn-controlled places.

"Would you prefer to be down there instead of her?" Riagán teased as I gaped at Sadb.

I looked down again. The mythborn had renamed the square Faoin Crainn. They grew magical trees with canopies reaching the roofs of the surrounding buildings, and thus created a natural ceiling. Charms swung down from the trees and provided gentle light and warmth, while guests sat at multiple tables underneath the evergreen branches. Mythborn servers brought food and drinks from a nearby building, and several musicians played a mesmerizing tune.

Cathal picked a table, and they both sat at a cozy bench, with Sadb leaning on her companion's side. Her hand was in constant motion, brushing against his chest and face, and Cathal gave her patient glances of someone who was getting tired of the attention, but allowed it for the sake of courtesy... or some other, ulterior gain.

I smirked. "I can see better from here than with my face stuck in your ceannasaí's chest," I replied. "Besides, I don't think I'd match Sadb's acting skills." If she was pretending in the first place. I'd never seen her and Cathal interact in a way that would suggest something deeper between them, but I wasn't an expert on mythborn relationships. I doubted any humanborn was.

Riagán chuckled. "She hates every single moment of it, but she's the one with the right looks. Can you imagine Cait in her place?"

I arched my eyebrow. By human standards, Caitríona was attractive and exotic, but her style and moves screamed of a tomboy. The nobleman Cathal pretended to be would never stoop to dating someone so unrefined. "And what about Laoise?"

I scanned the square again and fished out the three other members of the Scáthanna drinking at the table in the corner. Faolan, Lorcan, and Cait seemed like a group of friends enjoying a night out, but I had no doubt they were paying attention to everything that happened.

"Where is she, anyway?" I asked.

Riagán pointed at one of the streets leading into Faoin Crainn. "About to make an entrance." His voice rang with pride.

Laoise stood at the curb as if she was hesitating to enter

the busy area. Her clothes resembled those of the mythborn we'd found by the shriek's egg, and her eyes darted to the sides. She clutched an object close to her chest, and when I caught a flash of bronze, I recognized the Snake's triskelion. She took several steps into the square, then stopped again, her wide eyes searching frantically.

"She's good," I whispered in awe. If I hadn't seen her confident among the other Scáthanna, without a second thought I'd believe she was a scared and lost country girl.

Laoise tripped, and while she caught balance, she dropped the triskelion. She swiped it from the ground in a nervous gesture, but I was sure she'd delayed it enough for at least several guests to catch a glimpse of it. A risky move, because she drew the attention of both Snake supporters and those of the mythborn who'd fought against the Snake back in the other world.

"Movement in the south corner," Riagán whispered. "Tall, red-haired mythborn."

I pulled my eyes away from Laoise's show. As interesting as her act was, we needed to find those who reacted to it. "West too. Female, black hair." As I called her out, the mythborn gave a short nod to someone in the square, but when I followed her line of sight, I stared at the crowd of inconspicuous mythborn patrons.

"They're making contact." Riagán readied an arrow.

Another mythborn approached Laoise and whispered into her ear. She nodded wide-eyed and let him lead her through the square. I checked on her every other moment, but kept scanning the crowd, and several other mythborn seemed to be making their way in the same direction.

The black-haired female offered an encouraging smile when Laoise and her guide reached a side alley, but something in her posture kept tugging at my instincts. It might have been war-bred paranoia, but I called it out anyway.

"Female, hidden knife or other weapon." When I looked at the others who had now approached the alley, I caught similar cues in their movements—the soft moves of predators closing in on prey. "All of them!"

Riagán had either caught the urgency in my voice or come to a similar conclusion. His arrow tore through the air, and a subtle whistle followed its trace. At that sound, all the Scáthanna sprang into action and were in motion before the arrow reached its mark: the black-haired female's shoulder. She yelled out in pain when the shaft pinned her to the wall.

I watched the scene unfold with my nails digging deep into my skin. Even with their speed, Faolan, Lorcan, and Cait were too far away to make it to the alley before the other mythborn assailants had entered it, and Cathal and Sadb were both unarmed... Riagán loosed another arrow and got the red-haired mythborn before he disappeared behind the corner, but others took advantage of the crowd's panic and made it into the alley.

Cathal shouted something in Irish, and most of the mythborn froze and ducked down, while Sadb... The ethereal, empty-headed noblewoman she'd impersonated was gone, and in her place appeared fury incarnate. She darted through the square with speed that seemed to match that of Riagán's arrows and stormed into the alley.

I shifted, ready to start running as well, but Riagán didn't even move. "We wait here."

He was right. Before we made it three floors down, we'd lose sight of all the others and give up the advantage of having a bird's-eye view of the square. As the Scáthanna disappeared into the alley, my shoulders slumped. "I hate situations like this."

"They'll be fine." Riagán's voice seemed relaxed, but his eyes kept scanning the square. Down there, Lorcan unpinned the black-haired female and bound her. "Good catch with that knife earlier."

"Thanks."

Cathal walked back into the square, and after he looked up at our window, he headed toward several mythborn standing at the side. From a distance I couldn't tell what he showed them, but judging by their reactions, it must have been the Court's emblem or something similar. They stretched and offered bows while he spoke to them.

Riagán put away the arrow he had at the ready. "We can come down now."

He didn't have to tell me twice. I was itching to see whether we'd been successful. We had at least one prisoner, but who knew what had transpired in the alley? Did Sadb make it in time?

"Laoise and others are fine," Riagán said when I threw him an impatient glance.

"How can you tell?"

He smiled the smile of someone who was about to reveal something obvious. "Because if something went wrong, Lorcan wouldn't be wasting time with the prisoner."

"He's your field medic?" I guessed.

"Among other things." Riagán led the way down the steps.

We hit the bottom floor and rushed into the square. The mythborn around threw startled stares at Riagán, but one glance at his gray uniform seemed to put them at ease. For me, they had only displeased and hateful glares, and if I didn't keep close enough to the Scáthanna member, I'd likely be thrown out.

What a lovely place for mythborn high society to gather... I'd rather drink cheap ale in one of the Liberties' cozy pubs, where the only dirty look you got was when you were making trouble, no matter whether you were human-born or mythborn.

As we approached Cathal, he was still deep in conversation with what seemed to be the owners or managers of Faoin Crainn—if mythborn even had such positions—so I stayed one step behind Riagán. Nonetheless, my presence didn't go unnoticed.

"A humanborn! That's horrible!" A female with an elaborate hairdo pointed at me. Judging by the disgust that spoiled her otherwise quite attractive face, one would think Cathal had brought a shriek along, not one meager woman, maybe a bit underdressed for the occasion, but not particularly appalling. The flow of Irish words that followed her exclamation had an exaggerated tone, and I didn't even bother employing my linguistic skills to decipher her rant.

"Kaja Modrzewska accompanies us by Lady Eithne's personal request," Cathal replied in English, pronouncing my foreign name without a hint of an accent. "But, of course, we can leave if you find her presence unsuitable for this place."

The mythborn noblewoman threw me a displeased glance. "I'd prefer to not see the filthy..." Her voice trailed off and her eyes widened, as if the meaning of Cathal's words had finally reached her brain. "I'd hate to interfere with the duties of the Scáthanna," she said in a very different tone. "Please, pass my regards to Lady Eithne next time you see her."

She walked away in a stiff pose of hurt feelings and

offense taken, and I worked hard to keep my face straight with her act so obvious. I could admit that it'd been quite satisfying to see that pretentious mythborn put in her place, and I didn't hide it. Cathal glanced at me, but no reprimand came.

"You might be breeding a monster, ceannasaí," Riagán said with a huge grin.

Cathal glared back at him, his confidence unwavering. "I have six already. One more won't make a difference."

Faolan stood guard at the corner, his broad shoulders blocking the view of the mythborn in the square, and we walked over to the alley, where Laoise and Sadb, both with bloodstains on their clothes, pulled bodies into a line. Five mythborn, multiple weapons, and the two of them had taken them down barehanded. Not that I'd needed any proof of the squad's abilities after the fight with the shriek, but the effects of their work still stunned me.

I knelt down by the first body. They had some money, both Eireland currency and mythborn coins, cigarettes, few minor charms, but nothing else. Not even the triskelions I'd expected them to carry.

Riagán glanced at me when I let out a sigh of disappointment. "We still have one captive. I'm sure we can convince her to share the information with us."

"I guess that's all for tonight?" I asked.

Cathal nodded. "Riagán, get Kaja home before some oversensitive mythborn dies of horror at her sight." The sarcasm in his voice was clear. "We'll handle things here."

I followed Riagán through the alley, glad he didn't choose to go through the square. Staring contests with spoiled mythborn wasn't what I wanted to end my day with.

～

RIAGÁN LED the way through the back alleys of the North Side, and when we finally reached the river, we were around Ha'penny Bridge and Temple Bar, which meant a long walk home. He stopped, and the glance he gave the river was both thoughtful and calculating.

"Is something wrong?" I asked.

He rubbed his chin. "I'm trying to remember which bridge charges the lowest toll. The one we usually cross gets more and more expensive every time."

I chuckled. "It's because you try to argue with them. By now they remember you, so you're never going to get a discount." I inspected him. "I'd think you'd know their habits better than I."

He cringed. "Other mythborn don't get along with the bridge dwellers. They didn't help in the war back in the other world, and they didn't do much here either."

I couldn't relate, as the attitude of the bridge dwellers was the very thing that had saved my life. They might keep to themselves, avoiding contact with both humanborn and their fellow mythborn, but all in all, they weren't a bad bunch. Except, of course, for the human-eating ones, but every species had its bad apples.

"I think I can get us across without any toll." I gave him a firm stare. "If you keep your mythborn pride at bay." The snort he let out indicated that the very pride I mentioned had been hurt, and I chuckled again. "Let's go."

By habit, I walked onto the promenade, close to the railing and with my eyes fixed on the Liffey. The clouds had cleared a bit, and the twilight sky bled vibrant colors reflected in the scarce unbroken windows on the other bank, contrasting with the black tar of the waters.

"It can be quite beautiful when it's not scary." Riagán caught up with me and walked by my side.

I twitched at the softness in his voice, and the atmosphere of the evening walk by the river hit me. I shouldn't have taken that turn to the promenade as if we were taking a stroll. But I had, because I loved the Quays, and before the war, even when I rushed somewhere, I chose the by-the-river route and the wide promenades instead of crowded footpaths by the buildings on the other side of the street.

"It makes me nostalgic in a way," I replied. "I used to come here a lot."

"Before the war?" He didn't shy away from the topic. "What was it like?"

"Different. And in a way, the same." I stared at the ruined buildings. Maybe except for those. "In the evening the waters seemed as black as now, and they reflected the city lights. If it rained, everything would shine in the light of the street lamps."

Silence fell as I trailed off into memories.

"And then we came." His voice, nothing more than a whisper, carried a hint of regret.

I didn't have a good reply to that, so I stopped. Riagán joined me, and we looked at the river in silence for a time.

"It's still beautiful," I said. "The war is over and Dublin can become even better now with the magic you brought."

He didn't look at me. "Do you really think peace will last?"

I shrugged. "It's not impossible." I looked at him with a serious expression. "Unless it was only signed to buy time for another war." I couldn't avoid the accusing tone, though the Trinitians had used the peace to prepare, too. Just in case, as Albert claimed.

Riagán still stared at the water, silent. When I'd started losing hope of getting any reply, he finally spoke. "After we signed the treaty, after your winged vehicles... your planes landed, many mythborn hoped that humanborn would take the opportunity and leave. But many of you stayed."

"It's hard to abandon your history, your land," I replied. "Those who were born here didn't have anywhere else to go."

He lifted his head and locked me in his gray stare. "But you have somewhere to go. You're not from these lands."

"I was born elsewhere, but Ireland has become my home. Like others, I fought for my right to stay here." I leaned on the railing. The fresh paint on the wood reminded me that the promenade had been rebuild recently. "Besides, with the affliction..." I shook my head and left the thought unfinished. I didn't want to make it sound as if I had no choice and was unhappy with it. "Humans adapt easily. We've colonized the whole planet, so a magic-infested land is nothing but another challenge."

He let out a short laugh. "Are we a challenge as well? I've heard some humanborn talking about driving us to the sea."

"You are a different challenge," I replied. "We need to learn how to live with you and with magic. Besides, mythborn also have to adapt to the world they came into. It's only going to bend so much."

"What if we decide to force it to change more?"

Genuine curiosity rang in his words, so I answered with the gravity required. "Then you'll have war. The one that most likely will wipe out us all."

He didn't falter at my reply. "Let's hope for peace, then."

"Let's." My lips curled, though smiling didn't bring relief. We both knew hope wasn't going to be enough.

The sunset colors faded into dim grays, and wind herded more clouds our way. Their heavy and thick shapes foretold rain.

"We should get going," I added in a lighter tone. "We're not going to fix the world and how both the mythborn and humanborn think, so we might as well stop ruining our good mood."

I moved, but Riagán's gentle brush against my arm held me in place. "If it's any consolation, the Court doesn't want another war, and Lady Eithne's word has a lot of weight, even among those who'd like to see the humanborn bleed out."

I sighed. If only I could reciprocate with a similar certainty, but the truth was that I wasn't sure what Albert's thoughts were. He seemed happy enough with the peace we had, but many of his people craved payback.

"I don't think Trinity would attack unprovoked, but I can't speak with certainty anymore," I said. "My ties with them have loosened over time."

Riagán threw me an amused glance. "It's interesting to see a humanborn admitting that Albert might do something underhanded."

Of course, he'd read in my words what was convenient for him. I pouted, and he laughed.

"I apologize," he said as we resumed our walk along the promenade. "I appreciate your honesty. As for the Trinitians, Lady Eithne believes that as long as Albert leads them, they are the humanborn equivalent of the Court, and she prefers to deal with him than with the Eireland Office... Not that there's much left of the Office now."

I warned him with a wave of a finger. "Grim thoughts again. You should put on your kindest smile, as we're about to pay the toll."

Riagán chuckled. "Now that's something worth seeing. Kaja bargaining with the bridge dwellers."

I allowed myself a smug smile. "If we're lucky, no bargain will be necessary."

The dwellers at the edge of the bridge eyed us with suspicion, and I couldn't blame them. A humanborn in the company of a Court mythborn must be a rare sight. Especially when said humanborn wasn't clinging to her companion's side and batting her eyelashes at him every other moment.

"Is Three-Bones home?" I asked politely.

One of them grumbled several words in Irish, or rather the bridge dweller version of it, but he waved his bulky arm toward the shacks on the bridge, so I passed their makeshift checkpoint, nodding at Riagán to follow. The looks he got from the guards were even less friendly than the ones I was greeted with, and I hoped he would be smart enough to look away instead of giving them a challenging stare.

"Did you just lie to them?" he whispered as soon as we got out of earshot.

I laughed. "No way. I pass through here too often."

He eyed me suspiciously. "So that Three-Bones ...?"

"A friend, I guess." Nice to learn that there were things that the Scáthanna didn't know about me. We approached the shack, and the fire in front of it told me that Tee-Bee was indeed home. "Hey, Tee!"

A huge, clawed hand moved the rag curtain to the side, and the mythborn came out. "Kaja! Good see!" His face brightened, and he displayed his fangs in a wide smile. Then his eyes slid to Riagán. "Brought food again, eh? But not much meat on this one." Riagán tensed, and Tee-Bee burst out laughing. "No worry, willow-child. No eat," he said in his gruff voice. "Come in."

He disappeared in the shack, and I glanced at Riagán's face, frozen somewhere between disbelief and distaste.

"Willow-child?" I asked, approaching the shack.

"Not much strength," Three-Bones explained from inside. "Bend easy, too."

I chuckled and entered. Riagán hesitated only for a heartbeat and followed me. Tee-Bee pointed at a long bench by the table while he pushed a stash of rags onto his bedroll and closed a half-broken locker where he kept most of his food supplies. Above our heads, strange seaweed dried in bunches.

We sat down, and Three-Bones picked up an empty bowl. A clean one, at least by dwellers' standards.

"Willow-child want food?" he offered. "Kaja always scared of soup."

I smirked, though I couldn't argue. Most times I politely refused staying for dinner.

"I appreciate the offer, but we just ate," Riagán lied smoothly. With the initial shock gone from his face, he threw curious glances around. "I'm taking her home, and she wanted to stop by."

Three-Bones grinned and shook his head. "Kaja fishing information. Always." He made a mockery of a concerned face. "Poor Tee harassed."

While I tried not to chuckle, Riagán openly snorted. "Yes. I imagine Kaja can be quite fearsome."

"I brought you a seagull last time," I complained, though my voice betrayed me.

"Seagull good." The troll massaged his round belly. "Fat, a lot of meat. Not like a willow-child." He glanced at Riagán again, and I wouldn't call it a friendly look.

"Tee, this is Riagán," I said. "He saved my life. Just like you did."

The dweller's face softened a notch. A good sign. Three-

Bones could be reasonable if one had appealing arguments... or enough seagulls in stock.

"Maybe he saved to make soup later." He shrugged.

Riagán smirked. "Not enough meat on her, either."

Tee's face brightened, and he nodded eagerly. "Riagán smarter than other willow-childs. Seagull better than bony two-legs."

The mythborn archer nodded and relaxed. It seemed that he and Three-Bones had found some common ground, even if only agreeing that I wouldn't make a good soup.

"Any news on troublemakers?" I steered the conversation toward a more desired topic.

Tee-Bee pointed his clawed finger at me. "See? Kaja always fishing." He shook his head with disapproval, but headed over to a wooden chest of drawers. "A willow-child ran from the guards. Had a rag." He displayed a scrap of material.

Green, brown, and gold fabrics, weaved into a braid forming an armband. I glanced at Riagán.

"I know what it is," he confirmed.

"Can we take it?" I asked. "It might help us find the troublemakers."

Three-Bones gave me a serious look. "Kaja shouldn't search troublemakers. No good."

I sighed. How could I explain such a complex idea, that finding the evildoers so that they couldn't harm anyone else was worth taking the risk? Bridge dwellers had simple minds, and they kept together, so any threat hit them as a community, and as a community they retaliated with all their strength. No wonder both humanborn and other mythborn let them be and quietly paid the toll claimed for crossing the bridges.

His face softened. "Kaja not very smart," he said. "Maybe willow-child share smarts. Stay home, eat seagull. But take rag if must."

I pocketed the armband and stood up. "We better get going."

"Next time stay soup?" he offered, and then glanced at Riagán. "Willow-child Riagán come too."

I headed for the exit, but Three-Bones barred Riagán's way with his massive arm. The dweller's face became stern, and when he spoke, the sudden flow of distorted Irish had a threatening tone. Then he took a step back, but his eyes still stared with a murderous intent.

Riagán gave him a slow nod, and I caught something resembling respect on his face. He replied in Irish, but I caught the meaning: "I understand."

Three-Bones huffed, but his face lost the violent edge. "Smart willow-child. Go now. Come again."

We made it out, and I led Riagán through the bridge, and even though most of the dwellers ignored our presence, I kept him close.

"What was that about?" I couldn't help my curiosity, proving Tee-Bee's words right: I fished for information whenever I could.

"Your friend was kind enough to share a soup recipe with me." Riagán kept his face straight. "One that would be perfect with a certain willow-child as the main ingredient if he gets you killed."

My eyebrows must have turned into two perfect arches. "Tee-Bee? He's quite peaceful."

"For a bridge dweller," Riagán replied. "You two seem to have quite a history. Did he really save your life?"

I gave a nod. "In the war. I saved his right after it, so we're even, but a seagull every now and then gets me information I can't get otherwise."

The bridge dwellers at the next checkpoint must have assumed we'd paid the toll at the other end, because we walked off the bridge without being bothered.

"It doesn't seem worth the time," Riagán said. "It belongs to the Botanical Gardens Patrol. The mythborn who lost the armband might have been trying to avoid the toll or running late..."

"I know, but I wasn't going to ignore Tee-Bee's efforts. It's better he tells me too much than not enough." I handed the armband over to him. "And you're going to check the lead anyway, aren't you?"

He grinned and pocketed the cloth. "Don't expect miracles."

I laughed. "If Tee-Bee's clue helped us to catch the... one we're after"—I bit my tongue, since mentioning the Snake agents in public didn't seem a bright idea—"I'll buy him the biggest and the fattest seagull that has ever hatched."

Riagán shook his head, but said nothing, and after that we made it to my place in silence. As he stopped by the entrance, I caught hesitation in his moves. I could swear he was looking for an excuse to stay a little longer.

"I guess I should offer you some tea for ensuring my safe return." I pointed invitingly at the building.

A smile came on his face like a sun brightening the sky after a rainy morning. "I'd be delighted." He pulled out his set of keys and entered the building as if he lived in there, leaving me speechless on the footpath.

NOT ONLY DID I brew tea, but also shared the dinner I'd prepared for myself in the morning. Vegetable stew with rice, over-spiced to cover the dish's rather dull taste. Red meat or poultry would have improved it, but their price was still too high for me to afford daily, and I wasn't about to risk seagulls or fish. Food poisoning was one thing, but if a meal made my affliction worse, I'd have a hard time remedying it.

Riagán ate without complaints, and I didn't expect praise for something that wasn't an elaborate dish.

"So... How was it there? Back in the other world?" I broke the silence first.

He looked at me, surprised, then sat motionless in thought. "Different. I was told that when we arrived, it was a place of beauty. Enchanting, like some rare places over here." He shook his head. "My generation, like many others before it, was born into war. Ruins, ashes, and being alert all the time."

His gaze wandered across my living room. "Things like that, or like the Court... We didn't know them. Some of us were tasked with preserving our history and culture, but others never had time to learn much about it."

I looked away at the pain in his voice. "I apologize. I shouldn't have asked."

He put the fork away. "No need to. I just wish I could charm you with the tales of what used to be my homeland." He flashed a smile, and I caught a playful note in his voice, but his eyes remained serious. "But I only have stories of war, and you have enough of those."

I shouldn't have asked the question about the other world, my curiosity be cursed. Not only had I made Riagán recall his painful memories, but also got us back to talking about the war that divided my kind and his. If I didn't want the evening to turn into a grim session of sharing bad experiences from the past, I had to do something.

"But now I also have other stories," I offered. "Of annoying mythborn archers and shriek hunts gone wrong."

He leaned over the table, sparks back in his eyes. "Annoying, you say? I'd rather hear of the brave archer who jumped in front of a shriek to save a fair maiden, or who shielded her from a magical inferno."

I chuckled. "That would require a fair maiden, and I don't look the part." In a way, I preferred his games to the gloomy clouds of memories that haunted us both. "No one would believe such a story."

His rubbed his chin. "You're right. That wouldn't work. How about a cunning archer saving a rogue who constantly gets in trouble?"

I took the empty plates and dumped them into sink. "Keep trying," I called out from my kitchenette.

"A skillful archer aiding a beautiful scout in her quest for maintaining the peace?" His voice came from behind me, so he must have stood close, but he didn't touch me. Nevertheless, I felt pinned in the corner with his blocking the way out.

I turned carefully, avoiding physical contact. "Such plain flattery? I thought you were better than that."

Riagán grinned. "Didn't hurt to try. Besides, it doesn't seem you have a better suggestion." He walked back into the living room, so I didn't have to push past him.

"Maybe I should tell the story how it is?" I followed him. "A defiant humanborn scout helps the irksome mythborn archer and his companions uncover an evil conspiracy?"

He gave me a sarcastic glare. "That's not something anyone would believe either. Humanborn and mythborn working together? They'd sooner believe in a secret love between me and Orla."

The image and the thought of how the Trinitian bow mistress would react to such an insinuation made me burst out laughing. "If she ever hears about it..."

Riagán stared at me, then shook his head. "Even you wouldn't be so heartless. Peace or not, she'd hunt me down."

I chuckled. "She'd hunt me down as well for voicing such a suggestion. You'd be next on her death list, along with anyone she'd think might know about it."

"I guess I'm safe for now." He made an exaggerated gesture of relief. "So, Kaja, how much longer will you be able to suffer my presence?"

I narrowed my eyes. There had to be a trap coming. "Why are you asking?"

Riagán glanced at my games console, and I could swear he felt uneasy. "That game you showed me. I'd like to play more."

This was a reply I hadn't seen coming. His request sounded genuine, as if he had really enjoyed the game and had no other reasons to stick around. And, after all, he had keys to my apartment, so he didn't really have to ask for my permission to stay. Appreciating the courtesy of his request, I activated the power charms and launched the game.

Riagán made himself comfortable on the couch, and as much as watching him play would be entertaining, I resisted sitting down beside him. One cozy night spent on his lap was enough, and I didn't need to give him more reasons to tease me.

"I'll be upstairs. I have some work to do," I said.

He nodded, already focused on the game, and I couldn't help but smile as I climbed up to the den. It seemed I might have created the first mythborn gamer. How long it would take him to start cursing the game and complaining about glitches, bugs, and other things all gamers hated? I chuckled to myself at the thought, and then picked one of the amulets I'd been working on. The sounds of a virtual battle waged downstairs made my apartment feel a bit more like a home, and for once I didn't care whether Riagán had any hidden reasons to stay.

CHAPTER FOURTEEN

The evening was like any other, but instead of finding comfort in the familiarity of the walk back home, and the overcast weather that made the nighttime darker, I could only find disappointment. Information gathering always took time and patience, but having made no significant progress weighed on my mood.

As Laoise and I walked through the dark Dublin North after yet another raid, she threw me a curious glance. "You look disheartened," she said in that soft voice of hers, which contradicted her soldier-like appearance and the ash-gray uniform with the Scáthanna emblem on it. A sly smile curled her lips. "Is it because you'd prefer someone else to accompany you back home?"

It took me a moment to process her words. Riagán had an assignment, so it was up to Laoise to get me home safely, and even though I'd grown used to the arrogant archer's constant teasing, I definitely didn't mind a quiet evening for a change. "It's nothing to do with you," I replied. "It's just frustration. We're still no closer to finding our mark than we were before we started."

Her surprised expression made it clear she didn't share my feelings. "We're slowing them down and preventing a war. Isn't that a lot?"

"It's like pouring water out of a sinking ship while the breach remains unfixed," I mumbled.

"We'll fix the breach when we find it, but we need to make sure the ship doesn't sink before we do," she said. "You need to learn to cherish little victories."

I gave her a sour look. "Humans don't like to feel helpless," I replied. "We're not really the most patient kind, either."

Laoise grinned. "I find it hard to believe after what I've heard about you, Kaja."

I cringed. I didn't need to ask who'd provided the information. She wasn't the type to drink with humanborn veterans and swap war stories, which meant she could have had only one source.

Laoise offered me a shameless grin, and I almost forgot she was a member of the mythborn elite unit. I could imagine her in a bar, with that obsidian hair and big eyes, in a modest but flattering dress... She'd draw every male's attention, humanborn and mythborn alike. Until, of course, someone noticed she moved like a killer.

"We had questions, and Riagán was kind enough to oblige," she explained in a lighthearted way, as if she was asking me to not take it out on said archer. "Some of us wagered whether you'd flip when you saw our handiwork up close, especially on a humanborn."

I couldn't resist snorting. In some ways, the humanborn and the mythborn were alike. "I try to look at it as just another war we're waging. Only the allies and the enemies have changed." The humanborn the Scáthanna had killed were the Snake's agents, brainwashed and bent on destruction. I could have pitied some helpless civilians, but not the ones who had betrayed their own kind, their own world.

"Fair enough."

The conversation died, and nothing but our faint footsteps stirred the silence of an abandoned city block. Before the Magiclysm, Dublin had boasted a population of over a million, but both magic and the war took their toll on it, and then some immigrants had left for their homelands, so the number had withered to several hundred thousand at best. Many areas were abandoned, and buildings stood empty with most of the humanborn living in the city's South Side, while the mythborn claimed the north. The west part of the city was still the most volatile one, with both sides trying to slowly seize control of it without making it look like they were breaking the treaty.

As the echo of distant voices rose among the buildings, both Laoise and I tensed. Alone in an empty area, we both reverted to wartime habits. Whoever was coming our way didn't need to know we were around. Laoise sent me a knowing smile as if she was thinking the same, and pointed at the entrance of a nearby shop, as dark and ruined as everything else around. She moved like a ghost, putting my own sneaking skills to shame, but I made it inside without too much noise.

We squatted down behind a wall, and since the shadow of the shop's shattered display covered us, we peeked out into the street.

Three bulky humanborn armed with bats and rods walked past the shop. Even from the distance I sensed magic within them, and its chaotic flow told me they didn't have long before they'd become the Afflicted. I praised our caution. Even if they weren't a threat to us in particular at that moment, when they changed, they'd become a threat to *anyone*.

"Someone's hunting our friends," one of them said. "We've lost seven so far, including a courier."

Laoise reached for her knives but didn't make a move yet. We kept listening.

"You think it's the Court?" asked another one. "Humanborn don't know about us."

"We wouldn't have that problem if you'd taken out that Court bitch as you were told," the third one chimed in.

"I couldn't get past the gate, and their guards were getting suspicious," the other humanborn said. "The charge went off, so she should have died."

"But she didn't," the first one grumbled. "And now we'll need to use Brigh to get it done."

"And what about the other problem?" asked the third.

"We'll find those bastards who kill our own and show them how the Snake bites."

Their murmurs of anticipation resonated in my spine as a shiver, but seemed to have brought Laoise's blood to a boil. Even if I wanted to, I wouldn't be able to argue we should let them go, and in a way I wanted them dead as much as she did. But three against one, even a member of an elite myth-born unit? I didn't feel comfortable calculating Laoise's odds.

Before she moved, I put my hand on her arm, drawing her attention to me. She narrowed her eyes and then shook her head with a firm expression. At least we agreed that I wasn't a fighter.

I took out two of my trinkets. "I can help," I mouthed soundlessly as I showed them to Laoise, and she gave a nod.

We sneaked toward the shop's exit, and she left first, melting into the darkness as if she was nothing more than one of the shadows, and I could see where her unit got its name from. They *were* shadows.

I didn't try to be stealthy when I walked out into the street, but the humanborn were too engaged in what had now shifted into an excited brainstorming of the suffering that awaited their enemies, so I cleared my throat. "Heard you chaps are working for the Snake," I said when they turned toward me.

They gripped their weapons tighter as they fanned out to circle me, but before the first one got within swinging distance, I tossed my first trinket forward. I'd made it of a rubber ball, and it bounced cheerfully on the cracked asphalt. They all looked at it instead of dodging, which told me they had never fought against mythborn before. Sly little cowards hiding during the war who came out to destroy the peace.

One, two, three... The ball hit the ground repeatedly, and at the fourth bounce it released its magic. I'd been hit by a stun curse once and almost felt sorry for the human- born in front of me. The ground trembled below their feet, and they stumbled with their hands pressed to their ears. At such a short distance from the curse's source, the ringing must have been deafening.

Laoise darted from behind their backs, gray lightning with two blackened blades in her hands. She disposed of the first humanborn before the other two regained their footing and didn't miss a step approaching another target. I watched, mesmerized, but our opponents had already gotten back on their feet, and I muttered obscenities in Polish. I'd forgotten that since they suffered from the magic affliction, they were more likely to absorb the curse than to suffer from it... A useful trait, but it also brought one closer to the final stage.

The second opponent swung at Laoise, and they danced around, in search for an opening—a battle that the mythborn would win. Her blade cut low, at the man's leg, and before he could reach her with his rod, her other knife drew a line across his throat.

The third humanborn didn't lunge, and roared in pain instead. He shivered, and the magic within pulsated in a warning rhythm. It turned out that my stun curse was the final straw for him.

Laoise cursed in mythborn language, and in her widened eyes I saw the reflection of my own thoughts. There was no way we could bring down the Afflicted on our own. With their speed and strength enhanced by the magic warping their bodies, and with the instincts driving them, they could be a challenge even for a well-trained team.

Laoise corrected the grip on her knives. "Set the flare off and run. Others must know."

Once turned, this thing would chase us down with ease unless someone distracted him, and Laoise was making that call. Out of the two of us, she had a better chance to last longer against an Afflicted, while I could gain enough distance before she died. It was a good plan, given the circumstances.

So I ran, but not how Laoise expected. I lunged toward the humanborn, or rather toward the heap of lesions and bulges he was becoming, tearing another curse off my coat. As soon as I was in throwing distance, I tossed it and leaped back. The metal pin couldn't penetrate the Afflicted's hardening skin, but it didn't have to. Upon contact with such a magic-infused being, the curse activated in an instant. The Afflicted, now transformed, swung at me with his bat, but I rolled away, and he didn't come after me again.

Instead, he stood in place, his eyes swelling and all his muscles trembling.

I got back on my feet and watched him with a mixture of fascination and curiosity.

"I told you to run," Laoise barked as she lunged at the creature.

"Don't touch him!"

My desperate yell was enough to get her attention, and although she still stood battle-ready, she didn't attack.

It took three minutes of tremors before the Afflicted finally collapsed, his body now shrunken and fragile. The pin remained stuck to his back, glowing with magic like a firefly. Then it self-ignited and burnt into ash within a heartbeat, as if the metal it was made of was paper. From a distance, it seemed quite painless and quick.

Laoise took several cautious steps forward.

"It should be safe now," I said.

She knelt by the Afflicted, but the inspection didn't last long. "I've never seen a curse like that." The look she gave me was a mixture of respect and distrust.

"And you won't see it again anytime soon." Revealing I was the one who had crafted it wasn't easy, but better than trying to make up lies on the go. "It took me four months to make one." Using it on a random Afflicted had felt like a waste, but at least I knew it worked, and thanks to Eithne's drug, I had enough time to try making one more.

"You saved my life with it."

"You were about to save mine. I guess we're even." I looked around. All three humanborn were dead. "Too bad we couldn't get one alive."

Her lips curled into a cruel smile. "We didn't have to. They mentioned Brigh... I know her. She's an archivist at the

Court." She glanced at the last body. "That curse... It would have killed me if I touched him, wouldn't it?"

I met her eyes. "I don't know. I never tested it." I didn't see the point in lying after I'd already revealed everything else. "But since it absorbs all the magic within a living being, I guess both you and I would be dead. That's why I made it self-destruct."

"In the war..." Laoise said with caution, "it would have made a difference."

"I didn't make it for the war." My reply was snappier than I intended. "And I'd prefer it to remain the secret it was supposed to be."

Laoise looked at me in disbelief. "You didn't show it to the Trinitians?"

I sighed and weighed my options. If I wanted her to believe me, I needed to explain why I'd made it, but parting with my most guarded secret didn't sit well with me. "I didn't make it as a weapon. It's... for my personal use."

Her eyes widened, and she glanced at the Afflicted by her feet, then back at me. "I understand." Her voice carried only respect now. "Cathal will ask questions, but your secret will be safe with us."

I sat down on the curb while Laoise activated a familiar, tube-shaped charm, and a colorful magic flare rose above the buildings. We might finally have a better lead, but after what had happened, I wasn't looking forward to the Scáthanna's arrival.

THE MYTHBORN TALKED in a mix of Irish and their own language, which made it clear I wasn't invited to the discussion, but even with my limited knowledge of the language, I had no trouble figuring out that they were arguing about me. The often-repeated "humanborn," which was one of the words I recognized, and fingers pointing both at me and the dead Afflicted made it clear what the topic was.

Cathal stood with his face unmoving while Laoise's growing frustration suggested she was losing. The two other mythborn, Faolan and Sadb, both spoke with passion, and I caught anger ringing in their words. The other two of the Scáthanna saw to the bodies, searching through the dead ones' belongings. And Riagán, supposedly on lookout duty, leaned against a nearby lamppost, watching the scene with a hint of curiosity and a distinct lack of concern.

"I'm surprised you're not contributing." I pointed at the four mythborn still in the heat of discussion.

He arched his eyebrow in polite surprise, as if he didn't understand why I'd suggest such a thing in the first place. "It's pointless. Cathal has already made up his mind. He just lets them vent."

I held off a sigh. Although I wouldn't admit it out loud, I did wish Riagán would weigh in with an argument in my defense.

The three mythborn in the distance became silent when Cathal spoke. His voice didn't carry, and I couldn't guess anything from his expression. Laoise nodded and walked away, while Faolan and Sadb clenched their fists, and only when their leader barked at them did they leave to help with the bodies.

"They'll get over it," Riagán said in a light tone.

Cathal approached me, and I rose from my spot at the curb. Seeing as two of his people were unhappy, I hoped he wasn't about to kill me.

"Laoise said you didn't share the secret of that curse with the Trinitians," he got straight to the point. "Why?"

I looked him in the eye. "No one in Trinity knows I make my own gear. Actually, no one else knew until, well, now." I didn't mention Riagán. I still wasn't sure how much the others knew of his visits to my place.

Cathal nodded, but his posture didn't change, and I had a hard time reading him. "Can you make more of them?" he asked in a plain tone.

His question made me snort. "I'm going to remake the one I had and no more. I don't care if you think they might help you against the Afflicted, or if you find some other use for them. They're too dangerous to even carry one."

"You did," he pointed out.

"Take a wild guess why." I'd retreated to sarcasm. "You saw what this thing can do." I pointed at the last body, which in the dark looked like a piece of gnarled wood. "And it's better to not give anyone an idea that such a thing can even be made."

"Someone will figure it out eventually," he said.

I didn't point out it took me four months and mountains of desperation to get one right, and I only did it because I wanted it for myself.

"But I agree—no need to give them directions." He gave me a long, curious look, then he took a step closer and leaned toward my face. His presence was as uncomfortable as any other mythborn's, and the magic within him was calling to me, though in a different way than when Riagán was close. "I just wonder one thing... Why do you intend to remake it? Is Lady Eithne's offer not good enough?"

I cringed. "Does everyone at the Court know about it?"

Cathal didn't flinch. "You didn't answer my question, Kaja."

"I like to have a choice," I replied with reluctance. Pondering on the fact that I had given up my choice to save

Laoise's life wasn't a good idea. I never thought I'd need another curse, and I didn't want to risk leaving any notes, so re-creating it could take as long as making it the first time. If my affliction progressed or something triggered it before I was done... I shivered. "Besides, something could happen before I could... avail myself of the lady's offer." Eithne didn't make it clear whether her offer was a future reward for doing my job or not, and I wasn't ready to rush anyway, so I didn't inquire.

"Fair enough." Cathal finally seemed to relax a bit. "Since you proved yourself, we'll be your other choice if you accept. None of us will hesitate to bring you a swift death before you turn. But Kaja ...?" He looked me in the eye. "You might deceive anyone that you wish, even lie to Lady Eithne herself, but as long as you work with us... the Scáthanna don't keep secrets from one another."

"Understood," I replied with a serious face. As long as I worked with them, I had to follow their rules. And since I felt like I was already stepping on the very thin ice of Cathal's benevolence, I resisted the urge to ask how quickly those secrets I was to share with him would reach Eithne's ears.

He looked at Riagán. "I need Laoise to handle Brigh, so you get Kaja home. You can deal with your other task later."

Riagán let out something that might have been a snort, but Cathal shot him a warning glance, and the archer became serious within a blink.

"Let's go," Riagán said. "It's been a long evening."

When we'd put some distance between us and the other mythborn, I glanced at him. "The Scáthanna won't allow my having secrets, but they have some of their own," I said. Not that I expected to get any information out of him, but trying couldn't hurt. "Doesn't seem fair."

As I'd expected, he didn't take the bait. "You should work harder on sounding upset, Kaja."

"I saw the glances you and Cathal exchanged, and I noticed warning glares Eithne had sent you," I replied. "I'd be lying if I said I didn't think there was more to all of it. Things you're keeping from me. Being upfront and honest about it wouldn't be... Court-like."

"Now you sound bitter."

I held off a grimace and picked up my pace. I wasn't about to discuss with Riagán how I quietly hoped that working with the Court on finding the Snake agents would be a step toward bringing humanborn and mythborn together. I'd be naïve to think they really wanted to make Eireland into something more than a volatile island with a mockery of a government. After all, the other night he'd admitted many mythborn wished us gone.

He moved in front of me faster than I could catch it, and I almost walked into him. The scent of pines and campfire smoke enveloped me in an instant, and even though my instincts longed for his magic, my mind saw only another of his games.

"You didn't tell us you carried a curse around that could kill anyone who touches you when active." He looked me in the eye. "I'm quite surprised Cathal didn't drag you back to the Court for that... or worse. Instead, he gave you his trust and expects nothing less back. Yet there are things that are not relevant. As we have our secrets that will not endanger you, we don't ask why you insisted that the Court appoint someone else to liaise with Albert, even though you were the best person suited for it. We also don't ask why you've been recently avoiding Trinity."

My hands trembled in frustration, though I wasn't shocked they knew about it.

"You aren't hunted by them, and that's enough to leave it alone," he added in a lighter tone.

"And if I were?" I couldn't resist.

"We'd sort it out... one way or another."

The tone of his voice was more telling than his words, and I arched my eyebrow. I could swear Riagán had just suggested that if I didn't betray their trust, the Scáthanna would nearly go to war to keep me out of trouble, but he didn't elaborate.

We made it across the river, and before long we stood in front of my apartment building. The shadows by the walls moved, and I knew my neighbor mythborn kept guard.

Riagán looked at the entrance, and then sighed. "I need to go. Stay safe." And he disappeared into the dark without any other goodbye.

I stood in the street as his departure caught me in the middle of pondering whether I should invite him inside again. Well, at least I didn't have to make the decision between enjoying his company and despising his games. And, on the bright side, I'd have my video game for myself... Well, I'd have it in four months, when I would hopefully be done with my new curse.

With that grim realization, I entered the building.

CHAPTER FIFTEEN

I shouldn't have stayed up all night, but when I tried to lie in bed, sleep wouldn't come anyway, so instead I spent the long hours bent over my workbench in a vain attempt at re-creating the process that last time took me months to complete. I remembered the steps I'd taken, and even without any notes I was confident I could re-create the intricate structure of the curse I'd embedded into the trinket, but what I hoped for was a shortcut. The prospect of weeks or even months without my final insurance chased the tiredness away better than caffeine would, and pushed my thoughts toward Eithne's offer.

The curse was supposed to kill me before I transformed, before I became one of the Afflicted, but now it was gone, and my choice had become an illusion. While I appreciated Cathal's sentiment, the Scáthanna couldn't be around twenty-four seven, and I didn't want to risk that I'd hurt someone before they managed to put me down. Not to mention, dying by their weapons seemed a much more painful solution than a quick-acting curse.

When morning arrived, I made my way down to the

kitchen. Like tea, coffee remained a rare commodity, but as long as it was within my price range, I didn't care, so I brewed a whole pot. Tiredness had started to catch up with me, and I hoped in a couple of hours I'd crash regardless of the amount of caffeine I ingested.

The violent pounding on the door made it clear I shouldn't have hoped.

"Kaja! Are you there?" someone shouted. "Kaja!"

The accent sounded mythborn, and I abandoned the warm mug of coffee to open the door. The very moment I recognized my guest, I froze, but Faolan's golden face expressed only urgency.

"Brigh talked," he said. "The Trinitians are in danger. We need to go."

I stood motionless only for the seconds it took my brain to process the information, then I grabbed my bag and coat and stepped outside. It could be Faolan's ruse to lure me out of the safety of my apartment, but I was willing to take the chance. The mythborn didn't have to use deception to get to me, as I left my apartment frequently enough and wandered suspicious neighborhoods for a living. If he wanted me dead, he didn't need to put on a show like that.

I caught a glimpse of surprise in his eyes, as if he'd expected more convincing and wasting time, and then he gestured at me to follow.

"We'll take a shortcut," he said, climbing up the stairs.

That made me suspicious, but I wasn't about to argue, since I'd decided to trust him. "So, what's with the Trinitians?" I followed him.

"Brigh was indeed one of the Snake's agents, and she didn't work alone," Faolan replied. The quick ascent didn't seem to affect his breathing at all. "While she was to take out Lady Eithne, another agent set out to deal with Trinity's leader."

"They won't let a mythborn in..." A sudden thought struck me. "It's the messenger, isn't it?"

"He'd left the Court before we got to him, so the others went to find him, and Cathal sent me for you." Faolan's tone turned grim. "If we fail to intercept him, you need to warn the Trinitians."

I didn't need to ask why they wanted me to pass the message. Albert's trust in the Court and mythborn in general was limited, and if they started raising suspicions over one of their own, at the very one Lady Eithne had appointed to be her messenger, they would encourage questions rather than swift action, while my word still counted as solid. At least, I desperately wanted to believe it did.

We reached the rooftop, and Faolan led me toward a narrow plank that connected it to the next building. I didn't ask how it was supposed to save us time, since we'd have to climb down when we reached the end of the block. Instead, I followed him along the roofs, and the mythborn seemed to find his way across with ease... or with the expertise of someone who'd traveled this route multiple times. Even with all the talking about trust, I wouldn't put it past Cathal to have ordered his team to keep tabs on me.

Once we reached Meath Street, Faolan slowed down, and I saw no planks or walkways across the wide gap.

"What now?" I asked as I approached.

"Now we jump."

I didn't even have time to ridicule the idea, because Faolan wrapped his arm around my waist and activated one of his charms. Magic enveloped us in a cocoon, and he jumped as if we both weighed nothing. The descent, though, was faster than I anticipated and pressed the breath out of my lungs.

When we landed, Faolan let go of me in an instant, and while I fought to regain my balance, I caught his smirk. Once I was back on my feet, we resumed the race across the rooftops. I didn't get used to the breathtaking leaps, but I learned how to maintain my balance so we made quick progress, and I could see how going above saved us time in comparison to meandering through streets filled with pedestrians.

We slowly descended as we approached Christchurch. The buildings became lower, and when we reached the once-busy intersection by the cathedral itself, Faolan's last leap brought us to the ground. He looked at a building on the other side of the street, and I wondered if he was about to get us up there. With the straight route to Trinity, it seemed like a waste of time to continue on the rooftops.

"They didn't get him on the way," he said instead. "He might be already inside."

I didn't waste time spying the mythborn on the rooftop there, since she or he was probably gone by now. Instead, I sprinted down Dame Street, and Faolan followed me. People threw us startled glances, but they got out of our way, and we only slowed down when the guards at Trinity College's gate stood in our way.

"I need to see Albert!" I called out. "It's urgent!"

If that moron captain was around, he'd probably have me wait again, especially with Faolan by my side. Fortunately, it was one of the old-timers at the gate, and he waved at other guards to let me through.

"He's with me." I pointed at Faolan.

Nobody objected, and I wasn't sure how I felt about it. On one hand, Faolan could prove useful against another mythborn, but bringing him into Trinity without any precautions... Who knew what other charms and curses he had on him? I forced myself to exercise basic trust.

We entered the college, and I led the way through countless corridors. The armed Trinitians I passed paused at the sight of Faolan, and they moved their hands toward their weapons, ready to act. It seemed that only my presence prevented hostilities.

My bursting into the map room startled Orla and other officers, but the bow mistress regained her composure quickly and calmed the others.

"Where's Albert?" I didn't waste time.

"In his office," Orla replied, confused, not taking her eyes off Faolan standing behind me. "The mythborn representative wanted a private..."

I didn't wait for the rest. I spun on my heels, and Faolan leaped back at the last moment before I dashed again. Five corridors and three floors' worth of stairs were between me and Albert's office, and with each step I had more doubt we'd make it on time.

Faolan stayed on my heels, and the sound of other footsteps suggested Orla had joined us as well, but I didn't look behind me. We had almost made it to the top floor when the sound of glass being shattered and an angry shriek reached our ears.

"No ...!" I wasn't sure if the word even left my mouth.

The doors weren't locked, and when I barged into Albert's office, I froze at the scene. The commander stood by the window, bleeding from a flesh wound on his shoulder, and on the opposite side of the room slumped an unconscious mythborn representative, his forearm pinned to the wall by a familiar, gray-banded arrow. Whatever he held in his hand had broken, and purple liquid ate through his skin and muscles.

Faolan pushed past me but relaxed at the sight, which assured me there wasn't any immediate danger. "Show-off," he muttered while he looked at the arrow, but I caught pride and satisfaction in his voice.

Albert glanced at the broken glass in the window, at the mythborn pinned to the wall, and finally at me and Faolan. "That's going to be a mess to sort out," he said.

To my surprise, Faolan smiled. "Let me sort some of it out for you." He approached the mythborn.

"No! Don't kill him!" Orla shouted from the door.

Faolan winked at her and pulled the arrow out of the representative's wound, letting the mythborn slide down the wall. Then he turned to me. "I trust you have things covered here," he said.

His tone sounded almost like Cathal's, as if I was to follow his orders in the Scáthanna leader's absence. Then, before any of us could react, he lifted the unconscious mythborn with unnatural ease and leaped, pushing the rest of the window out and into the street. With his charm, he landed softly and dashed away as if his burden weighted nothing.

I gritted my teeth. Of course, I could ignore Faolan's words, but in the end I needed to handle things the way he wanted. I had no doubt he'd taken the representative to ensure the Trinitians wouldn't interrogate him and learn about the Snake, and leaving me behind to handle Albert seemed the best choice too, no matter how much I personally hated the prospect.

"Orla, lock the door," Albert said, and then looked at me. "I believe Kaja has some explaining to do."

"What about explaining all this?" Orla asked when the door separated us from the rest of the Trinity.

"The Court learned that the representative was working with the terrorists. I was asked to relay the warning, but I came too late. As for all this..." I scanned the office. "Albert got wounded when the representative assaulted him. The attacker had magic poison, and Faolan, the mythborn who came with me, took him out through the window to protect the humanborn in the room." Even as I said it, it sounded awfully contrived.

Albert gave me a dubious glare, but Orla nodded. "I can work with that," she said. "A better story than a mythborn archer shooting you through a supposedly ward-enforced window," she added. Those wards were supposed to ensure Albert's safety, after all.

"Fine. Let everyone know I'm all right, before someone goes on a revenge spree," he replied.

When she left, I walked over to the cabinet and pulled out a first-aid kit. He still kept it in the same place. "I'll have a look at your wound, and I'll explain everything," I offered while Albert pulled heavy curtains over the broken window.

In fact, I hoped patching him up would give me enough time to gather the scraps of information I could share and make them into a believable story. I really needed to convince Eithne to stop keeping things from Albert. It didn't help the mutual trust and seemed to stir more trouble than it prevented.

I SAT on Albert's desk, leaning over his shirtless torso as I cleaned his wound. What had seemed a good idea moments ago now brought unexpected discomfort. Last time I was so close to his half-naked body was in quite different circumstances... And it had been over two years since then.

"You aren't honest with me," Albert said. "All I hear is some sort of conspiracy among the mythborn who want to throw us back into the war, but I don't have to read your mind to know that's only a half-truth."

I leaned closer to avoid eye contact, but Albert held me by the chin and forced to look at him.

"Kaja."

I hated when he used my name like this, with a tone that was both demanding and reminded me of the intimacy we once shared.

"If I could tell you more, I would," I replied, "but Eithne needs to agree to that." I reached for the bandages and wrapped the cloth around his wound. "She believes some humanborn might be involved as well."

He snorted. "And you trust her."

I cringed. I didn't *need* to trust Eithne, since last night I'd heard three humanborn talking about the Snake myself, and I wished I could share it with him. But letting him know that the mythborn special unit wandered about and killed people Albert would consider civilians made me abandon the idea. The Trinitians didn't need more arguments against the Court, and I wasn't entirely blameless either. After all, the Scáthanna hunted the targets I pointed out to them.

"You don't have to answer this one," he said with a hint of sarcasm. "So can you at least tell me what you're doing in the company of the Court's elite murderers?"

I didn't even try to argue they weren't murderers. "It's part of the job I'm doing for Eithne," I replied. "I get the information, and they use it." I secured the bandage and moved away.

Albert's grimace made it clear what he thought. "Another vague answer."

"Then complain to Eithne about it," I replied with more ire in my voice than I'd intended. "I'll be happy to pass along that message." I gave him a mean glare.

He didn't say anything at first, but when the question came, it was like a poisonous sting. "The information you give them... Do they use it against the humanborn?"

There wasn't a good answer to that unless I wanted to give him a blatant lie, but remaining silent wouldn't cut it either. I forced the words out of my mouth. "When it's necessary."

"When it's necessary!" He raised his voice. "Can you even hear yourself?"

"They don't go about killing innocents. I'm making sure of that. Why do you think I took the job in the first place?" I reined my frustration in. Fueling the argument further wouldn't help. "They're effective at what they do. They saved your life today, didn't they?"

"Don't play that card." He grimaced.

I shrugged. It wasn't about winning the argument—it was about not having one. "I'll ask Eithne to let me tell you more," I said in a more mediating tone. "I think you should know all about that conspiracy, but my hands are bound unless she agrees."

As he gave me a long glare, I read in his eyes the inner battle he waged—doubt and concern mixing with the willingness to trust me no matter what. We had never betrayed each other in the past, and he must still believe I wouldn't. "You could turn down the job. It's not like you need more money."

"I can't." I resisted the need to turn my head away and

instead looked him straight in the eye. "Where did you think that vial I gave your scientists came from?"

Albert cursed heavily and ran his hand through his short hair. "So, she has you pinned down."

"Somewhat," I replied with caution. It didn't seem the best time to tell him about the rest of her offer. "You might distrust Eithne or question her methods, but she does it all to keep the peace. And today was proof."

He rose from his chair and paced around the desk. "I won't pretend that I like it," he said after the fourth or fifth lap. "But you are right, they did save me today." He looked at the broken window. "And it seems that if they want Trinity in chaos, they have the means."

Finally, the voice of reason! I held my breath and gave a cautious nod. "If you trust me enough, I'll take over the contacts with the Court. At least this way I'll ensure no more assassins sneak in."

He arched his eyebrow. "That would mean daily briefings, and lately you haven't been visiting much."

I couldn't resist smiling when I caught the accusatory undertone of the words. I wasn't about to deny I'd been avoiding him. "I'll be here, every morning and longer, if needed," I said instead.

Albert's clear laughter was like a remedy. "That almost makes me consider getting shot more often."

The door swung open, and two women burst into the room. Orla tried to stop Jemma, but Albert's lover was already inside, and I remembered too late that neither of us had locked the door again after Orla left.

"I heard you were wounded—" Jemma's words died as she took one look at the shirtless commander, then at me. She turned to Orla. "You didn't tell me he was with *that woman*!" she almost shrieked.

So this was what my name was: *that woman*. I bit my tongue. Snide comments wouldn't help, and I wasn't about to ruin Albert's relationship in the name of personal satisfaction.

"Jemma, I'm fine." He gave her a firm look. "And I'm busy."

Her lips trembled, but she didn't make any vicious remark, as I half expected her to. She spun in place and left the room faster than she had stormed in.

"You should have put your shirt on," Orla said. The emotional display seemed to have had no effect on her.

I glanced at Albert. "Go and talk to her," I said softly. "She deserves some explanation, and she needs to get over the fact that we not only work together, but we're also friends."

Albert hesitated, then nodded. "Let Eithne know you'll be handling communication from now on," he said. "And feel free to tell her what I think about her secrets and games." He offered a brief smile. "If you need anything else, Orla will sort it out. I'll see you in the morning."

He left, and Orla shook her head. "He's an idiot."

My eyes widened. Never during the war or after it had she shown disrespect to Albert, but apparently I was unaware of the depths her bitchiness reached.

"For trying to have a life?"

She snorted. "For letting you go." She looked me up and down. "I never liked you much, and I still don't. But if Albert wasn't such an idiot, you'd be at Trinity now, lending us your skills and knowledge instead of running around with the mythborn."

I rolled my eyes. "You know it's more than that. I don't fit in here. I'm hardly a human anymore, and Trinitians have quite a strict approach to... the purity." I gave her a challenging stare. In a way, I envied her the resistance she had to magic. Not only had it saved her multiple times during the war, but she was also one of the few immune to the affliction.

"That's why you should be here, changing it," she pressed. "Many of the veterans know you and trust you. You could make Trinity better." She glanced over her shoulder, at the closed door. "Or rather, you could have made it better."

I didn't miss the bitterness in the last sentence. In her mind, she must have already decided that I'd made my choice, and it wasn't in Trinity's favor.

"Until I changed, and you'd lose half of the people here trying to put me down," I fired back.

"Tadgh says he can reproduce the drug you've brought us," Orla said. "You'd stay as you are, which I believe is what you want anyway."

I smirked. Sometimes she did have accurate insights. "Tadgh? I thought—"

"I brought her a few drops." Orla shrugged, but a wide grin betrayed her. She didn't like or trust Jemma. Not that she liked me either, but at least we had some mutual trust. "So that she could play with it and make Albert happy. The rest stayed with Tadgh and the team he chose."

I shook my head in disbelief. One of the most resolute Trinitians, distrustful both of the mythborn and even those of humanborn who tried to embrace their affliction, preferred Tadgh over Jemma.

"I think I should get going." If I stayed, the conversation could take turns I'd rather avoid. I still hadn't told Albert about Eithne's offer... I knew he would become suspicious and argumentative, and I couldn't even begin to imagine what Orla would say about it.

She sneered. "Say hi to Riagán when you see him again. Tell him I'd love to see the arrow he shot today."

I nodded. "So would I."

We both knew the mythborn would never part with the secret of how his shafts were warded. In the past, we'd inspected the ones we recovered from dead bodies, but we never found anything except for standard balancing and empowering charms. I glanced at the broken window and the several pieces of glass still on the ground. It had survived a direct hit from the mythborn equivalent of a tank, but shattered with a single arrow.

"Do you think Albert will move his office?" I asked.

"We'll be lucky if he even moves his desk to the wall. But with that bloody archer out there, it doesn't really matter where Albert sits." She approached the window and pulled the curtains to the side. "I sent people to the roof I thought he was hiding on."

"And nothing?" I guessed.

"Nothing." She shook her head. "I hope we don't end up at war again, because I have a feeling last time they went easy on us."

I shared the sentiment. We'd lost many people, and the humanborn population had been reduced to a fraction of the five-million-strong country, but if the mythborn really wanted, they could have wiped us out. Instead, we had a budding peace and an imitation of coexistence.

I chased those thoughts away. In a way, the humanborn presence prevented the rest of the world from acting, and if they killed us all, nothing would keep the world's forces from retaliating. Even the magic shroud, affecting much of our technology, wouldn't protect them long. After all, humans were adept at overcoming obstacles. We'd already made amulets for planes to be able to land safely, bringing supplies and letting people come and go, so working out similar protections for advanced weaponry couldn't be far behind.

"Speaking of which," I said, "I'll check with the Court and see if I can get Eithne to be more cooperative. I'll be back in the morning, for the briefing. Don't let anyone else in."

Orla gave me an inscrutable gaze. "Albert still trusts you. Don't disappoint him."

I got the message. After all that had happened and all that she'd seen, she didn't trust me as much as she had in the past and was prepared to act if I turned out to be a traitor. I nodded and made my exit before the situation became uncomfortable.

Especially with all the secrecy and keeping things away from them both, I felt like a traitor already.

EITHNE STRETCHED ON HER CHAIR, and her face expressed sadness. We sat in her office, in the very heart of the Court, where ever-present magic teased my senses.

"I'm sorry, Kaja, but I can't take that risk," she said. "I understand that you trust Albert, but the relationship between the humanborn and the mythborn has been diffi-cult enough, and the Trinitians don't need another argu-ment against the Court, against all of the mythborn."

I should have expected her answer the very moment I asked for permission to reveal some of the mythborn's secrets. "I'd convince Albert to keep it a secret," I said. "And telling him would help build trust between Trinity and the Court."

"Would it now?" Her green eyes pierced me. "I can't see

how telling the humanborn that the mythborn brought something along from the other world, something that wants to push this country back into a devastating war, would help. It's bad enough that we didn't catch the representative in time."

I gave a slow, reluctant nod. I couldn't argue with her perspective, as I could see Albert would not trust the Court more if I revealed the truth about the Snake to him, especially after having kept the secret for so long. He'd see potential traitors in every mythborn, and would likely raise the threat level throughout the college, which in turn would make every other Trinitian more suspicious. The tension would spread like circles in the water, and at some point, someone would snap.

"I promise I'll speak with Albert as soon as we have everything under control," she offered. "I'm sure he'll understand."

I hid a grimace of displeasure. Telling Albert post factum seemed like a bad idea, but at least she'd be the one to bring the news to him. "Did you learn anything from Brigh? Or Domhnall?" I asked instead. "Because Faolan brought him here, didn't he?"

"He did. And we learned about a place outside of Dublin that might provide some information on the Snake's moves through Eireland," she replied. "The Scáthanna set out earlier to investigate. I apologize they didn't wait for you, but I wanted to make sure they got there before the Snake's agents move to another location." She cocked her head to the side as if inspecting me. "They won't be back until late. Maybe you should use that time to get some rest."

Getting the cue that the conversation was over, I rose from the chair and mumbled some courtesies. Nobody waited for me in the corridor, and Eithne made no motion to assign an escort to me, which I interpreted as a sign of trust. I took my time walking out to the exit and enjoyed the ambient magic of the Court. Somehow, it didn't flare up my affliction and had soothing properties. And when I inhaled the air, it brought about the faint smell I associated with my childhood, though I had a hard time pinning it to anything specific.

At that thought, I picked up my pace and made it to the gate as quickly as possible without raising suspicion. I still hadn't decided to take Eithne's offer, making an excuse to myself about the job not being finished, even though the mythborn lady hadn't implied the two were linked.

I crossed the river and didn't argue with the bridge dwellers who insisted I paid the toll. The river was black and restless, with its surface creased like an angry man's forehead, and its state reflected my mood.

With Eithne's refusal to let Albert in on the secret, I needed to consider what I could tell him to satiate his need for the truth while still keeping my side of the agreement with the Court. Avoiding him wasn't an option, not after I balanced his trust with my promise I'd be back in the morning.

My apartment welcomed me with silence, and even though most times the lack of sounds brought relief, on days like this one it reminded me I was alone, stuck with my own thoughts. I had no real life, few friends, and no future.

I couldn't confide in Albert, not anymore, and all my wartime companions had ties with Trinity, which also crossed them off the list. I considered visiting Three-Bones, but as helpful and friendly as he was, he didn't offer much in terms of an intellectual conversation, so his advice would be simple, unfit for the complexity of my trouble. It most likely would involve eating a seagull.

And even though I wasn't insane enough to confide in Riagán, since his loyalties lay with the Court and the Scáthanna, I missed his presence. If I had to focus on the conversation and dodging his questions or baiting, I'd have no time to overthink the morning meeting with Albert. I knew I had to go in, tell him the truth, which meant simply saying Eithne was a bitch and as distrustful of Albert as he was of her, and then hope for the best.

For an early dinner I picked one of the military-style rations still lingering in my cupboard, and while it heated up, I launched the game. At least hacking through countless enemies would help me relax. And then, perhaps, an early night... Since I'd been spending my evenings hunting for the Snake's agents with Eithne's elite murderers, as Albert called them, I hadn't been getting much sleep.

My eyes skimmed past the table and locked on the folder lying forgotten at its edge. *Emma Doherty.* Of course, with the bombings, Eithne's revelations about the Snake, and all the other fun of the past weeks, I had completely forgotten about the missing journalist. Not very professional of me, but Albert did say she was low priority... I meant to check what I could find after we got Jonas Byrne, but before I had a chance, Eithne had dragged me into the conspiracy hunt.

I picked up the folder, ignoring my game. I had a free afternoon, so at least I could check if any of my contacts had heard anything about her, and maybe stop by the Court again to see if they'd be willing to share their information. If I managed to locate her—or her body—that would definitely help with Albert. At least I'd have something to show for my time.

The folder didn't contain much to go on except for the several names that made up her contact list, three pictures, and an address. Or, rather, two addresses. One in the area once called Dublin 2, not far from the Trinity College, the other in Dublin 9... less than ten-minute walk from the Botanical Gardens. Of course, the second one must have been the pre-Magiclysm address, since during the war most of the humanborn had moved out of the northern part of the city—but with the peace restored, she might have gone back there. Especially if she was trying to sneak into the gardens...

I found the address on the map, and while I ate dinner I planned my afternoon. Check with the *Eireland Times* whether Emma was still missing, then head for her home in D9, and stop by the Court on my way back to check if the Scáthanna had had any luck on their assignment. If I hurried, I'd be back home by the evening and get some well-deserved sleep.

I put the bowl in the sink and ignored my more down-to-earth self who reminded me of the laundry. As long as I had more than two outfits to wear and a stash of clean lingerie, washing clothes could wait. Especially with the newfound excuse of searching for Emma. Not that I cared about some journalist who had most likely ignored the mythborn ban and tried to get into the forbidden area... If she was dead, it was probably her own fault, but finding her could score me some extra points with Albert, and I needed them bad, real bad.

CHAPTER SIXTEEN

The visit to the *Eireland Times* didn't improve my mood, as Emma's colleague made it clear he didn't appreciate my calling in weeks after they had reported her disappearance. I didn't bother with excuses or explanations and left the building as soon as I made sure Emma was still missing. I doubted I'd made a good impression, and the man I spoke to would likely complain to Albert later. He'd trusted the Trinitians with the search, and they passed it on to someone who seemed utterly unprofessional. Namely myself. Explaining how one missing person was less important than the future of the whole country was pointless. People always cared more about matters close to them than the good of the larger community.

I made it down toward the river. At the sight of a large bridge, built high over the river and over the low buildings, I let out a sigh. I remembered the times when trains used to cross it, carrying commuters back and forth. Back then, our only concern was the economic whirlwinds across Europe and our jobs' stability. The man at the corner of the street would hand out free newspapers, and I'd weave my way through the never-diluted crowds filling the city center's streets. After the war, with Dublin's population decimated, and with the new terrorist threats to add to it, most of the streets had become empty.

I walked along the river, reminiscing about all the things I used to hate. Not only the crowds, but also traffic, stuck in narrow one-way streets and so slow that sometimes a pedestrian could overtake a moving car. And trash everywhere, overflowing from full bins, carelessly tossed on the ground, and pushed around by wind. Even the automated sweepers couldn't keep up with it, and they took care only of the main streets, leaving the city's guts to slowly drown in garbage and filth. The war might not have changed things for the better, and had maybe even added to the mess with the debris lying about, but at least there were fewer human— and inhuman—beings to produce trash now.

I stuck to the southern bank of the Liffey, trying to delay the moment of entering what everybody considered mythborn territory. I might be the Court's guest and had a friend among the bridge dwellers, but it didn't mean all of the North Side's residents would be friendly. The darkening sky reminded me of how quickly nightfall came in winters, and I second-guessed my plan. But then, in the morning, I had a briefing in Trinity, and after that I'd possibly be visiting the Court again if Albert needed any messages delivered to Eithne, so I'd end up within a similar time frame. That was, if the Scáthanna didn't need me for anything, and since now Cathal wanted me around even when I wasn't the one to give them information about possible targets, I was truly left with this *one* free afternoon.

Commotion at the other bank drew my attention, but it didn't seem like anything important. Some woman collected a handful of insults from drunken mythborn she pushed through as she went somewhere in a rush. The wind tangled her brown hair, and her full shape made me think of Jemma.

As much as I wanted to like Albert's new lover, whenever I remembered the scene she'd made at his office, my frustration rose. As the war had taken its toll in lives, the choice of companions had become somewhat limited, but out of all the women available, Albert had picked one with a shitty attitude. I chased her away from my thoughts, as it brought more unpleasant considerations. I missed Albert, and I might feel slightly jealous of Jemma, but at the same time, I knew I'd never go back to Trinity.

When I finally decided to cross the river, I paid my toll and ignored the remarks in broken English of how tasty I looked, though I did make a mental note to avoid that bridge in the future. Whether they liked it or not, dwellers were a part of our society, and even though the Eireland Office had granted them the right to settle on Dublin's multiple bridges and ask for payment from anyone who crossed, mythborn and humanborn alike, it didn't mean I had to give my money to the creatures who still hadn't learned the basic principles of "coexistence". I'd rather walk further down the river and leave my money at Tee-Bee's bridge, where the dwellers seemed more amiable.

The North Side greeted me with crumbled buildings and silence, and I made my way through with caution. I fished out the Court's emblem and pinned it to my coat. I preferred not to make any mythborn guards nervous by trying to find it in my bag among many things that could look to them like weapons or curses.

As I ventured further north, I avoided the area that was once a commercial district. Back in the day, two large shopping centers towered over it, with a cinema multiplex around the corner, and many posh shops boasting their merchandise. For some reason, the mythborn favored the area, and it had become the heart of their social life, with places like Faoin Crainn drawing a lot of well-off patrons, and I didn't feel like dealing with the most arrogant and decadent bunch of our former enemies.

Only few blocks further to the west, Dublin North was showing its poorer and grimmer face with lower buildings and cheap businesses. Many places around here had closed down way before the Magiclysm came, and the war had done little to improve the state of the area. A few mythborn loitered around, but they left me alone, so I didn't pay much attention to them.

Nevertheless, I walked with one hand in my pocket, fingers clutching a minor stun curse, and made my pace fast enough to be out of the way before anyone could consider going after me. The mythborn around weren't like the semi-friendly bunch in the Liberties. They seemed more scarred by the war and less willing to adapt to the world they lived in, and I could bet that if I gave them any excuse, they'd jump on the chance, and I wouldn't get away with only a few bruises. In the eyes of some, I saw a promise of death: I only needed to give them any opening, any justification.

"Got lost?" A bulky mythborn stepped out from the shadows, and even though he could hardly bar the way in the wide street, his intention of stopping me was more than obvious.

I almost cursed. Saying I didn't want any trouble would most likely get me nowhere, except maybe making the mythborn laugh, and for a moment I sincerely regretted not waiting for the Scáthanna to return from their assignment and accompany me. I was almost certain they wouldn't mind as long as it didn't interfere with our job or their other assignments. Well, at least Riagán wouldn't mind.

"No." I gave him a confident stare. It didn't always work, but sometimes it made them doubt whether I really was the defenseless victim they saw me as.

His lips widened into an ugly grin. "Going to the gardens, then?"

"No." He must be stupid to believe I'd give an affirmative to that even if I was actually going there. The Botanical Gardens were off-limits to all the humanborn, and admitting one headed there was like handing the mythborn a permission to kill, because I was sure the bulky thing in front of me wouldn't bother dragging me to their authorities. "My friend has a place nearby."

"That friend, he a mythborn?" he asked.

I was about to deny it when a new idea presented itself. Of course, lying was risky, but the mythborn had already assumed I was on my way to a tryst, so it was worth a shot, and I nodded.

"Of the Court." I pointed at the silvery badge on my jacket.

I counted on the mythborn making the connection: someone from the Court, having an "exotic" humanborn lover but meeting her away from the prying eyes of his own kin, avoiding gossip.

He looked me up and down as if assessing whether I could be worthy of a mythborn's attention. I guess I should have put some makeup on in case I needed to rely on deception, but as I was getting used to the Scáthanna being around, I'd let myself forget the North Side wasn't always a safe place.

"He doesn't like it when I'm late," I added when the mythborn didn't move.

He gave me one more scrutinizing glare and then took a step to the side. "Have fun."

I sent him a meager smile and resumed my walk before he changed his mind or decided to inquire about my supposed lover's name, but the Court's emblem must have convinced him I told the truth. They didn't give those to just anyone.

For the rest of my journey, I paid more attention to my surroundings, and whenever I spotted mythborn lingering in the shadows, I crossed the street or changed my route. Losing time on a detour was more appealing than losing my life only because someone decided I'd ventured too deep into the mythborn territory.

WHEN I FINALLY STOOD IN front of the ruined building, its windows broken and dark, it became clear I'd come in vain. It must have been abandoned for years, and Emma had probably never visited it after the war. But since I was already there, looking around wouldn't hurt. If I was lucky, maybe she'd stopped by and left a clue behind—*anything* that would point me in the right direction.

Cracked bricks from a collapsed wall rattled under my boots as I made my way inside. In the day's receding light I scouted the ground floor, recognizing the typical layout: the dining room merged with the kitchen, the living room, and the stairway, the last still mostly intact. Nothing around indicated Emma had visited, but the stairs caught my attention. Some bricks and pieces of plaster lay about, but it wasn't rubble like the rest of the ground floor. Somebody had used them often enough to make clearing the debris worthwhile. Someone had put crude boards in place of the missing steps and reinforced the railing with metal rods and pieces of wood.

Upstairs, I discovered a makeshift bed covered in ragged blankets and a stash of half-rotten food. But what caught my attention was the symbol on the wall—the three-headed snake, a mockery of a triskelion, crudely shaped but taking all the available space, as if its painter wanted the whole world to know. It seemed I'd come across another of the Snake's followers.

With my heart pumping adrenaline into my veins, I scouted the rooms, expecting to see a similar setup to what I'd seen in Byrne's apartment and during the raids with the mythborn: some leaflets and ready-to-rig explosives. And sure, I found them all. What I didn't expect was the size of the stash.

I didn't need to poke around any more to realize what I'd stumbled upon, on that one evening when the Scáthanna were out of town, and I was on my own. We'd spent days looking for the Snake's agent, for the one who controlled all the other followers, and here I was, in the middle of his or her lair: alone, bloody alone, and without any hope for backup.

My charms remained silent, which meant I might have been lucky and not triggered any magical alarms, provided there were any around. If I backed out and headed straight for the Court, we had a chance of setting a trap. I bet Eithne would spare no resources if she could cut off the Snake's head in one swift move. Even if Cathal and his squad were away, she had enough mythborn warriors with plenty of charms and curses to take down one person.

I made my way down the steps with more caution than I had climbing up. I might be paranoid, but I feared that one misplaced brick could reveal I'd been upstairs. I hadn't found anything there that would tell me of the agent's identity, which meant we only had one shot at catching him or her.

I'd almost made it to the door when I heard a song.

"*Siuil, siuil, siul a run, siuil go sochair agus siuil go ciuin. Siuil go doras agus ealaigh lion.*" A female voice.

I knew the melody and some of the words: a traditional Irish love song. Some of the Irish humanborn used to sing it by campfires, and I wouldn't be surprised if the mythborn sang it as well, since the lyrics were partially in English, partially in Irish. As the voice drew nearer, I sneaked over to the kitchen and stood against the wall, hoping to hide in its shade.

"I wish I was on yonder hill. 'Tis there I'd sit and cry my fill, and every tear would turn a mill." The sound of steps crushing the bricks told me the female had entered the building, but then the song stopped, and instead a doglike sniffing reached my ears.

I didn't need to peek over the corner to recognize the chaotic pattern of magic that spread from the entrance. The Irish lyrics might have confused me, but now I was certain it wasn't a mythborn on the other side of the wall, and she'd find me soon enough.

I stepped out. "Emma? Is that you?" I kept my voice gentle and made no sudden moves.

I'd never heard an Afflicted sing before; no wonder, really, since we tried to kill them before they became deadly, instead of making a polite conversation or engaging in artistic pastimes. But it seemed that now all I could do was talk my way out of this situation—or die.

The creature in front of me was every bit an Afflicted. When the change came, the magic within her had made her flesh grow uncontrollably, resulting in a bulging body and twisted limbs. Her eyes, all yellow, resembled those of a cat, but her irises spun around instead of staying vertical as she inspected me. Her hair was nothing more than handfuls of blond strands on her head, which was covered with scute-like scabs.

"Emma?" I repeated.

She looked at me with no recognition on her twisted face. "*Siuil, siuil, siul a run, siuil go sochair agus siuil go ciuin. Siuil go doras agus ealaigh lion. Is go dte tu mo mhuirnin sla.*" Her body rocked back and forth as she sang. Then, with a flash of sanity, she focused on me. "Emma is gone. All gone. Not a little piece left."

"I'm sad to hear that," I replied. "I'm sorry I interrupted your song." I hoped the prompt would push her back into a semi-trance state.

The Afflicted nodded. "All gone. And you better be gone too. You can't see—" She glanced down at her own hands and at box full of the magic devices she held.

Of course I followed her gaze, and when I looked up, her narrowed yellow eyes watched me intently. I didn't like the expression on her face and the threat hidden in it.

"I'm sorry," she said in a soft voice that contradicted the declaration of violence in her body language, "but you can't see that." She went back to humming while she put the explosives down, and then faced me with her hands empty. Even in the falling darkness, I couldn't miss her long, claw-like fingers.

I didn't wait for her to lunge. I threw a stun curse right at her and darted for the stairs. If only I had my special curse... but I'd settle for as little as Faolan's jumping charm. Anything to give me a chance.

Downstairs, Emma roared in pain, and I headed for the window. Jumping through it wasn't a perfect solution, but I had no time to stop and consider other options, not with a raging Afflicted on my back. The amulets shielded me enough to prevent any broken bones, but I still felt the impact as I rolled on the pavement. While I scrambled to my feet, Emma appeared in the window I had just vacated.

Our eyes locked, and for a moment I wondered whether Laoise had felt the same facing the Afflicted I'd killed not so long ago. She knew she couldn't win the fight, but had to stand her ground to give me time to escape, to warn others... Too bad I didn't have anyone by my side, and no one would carry the message. All I could do was to fire up the magic flare from Cathal and then last long enough for someone to notice the fight and investigate. Even if Emma left, the Snake's symbol on the building's wall would give the myth-born a clue of what had transpired... But that also meant I couldn't run. I had to fight and die where I stood.

Who cared? No one could outrun an Afflicted anyway.

Emma landed in front of me with ease, as if she'd jumped off a curb, not out of a window high above the ground.

I flicked another stun curse in her direction when she dashed at me, and magic exploded between us. Then I had only enough time to lift my forearms. The amulets sewn into the hem of my jacket protected me from the most of the impact, but it still pushed me backward, and I lost the grip on the magic flare. It rolled away, and I didn't risk watching its trail.

Thankfully, Emma stumbled and paused, giving me a few seconds to fish out another trinket. Toss and duck, that was all I did. Fires enveloped her, and an inhuman scream of pain echoed within the street, but she kept moving.

I didn't have many curses left, and most were designed to keep the danger away from me, not to kill. Another stun curse bought me few more breaths, but I was running out of options.

My last fire curse flew toward Emma, and the air filled with the pungent smell of her burnt flesh. But when the flames died out, she was at me again. Her eyes glowed with the fury I wished I didn't have to taste. She slashed at me with her claws.

I rolled on the ground, but it was a matter of seconds now. My fingers clutched the last trinket as if it could change anything... The curse I'd never had a chance to test, as the war ended and it was geared toward stopping mythborn. I had no idea whether it would work on an Afflicted.

Emma leaped.

She was faster than me, but I wasn't exactly trying to dodge. She dug into my arms and chest and left deep gashes. The wounds brought pain, but what made me scream was the chaotic magic entering my body. I should have known her claws carried this kind of poison.

A satisfied smile stretched her face, making her look like a monster from a cheesy movie. Then I buried the curse, a silvery triangle of a scrap metal, straight into her eye.

She shrieked and stumbled backward, dropping me onto the cold asphalt. My vision blurred from pain, but I never took my eyes off her.

The curse activated upon contact with her body and enveloped Emma in a cocoon of lightning bolts. It sucked the magic directly from her body, feeding it into the trap. She spun around and tried to push her way through, but with the curse deep in her eye, she was immobilized... that was, until she figured it out and pulled my trinket free.

For the time being, she seemed blinded by pain, and her instincts took place of what little reason she might have as an Afflicted.

I crawled away, more to avoid getting caught in the lightning cage than in the hope of saving myself. Even if I could tend to my wounds, I had no antidote for her magic poison. And that meant that I'd become like Emma soon enough.

A quiet whiz tore the air, and I only caught it because in the war I'd learned to listen for it. But this time it wasn't a messenger of death, at least not of mine.

One by one, three arrows were buried in Emma's chest, and another one sank right between her eyes. They flared up with magic from the charms engraved into the shafts, and the Afflicted dropped to the ground. The magic trap around her waned at the same time the magic died with her body.

"Kaja!" Riagán called out from the dark.

I smiled and rested my head on the ground. We'd won. The Scáthanna were here, which meant that not only would they deal with the Snake's mess, but they'd also keep their promise.

Riagán knelt beside me. "Why did you come here alone?!" His face betrayed him, and I knew that I was in a bad shape.

"Emma Doherty," I said. "She went missing weeks ago." My hand jerked when I tried to point at the motionless Afflicted. "She was the Snake's—" Instead of words, a scream came out of my mouth when pain pierced my muscles.

Riagán held me in place. "Don't talk. I'll get you patched up."

I forced a smile. "Emma's claws. Magic poison." Speaking became difficult, but I hoped he'd understand.

His face, changing into a mask of horror, told me he did. What followed was a string of curses in Irish. I'd never heard Riagán expressing himself in such an exuberant way, and the rant didn't match the image of the always composed master archer.

Last thing I saw before the pain blacked me out was a magical flare rising in the sky.

PAIN TOOK my consciousness away and pain gave it back. I didn't know how long I was out, but the sky had become really dark when I wasn't watching. The cold stone pressing against my back suggested I still lay where I'd fallen, but when I tried to move, I discovered multiple binds holding me.

"She's awake," Riagán said, his voice plain but with undertones of torment.

At the sound of footsteps, I twisted my head. Cathal squatted beside me. "Kaja?" he asked. He inspected my face as if in search of something.

"You promised," I said to him, not to Riagán. "I don't want to... Not like her." He was the commander of the Scáthanna, and he wouldn't fall for cheap sentimentality. He would keep his word. He had to.

"I remember." I caught a hint of satisfaction in his voice. "But you're coherent, which means you haven't turned yet."

I might have wasted my breath on the following string of insults in Polish, but it felt good. Then I gave him a firm stare. "So you're going to wait till I change? That's an unnecessary risk."

"Do you have any more of your amulets?" he asked. "The ones that slow the affliction?"

"Five or six more," I replied. I wasn't surprised he knew how I protected myself. "But they're back at my place."

"I'll get Faolan to bring them here. Where do you keep

them? Any protective wards he needs to look out for?" Cathal asked.

I let out a laugh that turned into a violent cough. My lungs burnt, affected by the poison that kept messing with my body. "That's not going to work."

I didn't even mean the amulets—I doubted they could improve my condition, but I kept them in my den anyway. Riagán must have caught the meaning, because Irish words flowed between him and Cathal. I could barely follow the conversation, but he must have been explaining the nature of the wards I'd made.

More Irish followed, and I stopped trying to figure out what they were talking about. Their voices, Riagán's expressing frustration and Cathal's much calmer, melted into one, like a radio show in the background. I closed my eyes again.

Cathal called Faolan over, and his angry voice joined the conversation. Something about my being a waste of time if I understood correctly—and in a way, I agreed with him. No one ever survived long in the final stage, before the affliction claimed them, and few more amulets couldn't change that.

"Kaja." Riagán leaned over me. "Those amulets. You need to tell me where they are exactly. And how they look."

I looked at him. "You can't enter the den. You'll die."

"Amulets, Kaja." His voice rang with urgency.

I sighed. Why did mythborn have to be so stubborn? "The table to the left of my collection. Everything that's in a red box."

"Let's get going, then," he replied in a lighter tone.

"What?" I stared at him.

"The binds stay on," Cathal said.

Riagán's face remained serious when he replied, "I know. Thank you."

He lifted me as if I weighed nothing and, without any more words, set off through the streets. I sensed the magic around us, so he must have used some sort of a charm to enhance his strength, and maybe speed as well, but it didn't resonate with the poison in my blood.

"What did you do to me?" I asked as he carried me toward the river.

"We stabilized you," he replied. "Mythborn are not resistant to the magic poison most of the Afflicted produce, but we react to it differently. It doesn't change us. I poured everything I had with me onto your wounds, and when the rest arrived, they added theirs. It seems to have worked well."

So that was why I hadn't changed yet... I looked at him. "But it's not going to reverse what's happening."

At first, he didn't reply, but his grim face told me enough. "If your amulets work, it'll give you few weeks more. Maybe a couple of months," he said after the initial silence. "Cathal sent Lorcan to get more antidote from the Court, and the affliction medicine Eithne shared with you already." He glanced at me. "But no one knows if it'll help."

"So, bury me under amulets, pump me with magical drugs, and hope for the best?" I offered in a lighter tone.

He nodded, but didn't smile. "That's why the binds stay on. Not even the Afflicted can break through them."

That sparked my curiosity, and I regretted I wouldn't have a chance to have a closer look at them. If the humanborn could duplicate its properties, we would gain an upper hand in the fight against the Afflicted who regularly threatened civilians' lives.

"You're not getting your hands on them," Riagán grumbled, but I caught amusement in his voice.

"That obvious?" I asked.

"I saw your workshop. I saw two of your curses that weren't of mythborn make," he replied. "Not to mention the amulet you gave to Eithne." He glanced at me again, and a familiar sarcastic smile flashed on his lips. "If I left you with the binds for longer than a heartbeat, within a month, all Trinitians would carry a copy," he teased.

I smiled.

Talking helped—it kept both of us distracted. I could focus on something other than the rising pain, which suggested the strength of the mythborn antidote was fading, and Riagán wouldn't notice I could hardly keep from shivering.

Until I jerked in his arms, and a moan sneaked out through my clenched teeth.

"Stay with me, Kaja!" he called out.

I didn't.

CHAPTER SEVENTEEN

Either the Afflicted had more coherent thoughts than we'd been led to believe, or I wasn't one when I woke up. My eyes snapped open at the first flash of consciousness, and I stared at a familiar, warded ceiling of my den. My body ached and my arm was twisted in an uncomfortable way, but other than that I felt quite alive… and still myself.

I pushed the blankets to the side, unable to understand why I was on the floor instead of lying in my bed, but when I tried to lift myself up, my arm held me in place.

"Don't move!" a voice called out from downstairs. Riagán.

Of course, instead of listening, I tugged on my arm once more, and only then realized it was bound to the ladder leading downstairs, and my hand, immobilized by one of my scarves, was reaching past the wards. Riagán's fingers skimmed across my skin, and he climbed up.

"I'm sorry, I went down to make some food." He reached to the side, and the clanking of tableware reached my ears. "Here, drink this."

He pressed a vial to my mouth and poured its contents in as quickly as I could swallow. The familiar taste of the mythborn drug teased my tongue.

"Isn't it supposed to be taken in drops?" I teased.

He looked away. Enough of a tell how bad my state must have been.

"So, how much do I have?" I asked. We might as well get it out of the way.

"Lorcan says days. Maybe a week. When I brought you here, your wards all lit up and you seemed a bit better."

Days. Not exactly what I'd consider a luxury, but at least it gave me time to talk to Albert and a few other friends.

"The wards pull from chaotic magic. They help to keep me stable," I replied.

Days. This word kept coming back to me. At most, I had a week left. Was this how patients in the final stage of a terminal disease felt?

"They might have saved you," Riagán said. "I think you'd start turning if they didn't activate. Do you want more of the drug?"

I shook my head. "I feel... fine for now." I glanced to my side, at two large stashes of vials, empty and full. I wasn't ready to ask how often I would have to drink them. It didn't matter if I had so little time left, but it seemed the Court had been grateful enough for my finding Emma to provide me with enough of the drug for the very short rest of my life. "Any chance you could unbind my hand?"

He sent me an apologetic smile. "I needed to make sure I'd still be able to get up here when you were unconscious." He untied the bind and put my scarf away.

I lifted from the floor with caution, but the wounds didn't cause as much pain as I'd expected.

"We get the best salves, and Cathal decided you could

benefit from them," Riagán explained, as if reading my mind. "Though he said that if you ever try to take an Afflicted on your own again, he'll finish you off himself."

As if there would be any "again." I snorted in appreciation of the joke, then made my way to the worktable and picked up a crafting knife.

Riagán narrowed his eyes. "I don't think you should be working with magic."

"I won't." I knelt by the wards surrounding the entry to my den and waved him over. "Carve your name, here." I pointed at the spot. "I'll connect it to the rest of the ward, and you'll be able to enter and leave freely."

He didn't say anything else and took the knife. I admired the precision of his symbols that put my work to shame, and once he was done, I pricked my finger with the blade and smeared blood over his name, drawing lines toward other symbols. The intricate ward lit up for a blink.

"There, done." I rose from my knees. "So, what about that food you mentioned?"

"It's a work in progress. Humanborn kitchens are complicated." His eyes were still on the ward. "This is... an untraditional approach to wards."

I grinned. "I had to figure it out myself, from the scraps of knowledge I found. Let's see what mess you've made in my kitchen." I let him help me down the ladder.

I somewhat expected broken appliances, but either Riagán had exaggerated his unfamiliarity with human kitchens, or he had only started when I woke up. Freshly baked bread teased my nostrils, and I didn't even ask whether he'd gotten it from the mythborn bakery at the corner.

"How long have I been out?" I fished out cheese and a bit of meat from the fridge, then took out my stash of flavored tea I'd scavenged years ago from a ruined shop. No point in saving good food for later.

"The whole night and most of the morning." He filled the kettle and only flipped it on after a careful inspection of the charm attached to it. "Lorcan dropped off the medicine and said Eithne was furious about what happened." He gave me an inquisitive stare. "Why did you go there on your own? Why didn't you wait?"

I sighed. "I was looking for a missing humanborn journalist. I had no idea she was an Afflicted and the Snake's agent. I checked the house, found the explosives, and wanted to get to the Court, but that was exactly when she came back. The rest you know." A thought sparked in my head. "How did you find me, anyway?" I never got a chance to use the flare, and though my curses going off might have drawn attention, he must have already been around.

Riagán gave me another apologetic smile and took my silver brooch out of his pocket. The very one I gave him after the explosion at the Court. "I asked Connor to play with it and see if he could make a locating charm out of it." He glanced down at it. "When we came back from the assignment and I realized you were deep in the North Side instead of home, I got... worried."

I stared at him, speechless at first, then shook my head. "I got what I deserved for trusting you." I should have expected that his offers of settling my debts were never what he'd made me believe they were. Getting the keys to my apartment had most likely served some ulterior motives too, and on top of that, I had just added his name to my wards. But removing it would require too much effort, and in the end, I wouldn't be around for long enough to worry about it.

"It's one of those things you weren't supposed to know." His voice offered something resembling remorse.

I prepared sandwiches and brewed the tea. Throwing a tantrum about it now, when he had saved my life, seemed like a waste of time. And time had become as much of a luxury commodity as grapes.

"I guess I'm also not supposed to know why?" I didn't look at him when I asked the question. "Why the Court is so interested in me that they made you spy on me? Why give me the drug to keep the affliction away? Why save my life?"

Riagán shrugged. "Eithne appreciates your work."

"If there was a reward for the most evasive answer, you'd win a grand prize." Beating the current trophy holder—myself. But I wasn't about to give him ammunition, especially given if he hadn't saved my life, I'd kick him out this very moment. "I don't feel like playing your games. Nor the Court's, for that matter."

"It's not a game," he replied, his voice solemn and serious. "Eithne appreciates your work, and she wouldn't have made you an offer if she didn't see value in you. Even with what happened during the war, you were able to work with us." He looked me in the eye with a sincerity I didn't expect. "And the charm was my idea. With your line of work you're rarely home, and if the Scáthanna needed you, we had to have a way to find you quickly. If Eithne knew about it, I'd most likely be suffering some sort of humiliating punishment. Like a street patrol in Luimneach... Limerick," he corrected himself, to use the English name of the town.

"Eithne doesn't know?" I didn't want to believe he'd kept secrets from her, but then I remembered the warning glances she threw him once.

"I was ordered to stay away from you." He grinned. "And for all Lady Eithne knows, I did until last night. She wasn't happy with Cathal's decision to send me with you."

I digested the new information. It made no sense. "Ordered to stay away?"

Riagán shook his head. "I'm sorry, Kaja. I was told I should stay here only until you wake up, give you the rest of the medicine, and extend Lady Eithne's invitation... There's still time for the ritual." He paused and offered a teasing grin. "So how about that: I promise to tell you next week."

I opened my mouth, then closed it when the words sank in. My anger evaporated at the true meaning of his message. "Do you really think I could survive it?"

He offered a shrug. "You're as good as dead already, so what difference does it make if the ritual fails?" Strange pain and bitterness rang in his voice. His face shifted, but the smile that stretched it seemed forced. "I should leave you to your matters." He offered a bow.

"Thank you," I said with sincerity. "For trying to save my life."

His smile came again, and it had a genuine feel to it with that hint of sarcasm Riagán always seemed to have at the ready. "This time you're not going to get out of your debt easily," he promised.

I laughed at his playful tone, so familiar by now, and for a moment I forgot about my wounds, the affliction, and the decision I had to make. And that I'd most likely die before I ever had a chance to repay that debt.

Riagán left, but before the door closed behind him, he threw me one last glance, his face serious again. I stood puzzled both with his sudden departure, and his strange, pained expression I couldn't quite place.

THIS TIME I didn't rush to Trinity College. Instead, I took a long stroll along the Quays, by the river, and used it to sort through both my emotions and things to do. I was about to die, and I wasn't ready, but hardly anyone would be. Yet I needed to focus on what had to be done, not on feeling sorry for myself. I'd known this was bound to happen.

I didn't need to contact my family. After the war, when I learned what my affliction really meant, I made Albert lie for me. When he was sending a death notification to my parents, I asked him to add my name to my sister's. I would be dead soon enough, so there was no point in their going through the same suffering twice: first with Ela, then with me. Albert didn't approve but sent the letter, and that was all I cared about.

There was still the matter of my apartment, but I could ask Riagán to take care of it, since he already had the keys and I'd weaved his name into the wards. I wanted to give some of my amulets to Albert, or donate them to Trinity, but I could deal with it another day. Especially since I still had to sort through some junk... I made a mental note to take care of it in the evening, as I didn't trust Riagán to bother with my request to share the den's contents with the Trinitians. If he even went back to my place after I was gone.

As I took a turn south, and away from the river, memories of my arrival to Ireland, back then a normal European country, swarmed me—among them, the image of O'Connell Bridge, the one I'd just left behind but so different: filled with crowd like a human anthill, and English language everywhere, sometimes accompanied by accents so unfamiliar it was difficult to make the words out. More memories flocked into my mind, and I chased them all away, because if I let any of them linger, they'd bring back the pain of losing

Ela and the atrocities of war. I didn't need or want to dwell on that.

The Trinity's gray walls in the distance brought me back to reality, but I still almost bumped onto a woman taking a turn with the speed of a greyhound. She hardly noticed me, muttering some generic apologies as she rushed away toward the river. I stood dumbfounded when my brain caught up with the event, offering recognition, but the woman—Jemma—didn't even look back. She didn't seem upset, just in a hurry, so I could hope that it wasn't anything to do with Albert.

I smiled at a sudden thought—since she was going somewhere, at least I wouldn't have to deal with scenes of jealousy if she walked in on Albert and me again.

My stroll ended at the college's entrance, and I hesitated. If I could find any valid excuse to turn away, I would, but I owed Albert an explanation, and without the luxury of having more time, it had to happen as soon as possible. The guards eyed me as I stopped before the gate. I searched for a familiar face among them, but no veteran I knew was on duty.

"Can we help you, ma'am?" one of them asked, his politeness awkwardly covering concern.

"My name is Kaja Modrzewska," I said. "I need to speak with Orla or the commander."

He gestured for me to get closer, and his companion reached for the curse detector.

I shook my head. I'd brought several vials of the drug with me, but I couldn't risk their device triggering the change. "No magic. Please tell Orla that Kaja is waiting here. She knows I'm not a threat."

They exchanged concerned glares, but one of them tore away from the group and rushed into the courtyard.

I stepped to the side and leaned against the metal fence. Humanborn passersby threw me curious glances, and I did my best to offer smiles in response. I'd made the mistake of looking into the mirror before I left home and had no illusions about how I looked: a junkie in the last stage of addiction who had been sleep-deprived for weeks. At least whatever Riagán and the other mythborn did had stopped my wounds' bleeding, so I didn't scare people away with red stains on my clothes.

"Step aside—take all the magic items with you," Orla said from the gate. "You can come in, Kaja," she called out.

She kept her distance, and I nodded with appreciation. She carried quite a few amulets on her, and her bow was heavily charmed. I didn't think they would trigger the change, since, unlike the curse detector, they were dormant until she loosed an arrow—but nevertheless, it was thoughtful of her.

She took in my miserable state without a word of a sarcastic comment. "We've heard what happened," she said before I opened my mouth. "There's a room ready, the first one on the left through this door." She pointed at the nearby entrance. "I'll get Albert."

Left alone, I headed for the door, and as soon as I crossed it, pain choked my throat. I didn't even have to glance at the marks of magic-nullifying wards to know they were there. Uncomfortable to cross but keeping anything within their reach stable. In the past, Trinitians had used such spaces for veterans suffering through the final stages of affliction, and I couldn't help wondering whether a vial of fast-acting poison, the last courtesy for the ones who'd risked their lives in the war, would be waiting there for me.

I entered the room, nauseated from crossing the ward. The table in the middle was empty. Several chairs stood around it, and I picked the one facing the door. Anxious as I was, I still preferred to see Albert's face when he came in.

I didn't wait long, and then he stood at the entrance, his face twisted in torment.

"We knew this day would come," I offered in a gentle voice. "We just pretended we didn't remember."

He sat down, his eyes never leaving my face. "Knowing doesn't make it easier."

"No, it doesn't."

Silence fell, and I stared at my hands. Watching Albert's face brought unexpected pain and made my acceptance of the inevitable more difficult.

"Lady Eithne visited us in the morning," he said. "She told me that you found... Emma. And what she had become."

"Did she tell you anything else?"

He hesitated, then nodded. "She told me what you've been doing lately, and why. And that your search was successful."

I exhaled. Small blessing—Eithne had finally seen some reason and included Albert in the secret. Which, judging by his careful choice of words and avoidance of any details, was still a secret for the rest of Trinitians.

"We both agreed that it would be best to keep the story simple," he continued. "All the public will know is that the Court found the anti-Eireland extremists and dealt with them. They'll also compensate Emma's family for an unfortunate incident in the Botanical Gardens."

Right, an unfortunate accident... That journalist had probably tried to sneak in there and paid dearly. And with her, as it turned out, we all did. But the mythborn covering it up and offering compensation would ease any tensions.

Otherwise some hothead could think of revenge and get the spiral of retaliation going.

"At least that's sorted." I looked at him. "I'm sorry I didn't tell you earlier."

He waved it off, as if my past evasions didn't matter anymore. I hoped it was so, and that he understood, but I didn't feel like pressing.

"So, what now?" he asked. "Will you stay with us?" He gestured around. "We could make the room more comfortable, and—"

My head shake cut him off, and I held up my hand before the bitter comment I sensed coming made it off his lips. It wasn't about my stubbornness anymore. "There might be a way... to help me." I chose my words with caution. To give him hope when he might already be coming to terms with losing a friend felt almost cruel.

He inspected me as if searching for deception. "But there's a catch, isn't there?" he asked.

"There always is." I couldn't help but smile at his question. We'd both gone through too much to believe in miracles. "It's Eithne's offer. I still might die, and if it succeeds..." I didn't finish. I didn't have to.

A grimace twisted his face. "She'd have you dancing on her strings." His stare pinned me. "But you'll do it, won't you?" His tone made it clear that only one answer was acceptable.

Surprised, I gave a reluctant nod. I'd expected him to argue, but maybe with my otherwise inevitable death, he was ready to agree to any means that could bring me salvation. "I saw Emma up close. I don't want to end up like her," I replied. "If their ritual goes wrong, at least they'll ensure I die before I can do any harm."

He cringed at my last remark, but then he offered a

smile. A meager one, but nonetheless the first one since he had entered. "You could take over the contacts with us from Eithne. You'd have a reason to visit us, and I'd rather deal with you than with her."

"Even when I'd be throwing mythborn demands at you or saying things you don't like?" I teased. Anything to keep him in a good mood and not make him ask what my chances were.

"You've been saying things I don't like since we met," he said, not without sarcasm. "If you keep doing the same with the mythborn, they will kick you out of the Court soon enough."

I smirked, then rose from the chair. "I hope I'll see you soon." I didn't intend to explore the other option.

"Kaja."

Albert stood up, and before I could move away, he hugged me tight. We stood motionless, and I remembered how much support his touch provided. Even if we'd stopped being lovers, even if we argued... the deeper feeling of friendship that formed during the war had remained the same. I stayed in his embrace for a little longer, enjoying the feeling of safety, then I peeled away and headed for the door.

Words weren't necessary.

CHAPTER EIGHTEEN

The gray walls of the Collins Barracks looked more disheartening than usual, and even the memories of the beauty the mythborn had brought with them when they made that place their home couldn't brighten my thoughts. On a winter day like this, with the sky almost matching the walls' hue and clouds hanging so low that they seemed to scratch the rooftops, I couldn't call the building by its current name. This wasn't the Court—these were the Collins Barracks, Dún Uí Choileáin, with its rich history.

I let myself get lost in memories, since for the last two days I'd been handling all the urgent matters in case I didn't survive the ritual. I still had more to do, but it felt like I was living on borrowed time and testing my luck, so instead of putting off the visit to the Court for one more day and dealing with less important things, I'd made the trip.

"Welcome, Kaja." One of the guards by the post recognized me. "I'll let Cathal know you've arrived."

Of course, the amount of time I'd spent around the

Scáthanna made him assume I was to set out with them again.

"Actually... I wish to speak with Lady Eithne."

Confusion flashed on his face, but then he nodded. "I'll have someone let her know. Meanwhile, you can wait inside." He indicated a door in the archway. Even from this distance I sensed the powerful wards on it, but they weren't the magic-repelling ones.

"I'd rather wait outside, if you don't mind."

His companions tensed at my words. I should have expected such a reaction from a mythborn likely not used to humanborn who didn't follow his orders veiled as requests. Though on the other hand, I'd seen quite a few Trinitians with similar attitude, Captain Boyle being a shining example. My instincts urged me to take a step or ten back, but if they thought I had something to hide, it wouldn't help. I should have said I was going to the Scáthanna instead, and asked *them* to escort me to Eithne.

"Came to see the lady, humanborn?" a familiar voice asked.

Sadb, the ethereal beauty and a deadly killing machine, stood at the courtyard. Her hand rested at the hilt of her sword, but otherwise she seemed relaxed.

"Yes." I chose a simple reply that wouldn't antagonize her or give her any openings. The memory of the angered glare she gave me that night when Laoise and I fought the Afflicted, and the Scáthanna learned about the curse I'd crafted, was still fresh in my memory. I didn't need to give her excuses to kill me when I was less than a step away from becoming the Afflicted.

She smirked. "Let's go, then." She shot one glance at the guards, and none of them spoke even a word of protest. It seemed that Sadb intimidated her fellow mythborn as much as she intimidated me.

I crossed the archway and expected Sadb to lead the way, but instead she waited until I caught up with her. I couldn't decide whether it was a courtesy or if she preferred to keep an eye at me instead of having me behind her back. We walked through the courtyard arm in arm.

"Took you a while to come here. Fear of dying finally got the better of you?" she mocked me as soon as we got out the guards' earshot.

"Being alive is definitely more appealing to me. But yes, I'm scared... of becoming a Léanmhar." I didn't need to compete over who was the bigger badass, because the winner couldn't be more obvious. Besides, fear was a part of every human, every humanborn, and I wasn't about to deny it. "Are you regretting that Cathal didn't order me killed the other night?"

She arched an eyebrow and gave me a rather cold stare. "That's 'ceannasaí' to you."

No way—she wasn't getting away so easily. "Regretting that your *ceannasaí* didn't order me killed the other night?"

My rephrased question brought a smile to her face, and for a moment, she looked almost friendly. "A bit. But if you survive, I'll have plenty of time to make *you* regret he didn't give that order."

I arched an eyebrow—not at her words, but at the lack of a threat in her voice. As if she was casually talking about us having lunch together, and not about making me miserable for possibly the rest of my life.

I expected more baiting and teasing, but she walked in silence with quite a smug expression on her face, as if she were enjoying a secret I wasn't allowed to know. I stared at the cobblestones under my feet and sank into my own thoughts. But I didn't linger on my future prospects. No matter what waited for me at the end of the ritual, if I was still alive, I'd deal with it one way or another. I wouldn't give up a chance to live at some vague suggestions that my life would suck afterward.

When we got to the building's entrance and the Court's magic reached me, I hesitated and earned a sarcastic glance from her.

"It's not going to kill you. It's not going to trigger your turning, either," she said.

It might be a trap. She might be lying to initiate the final stage of my affliction and thus have a reason to kill me. But she was one of the Scáthanna, and so far they'd offered no deception. I had no doubts that if Cathal gave an order, she'd draw my blood with no hesitation or remorse. Without it, though, Sadb wouldn't cross the line... at least, I hoped she wouldn't.

I stepped into the door, and the Court's magic enveloped me in a subtle cocoon. Sadb gave me something that I could only interpret as an approving smile, as if I'd done better than she expected.

"The whole Court is protected like that, and no human-born can turn within its walls," she said as we walked through the corridors. "If Cathal was certain you were stable enough, we'd have brought you here." She snorted. "But we all expected you wouldn't survive even half the way."

I gave a nod. I wasn't surprised no one had believed I'd live through that evening, since back then I didn't see it happening either. I couldn't blame them for wanting to protect their home. Even if I couldn't become the Afflicted within the Court's walls, it would be enough to turn within its vicinity to bring trouble to the mythborn home's doorstep. The Scáthanna seemed adept at killing changed humanborn, and they had supposedly unbreakable binds, but the risk was always there.

We stopped by Eithne's office, and Sadb knocked. "Lady Eithne, the humanborn Kaja is here," she called out.

"Let her in." Eithne's voice came muffled by the door.

Sadb pointed at the door and then walked away. "See you around," she said over her shoulder. "Maybe."

I offered a shallow bow to her, just enough of a bend to be considered courteous, and entered Eithne's office.

The lady sat at her desk, her body wrapped in a silk dress of elaborate making, her hair flowing with almost unnatural perfection. But it was her eyes that, as always, caught my attention: two pools of a piercing green glare.

"I was wondering whether you'd come." Her voice was calm and almost plain. "I'm not happy how things unfolded, but I can't deny you did well. Without you, we would've been chasing the Snake's agent for weeks, if not longer."

"It was by pure chance." I didn't want to take credit for what had been luck—very bad luck, to be precise. "If I knew what I was getting into, I'd have waited for the Scáthanna to return from their assignment," I admitted.

She let out a short laugh, but then became serious. "So, why did you come today, Kaja? What do you expect? I can reward you for your services, but I believe that in current circumstances it would be an empty gesture."

"I want to take a chance with the ritual," I replied. "If you're still willing to offer it to me."

She inspected me in silence, and fear clutched my throat. She held my life in her hands, because if she decided to refuse, and even I saw reasons to do so, I had no other hope.

"That I know," she said. "I'm wondering why. Is this only

fear of death or something more? I made this offer weeks ago, yet you come now, in the very last moment."

"Your offer, no matter how generous, comes with strings attached. The time I've spent working with the Scáthanna helped me to accept them," I said. "But I'd be lying if I said I didn't want to live or that I didn't fear turning into a Léan-mhar." If I ever had a chance, I'd have to ask Riagán or maybe some other mythborn what their fixation with fear was. For humanborn it always seemed obvious that premature death was not welcomed, and we always lived with its shadow hanging over us. The trick wasn't to avoid being afraid but to overcome it.

"I wouldn't have made an offer if I didn't think you'd be able to shoulder the consequences of the ritual, but your taking time to consider them yourself makes me believe that you think so too." Eithne shifted in her seat, and a smile came on her face. "I've received a report from Cathal regarding your time with the Scáthanna. He has concerns about your being distrustful and unwilling to share secrets at times, but otherwise his opinion was good."

My eyes widened when everything came together in my head. "You set this up, didn't you?"

Her overbearing and almost suspicious friendliness in the last weeks made sense now, and other things fell into place too. First, she'd made me investigate the bombings, then she asked me for help with the Snake agents and forced me to work with the mythborn I was most likely going to hate. Just like when Cathal teased me to see how much I could take, she'd been checking if I'd be able to come to terms with what would come after the ritual. I'd never thought she would make me part of the Court itself, with only the powerful and proud mythborn as its members, but I'd become associated with them in so many ways that it wouldn't really matter in outsiders' eyes.

She nodded. "The ritual is our gift to the humanborn, but we prefer to bestow it upon those who understand the need for our coexistence in this world." She rose from her chair. "The Court keeps an eye out for those humanborn who suffer from the affliction, and we weigh each decision separately. You were able to overcome your adversity toward mythborn, your distrust of me, and the wartime experiences, which means my offer is still open for you." Eithne walked to the door and indicated for me to follow. "If you're ready, let's not waste time."

She led me through corridors and down stairways, until we reached an underground level I never knew existed. Or maybe it didn't until the mythborn took the place over.

Stone and crystals had replaced the wood and tapestries of the floors above the ground, but the architecture and embellishments remained as stunning as everywhere else in the Court. And magic felt more intense, as if it emanated from the luminous crystals.

"This where I have to leave you." Eithne stopped by the doorway carved in green marble, like the marble I'd seen in Connemara years before the war. "This corridor will lead you to a chamber, where you'll remove your clothes and all your other belongings. A mythborn will come. She'll prepare you and show you the way to the ritual waters. All you have to do is walk through the water and reach the other door. It'll be done by then."

I offered a half-smile. She made it sound easy and simple, but I suspected it was nothing like that.

"Should you survive, you'll enter a mirror chamber," Eithne continued. "Spend as much time as you need there and get used to the new you. I'll meet you there." She pointed at the doorway, making it clear she wouldn't answer any of my questions.

"*Go raibh maith agat.*" My accent must have hurt the mythborn's ears, but at that moment, saying "thank you" in English didn't feel right.

She offered a smile. "Good luck, Kaja."

And then I was alone, with her footsteps fading as she walked away. I took a deep breath and entered the corridor.

THE CORRIDOR SEEMED CARVED in a huge block of crystal, and no one had bothered to polish its edges, which gave the walls an eerie, distorted look. The light seeped through the semi-translucent matter, so it wasn't dark, but the colors shifting and pulsating like the magic I sensed caused shadows to form in the less illuminated nooks.

Then, after a turn, it unexpectedly opened into a small chamber as empty as the corridor. No other doorway led out of it. I walked into the middle and looked around, but no one came, so I took my clothes and accessories off, pilling them on the crystal ground. The fear of triggering the change accompanied me while I removed each of the amulets, but then I remembered Sadb's words. I couldn't become the Afflicted within the Court's walls.

As soon as I stood naked, shivering in the air that turned out chillier than I'd thought, a mythborn female approached me. I could swear she walked out of the solid wall, but it must have been the crystal and the lights playing tricks on my eyes.

The mythborn, whose age I couldn't nail, wore a dress that looked like it was weaved from spiderwebs and embellished with dewdrops. Her milk-white eyes didn't focus on mine, and I couldn't help wondering how much she could see. The texture of her skin resembled the crystals, though when her fingers reached for me, her touch felt soft on my arm. She walked around me, dipping fingers in a marble bowl she held, and left multiple marks on my skin—face, chest, limbs.

At first, it seemed random, but the closer I looked at the irregular shapes, the more symbols I recognized, and I understood the purpose of her actions: she was making me into a living ward! In the silence of the chamber I didn't dare to ask whether those markings would stay with me forever like tattoos.

Whenever I moved, her firm touch made it clear I was supposed to stand still. Only when she was done, or I thought she was, did she face me, with her short white hair that resembled spikes and her bleak eyes looking past my face, into nothingness. I found it hard to believe she was blind, especially when she ran her finger across my collarbone in a single smooth move, and her nail broke my skin. She drew hardly any blood, but even those drops were enough to activate the ward she had put on me.

The chaotic magic within me stirred, and my stomach turned, but the symbols on my body held it in check. I fought the retching, but the mythborn pushed my head down in a telling gesture, so I stopped resisting and threw up as soon as she stepped out of the way. My legs were trembling, and I focused on keeping myself upright.

The mythborn held out the container and indicated my lips, but when I drank, the trembling didn't cease, and instead my stomach grumbled in protest. I balanced, bent over, ready to throw up again, but the female by my side pushed the container to my lips. It seemed I wasn't allowed to throw up until I drank the rest, so I did, and every sip unsettled my insides even more.

Then the mythborn took away the container and pointed at the wall. It shimmered and flowed, as if the crystal had turned into water. A nudge encouraged me to get going, so I took several steps on shaking legs. With the weakness overwhelming me and my stomach twisting, I wondered whether I'd even make it to the next chamber.

I stepped through the curtain of magic mist that concealed the exit, and the power within it prickled my skin, stirring the chaos trapped within my body. The Court's protection or not, if I didn't have the ward on me, I'd likely be turning into the Afflicted that very moment, but I kept walking, one wobbly step after another, following the path carved in crystal.

To my relief, the corridor soon opened into a circular chamber, maybe thirty steps in diameter, and I stopped at the edge of what looked like stone steps leading into a pool. Its water was milky white, as if frothed, and in some places it rose above the edge, resembling puffs of mist or steam. As my legs were betraying me, I gave up the thought of trying to catch my breath. If I waited any longer, I wouldn't find the strength to walk into the pool.

I took the first step in, and only the overwhelming shock prevented me from shrieking when the pain pierced me. The pool wasn't full of water... I'd walked into pure magic! Now Eithne's words made sense, and the other end of the chamber seemed much farther away than a moment ago.

I kept walking, and with each step a moan escaped through my clenched teeth. My stomach still rebelled and the magic within me was like a squall, twisting my guts and thrashing against the cage of the ward on me. The rising ribbons of mist teased my eyes and blinded me, so I could only hope I was moving in the right direction.

Halfway through the pool, my legs gave up, and I collapsed. The not-water hit me in the face, and before I could resist, my stomach returned all the liquid the mythborn had made me drink in the other chamber. But even with my head below the surface I could still breathe, so I continued on all fours while magic thrashed at me from the outside and from the inside.

Then, when I couldn't stay on my knees anymore, I crawled, blind and helpless, moaning with pain, because I didn't have enough strength to scream. If anyone was there with me, I'd beg them to show mercy and finish me. How long would my suffering last?

My fingers scratched against the wall, which meant I'd lost my direction, so I kept crawling alongside it, but if I knew staying motionless would bring relief, even in death, I'd have lain at the bottom of that cursed pool.

I crawled with my fingers like soft claws grabbing the crystal beneath me. I crawled because I couldn't give up, even when I felt the affliction had started claiming me and my body began to change.

I crawled.

And then, quite unexpectedly, all the pain ended. That was the last thing I remembered before fading off.

CHAPTER NINETEEN

When I came to, a mythborn female was looking at me. She was lying naked on the floor not too far away from me, and her face seemed strangely familiar. I must have seen her somewhere around the Court, though I couldn't quite place her triangular face and brick-red hair that reminded me of the buildings in Dublin.

I opened my mouth, ready to ask questions, because I had no idea where we were or why we were here, but she opened hers at the same time, and I paused. I figured she knew better than me what was going on. She didn't speak, and instead inspected me with narrowed eyes.

Then I finally placed her face within my memories. If the hair were brown, and the face a bit rounder, it could be me. I stared at myself-not-myself in the mirror. All the walls in the chamber were reflective, and no matter which way I looked, I saw myself... but only one at a time, as if some magic prevented the images from multiplying to the other mirrors.

I scrambled to sit up, unsure of my body—but at least the pain was gone—and inspected my reflection close up.

Now that I knew I was staring at myself, I recognized my own features, but magic had left none of them unchanged. My own eyes inspected me with the intensity of a mythborn glare, their color deeper and uneven, as if they reflected the clouds over Dublin, and my skin... Getting tanned in Eireland was quite a challenge, so I'd always had been pale, but now it seemed my skin became somewhat translucent. Not that I could see anything underneath it, but when I looked at the right angle, there was a layer of a water-like surface along my arm. I dragged my finger along it, and it felt cold to the touch first, then like my own skin.

I caught the sound of footsteps behind me, and I spun on the floor to meet whoever entered, even though the mirrors claimed I was alone in the chamber. More sounds reached my ears: some conversations in Irish and the clanking of armor, but I didn't see their source. I'd survived the mythborn ritual only to go insane and start hearing voices.

Then a knocking came, and a soft voice. "Kaja?" Eithne —I was sure of it. "May I enter?"

"Please." My own voice had changed too, but I should have expected that, since it seemed that the magic had affected my bone structure. Human skulls were resonating boxes, so if the ritual had altered my face, my voice would sound different without any magic involved.

That thought, both amusing and absurd, helped me relax, and when Eithne entered through the door behind one of the mirrors, I offered a meager smile.

I was sitting on the ground, cross-legged and naked, and she inspected me without a word. My sarcasm kicked in, a clear sign that, regardless of my looks, I was still myself, and I itched to ask her whether I should stand up so she could examine me more thoroughly.

"I can see that glimmer in your eyes." Eithne smiled with satisfaction. "The ritual hasn't changed you much."

I arched my eyebrow, because my face, hair, and the rest of my body had changed plenty. I just got to keep my personality, probably along with all my nightmares and other problems. Not that I believed she expected me to become noble and composed like the mythborn were. Or to start speaking perfect Irish.

She laid a piece of cloth on the floor, a long piece of green, silk-like fabric that resembled something between a nightgown and a bathrobe, and then sat beside me. First time I'd seen her get down on the floor like this. She seemed almost casual and unladylike. "Don't worry—you'll get your belongings back. I'd have brought them with me if I knew you'd be able to fit in..."

Her voice faded, and she didn't have to finish. I might have changed more, and if my old clothing didn't fit, it would only add to the trauma of adjusting to my new body.

Laughter sounded right by my shoulder, and I snapped my head around, but of course no one was there.

Eithne's eyes narrowed as if she was figuring out what was going on, but she didn't ask the question I expected. Not that she had to—her posture made it clear I couldn't avoid an explanation.

"I hear... sounds and voices." If there was anyone who'd believe I wasn't going crazy, it would be Eithne. "Steps, laughter, sometimes words in Irish."

She didn't seem surprised or concerned. "It may pass or it may stay with you."

That wasn't comforting at all, but I didn't reply. I'd known the ritual would change me in unexpected ways, and I could learn to live with voices around me as long as they didn't try to interact with me or whisper disturbing things in my ear. At least I looked like a... well, not a human being anymore, but not like a monster either. A memory of how Emma had ended up made me shudder, and then relief washed over me. No matter what the future would bring, I was still mostly myself.

"So, what happens now?" I asked.

"You take your time here. Get dressed. Learn once more how to move and walk." She gave me the smile of a concerned mother. "I'll send a word to Trinity, so Albert doesn't worry himself into something foolish, and in the evening I'll introduce you to the Court. I'd like you to stay with us for at least several days. We have quarters ready for you."

Stay with them? Quarters? I expected I'd be tied to the Court, but it seemed that Eithne intended to make the bond more serious than I'd thought. "No lessons in your language?" I asked to cover my sudden concerns.

"Only if you want to. Most of us use English and Irish anyway, and I'd rather see you spending time with Connor." A smile came to her face. "Cathal mentioned you've been dabbling in our magic and could teach our craftsmen a thing or two." She must have caught my glare, because she added, "He didn't impart any secret of yours, if you're worried. It seemed quite obvious after you gifted me with that amulet of yours. It wasn't of mythborn make."

I snorted. "I should have known it wouldn't escape your attention."

"Your skill is remarkable for someone without a tutor, but you could learn much more from Connor and others, if you desire to."

I gave it some thought. The first meeting with the myth-born whom I had saved was awkward enough, but if we were to work together and share knowledge on charms and curses, it could improve, and I needed friends at the Court.

"I'd be honored if he finds me worthy of his time," I replied.

Eithne rose from the floor. "I'll arrange everything."

She left, and I reached for the robe. Even if I was alone, I didn't feel the need to stare at my naked body. Especially if Eithne was right, and I had to relearn all the simple movements. Dressing up didn't turn out to be a challenge, but I couldn't be so optimistic about things that required balance, and in a way I felt grateful to have been left alone in the room. At least no one would witness my humiliation if I tripped over my own legs.

"Why am I not surprised you're here?" Eithne asked, and I almost jumped up.

But she wasn't in the chamber, and I didn't think she had said that to me.

"I thought I'd check on Kaja before we set out, my lady," Riagán replied.

My eyes widened. I wasn't hearing things! I heard *real* mythborn walking and talking outside! As if my hearing reached farther, even though Eithne's and my own voices had come at a normal volume, so I hadn't become super-sensitive. I simply heard more, farther. And since the conversation I was accidentally catching seemed interesting, I focused on it. Testing my new body's limits could wait a little longer.

"You could have at least lied that Cathal had sent you." I caught displeasure in her voice.

"I could've. But I don't think it matters anymore, does it, my lady?"

Silence followed, though I was almost sure I caught Eithne sigh. There was something eerie about sitting on a floor in a room with nothing but mirrors and eavesdropping on a mythborn conversation.

"So?" Riagán said. "Does she like it, my lady?"

"I'd think you'd ask whether *you* will like it." I got so caught up on the meaning of her words that I almost missed that they reeked of sarcasm.

"I know I will." His confidence surprised me. Did he mean the change I'd been through or something else? "Can I go in, my lady?"

"That's up to her." Fabrics shuffled. "I have matters I need to attend."

"Of course, my lady."

I caught the sound of footsteps, and then knocking echoed through the mirrors. "Kaja, may I enter?" Riagán asked.

"Come in," I called out as I ensured the robe's belt held the garment in place. No reason to send him away after he'd done so much to keep me alive. Besides, I hoped for some answers.

He stepped through a different mirror than Eithne had, making me wonder once again about the magic that protected the chamber. He scanned me quickly, as if he didn't want to make me uncomfortable by staring.

"Welcome back among the living," he offered with a smile as he approached and squatted down.

His fluid movement sparked my envy... But maybe now, changed and all, I'd be able to learn how to move like that too.

"I see Eithne lifted her ban," I teased. "Does it mean I get to ask some questions?"

I expected another game, but instead he nodded. "Did Lady Eithne tell you that the Court keeps an eye on some humanborn? The ones who might be offered the ritual."

"She mentioned it but didn't go into details." I hoped he'd get the hint.

"Ever since you saved Connor, the Court had been watching you." No shame nor discomfort rang in his voice, as if he hadn't just confessed that the mythborn had had me under surveillance. "Eithne wanted you in the Court, but after you left Trinity, you seemed quite adamant about being independent. She also worried that if you joined us for the wrong reasons, this would cause trouble in the future or you wouldn't stay..."

"Wrong reasons?"

He gave me a skittish glance. "We weren't... oblivious that you left Trinity after you and Albert split."

I burst out laughing. They might have been watching me, but they didn't know everything. "I left Trinity *before* Albert and I split. Half a year or so." I allowed myself another chuckle. My voice sounded softer now, more pleasant to the ear, and I enjoyed it. "But it doesn't explain how it would translate to my leaving the Court."

A smile danced on Riagán's lips. "Take a guess how."

He still squatted beside me, relaxed and casual, but his gaze had unusual intensity, and my gears started turning.

Always close, sometimes annoyingly so, but never truly crossing the line. Teasing, playing games, and nudging me out of my comfort zone, but at the same time ensuring I was safe. He'd kept from me those secrets that would reveal too much and wasn't above deceiving Eithne, who'd ordered him to stay away...

I stared at him while I put things together. Then the silence lingered as I considered the consequences of his words. Namely, my own feelings surfacing. He'd gotten me to where he likely wanted me to be: curious, fascinated, irked with him just enough to add spice to the mix. And—

what was the most important—he'd made me trust him. He'd saved my life multiple times, never asking for anything serious in return, and I had no doubt it was his insistence that made Cathal go through the trouble of keeping me alive instead of giving me a quick and merciful death when I was about to become the Afflicted.

"I should have waited." His tone was serious and somewhat apologetic. "There was no need to add to your current discomfort."

Riagán shifted, but before he got up, I grabbed his arm and held him in place. To my surprise, hope flashed in his eyes, only to be covered by playful sparks. If I was to make a bet, he'd revealed more than he ever had before, and if I wanted to keep my distance, I'd never see those emotions again, concealed forever under his mask of playfulness and confidence.

"Taking your revenge on me?" he teased.

I offered a smile. "You surely deserve it, but... I just don't want you to leave." I'd never bothered with playing games, and even if I looked like a mythborn now, I wasn't about to change my habits.

He leaned forward, and I recognized the hunter within. The hunter who'd found an opening. "Is there anything else you don't want me to do?"

With his face so close, the scent of pine and campfire smoke enveloped me, and I drew a deep breath. Last time I only got a glimpse of what it would be like to kiss him, and the addiction aside, it had been promising. "I could make a list."

He didn't move back. In a way, I'd missed his games and the attitude of someone who couldn't be defeated. In a world of too much death, it brought eerie hope and comfort. "And will you?" he asked.

At this point, with his body stretched toward mine, I wondered how he managed to keep his balance. Maybe one poke would send him onto his backside... But as amusing as it could have been, trying to do so would ruin the moment, and I didn't want it ruined. Still, I didn't resist the tease. "If you insist."

He reached for my arm and pulled me closer. Unprepared, I spun on the floor, and before my brain processed it, I had Riagán squatting behind my back and his face against mine. One day, I promised myself, we'd have that discussion about personal space. Not that I minded him invading mine anymore, but in a sudden outpouring of selfishness, I didn't want to see him doing it to others.

"You better hurry, then." I heard a promise in his whisper. He held me close, and the warmth of his body reached me through the thin silk I wore.

"It might not be the best time to kiss a mythborn," I said. Eithne would be coming back soon, and I was supposed to practice walking and other boring things.

"I'll get us the remedy if it turns out we need it." His fingers skimmed across my forearms impatiently.

The magic within me responded to his touch, but his words gave me pause. "We?"

When Riagán laughed, his breath brushed my cheek. "You've changed, Kaja. You might not be a mythborn, but now you share our magic, so I'll react the same way as you do. Though the side effects shouldn't be as intense as the last time." He let out a short laugh. "I was surprised that you made it all the way to that alchemist's shop."

I didn't even cringe at the realization he had followed me back then. After all, Riagán and the Court stalking me was old news, and he'd probably just wanted to make sure I was safe. Besides, I had a more interesting—and I admit, also appealing—twist to consider. Riagán getting addicted to my magic, *to me*, was unexpected but exciting. On the other hand, if Tadgh's theory on mythborn kisses was anywhere near truth, it made sense that they reacted to one another in a similar way humanborn reacted to them.

I shifted, and he released me from his grip, but I only moved enough to face him again.

"I guess it's as good a revenge as I can get." I lifted my head and looked in him the eyes.

Riagán took the clue. He pulled me closer, and I could say I got to experience my first full kiss with a mythborn. But then, that would be a lie.

All I remembered from it was that he tasted of summer fruits and magic.

CHAPTER TWENTY

T he sound from behind the mirror was more pounding than knocking, and I tore away from Riagán, startled like a teenager caught doing something she shouldn't be.

He snickered at that. "No one would enter without your permission," he said quietly.

The pounding repeated, and this time a voice came as well. "Riagán! Meeting at the lady's office!" Laoise called from outside. She didn't even ask whether he was with me, as if it was obvious. "Cathal said you better hurry!"

His face changed, with a shadow across it like a cloud on a summer's day. He stood up. "We have an assignment. If she's calling us in, something must have happened."

"Go." Of course, I didn't want him to go, but the mood of careless moments had waned anyway, and reality had caught up with us. He had a job to do, and I had to get used to the new me, so I could do my job too... whatever it was now.

"I'll see you when we're back." His eyes devoured my face, and something new sparked in them. The usual playfulness was still there, but accompanied by an intensity of emotions he hadn't revealed before. "Don't get in too much trouble until then."

I chuckled at that. I definitely had had enough trouble recently. I could do with a little bit of quiet. Besides, I didn't expect Eithne would let me out of the Court in the next few days, maybe even longer. I snuffed that thought before it showed on my face. Spoiling my last moments with Riagán by revealing my concerns about my future didn't feel right.

"Should I find someone to bring you the antidote on my way out?" He must have sensed, too, that our moment of carelessness was slipping away. "Or will you manage to bear the consequences of kissing a mythborn?"

I gave him a glare. We'd kissed long enough for the magic within us to settle, and even though I still liked the idea of doing it again, my mind wasn't obsessing over that thought, and my body didn't show withdrawal symptoms. He was right that after my transformation the reaction had turned out less intense. Come to think of it, Max had been right too: seeing things through seemed to have fewer unpleasant side effects.

Of course, I hadn't really seen it through—at least not yet, as my treacherous mind whispered—but an hour or so of kissing and caressing had done the trick well enough.

"I thought so." Riagán leaned over, and his lips brushed mine once more. "I won't be getting any either." Then he stretched and headed for one of the mirrors. Upon his touch, it parted, and he disappeared outside.

I allowed myself another moment of dreamy recollection, tasting the memory of his touch, and then looked at myself in the mirror again. My new face would take getting used to, but checking if I could move and find my balance was more important. My voice of reason suggested it should have been the first thing to do instead of playing with a mythborn's tongue, so I told it to shut up. Eithne wanted me to stick around, and I had no doubt I'd be stuck at the Court longer than those few days she'd mentioned, so I'd have plenty of time to practice how to walk.

But I still needed to be at least presentable when she came back.

I rose from the floor, my body light and flexible, which came as a relief. I'd liked the agility I had as a humanborn, and my speed while running, so I hoped I could get my new body to a similar level, if not better. Several cautious steps reassured me I wouldn't fall over my own legs, so I proceeded to jumping and spinning, indulging myself with an improvised dance. Magic within sang to the rhythm with which my muscles moved, harmonized and steady for the first time I could recall, without the tint of chaos that had bothered me like a splint in the skin and grown with each passing day. I heard a promise weaved into its steady flow: if I practiced, I'd surpass the abilities I had as a humanborn.

A smile stretched my new lips. I was alive, I wasn't a monster... and I was forever tied to the mythborn and the Court. With a screech of immaterial mental tires, my thoughts took a sharp turn again, crashing at full speed into reality. Not that I had doubts about the decision I'd made, the only one I could have made, but the prospect of being thrown into unknown waters, murky with the mythborn's politics and games I didn't understand, spoiled my mood.

At least I could count on Riagán's help, and maybe others from the Scáthanna would offer their advice. Eithne wanted me here, so she'd likely give me directions, and if I made friends with Connor, I wouldn't be in a bad situation.

Footsteps echoed in the corridor outside, and I caught scraps of a conversation, this time in English. I remembered my enhanced hearing. With it, I'd be able to learn more of what was going on in the Court, and it could keep me out of trouble. It also meant that, whether I liked it or not, I should get some lessons in Irish and the mythborn language, as many still used it. I didn't have to speak it, but understanding it would make a difference.

I stretched my arms and spun in place, with my balance close to perfect. I wanted to jump and run, to test my new limits. I'd worry about intrigues later, or find a way to get away from the Court as often as possible. After all, I'd managed to convince an overprotective Albert that my place was outside Trinity. Even if Eithne proved equally stubborn, I'd find a way.

The sounds of footsteps and knocking pulled me away from my pointless considerations.

"Kaja? May I come in?" I didn't recognize the female's voice, soft and warm. "Lady Eithne sent me to help you."

"Come in," I replied.

A young mythborn female stepped through the mirror. Her hair was an obsidian frame to her copper skin that shone gently like actual metal, and she wore the simple clothes of the Court's servants. Hesitation in her moves made me gesture her closer with a friendly smile.

"Lady Eithne apologizes she couldn't come," the mythborn said, "but urgent matters required her attention. My name is Dearbháil, and I'll be honored to help you prepare for the reception."

"It's nice to meet you, Dearbháil." I offered a curtsy. She seemed fragile and bashful, and so different from the Court mythborn I'd met so far. "Tell me what I need to do."

Her face relaxed a bit. Up close, I noticed a weblike pattern on her skin, but I tried not to stare. "If you're ready to leave the mirror chamber, I'll show you to your quarters."

I was more than ready. "Lead the way,"

A smile followed her words, her first one. "Do you think you'll be able to find your way out of here?"

A test? I wasn't sure, but I looked around in thought. The mirrors all looked the same, and since both Eithne and Riagán had entered through different ones, I needed another clue. I guess I cheated a little bit, since I listened to the footsteps and hushed conversations outside as I walked around, having my own reflection as a faithful companion. I stopped by the mirror where the sound was the strongest. The door had to be thinner than the walls.

"Impressive." Dearbháil joined me, and the mirror cracked open with the touch of her hand.

We walked into a corridor like many others in the Court, and the wooden door closed behind us. Dearbháil led the way while I glanced out at the courtyard. The gray sky outside suggested daytime, but didn't help me in figuring out how much time had passed. Had I been out for mere hours, or had I spent days crawling through the pool and unconscious?

"What day is it?" I asked.

At first, she gave me a confused glance, but then smiled with understanding. "Tuesday."

Suddenly, Eithne's remark of letting Albert know made sense. I'd lost four days, and in this time he'd probably contacted the Court multiple times. I didn't dare to ask whether the ritual was meant to take that long. When I went in, I'd expected it to be several hours at most, but I didn't care much. Without it, I'd be dead anyway, and however long it took, I'd come out alive and free of the magic affliction, so all was good. All *had to* be good.

We stopped by a door like many others in that corridor. Except that on the wall to the side, a small silver emblem hung: the Court's symbol, and my name both in English and in mythborn runes under it.

"All your items are already in here," Dearbháil said, "and I've brought several formal dresses that might be to your liking. I'll also help you with makeup and hair, if you wish me to."

I arched an eyebrow. I wasn't a dress kind of girl, and I'd prefer to put my own clothes on, but the reception the mythborn had mentioned earlier sounded like something quite formal, and my chosen outfit wouldn't cut it even if I had it cleaned and pressed.

"I'll gladly take your offer," I replied. At least she'd make sure I looked "proper" for the occasion. I opened the door and invited her in.

THE BROWN DRESS I chose from the ones Dearbháil had brought was modest and comfortable enough, but paired with an elaborate hairdo and makeup, which I'd fought to keep at a minimum, it made me feel out of place. Like a curious animal on display. Maybe aside from the fact that no one in the vast dining hall was actually looking at me.

I felt the mythborn's stares stabbing my back, but whenever I turned to confront them, their eyes focused elsewhere, and I grew tired of their games. I caught their whispers in Irish. I didn't get the words, but the tone of their voices, so full of sarcasm and mockery, told me enough. If I didn't need to wait for Eithne's arrival and her official introduction, I'd be out of the room in a heartbeat. Last time I'd felt so uncomfortable was before the war, at my acquaintance's Christmas party... but it hardly was a memory I wanted to dwell on.

"When you faced that giant, you seemed more relaxed than you are now," a familiar voice said behind me.

I turned and sent Connor a smile. He wore more formal clothes than what I'd seen him wear at the workshop, and like me, he seemed uncomfortable. I would bet the magical harness around his leg, openly hugging his thigh instead of being concealed under his pants, had a little to do with it.

"At least we both knew what the danger was back then," I replied. "Here... not so much."

His laughter disturbed the etiquette-imposed quietness, drawing mythborn eyes toward us. Their noble faces twisted in distaste, but Connor's stare remained defiant and some-what challenging. With every passing minute, I liked him more and more.

"They boast of their bloodlines and noble ancestry," he said when most heads turned away, "but they have nothing to show for it. They thrive on politics and intrigue, but this rarely affects the Court."

I arched my eyebrow. "How so?"

Connor indicated the food table, and we walked over to it. "The Court is made up of two groups: those who are enti-tled to be a member and those who are valued by Lady Eithne."

"That's quite a sharp line." I wasn't hungry, but a partic-ular fruit had caught my eye. Grapes were definitely in the "benefits" column when it came to joining the Court.

"Some, like Cathal, belong to both groups, but that's rare." Connor filled his plate with various foods. "Most nobles did little during the war, and even less after it ended. In her wisdom, the lady recognizes those who contribute to the Court's growth, mythborn and myth-touched alike."

The new term caught my attention. "Myth-touched?"

His lips curled at a joke I didn't catch. "The ones like

you. Born of human, but changed with our magic," he explained. "Over the past years, quite a few have joined the Court, though they're not around. Most are away, pursuing the skills that drew them to us in the first place. As you will, I suppose... From what I've heard, you might be visiting my workshop soon."

The curiosity in his voice sounded genuine, so I nodded. "I've been trying things on my own, and I've had some results. But it's nowhere near mythborn craft work."

Connor shrugged. "As long as it works." Apparently, the practical side of the magic was more important to him than the fancy look of the crafted items. We could definitely get along.

Commotion at the door caught everybody's attention, and mythborn stepped to the sides as Lady Eithne made her entrance. In a flowing gold dress, shining as if it captured the sun's rays, and with her hair up, she looked every bit the queen I suspected her to be to her people.

Behind her, the Scáthanna came in, all seven of them in full gear, which suggested they wouldn't be staying long. They also kept to themselves, and no other mythborn dared approach their group. No one even threw more than a glance in their direction, and I envied them. I looked at Riagán, but our eyes didn't meet, and I avoided staring for too long. Who knew how much he'd revealed to his companions? Laoise had come searching for him in the mirror room, and looking back at some of the events, I believed at least Cathal also knew what was going on, but it didn't mean I had to make it clear to everyone around.

"Kaja, there you are!" Eithne headed straight for me. Her face had a friendly expression and a warm smile, but her emerald eyes stared intently, and she gave me a nod. It seemed that making the sacrifice of wearing a dress and letting Dearbháil paint my face had paid off. "Let's get you introduced."

She held me by the elbow and spun in place, facing most of the mythborn in the hall. Many kept neutral expressions, but it wasn't hard to spot some grimaces of boredom or disapproval and catch irked whispers in the back.

"Everyone, I'd like you to meet Kaja," Eithne said in a formal tone. "Her services to the Court and her sacrifices have been nothing but praiseworthy, and I'm delighted she accepted my invitation to join us. Please, give her a warm welcome, and I hope in the future you'll find her as helpful and trustworthy as I do."

Thank heavens mythborn didn't clap. I had no idea whether it was part of their culture or a veiled insult toward me, but as soon as Eithne's words faded and she left my side, the mythborn stirred and went about their business.

I breathed out, ready to go back to conversation with Connor, but my relief turned out to be premature. A mythborn noble approached me, and I did my best to not stare at his pure gold hair and complexion so pale it would put Snow White's skin to shame. His clothes, of the finest quality, made it clear he counted himself among the best.

"Welcome to the Court," he offered in a rather dry tone that could easily be taken as slightly hostile. "I hope you'll be as useful as the lady says."

He didn't even bother to introduce himself, as if, no matter how useful I was, I hadn't earned the privilege of learning his name. "Thank you," I replied, a notch louder than I had to. "I hope to learn the mythborn ways, including your famed art of polite conversation."

I could swear I heard a snort somewhere in the room, which, along with the nobleman's suddenly sour face, told me my jab hadn't missed the target. I might not be a master diplomat, but the insult game was one I could play well enough.

Another mythborn approached, a female in a much less elaborate dress. She offered warm words and quite a genuine smile, while the next two eyed me as if they were looking for any fault in my behavior to gossip about later. With more and more mythborn greeting me, the line that Connor had mentioned became more than clear.

I still listened to conversations in the hall, but even those in English brought nothing of interest, and I found it hard to follow so many of them when they happened at the same time and I couldn't match voices with faces. But one conversation caught my attention, since I already knew the mythborn who spoke.

"She looks miserable." Faolan's voice offered no sympathy. "Faced a shriek without fear, almost died under the claws of a Léanmhar... One would think a bunch of stiff mythborn wouldn't be an issue."

"As if you would do any better in her place," Caitríona chimed in. It seemed the Scáthanna shared both Connor's sentiment toward the nobles and my thoughts on how official parties sucked.

I glanced at them and caught Laoise's smug grin when she said, "Maybe you should save her, Riagán?"

"I'd have to remove you from the picture," the archer replied, amused, "otherwise no one would believe we urgently need another scout to fill in."

I nearly smirked at that, because I had no doubt that at short range he'd lose against Laoise. After all, I saw her knife play up close. I also had no doubt that Riagán would never admit openly that she was better than him.

The nobleman in front of me gave me a strange look, as if not paying attention to his empty phrases was a deep insult and a violation of etiquette. Well, he shouldn't have expected anything else from a myth-touched who had not a single drop of noble blood in her veins. Magic, sure—more than enough, but nothing more.

As he left, I caught the last bits of their conversation.

"At least we could make her less miserable, eh, ceannasaí?" Laoise said. "And teach those stuffy pricks a lesson."

I didn't get what exactly she was suggesting between the lines, but I had to focus on another mythborn approaching. Her meager words of greeting were full of warmth, and I did my best to reciprocate the courtesy.

Then, before I realized, Cathal stood in front of me. "Welcome to the Court, Kaja." His confident voice carried through the hall and drew attention to us. It also carried a notion of familiarity instead of formality, as if he wanted to make it clear to everyone I wasn't a stranger. "The Scáthanna are looking forward to working with you again."

"So am I, ceannasaí." I offered a bow.

His eyes flashed when he extended his hand in a humanlike gesture, and when I gave him mine, he—without any warning—kissed it. Whispers rose and gazes followed Cathal's departure, even after he and the other Scáthanna left the hall. I couldn't catch their conversation clearly through the walls, but the amused tone and laughter left no doubt they'd enjoyed the show Cathal put on. Though the glance he threw me over his shoulder before leaving made it clear this was an exception, and I shouldn't expect such treatment in the future. Nevertheless, I was grateful for that one-time rescue.

Eithne stood far off, surrounded by a group of myth-born, but she didn't miss what was going on. Her lips trembled slightly as if she was holding off laughter.

The mythborn gathered in the hall stirred, and discussions rose around me, with my and Cathal's names returning every other sentence. Apparently a myth-touched regarded by the Scáthanna was someone entirely different than another ex-humanborn to whom Eithne had granted the privilege of the ritual, because when more mythborn came to greet me, they were either polite or friendly. I'd still prefer to be out and gathering information or in Connor's workshop learning the craft, but at least I didn't have to worry about veiled stabs and intrigues. Cathal had indeed made me a bit less miserable.

His words, which I took as a promise of working together again, also helped to lift my mood. He wouldn't have said it if he didn't mean it, so I wouldn't end up stuck in the Court's building forever. I'd be out there, doing what I did the best. I had no doubt that the elite Scáthanna wouldn't hold back with comments about my shortcomings, but I'd learned enough about them to deal with it. With that thought, after the last mythborn offered their greetings—or at least the last of those who wished to acknowledge me in the first place—I picked up a glass of wine and mingled with the crowd. Maybe Connor had stuck around, and we could talk about amulets and charms.

Some mythborn still threw glares of half-concealed discontent at me, but I didn't care anymore. I wouldn't let them question my right to be there or try to belittle me in any way. I might be only a myth-touched and a commoner in their eyes, but I was one of them now.

Kaja Modrzewska of the Court.

I liked the sound of it.

THANK YOU FOR READING!

Thank you for reading! If you enjoyed the book, please
consider leaving a review.
Kaja's adventures continue in
Myth-touched

Sign up for the author's newsletter and receive your
complimentary copy of Scourges, Spells, and Serenades – a
collection of fantasy short stories:
authorjm.com

ABOUT THE AUTHOR

Joanna might be a bit too cautious to do anything even remotely daring or dangerous herself, so she writes about daring adventures and dangerous magic instead. Yet, she found enough courage to abandon her life in Poland and move to Ireland, and then some years later, she abandoned her life in Ireland to move over to the US. She's determined to settle there, once she finally chooses which state to reside in.

When she's not writing or thinking about writing, she plays video games or makes amateur art. She lives the happy life of a recluse, surrounded by her husband, a stuffed red monkey, and a small collection of books she insisted on hauling across two continents.

facebook.com/AuthorJMac

x.com/AuthorJMac

instagram.com/authorjmac

goodreads.com/authorjmac

bookbub.com/authors/joanna-maciejewska

You can find the full list of her publications and more about
her at:

http://authorjm.com

and connect with her via social media:

- facebook.com/AuthorJMac
- instagram.com/authorjmac
- indiepocalypse.social/@AuthorJMac
- bsky.app/profile/authorjmac.bsky.social
- threads.net/@authorjmac
- x.com/AuthorJMac
- goodreads.com/authorjmac
- bookbub.com/authors/joanna-maciejewska

www.ingramcontent.com/pod-product-compliance
Lightning Source LLC
Chambersburg PA
CBHW030758210726
48290CB00002B/314